D1082708

Down Here in the Warmth

Euel Arden

Down Here in the Warmth
© 2020 by Euel Arden

ISBN (Print): 978-1-09831-925-0
ISBN (eBook): 978-1-09831-926-7

BOOK I

CHAPTER 1

"Nigga..."

That's what they said.

That's what they always said.

Nigga this and *nigga that* and...It was how they greeted Virgil every morning on his way home from work.

Exhausted and depressed after sitting alone at an empty desk for eight hours straight, he'd be greeted with glee by a group of teenagers on their way to school or who knows where—high as fuck at eight in the morning and smiling as wide as the skin on their black faces would let them.

"What up my nigga!" they'd run up and shout—before quickly leaping back into the safety of the crowd.

They thought it was funny.

Virgil: Iraq War veteran, trained security guard, ex-churchgoer; greeted every morning by this stultifying word. A word so reviled by decent society, that it had been stricken from the common lexicon.

A word referred to, only in the direst of need…after an appropriate amount of squirming, as…the N-word.

With one hand buried in his pocket and the other gripping a straining plastic bag holding his breakfast, Virgil drifted east along 8th Street, staring vacantly down at the sun-bleached sidewalks. He was deep in thought; so deep that for all intents and purposes, he was blind.

He was thinking about Raj and his crew, and their daily greeting.

He was searching for a comparable word: not in meaning, but in power…another word that had been elevated to unutterable, even, un-inscribable status.

Nigga.

When you really looked at it, it seemed kind of weak; silly actually. Like you could flick it in half at the *gs*—but it was powerful. It broke hearts, and ruined lives. It ended careers.

It took Virgil an entire block to come up with an equally powerful word: *Yahweh*, from the Hebrew texts. *Yhwh*: the proper name of the God of Israel. A word whose expression was forbidden. A word so terrifying that even writing it out fully, was anathema. A word that if spoken aloud, who knows, maybe the Lord Himself would strike you down…and yet, here it was, his own blasphemous word every morning, from his own people, spewed out like spittle in his face.

As he did every morning, Virgil had planned to avoid this meeting. He'd slide up the avenue, instead of walking down the street. He'd linger at work. Or maybe he'd eat breakfast at the diner, in a deep booth, far in the back, but in his usual anxiousness to rush back to the safety of his apartment, he ordered his breakfast to go, and made a beeline for home. Now it was too late to change his mind; he was already within view of the Riis Projects. He'd be running into Raj and his crew shortly.

They knew it bothered him. That's why they did it. Virgil had made the mistake of trying to bond with them one night before setting off to work. And though he tried his best to hide his disgust at Raj and his friends, who spent most of their free time sitting on the benches in front of the building and creating a general nuisance, he knew they could tell. A wrong word, an off look…a misplaced attempt at advice, and Raj quickly picked up on what Virgil's real opinion of them was: *Nigga think he too good for us.*

They parted ways awkwardly, and now, any time Virgil ran into them, they over-exaggerated their offensiveness just to rib him.

It wasn't that Virgil was scared of them; they were really just kids, while Virgil was a grown man: plus he had half-a-foot and a hundred pounds over the biggest of them. It was just that…he hadn't been good with any people of late…not since returning from Iraq. And they could sense it.

Then again, what balding, overweight, thirty-something-year-old man with horn-rimmed glasses, had ever been good with a group of teenagers?

By the time Virgil reached the end of the block, he had become so embroiled in his thoughts that he was stopped in his tracks when he looked up.

A few thousand people were packed onto the sidewalks and into the common area of his apartment complex. Most of them were young—high school and college age, but there were older people too.

He wasn't quite sure what to make of it. He struggled to remember the date.

Is it a holiday? he wondered.

He crossed the avenue, then squeezed between two parked buses to get up onto his sidewalk. He skirted the edges of the crowd, making his way toward his building's front door.

He was about to ask someone what was going on but he figured it out as soon as he read the first placard: NYPD = Guilty

Apparently everyone was gathering at the Riis Projects before marching over to a protest at City Hall. Virgil scanned some more signs: We Are All Martins. Guns Don't Kill People—Cops Kill People. 42 shots. And the most popular one: an image of Mayor Davis with a Hitler mustache.

A few days earlier, on a Saturday evening, there had been another police shooting—the second, high-profile police shooting in the past few weeks. Four white police officers, responding to a call of "shots fired," had fired forty-two bullets into a car they had mistakenly thought was trying to run them down. It turned out to be a respectable African American family leaving a birthday party.

A young married couple sat in the front seat of the car; in the back, in a child's seat, slept an eight-month-old baby—the Martin family.

The couple had died in a bloody mess. The pictures emblazoned the front pages of every newspaper and news website the next day. Miraculously, the child had suffered only a scratch on the cheek from flying glass.

Virgil vaguely remembered hearing something about the tragedy, but he didn't follow the news much anymore. Ever since he had started working nights, he had effectively retreated from the world.

He watched the crowd start to file out along the sidewalk and head toward the protest, but it was slow going, and had little effect on the mass still packed in between the buildings.

He heard someone shouting from a bench in front of his building. It was Howard, a resident of his building and a student leader at Columbia. Virgil had known Howard and his family for years. Howard's mother used to drop Howard off at Virgil's grandmother's to babysit.

Howard stood on the bench with one foot up on the backrest. He leaned out and roused up a group of students he had organized. Already his voice had gone hoarse.

Virgil smiled proudly. He liked Howard; he had always been bold. He was one of the good kids from the building, and secretly, Virgil had always been proud of him, as if Howard's success somehow reflected on him. As if, in the few times he had helped babysit, he had imparted some sort of wisdom to him. They didn't talk much nowadays, but Howard was always respectful when they ran into each another.

Virgil slipped by the group of students and ducked into the front door of his building without being seen.

When the door snapped shut behind him, the commotion from outside muffled. He walked across the lobby and was about to enter the stairwell when a hushed voice stopped him.

"Yo, Virge."

Raj peeked out from behind the basement door at the back of the lobby. Raj's friends crowded behind him.

"They still out there?"

"Yeah," Virgil said. "There are tons of people out there. You're not going?"

"Hell no!" Raj said indignantly. "We got the whole day off cause' a this thing. I ain't wasting my time marching around in this heat… Hell no!"

He stretched his neck out from behind the basement door to get a better view of the front of the building. A few of the other kids also poked their heads out to scan the empty lobby; then all at once they pulled their heads back in and shut the door.

"So you'd rather spend the whole day hiding in a basement," Virgil muttered. He turned and trudged up the stairs. By the time he reached his floor, he was winded. *It's only three flights,* he thought while catching his breath. Sooner or later he'd have to get back in shape.

He took out his keys and walked to his door. He stopped to catch his breath again before putting his key in the lock.

He used to be an athlete. He used to bound up those stairs four at a time after a full day of playing ball; but now with the extra weight, and his asthma worsening, he tended to do things more slowly and deliberate.

He had weighed a hundred and ninety pounds when he enlisted, and he stayed close to that weight until he was discharged. Since then he had packed on a hundred extra pounds. But he had never considered himself obese. His waist was wider than his chest, that was true; but the roundness of his face was what gave him the impression of being heavier than he really was. He carried a lot of weight in his jowls, and that, combined with his thinning, close-shaved hair and his army-issue glasses, made his head look small atop his very large frame.

Still, at six feet four, he didn't think he looked too bad overall. But he felt it: he needed more rest, and he could feel his heart working harder than it should.

He unlocked the door and stepped into his dark apartment. He put his bag on the kitchen table and sat. With a ponderous hand, he reached out and sifted through a litter of papers on the table. He stopped when he found what he was looking for—a photocopy of a page from a book he had read.

Here it is.

He had underlined one sentence in black marker. It was a James Baldwin quote, from a letter he had written to his young nephew: just about Raj's age. It was something along the lines of…your greatest danger, is *believing,* you were what the white world called, a nigger.

He had planned to show the quotation to Raj. He didn't know why; maybe to prove some point, or maybe just to give the kid some advice…the way sometimes you want to tell somebody something about themselves that is so obvious, but for some reason they can't see it—and that *something* would be so simple to fix, and would make their lives so much easier; but, in actuality, it was almost impossible to bring up, as if that person's whole persona had been set up to defend against receiving that one bit of information. And so the right moment never came up.

He probably has no idea who James Baldwin is, Virgil thought as he stared at the paper. *He'd just get more insulted.*

It was best to leave it alone. What right had he to give advice anyway? Who was he? Just some weirdo recluse who only came out at night; a man afraid of loud noises; a man afraid of people. No. It was none of his business. And so the quote lay on Virgil's table for weeks, while he decided what to do with it.

He put the paper down and unpacked his breakfast. Then slowly and methodically, he began to eat.

Working nights hadn't made it any easier for him to get into shape, and though he only ate two meals a day—one in the morning, before he went to sleep, and the other at night, right before he went to work—they were substantial. Every morning he had two breakfasts at once.

Today it was pancakes smothered in syrup, and a cheese omelet with home fries—not to mention toast with butter and jam…and everything else that came in the bag from the diner. In the mornings, he was famished.

At night, his cravings tended more toward meat and sugar. He ate lots of bacon and liverwurst. Cheap chocolate cakes slathered with icing. And, of course, two large mugs of coffee with six sugars each.

He had been on the midnight-to-eight tour for over two years now, and was glad of it. He had needed the silence and solitude. It gave his traumatized soul a chance to heal, and hopefully, rise from wherever it had retreated to during the war. Maybe, just maybe, there was a chance for him to regain what he once was.

And while he felt that all this time alone was necessary, he also realized with trepidation, that it was pulling him away from the people he loved—his mother, his sister, his sister's children; they were all beginning to forget him. But he had no choice. This was a price he had to pay.

In the parallel world of night people, life was simpler. It was softer: less harsh… people didn't hurry. People didn't worry about being "professional" at four in the morning, and everyone spoke in familial tones…

He would sit at a diner late at night, and the workers, when not serving, would not even see him. They would chat loudly, airing their business across the counter as if there were no one else around…and this was when he found his peace.

He was about to butter his toast when he stopped, lifted and aligned his upper carriage as straight as he could, and took a deep, unconstricted breath.

I'm not relaxed enough to sleep.

This he determined by monitoring how deeply he was able to inhale. That, and his perceived heart rate.

He reached for a bottle of aspirin on the kitchen counter and popped a couple of pills.

Aspirin had been the key; it had become his sleeping pill. He wouldn't touch anything stronger. Aspirin calmed him and helped his blood flow, and if he were having one of his daily panic attacks, he would take more…five or six. And if he were still up half an hour later, he'd take even more—eight, ten…twenty?

Sleeping had been the hardest part of working the night shift. He did not sleep well during daylight hours. It took concentration to stay under, and the struggle played out in his dreams: *Calm…calm,* rolled over in his sleeping mind.

The summers were the hardest of all: the days were brightest, and sleep deprivation drove him to climb the furniture and staple heavy blankets over each window in his room. It was the only way to quench the flaming coronas that broke around the edges of his new wooden shades.

Virgil finished breakfast and cleaned up. He shaved—carefully tightening his pencil-thin mustache—then took a cold shower to help further calm down. It wasn't until he turned off the lights and settled down to sleep, that his mind was finally free enough to see the beast of solitude, sitting in the shadows before him.

He needed the night shift, it was true, but sometimes the loneliness took him to the edge. Sometimes he didn't speak for days. He'd pace away the long punishing weekend nights, never leaving his apartment, until his mind became so lost that he began to wonder if he were not just another ghost, haunting an empty world.

And then something would set him off: a baby crying, a disturbing news report…a loud crash from outside, and a flood of ice water would wash over his heart, and he'd start to obsess. *My sister needs help with her kids. My mother is getting old… They've given up on me.*

And then there was the dawn. Every morning, near the end of his shift, he'd step outside to face it. And even mighty New York with its buildings thick as gravestones could not stop the terrifying colors from bleeding through him. He'd stand, back against the brick wall, and wait…while from across the darkened ocean, a leviathan strode toward him, only him, gathering nightmares along the way.

Each dawn he stood, soul bared, willingly awaiting God's wrath, or absolution. By degrees the light would arrive, moving implacably, until all at once it stood over him: a sky of horrifying infinity.

No. Sunrises were nothing like sunsets: peaceful and soft: the back of Colossus, striding safely away over the horizon. A dawn was just a start.

And every dawn, Virgil stepped into the same Iraqi village he had shelled the night before from miles away—badasses, roaring their war cries from inside their armored shell; howling along with blaring bloody music.

We, the line of warriors who have trod this ground since ancient Babylon…

As an afterthought their platoon had driven through that same village the next morning. By dawn's early light, their caravan crawled beneath a soul-stretching blue horizon ripped across with torrents of colors; the air around them scintillated and seemed alive. Virgil was in high spirits.

The day before he had spoken with his mother and learned of the birth of his niece. He recalled the conversation with a warm smile as they entered the town. They rolled past crumbled buildings. His eyes fixed upon a small dark pile, laid out prominently at the base of a concrete hill—a hill that had been a home the day before, and he knew right away what it was—almost as if he had always known his future.

He had seen bodies before, and other bodies could be seen here and there, even that morning, laid out on the sides of the road: black sacks of cloth, really; but that morning his mind would never make it past that one; a mountain. Alone, in front of its home, a tiny body lay facing the sky, its trunk too small to be twisted and awkward, like an adult's. The baby lay neatly, marveling at the dawn, snow white, blackened eyes….

Forever. The image would forever be tied to his own niece. He would never be able to enjoy her company. He was cursed. He would bring her only bad luck.

He found himself standing there. The weapon he was holding dropped from his hands as the weight of what he'd done—*for how long?*—struck him dumb. He dropped to his knees.

His crew stood close, but no one laid a hand on him. No one said a thing.

"I don't care if you kill me," he finally said. "I will not roll again,"

His lieutenant stood among the men.

What could he say?

Back at camp they kept him around for a while. When a new commander came in, they packed him off for home.

Since then, his life had been one long struggle to balance the turmoil in his head.

Peace. That was all he sought now. *A little more peace. Please. Everyone, just hold on. I just need a little more time—alone.*

The phone rang and Virgil sprung up from his sleep, every nerve screaming.

He was confused.

He had forgotten to take his phone off the hook. He looked at his clock radio across the room.

9:44.

Nine hours late! was his first thought.

He stumbled around his room half-conscious, knocking things off his dresser. He was checking clocks. He looked at the time display on his television—then his watch, lifting it an inch from his weak eyes. Neither of them indicated either A.M. or P.M.

The phone rang again.

He still didn't know if it was morning or night.

"Why are you fucking calling me?" he shouted and slammed his fist against his thigh.

He grabbed the phone, thinking it must be his boss.

"Hello?" he said sheepishly.

"Virgil." It was his sister. "Turn on the television."

She turned her mouth from the phone and said something to someone else on her end.

"What?" Virgil asked, still confused.

"Virgil!" she snapped. "Turn the television on! I think your job is cancelled for tonight."

CHAPTER 2

As Lestor slipped out the backdoor of his parents'
Brooklyn home onto the unlit porch, he had to remember to duck to
avoid the bamboo wind chime that hung from the center of the rusted
awning. After a lifetime of ducking to avoid them, it just then occurred
to him how strange it was, that the chime had always had right-of-way
over people on that porch. Wind chime, stacks of flowerpots, piles of
tarps, everything, on that cluttered porch, had always had precedence
over people.

They come down tomorrow, he determined.

He closed the door quietly and crouched down low. He wanted to
make sure his silhouette could not be seen above the short brick walls
of the porch. But in that darkness, it was doubtful that anyone could
have seen him. The small backyard at the foot of the porch, his laager,
was surrounded by a ring of tall, stoic, backs of other houses: all high
and deep enough to block the light from the streets.

Lestor moved cautiously, trying not to disturb any of the piles
teetering around him. With a final, high, wide step, over a plastic tub

filled with gardening tools, he landed on a clear patch of terracotta tile, at the top of a small set of steps that led down to the yard.

He sat for a while in the stillness, leaning his head against the cool crusted brick wall. From out on the street in front of his house, he could hear the low rattling generators of the television news trucks. A clearly spoken word rose above the drone of the trucks every now and then, but mostly the voices were muffled. Weary reporters and camera crews sat about drinking coffee and awaiting signs of life from Lestor's house; the klieg lights of their cameras bathed its façade in perpetual white light. But the powerful lights managed to reach only halfway down the side alley to where he sat; the rest of his backyard was deep dark jungle. The twenty square feet of concrete that had been his childhood basketball court, had been taken over long ago by large wooden flower boxes overflowing with a tangle of flora.

This was the house he grew up in, in the neighborhood he would always think of as home. These streets were all he knew until college, and he knew them well: all the kids did. The backyards, the alleys, even the trees; every inch of that whole neighborhood had been explored. What he no longer knew were the people.

It started in high school: the change of the neighborhood. One too many black families had moved in—and *poof*, all at once, the white people vanished. Within a few years, the neighborhood had gone from almost all Irish and Italian, to black: white flight. By the time Lestor graduated from college, he barely knew a family on the block.

Lestor's family had stayed though. His parents would never move. It was a secret point of pride to them: to live in an all-black neighborhood.

"What is the big deal?" his mother would say, when he suggested that…maybe…they might want to move. "Everyone on this block owns their homes. We are all invested in this neighborhood. We all want a better life for our children."

But still, things were different. Sometimes when Lestor visited on the weekends, he'd hear gunshots at night.

"So fuckin naïve," he whispered through clenched teeth.

In his hands, he held a black nine-millimeter pistol. He toyed with it—unconsciously picking at its handgrip with his fingernail. The weapon had been in a paper bag that a complete stranger had shoved into his arms the day before. At the time he hadn't known what to think, only that something important must be in that crumpled bag. It was heavy. It was solid. It had to be something *substantial*. And, given his current circumstances, something even *terrible*. And so he held onto the bag for hours, not daring to peek into it until the time was right; until he was absolutely certain no one was around.

When he finally did, late that night, in his old room—with his door shut, his phone off, and all the lights off but one—he dumped the contents of the bag onto his childhood bed: a box of ammunition, two clips, a nylon waist holster, and that portentous weapon.

The funny thing about the whole situation, was that it didn't seem so strange: that someone would hand him these things. It seemed almost natural, as if it were supposed to happen. But then again, ever since his parents had been murdered two nights earlier, nothing seemed strange anymore. Everything felt unreal—unreal, but at the same time, moving along smoothly...

That night, he had meticulously examined the gun: breaking it down, rebuilding it, loading and unloading it, wiping down each bullet with a clean rag. It was fascinating. He tried scratching the gun's inexplicably hard, plastic-like surface, but his nail wouldn't bite. *What is this?* Seventeen rounds. He didn't even know a pistol could hold so many bullets. That night, for the first time, he slept with a loaded pistol on the floor next to his bed.

Lestor stood and made his way to the wooden fence at the back of the yard; the gun felt comfortable in his hand.

The equalizer. That's what they called it in the old west. Now he understood why. He was fearless with that gun in his hand. Like a God, he could now hurl lightning.

He slid the gun in his waist holster and climbed the wooden fence, hopping onto his neighbor's garage roof.

He hadn't been roofing since he was a kid. They used to go all the time—always during daylight hours though. A pack of them would stealthily make their way down the block by way of backyards. The objective was to make it to the end of the block without getting caught. They'd travel by means of garage roofs, fences, cinderblock walls, and, without setting foot to ground, they'd try to make it to the last house on the block.

That last house was exactly where he was headed—the house of his childhood friend, Colin.

Lestor moved faster now. It was easier than when he was younger: he was taller, and stronger. He passed through the yards with resolve, using all four limbs to move along effortlessly.

The midpoint of the journey had always been the tricky spot: the cable, a cluster of telephone lines ran through an old metal tube. The span was the length of a yard: twenty feet. It was the spot that had always stumped them; none of them had ever been able to carry themselves more than a few feet along the cable before dropping, and sprinting the rest of the way across the yard to the next roof.

He stopped for the first time when he reached this spot. He had forgotten about it. He sat at the roof's edge and stared down at the now well-manicured lawn. The drop was only ten feet. He let slip a chuckle when he recalled how Colin had fallen there once, long ago.

Always a bit overweight, Colin's hands slipped right away…but he didn't outright fall. The arm of his sweater had snagged on the cable and hindered his descent… Lestor remembered the fear they had both felt: perched, right where he crouched now, he had stared into Colin's eyes as he fell…slowly, the arm of his wool sweater stretching longer and longer. Fear and panic contorting Colin's face as if he were falling from a cliff—and then, he was standing on the ground with an eight-foot-long sweater arm, still stuck to the cable.

Lestor shook the smirk from his face. He had to refocus. He closed his eyes, and the nightmare image of his parents' death reappeared. He reached up and grabbed hold of the cable. To his surprise, he was able to carry himself across the whole span, over to the next garage.

Lestor's parents were lawyers. Famous ones. His mother and father were what some people derisively called "civil rights ambulance chasers." They had been involved in a number of high-profile civil rights cases: against the police, against the state.

They were well known in New York, and, of late, they had become nationally known. They had a book on the *New York Times* bestseller list, and they regularly appeared on cable news programs to provide legal commentary.

Lestor picked up speed as he moved along the fence line: roof, roof, wall, roof, wall, roof, fence. He hadn't done this in fifteen years. He bounded over obstacles and traversed tall cinderblock walls that used to daunt him. When he finally hopped onto the last roof overlooking Colin's yard, he slowed, then crawled under the shelter of some low-hanging maple branches.

Colin's backyard was a box: a small concrete square, enclosed on two sides by cinderblock walls, plus the garage Lestor was on top of. The forth side of the backyard was the back of Colin's brick house. A short chain-link gate led out to the driveway and street.

Lestor lay on the asphalt shingles and peered over the hip of the roof. Colin's apartment was in the basement of the house. Lestor couldn't see directly into the basement window, but he knew Colin was there; he could see the flickering lights of the television set, dancing in the window.

The last time Lestor had seen his parents alive was two nights ago on the evening news. He hadn't looked at a television since. By now most of the country—and, for all he knew, most of the world—had seen the footage of his parents' murder. For two days straight it had been the only thing on, and if you managed to turn off the TV, it was all over the internet as well: there was no escaping it. As long as the ratings rolled in, no one seemed to mind the pain it was causing, and no one seemed to mind what it was doing to the country.

Now the whole world seemed to be waiting for the next act.

Near the end of the first day of riots (which still sputtered along), News Chopper 1 was flying high over lower Manhattan. It hovered for a while over the deserted downtown area, but the police had cordoned most of it off, and all that could be seen were well-lit dead zones, and scattered clusters of police officers.

Moving on, the chopper crossed the river to Brooklyn, where most of the later action had taken place. It shot footage of small things: crowds milling about intersections, a store long since looted, the lapping orange flames of a neatly contained car fire, and then, jackpot: reports of blood nearby.

It was early evening when the chopper arrived at the scene. An elderly white couple had been dragged from their front door by a mob of young black men. Chopper 1 went live.

It was a terrifying and confusing scene: a loose cluster of young men swarmed around the couple kneeling in the middle of the street. The crowd seemed torn between protection and aggression. For some, dragging the couple from their home had been enough, but there was an ugly force at work within the mob. While a few people tried to help, a small group of younger attackers danced mockingly around the victims.

A middle-aged black woman tried in vain to hold back the stream of attackers. She strove to gather the couple in her arms, as if trying to enfold them in the protection of her bosom. At one point an attacker lunged in, and the woman held out a defiant palm—draining the courage from the youth and forcing his retreat.

An older man had been there too; a thin man in a brown suit and hat. He held a small Bible in one hand and stood tall at the center of the small, open clearing that formed around the victims. In the camera's lens, he stood alone, holding his Bible out; one could see his head moving as if he were preaching, but the mob's collective mind seemed to be turning the other way. The attacks were becoming more brazen.

"Get the shot! Get the shot!" could be heard from the helicopter's news crew.

Faster and faster the attacks came, the attitude of the mob turning from bawdy and mocking, to sinister and focused. A broken broomstick came down from one side of the crowd; a kick from the other. A hand reached in from out of the darkness and brutally yanked the woman's hair.

By this time, the defenses had totally broke down. Someone grabbed the woman by the ankle and dragged her away ungracefully. She was released a few yards away—her dress had ridden up, exposing her pale, unfit legs. Her long gray hair fell in a tangle over her face.

Once the couple was separated, everyone who was watching knew the game was lost.

The man had fallen facedown and had stopped moving, it wasn't clear why; he had been crawling toward his wife.

You could hear the confusion in the helicopter as someone let out a gasp: *Oh my God!* they said, as if it had just occurred to them: real people were down there.

"The police have been notified. The police are on their way," the anchor from the news studio said on air, to calm their coworkers in the helicopter.

And then somehow, somebody in the news studio realized, at the same time as Lestor, who the couple was.

"That's Theresa Milgram!"

The attackers now had pulled up their shirts to cover their faces. They knew the cameras were on but didn't care.

Theresa Milgram, her face bloodied, managed to pull herself to her knees. She was trying to speak to her attackers.

A pool of blood appeared on the ground around the man's head, and most of the crowd had moved away, as if the blood had quenched their anger. The sight now frightened them. One last brazen attacker flashed into the chopper's spotlight. In one quick move, he ran up to the kneeling woman and threw a brick, full force, into her temple. Lestor's mother dropped like a stone.

It was over.

The woman, who had been trying to stop the attack, was now down on her hands and knees, trying to help his mother. Lestor now recognized her as their neighbor, Mrs. Greene. She was the only moving actor on the screen now, but for some reason, Lestor could focus on only the single painted white brick lying on the ground beside her. It was one of the bricks from their front garden. He had helped his mother paint them one weekend long ago.

The camera panned to the right, and there, standing in the corner of the screen, clear as day to anyone who knew him, was Colin; he had witnessed the whole thing. Now he stood sheepishly on the sidelines.

How would he ever forgive himself?

Lestor found himself kneeled in front of his television, his hands covering his mouth. A wall of adrenaline washed through him like a tsunami—and from that moment on, nothing seemed real.

For the next two days, the media circus was up and running; a hornet's nest had been stirred to righteous action by the jolt of this event. Not merely because the vicious murders had been caught on film—enough on its own—but because of who the victims were: Stanley and Theresa Milgram.

Eventually, somebody up high made the decision to stop showing the clip. A rare altruistic decision had been made by the media, as had been done after 9/11, when the media finally broke the interminable visual loop of *Airplane into tower, airplane into tower.* It was causing mass psychological distress.

The Milgrams' end, had stopped being shown on television. But the froth continued.

Lestor had seen the footage only that one time. After that he cut all connections with the outside world. His girlfriend had gone to her parents earlier. His brother, Shazz, was in Florida. Lestor was alone.

More than once during that hellish first night, out of habit, he reached for his phone to call his parents. And each time he caught himself, and debated whether to call or not. Could he bear to hear their voices on the answering machine? No, no one should.

The heat in his apartment crept up slowly until he realized he could barely breathe. He had to get out of there and get some air. He went downstairs and sat on the stoop for the rest of the night.

At dawn, two plainclothes police officers found him sitting there, legs stretched out lengthwise along one step. They had come to escort him to Police Plaza. The Mayor wanted to see him.

Lestor stood and followed.

The officers talked among themselves on the short drive to Police Plaza. Lestor sat quietly in the back of the unmarked car. When they arrived, they drove up onto the sidewalk behind the large brick building and parked.

Lestor was led through the back entrance of the building and then onto an elevator. The doors closed. When they opened, Lestor found himself in the middle of a bustling command center. He was taken to a smaller room off to the side and dropped off just inside of the door.

The room was wider than it was deep. Tall windows took up most of the walls around him.

Mayor Davis stood behind a monolithic wooden desk at the front of the room. In the midst of an animated phone call, he waved and jabbed his finger in the air as if slaying an invisible dragon. The police commissioner stood by the side of the desk, anxiously awaiting orders.

Lestor stood like a stone in a stream: people flowed around him, hurrying in and out of the office. Others moored in quiet eddies at various points around the office, feverishly working their own devices.

The room stopped when the Mayor put his phone down: he walked around the desk and came to greet Lestor. He took Lestor's hand in both of his and expressed his condolences. When the pleasantries were over, everyone in the room, but the Mayor and the police commissioner, resumed their roil.

The Mayor led Lestor to a high-backed, red-leather chair in front of his desk, and though the chair faced the desk, it was uncomfortably close to the center of the room. The Mayor pardoned himself and went back to wrap up his call.

Lestor sat quietly, feeling small. He couldn't see what was going on around him anymore, and was too self-conscious to lean to one side or the other and look around the wing of his chair.

Mayor Davis was quick. He finished his call then came back around and took Lestor's hand again. He spoke with an unnervingly loud tone of confidentiality. Lestor was too exhausted to fully understand what was being said.

"…much for you to do, Lestor…

"…grab hold of the moral reigns your parents had wielded…

"…to settle down or more people will get hurt…

"…reports of civil unrest in other cities…

"…Lestor, *you* could end it all…

They had a prepared statement for him to read.

The media had already assembled in front of the building for a 9 A.M. press conference.

Lestor was handed a sheet of paper with two short paragraphs on it.

He suddenly noticed that everyone in the room was moving... Had they all stopped?

He stared down at the words on the paper but couldn't read.

When he looked up again, he saw a local celebrity religious barker, peering over the Mayor's left shoulder.

He glanced back down at the paper; when he looked up again the religious leader was gone.

Lestor knew they were right...but something was gnawing at him. It didn't feel right.

Are my parents' deaths to be just another news story, to be swept aside after a few days?

He had always been quick to forgive: that was the world he had grown up in, but just this once...just this once...

The focus on him had receded.

He sat with the statement dangling from his fingertips as people rushed around him again. He was getting a bad feeling.

If you don't have a plan, you become part of somebody else's plan.

He wished his brother was there. He was strong. He would know exactly what to do. But he had not even talked to him yet. Shazz was still in Florida.

Lestor stood and excused himself to use the restroom. When no one followed, or even paid attention to him, he knew he was going to leave.

Let them do what they want, he told himself. *I want no part of it.*

The stairwell door stood just past the bathroom door. Lestor walked through it.

He moved down the cavernous stairwell two steps at a time, concentrating on making sure his large feet didn't miss a step. At the bottom, he popped out into the building's lobby and walked out through the front door: past the cameras and chairs set up for his press conference.

It was while navigating the busy plaza that Lestor ran into the man with the bag. At first, it seemed he and Lestor were just getting into each other's way; but after the second parry, Lestor realized that his moves were being matched. He stopped and looked in the man's face… There seemed something "off" about him. He was average height, and rather thin, but his clothes seemed too big.

He wore a plain white baseball cap, which sat high on his head and tilted down jauntily, and a bright red velour tracksuit. The top half of his face was obscured by a pair of amber-tinted glasses, which seemed more suited to a grandmother than a middle-aged man…which is what Lestor figured he was. He found himself staring at the only exposed area of skin on the man's face: a waxen angular jaw, which was even more off-putting because the man's lips seemed to be unevenly drawn onto a powdered white canvas. Lestor figured he was some security official sent to bring him back.

He was about to step back when the man reached out and plucked the statement from his fingers (he had forgotten he still had it) then shoved a brown paper bag into his gut. And then he was gone.

Lestor stood unmoving for a moment, feeling a little queasy, but he had to get out of there fast. He had no time to wonder. He had to disappear: back into the crowds, down into the subway. He needed to get home; not to his apartment in Manhattan, but home to Brooklyn… to the house where he was raised.

Since then, his silence had become deafening. He refused to be interviewed. He refused calls from the police commissioner. He refused calls from the Mayor. When the police knocked at his door, he politely asked them to leave. He knew what everyone wanted, but he couldn't oblige. He couldn't let his parents' lives be swept away so easily.

Lying on the garage roof overlooking Colin's backyard, Lestor swore that something was about to change in this equation…Colin was going to die.

He has to. He has to. He was right there. He was right there and did nothing. He just watched.

"He's a young man," Lestor thought, "a strong man. He could have done something. He could have tried."

Lestor dropped off the garage roof into Colin's backyard. When he landed, Colin's dog began to bark.

Bruno was a full-grown Rottweiler, but Lestor had known him since he was a pup. He and Colin had driven up to Washington Heights to pick him up. Colin worked up there; he had gotten the dog for free from a bodega owner he knew.

Bruno must have been too young when they first picked him up: his eyes were barely opened. He was so small that Lestor had cradled him inside his jacket during the ride back. So Lestor was one of the few people who could get near Bruno.

Colin's door was set two steps down and led to a basement apartment in his parent's house. He and Lestor had hung out there since they were kids.

Lestor tapped lightly on the heavy door.

Colin didn't answer right away.

Lestor could picture him on his couch, sitting at attention and staring at the door. These past few days had been dangerous times.

"Who is it?" Colin finally called.

A few moments later, Lestor could hear the commotion of Colin struggling to control Bruno, who was hurling himself against the door.

"It's me," he said, in a hushed tone. "Lestor."

Colin and Bruno stopped their struggling. "What are you doing here?" Colin asked, matching Lestor's tone. Half the world was looking for Lestor.

"Just open the door!" Lestor snapped.

"Wait, wait. Hold up," Colin said.

He managed to get Bruno to sit; then he turned to scan the apartment quickly. He winced when he saw that his television was tuned to a news station. The network had been periodically switching over to a live feed outside of Lestor's parents' house, right down the block. He ran and turned the channel to a baseball game.

What does he want? he thought anxiously, before heading back to the door.

"Okay, hold up!" he said again, as he cracked the locks and opened the door just enough to peek out. "Bruno!" he shouted while struggling to restrain the dog. Bruno's aggression had turned to excitement.

"Get back. It's Lestor, calm down."

Colin pulled the door open a little farther to let Lestor slip past. Bruno followed Lestor as Colin stuck his head out the doorway and did a quick scan of the yard; then he locked the door. Lestor was sitting on the couch, petting Bruno, when he came in.

Colin stood in the center of the room, rubbing his hands against his hip pockets. A rectangular coffee table stood between him and Lestor.

"I don't know what to say, Lestor," he said. "It's a horrible thing… everything is horrible right now."

"I don't want to talk about it," Lestor said. "I just need some breathing room."

"Yeah…okay," Colin said, without moving.

Lestor could have tried to find out who else was involved. Colin's family had been the first black family to move onto the block. They had not panicked and run when the neighborhood began to change, and so Colin knew all the new people who had moved in. But at that point, Lestor didn't care. The police had quickly rounded up the four principal culprits.

"Do you want a beer?" Colin asked and turned to go into the kitchen.

"No…I'm not drinking anymore. I need a clear head."

But he longed to just sit back on Colin's couch and forget everything, the way they used to. The way he and Colin, and a few other of their friends, used to sit back on weekends and watch a fight, or a playoff game, and drink imported beer and smoke weed and be safe and secure in their underground den.

Colin stood in front of his opened refrigerator, holding a cold beer in his hand. "Has Shazz been around?" he asked.

"No." He still hadn't talked to his brother. "I don't even know if he knows."

Lestor got up and went to the bathroom. He sat on the closed toilet seat and took out the gun. He cradled it in his hands, examining the weapon once again. He didn't even know if it would work. What if he pulled the trigger and nothing happened? He had never shot a gun.

He heard Colin return to the living room and sit on the couch. He wanted things back to normal too, but there was this thing between them now. They had become colors, relegated to different teams.

Lestor heard Colin admonishing Bruno, who was trying to play. Bruno would take a tennis ball and drop it between your legs while you sat on the couch; then he'd give the ball a sharp jab with his snout, causing you to jump. After that, you had no choice but to toss the ball away…then he would bring it right back.

Lestor listened to the struggle and let out a laugh. Once more the anger seeped out of him. He couldn't stay angry in the presence of his friend.

He thought back to when they were kids—the Yankees had won the World Series—and how they had run out of that apartment and stomped and goose-stepped up and down the block, celebrating, and how none of the other kids (or parents) came out of their houses— *the Mets fans*—and those kids had hid behind their front doors and grumbled, while listening to the hooting and hollering, daring them to step outside.

Quick!

He needed to concentrate…the pictures, the scenes…

He stopped.

"This is ridiculous," he muttered, and he stood up and shoved the gun back in its holster.

Lestor didn't bother to go back to the couch when he came out of the bathroom. He stopped in the middle of the room and faced Colin, their places now switched.

"Colin, I need to go," he said. "I need to get back to the city."

Colin stopped his struggles with Bruno and they both looked up dumbfounded. But Colin also felt relief. He sensed something was not right.

He got up and walked Lestor to the door.

"Are you okay?" he asked, opening the door.

Bruno ran out into the yard. Lestor stepped out after him and turned.

"I don't know," he said, "…No. I'm not okay. I have no idea what to do."

"Are you sure you don't want to hang out for a while," Colin asked, "and watch the game?"

"No," Lestor said. "I can't relax now. It's too soon."

"Lestor," Colin said. "I'm sorry. This whole thing…was just so crazy. I didn't know what to do."

Lestor paused.

"What was she saying, Colin?"

Colin froze. He knew exactly what Lestor was talking about…the scene, the scene etched into everyone's mind: Lestor's mother on her knees, arms opened to her attackers until…

Colin stared at the ground, an expression of pain flashed across his face, and he spoke her words in a whisper.

"'You don't understand'," she said. "'You don't understand'."

Lestor turned quickly to leave then stopped.

"…You should have done *something*," he said, then left, leaving Colin alone with his blunt statement.

Lestor walked down the unlit driveway leading toward the front of the house. Once on the sidewalk he turned toward his parents' house at the other end of the block. He could see the glaring lights of the press. They were camped out, waiting for him. Their equipment and trucks reached out into the middle of the street, leaving only a thin lane for cars to get by.

He thought of his mother. Her arms held out till the end…No, he couldn't let himself get weak now. It was too soon to forgive.

He walked toward the bright lights. They would bring him back.

CHAPTER 3

When Lestor returned to his apartment in the East Village the next morning, he found his girlfriend, Casey, waiting for him. They both lived there, but Casey had left the city the moment the riots started. Her mother had insisted that she go right to Grand Central and hop on the first train north.

Lestor agreed; their apartment was not far from City Hall: ground zero of the riots. But he didn't really think they were in any danger.

That night, Casey had witnessed the events live, just as Lestor had. She had been close to his parents, especially his mother, and her first instinct was to run back to the city, but her parents forbade it.

She paced her house in agony for the next two days, trying to get through to Lestor in ten different ways, but he never answered, and he never got back to her. And the longer it went on, the worse she felt. She began to have the unsettling feeling that maybe...Lestor held some resentment toward her, because of her background. Casey was black.

Her heritage had never been a problem. In fact, their integrity had been so pure that it had never come up, until now—and now it was the only thing she could think about. For two days, she obsessed herself into a frenzy until, for the first time in her life, she outright disobeyed her parents and raced back to Manhattan.

And so when Lestor returned to his apartment and saw her standing alone at the back of their kitchen, he realized how big of a mistake he had made. Her eyes told it all.

How could he have been so cruel?

They both broke down, falling into each other's arms then sinking to the floor; neither of them saying a thing until they were all cried out.

Afterwards, Casey helped him to their room so he could get some rest.

They had met in college. Lestor was two years her senior at NYU. They had dated all through school then continued on afterward; and when Lestor's parents realized how serious they were, they let the young couple move into their old apartment in the Village. It had been *their* first apartment too.

Lestor taught high school in Spanish Harlem, while Casey worked on her master's at Columbia. They would marry when she graduated.

Lestor spent the rest of the day in fitful sleep, while Casey spent the day ducking in and out of the room like a worried mother over a sick child. Lestor would open his eyes and she would be there, hovering over him, holding a cool glass of orange juice to his lips…He'd close his eyes…Next he'd see her pacing the living room in worried conversation on the phone.

At one point he opened his eyes, and she stood at the foot of his bed: "I just saw my old college roommate interviewed on TV," she told him.

But Lestor didn't understand; all he could do was wonder: "What time is it?" Because daylight still filled the room. With his body drained and his mind unsettled, he hadn't the energy to tell real life from dream.

"You're invited to a peace rally at Union Square…" he heard clear as a bell.

"…The President just said your name…" he wasn't sure he heard at all.

And then, at last, he opened his eyes and the room was filled with cool blue night. He looked down, past his feet, through the opened door to the living room, and didn't see Casey.

The couch was out of view, to the left of the doorway; the television to the right. If she had been there, he would've caught a glimpse of her legs on the couch. Opposite the couch, also out of sight, a muted screen washed the empty room with a flickering, underwater blue.

"Case…?" he called weakly.

Without pause Casey stepped backward into the door frame; she had been standing in front of the television. She stared at him without a word, and Lestor knew something was wrong.

Oh God! Why can't this just be over already?

"What's wrong?" he asked as he sat up.

"Lestor," she said, slipping into tears, "I don't think it's over yet."

Lestor hopped out of bed and made his way to the living room.

He looked at the television. More flames, more live footage from helicopters: silhouettes leaping before walls of orange.

"Enough!" he blurted, as he stumbled back in revulsion.

Casey grimaced as she watched him struggle. She had been trying to keep him from any bad news today. She didn't tell him that the media had tracked down her parents and called them for an interview, and she didn't mention the police car that was on fire in broad daylight, in front of the courthouse in downtown Brooklyn. She didn't tell him about the news specials on his family, and the Martin family, and that, basically, this story was the only thing the entire planet was talking about.

But there was only so much she could hide from him. This was becoming too much for her to bear alone.

"Lestor! Look!"

She grabbed his wrist with one hand and pointed to the television with the other.

Lestor stopped and turned back to the screen. He leaned in and squinted. Casey watched the awareness grow on his face.

"Oh my God!"

It was his parents' block. It was on fire.

It's Shazz.

Inexplicably, he struggled to suppress a smile. "What the fuck?" he said.

He stepped closer to the screen.

Firefighters ran to and fro in a scene that seemed reminiscent of a World War Two documentary: the bombing of London.

Shazz is here.

There was no more hiding.

He sat down and watched as the scenes rolled by like numbers on a roulette wheel. Casey sat down beside him.

…In Brooklyn, reporters spoke before backdrops of jittering flames…In Union Square, people had already begun to gather for the next day's peace rally…A reporter stood beside a burnt-out car, a reporter stood in front of the blown-out windows of a looted store, and always, every time the wheel stopped, it landed on the same static image: the outside of Lestor's building, its façade blanched white by the lights of the camera, solitary as a monument.

After the third time on double zero, Lestor leapt to his feet and pointed at the screen: "What's this got to do with me?" he shouted. "This has got nothing to do with me!"

Casey didn't say a thing. She put her hand on his forearm for assurance.

"Even if I went out there and told everybody to calm down," he said, "and then went to the peace rally and told everyone to forgive those…those *devils* that killed my parents, this will not stop. This will *never* stop."

At that moment, on the screen, a flustered correspondent in front of their building directs her cameras toward the sidewalk. Two men are approaching from down the block. They step out of the shadows of a large tree. Immediately, a crowd of reporters swarms them. Lestor starts. It's Shazz and his friend, Roddy. There is some jostling among the reporters as they try to talk to the two men, but Shazz and Roddy don't slow.

A reporter shouts: "What do you think about the fire in Brooklyn, Shazz?"

"I couldn't care less if that whole neighborhood burned down."

"Are you going to tomorrow's peace rally?" another reporter asks.

Shazz stops for a moment.

"Are you kidding?" he says. "You saw what happened. Would *you* go to a peace rally?"

He resumes walking.

The men turn onto the front stoop of Lestor's building and climb the stairs.

Questions continue to fly, but Shazz and Roddy are already inside the building.

Lestor and Casey stood dumbstruck in the middle of their living room. They had been watching the scene as if it were a thousand miles away. They didn't react to what was happening until the television screen showed the front door to their building close behind the two men. Then they started running around and straightening up the apartment. They had only a few seconds before Shazz would be at their door. By the time they fixed the pillows on the couch and threw a glass or two in the sink, a knock was already sounding at the door.

They froze and looked at each other.

After a short pause, they heard the sound of a key in the lock.

Casey ran to get the door.

CHAPTER 4

You pray to God for relief but it never comes. Drugs won't do it; exercise won't do it; meditation won't do it…Taking a few days off from work and hiding from the world, sort of does it, for a while; but then the world squeezes back in through the cracks, and the pressure is back.

Virgil sat on his living room chair, concentrating. He did this often. It was a type of prayer. Any time a terrible thought entered his mind, he'd close his eyes and concentrate on killing it. Through constant practice, his abilities had become so focused, so perfect, that he could encapsulate a malignant thought in an instant, and keep it from touching others. He would box these personal memes so tightly, that they would quickly shrivel and die from lack of air, and then they could be safely ejected from his mind. This had to be done. It was the only way for him to move forward through daily life.

Schools in the city had been closed after the first night of the riots; most of the businesses too, and the hallways in Virgil's building had taken on the air of a college dormitory during a weekend snowstorm.

The stranded residents spent their days wandering the halls and dropping in and out of neighbors' apartments.

Virgil had been told not to report to work until things had settled down. What good would a single unarmed security guard be anyway, against a rampaging mob? So he spent the next few days shuffling around his dusky apartment, never opening the door.

After he had calmed his thoughts, Virgil got up to check the hallway. He did this regularly. His apartment was set at the end of the hallway, next to the stairwell entrance, and when he looked through his peephole, he could see the full length of the hallway, straight down to the stairwell at the other end of the hall. He noted that every door on the hallway stood wide open…Gatherings ebbed and flowed in front of different doors during the course of the day, as people spontaneously collected to discuss the latest flare-up in the news.

At first, everyone had been shocked into whispers by the horrific footage of the Milgrams' murder, but as time went on, various opinion makers—on television, on social media, in the newspapers—made it socially acceptable to gloss over the bloody scene and focus on the injustices that had led to it: *Where was the coverage of the Martins' murder? Where was the outcry over the police brutality during the protest?*

Which, in turn, caused others to jump to take up the opposite positions: *How can you justify the killing of two people on the street like that?*

Sides were being chosen.

And while this debate was being wrestled out over the airwaves, a constant supply of new incidents was being fed into the furnace: a white police officer was shot in Texas, a black teen was shot by a cop in Chicago.

On the night of the great Brooklyn fire, a new, almost visceral, tension could be felt in the air. The entertaining television event had become serious, and a small kernel of real fear dripped into people's thoughts: *maybe this situation is not in control.*

It was at this point that Virgil could no longer bear hiding in his apartment. And so around midnight on the night of the fire, he opened his front door and joined the ranks of hall walkers. He had to talk to someone.

When he finally stepped into the bright hallway, he was surprised to see how many people were still up at such a late hour. He spent the next few hours talking with neighbors from every floor and wing of his building. He spoke to some people he hadn't seen in years.

It felt good to open up and talk again. He talked for hours—and could have talked more. But by 4.30 in the morning, most of the doors on his hallway had closed, leaving him alone once more. He reluctantly lumbered back into his apartment. He turned on his computer. He turned on his TV, and he waited for the early risers.

The fire in Brooklyn had been doused hours ago: news copters no longer had flames to buzz around. So by dawn, the latest chapter in the citywide turmoil had already begun focusing on the arrival of Shazz Milgram: the older son of Stanley and Theresa...

How will Shazz Milgram's arrival on the scene affect the situation?

Is Shazz's arrival what Lestor Milgram has been waiting for, before making a statement?

Like it or not, Lestor's brother had become the topic of the early morning news shows.

Virgil had an uneasy feeling about this new variable in the equation: Shazz had snorted at the idea of a peace rally, and he might have had something to do with the fire.

His words certainly were not helping the situation.

The media was saying that someone may have died in the fire.

First the youngest Milgram son had disappeared, and now this. To Virgil, it seemed like an endless parade of bad news.

He went into the kitchen and made a sandwich. He was running low on food.

A neighbor had told him that the deli on the corner was still open. "It'd take more than a riot to stop them Koreans from opening," she had said.

I better go tonight, Virgil thought, as he ate his sandwich and clicked away at his computer. The situation might go on longer than expected.

From the start, the protest at City Hall had gone all wrong. More people than anticipated had shown up. Bound by social media, the students of New York were well-organized.

The police, on the other hand, had prepared as they always had prepared for this type of rally: by closing off a small section of lower Broadway next to City Hall. They had set up a series of pens, into which they efficiently herded the protestors—and from which the protestors were allowed to harmlessly vent their discontent.

All morning, the sun had beaten down on the caged protesters. They chanted and listened to speeches, while crammed into their pens.

"How many times has this same protest, for this same reason, taken place?" was said. "Is anyone even listening?…Are our lives worth nothing?…Are we shouting into the wind?"

It was around noon that, here and there, people began fainting. Those who had passed out in the back, were carried off to a shady spot for some water and medical attention. But when a young woman up front passed out, up against one of the metal barriers, things became more complicated.

Behind the woman stood a packed and protesting crowd. On the other side of the barrier stood thirty feet of clear asphalt, lined by a phalanx of police officers in full riot gear. The officers themselves were boiling in the heat.

Most people would point to this moment as the catalyst that started the riots.

Patty, the young woman who passed out, was a delicate-looking thing. She couldn't have been more than five feet tall and a hundred pounds. She wore boxy shorts, too big for her skinny legs, and an oversized white T-shirt with a logo of her own design: a large peace sign scrawled in black marker.

As the protest had worn on, she had started leaning heavily against her roommate, who thought she had been joking, until she realized that Patty was not responding to her. She shouted for help, and a group of nearby friends had held Patty up, as they tried to work their way toward the back. But the pen was too crowded. Reluctantly, they were forced to lift Patty over the barrier and set her down on the hot asphalt, her back upright against the barrier.

Arms reached through the bars to hold Patty steady; more reached over the top to proffer water and tamp her burning forehead with a cool, damp cloth. Others shouted to the police to come over and take Patty out of the sun. But after a long ten minutes, Patty was still sitting there.

The police officers' job that day was to hold their ground, not to administer first aid, and one of the images burned into people's minds—and printed on front pages—was that of a line of burly white police officers standing idly by, while a frail, semiconscious brown girl lay helpless at their feet.

The longer the scene played out, the more the crowd's outrage grew. Until it became too much, and someone stepped up to do something.

"You see how much they care about us!" Howard shouted, as he put a foot on top of the barrier and prepared to jump over. "They would let this girl die, right here in front of them, without lifting a finger." He swung his body over the barrier and landed with a bounce on the open street, all the while keeping a wary eye on the police.

"Protect and serve man! Protect and serve!" he barked over his shoulder at the unmoving wall of black.

Patty was one of Howard's people: she was one of the students he had organized. He felt responsible for her. He had hopped the steel barrier with the intention of helping her to her feet, then peacefully walking her out of there. His gesture seemed obvious to him: it would help both sides. He hoped it would be obvious to the police officers too.

Howard had just knelt in front of Patty, when all at once, the police line moved forward.

A great roar went up in the crowd.

Here we go!

Howard barely had time to turn his head, and when he did, he turned full face into a blast of pepper spray.

A collective scream of outrage rose from the crowd.

Howard collapsed instantly. Every membrane on his face became inflamed. His eyes were on fire. He couldn't breathe. He couldn't see. For a few seconds, he thought he was going to suffocate… until he quickly figured out how to get air into his lungs: he got on his hands and knees and began taking huge gulps of air like a fish out of water.

Meanwhile the crowd had shoved forward, and the police were shoving back, and Howard was on the ground between them, getting kicked and crushed by both sides.

It took him a moment to regain his composure. He was still blind, but breathing had become easier. When he realized what was going on all around him, his first thoughts were to get out of there.

He reached out a hand to feel for Patty… but she was gone.

Probably cleared out by the police, he hoped.

He was getting to his feet, trying to stand up, when in a burst of defiance the crowd surged again. Howard was hit hard in the rear, and shoved forward in an awkward, arms flailing, running fall. He soared out of control; his feet desperately trying to catch up to his almost horizontal body, until he slammed headfirst into the soft belly of a street cop. They each dropped in opposite directions.

In an instant, three cops pounced on Howard and started beating him about the arms and legs. A few seconds later, he was dragged off in plastic cuffs then tossed into the back of an empty police wagon.

It wasn't until he was face up on the steel floor of the wagon that the pain caught up to him. He had been removed from the situation so fast that his cuffs hadn't been secured; one hand had slipped out.

He immediately turned over onto his knees and began wiping his face with his T-shirt. Then he pulled off his shirt so he could thoroughly wipe down his whole head; and as the pain receded and he was able to pay attention to the world outside, he became aware of a sound like breaking surf all around him.

Outside, the sounds of struggle roared and rocked his prison cell. He heard the screams of men and cries of anguish, resounding off the canyon walls of lower Broadway and breaking up into the clear blue sky.

He jumped up and began hammering the walls of his steel cell, howling to the heavens.

CHAPTER 5

At eight the next morning, Virgil heard the thumping bass of someone's stereo from down the hall. No doubt it was the Boneheads: Chris and Ray.

Virgil moved quickly to his door to look out the peephole. The floor was empty, but he could see that the Boneheads' door was already open. Chris hopped out of the apartment. He stood in the center of the hallway wearing only a towel; he had apparently just gotten out of the shower. He looked down the hall one way, his body bouncing with the music, then he spun and faced the other way. Seeing no one around, he hopped back into his apartment.

A minute later, Ray did the same thing.

Virgil grabbed the doorknob, about to venture out into the hall, but he quickly thought better of it. One had to prepare oneself for the Boneheads; they were forces of nature: super-human, ex-college football players. They weren't the type of people you could just sit and have a conversation with; especially not now, since, according to Virgil's internal clock, it was late night, while to the Boneheads, the day had just started, and they were at full power… Then again, the Boneheads were always at full power.

The Boneheads were the great curiosity of the building. Not because Ray was black and Chris was white, and they were room-mates; or even that they acted so alike, though Ray was raised in the next building over, while Chris had grown up on a Long Island sod farm. It was just that, they defied everyone's understanding of human physiology. How was it possible for one human being to have so much energy; let alone two?

Every night they'd be up late, clowning with a pack of friends until two in the morning, at which time, like clockwork, they'd go to bed, falling asleep the instant their heads hit the pillow. And then a calmness would descend upon the hall… until eight the next morning, when they'd hop up and hit the ground running at full steam.

They had met at college in Michigan, where they both had full football scholarships, Ray as a quarterback, Chris as a safety and surprisingly good punt and kickoff returner. But neither of them had ever taken it seriously; mostly, they had enjoyed one big party for four years.

Now that they were graduated, the party simply continued.

Virgil went back into his kitchen and poured out a bowl of cereal. He'd have to wait for a few more of his neighbors to awaken before he entered the hallway. A few extra people would help to dissipate the energy of the Boneheads. The last time they had caught him alone, they literally dragged him into their apartment to watch highlights from Ray's high school playing days. "This is the tape they sent to his recruiter," Chris had said, filled with pride for his friend's accomplishments.

On the screen, Ray ran one way or another; tossing the ball over groups of players into end zones, or running into end zones himself.

The video was of poor quality and played like an old-time, sped up, black-and-white movie.

Virgil remembered being sandwiched between the two on their tired red corduroy couch. An empty beer keg sat in front of them on the bare floor.

It was just last night that Chris told Virgil it was Howard, who had been the person on the news getting maced by the cops.

"Yo Virge," Chris had shouted, stomping his feet in excitement. "You see Howard knock that cop on his ass with his head? He Earl Campbell'd him!"

He was referring to a famous run by the ex-Houston Oiler, but Virgil didn't know that.

"That was Howard?" Virgil said. "Are you serious?"

"Yeah man!" Chris shouted. "We could have used a noggin like that back at school."

Virgil was shocked. He had seen the footage many times but hadn't realized it was Howard.

When he went back into his apartment later that night, he logged in and watched it again.

Already, internet jokers had edited the video to add their own sound effects. Howard now moved to the sounds of Curly from the Three Stooges: wiping the pepper spray from his face in a frenzy, *woo woo woo*; getting knocked in the ass by the metal barrier, *bonk*; giving the cop a running head butt to the belly, *oof!*

It was definitely Howard: his jerky mannerisms, his squared jaw, and his close-shaved head.

There he was, his Howard, at the start of a huge riot.

In a way, he was relieved. It was far better than if Howard had been at the end of the riot, in Brooklyn... After Howard had been thrown into the police wagon, the protest had turned into a full-out battle. The small triangular block that City Hall sat on had been locked up tight, so the only way for an angry crowd to move forward, was to flow around it. And as luck would have it, Police Plaza was right there. And so, without actually planning it, the large crowd found itself right where it needed to be: in the wide-open space of One Police Plaza.

"*Virge!*" Ray shouted when Virgil opened his door, a few hours after he had first looked out the peephole. Ray had been standing in front of his door, keeping an eye out for people.

"*Virge!*" came a similar shout from inside the apartment... followed by Chris popping out into the hallway.

"Boneheads!" Virgil answered, with as much enthusiasm as he could muster, as he walked down the hall.

"Hey, Ray," Chris said, turning to his roommate, "Virge was in the army, right?"

"Virge, you were in the army, right?" Ray asked in a confidential tone.

"Yeah," Virgil answered. "What for? Why do you ask?"

"Come here, we want to show you something." Ray said, and put his arm around Virgil's shoulder and guided him into their apartment.

Ray was the taller of the two men, though still not as tall as Virgil, and Virgil looked down admiringly at Ray's full head of dark dreadlocks, perfectly trimmed to shoulder length. The dreds only added to Rays contrast to Chris, who had a small blond mustache and naturally bleach blond hair that grew in tight wavy curls, right up against his scalp. And though at first glance, the two men appeared to be complete opposites, if you spent any time with them at all, your brain would simply overwhelm your eyes, and you'd think they were related.

Inside the apartment, three of their friends were sitting on the floor, playing video games. Their attention didn't waver from the screen when Virgil walked by.

There was always a contingent of video game kids in the Boneheads' apartment: friends from their old school dropping by for an extended visit, or other gamers from the building—all watching a sporting event… or playing video games.

Ray led Virgil into the apartment's only bedroom. It was set up like a typical college dorm room: a twin bed on each side, and not much else. Chris was standing in the room. A flat, square box lay on the bed closer to the door. Ray reached over and flipped the lid open. Inside was a black pistol.

"Whoa!" Virgil jumped back, as if the gun were a snake. "What the heck, man! What are you doing with that?"

Both Chris and Ray looked earnestly at Virgil's face, as if uncertain about whether this new thing in their apartment was good or bad.

"Is this what you had in the army, Virgil?" Chris asked.

"No," Virgil answered without thinking, "we had M-9s… 9 mms. That looks old….what the heck. Where did you get that thing?"

Virgil pulled slowly away from the pistol, thinking: *This thing can shoot through walls. I'm not even safe in my own apartment.*

He needed to get away from it.

"Raj and his friends found a van loaded with them; boxes of them. Right outside. Right on Avenue D," Chris said, pointing at the wall of the room that faced the Avenue. "Someone broke the window and they all got grabbed up."

"They were shooting them off on the roof last night," Ray said, "while watching the fire over in Brooklyn."

"You know how to use it?" Chris asked.

"Yeah well… hell no!" Virgil said. "What are you doing with this thing? This is very dangerous. You need to get rid of it. You're going to end up killing someone."

Virgil turned and left the apartment. He felt sick to his stomach.

A poison had found its way into his garden.

Virge! he heard, as he left the apartment.

"Get rid of it!" Virgil yelled over his shoulder, as he went back into his apartment.

But he knew they wouldn't; even he had felt its pull. "What is wrong with people," he said, after he had slammed the door behind him.

Everyone was moving in the wrong direction.

He thought about how the protests had so quickly become violent. How the police had moved forward, swinging and swinging and moving through clouds of teargas; how the protesters, who were usually moved to fear by something like this, had resolutely stood their ground. Rocks and bricks and anything else that could have been pulled up from the plaza's landscaping had been hurled at the police. There were scores of injuries on both sides. Bloody students were carried to a small grass field nearby; a field that turned out to be the African Burial Ground National Monument—a fact that was not overlooked by the protesters—and both sides were growing more and more filled with dangerous, self-righteous rage. By early afternoon, knowledge of what was happening downtown had spread, and everyone who worked in the city was well aware of the situation. People began leaving work early.

By the time most people got home, they were shocked by the intensity of what they saw on the six o'clock news.

Where did this come from?

By the eleven o'clock news, what had been born in lower Manhattan had been pushed across the Brooklyn Bridge, culminating at the Milgrams' front door.

"What the hell was a van filled with guns doing outside anyway?" Virgil thought, as he sat quietly on the hallway floor inside his apartment, his back against his front door.

CHAPTER 6

The first time Casey saw demon was in her boyfriend's face. Actually, "boyfriend" was not a strong enough word for their relationship. To Casey, that word had always smacked of two-month-long, suburban high school relationships. Ones that she could never quite understand: how could you give your soul to a new person every few months? It made no sense at all. When Casey gave, she gave for good.

They had been dating only a few months when she had seen it: the demon. They had been out to dinner, and though it was a Monday night, Lestor had convinced her to go out for one more drink afterwards. It wasn't until the bar had emptied, that Casey realized Lestor had had too much to drink. The situation was starting to feel ugly and she wanted to go home. He wanted to stay. In a brief, furious flurry, they argued, and Casey stood to leave.

That's when Lestor spun around in his seat and, in a panic, held onto one of Casey's hands with both of his. He stared into her eyes and pleaded, "Don't leave me. Please don't leave me here," as if he were powerless; as if he were bolted to the stool… and that's when she saw it—or rather, that's when she saw him, beneath it. His tawny features, helplessly imprisoned beneath a shimmering, gossamer veil of some force, some… demon, who, in its arrogance, in its supreme confidence in its absolute control over Lestor, had carelessly risen to the surface.

It all happened in an instant, because as soon as this demon realized it had been perceived, by the instant flash of recognition on Casey's face—it shot back down like a night crawler surprised by a flashlight, once again wrapping itself tightly, somewhere deep within the bowels of its unsuspecting victim, once more, firmly in control.

That was the exact moment when Casey realized that Lestor was an alcoholic. It was the first demon that Casey had ever encountered, and she should have had no way of recognizing it, but some atavistic instinct, left over from primordial days, had kicked in hard at that first meeting. Instantly, her heart had been seized with terror, and instantly, she felt rage: this was something to be killed immediately.

Since then, they had starved the demon out. They had quit going out three or four nights a week; they stopped having bottles of wine with dinner, they had gone for help together. And slowly, so slowly, the parasite atrophied away. It was the only way they knew how to rid themselves of it. There were no miracles; no… laying of hands, that would magically eject this demon out of him. No. Time was all they knew: little by little; step by step, ever vigilant.

The night Casey opened the door for Shazz and Roddy, she felt that fear once again, and realized right away, that a different type of demon had entered their lives. This was not the Shazz she had known for years; *that* Shazz was not in control.

The two men walked silently past her as she held the door. They were tall and gaunt, like wood-hewn statues from a medieval church, come to life. Lestor stood silently in the living room. He had known his brother was on his way the moment he saw the fire.

The two brothers embraced, and for the first time since the nightmare began, Lestor felt his strength returning to him. He felt like crying, but he had to stay strong in front of his older brother.

"Was that you?" Lestor asked quietly, nodding his head toward the television.

Shazz looked at the flames on the muted screen. Lestor watched his face closely to see if his expression would change; it didn't. His gaze remained hard and impassive, the only movement, the flickering reflection in his eyes. He nodded and turned back to his brother.

"Yes," he said, "I did that."

In his heart, Lestor had already known; but still, it came as a shock. It seemed unreal that this person in front of him could be responsible for an event being televised throughout the world.

"…and Mom's house?" Lestor asked.

"No. Not our house. Our house is fine… and Mrs. Greene's. You'll see. Tomorrow morning they'll be the only undamaged houses on that side of the block, and then everyone will know."

"Know what?"

"Know that it wasn't an accident."

The statement stopped Lestor in its tracks. It was all too much to digest.

Shazz saw the look of consternation in his brother's face and moved on.

He went over and greeted Casey. "You remember Roddy?"

Roddy had been standing a respectful distance behind as the reunion took place; he had been trying hard not to stare at the flames on the screen, but he couldn't help himself. He snapped out of his

trance as soon as Shazz mentioned his name. He nodded his head
in greeting.

Roddy was a longtime friend of the family. Lestor had known him
for years; Casey had met him a few times as well. Roddy was tall—taller
than Shazz, who stood at an even six feet—but he didn't seem as tall
because of the way he carried himself. He leaned slightly forward at
the waist, as if trying to keep eye level with the rest of the world, and
when he walked, the long upper half of his body swayed with each
step, the way a giraffe's neck moves when it walks. He had long blond
hair that he kept in a ponytail, and more than a few earrings in each
ear. The loose gray sweatshirt he wore was sleeveless, and his skinny
arms sported random old-school tattoos, as if each had been tossed
on without much forethought at the end of a long night of drinking.
Lestor noticed a new one in the center of his left forearm: a classic
black panther.

"I just found out last night," Shazz said. "We'd been out fishing
all day, and were just sitting down to eat at the marina when I looked
up at the television and saw it." He waved a finger toward the screen
and shook his head in disgust.

"We hopped in the truck as soon as we saw it," Roddy added, "and
drove straight through."

They moved into the kitchen and sat around the table. Casey
brought out food and drink, then sat down next to Lestor. She hadn't
heard everything Shazz had said to him when he first came in, but
she got the gist of it.

Shazz didn't mention the fire again while they talked. He was
more interested in what had been happening with his brother for the
past few days. He asked questions, and Lestor told his story, minus
the gun and visit to Colin's house. He told Shazz about his visit with

the Mayor and police commissioner, and how it didn't feel right, and how he had snuck out of the building and gone to their parents' house in Brooklyn.

"Good!" Shazz said. "They were gonna use you. They want this mess behind them as fast as possible, and they need us to make it okay to move forward. They don't give a shit. It's political theater: we go out there and beg the world to accept *our* forgiveness, and they bow their heads at the funeral and say how wonderful we all are and what great examples we all are, and then they move on.

"Thank God you didn't give that speech," he concluded. "Mom and Dad would have been forgotten already..."

They spent the rest of the night catching up. They spoke of old times, and everyone—Casey and Roddy included—told stories; and without planning, sitting around the kitchen table became their parents' memorial dinner, and warming hearts blossomed smiles. But every so often they would stop, and turn toward the television, and wonder at the world and their new role in it.

How had it all gotten so hard?

Casey listened and joined in, but when she saw the turmoil on television, she worried. With Shazz's attitude, she saw no good way for the situation to resolve, and she knew Lestor's fate was tied to his brother's. After a while, she started to get a headache, and she turned in for the night.

The others stayed up for a while longer. Lestor could see that Roddy and Shazz were exhausted. They had been up for two nights straight. The front room was already made up for Shazz, and after Roddy nodded off on the couch, Lestor got out some sheets and a pillow for him. Then he turned in.

Evening had always been Lestor's favorite time of the day. Lying down beside Casey was bliss. With her next to him, he felt perfect satisfaction: nothing outside their room could make him happier. He'd lie half-buried among pillows and gaze up at her fixing her hair, or flipping through a magazine, and he felt his soul being nourished. She was all his in those moments.

I won't enjoy my oasis tonight, he thought as he entered the bedroom and saw her sitting on the bed, staring down at her laptop. She had been gathering news. She looked worried. Lestor was worried too. He left the room to brush his teeth.

Shazz was sitting on the edge of the living room chair, fixated on the television; something about it scared Lestor. Shazz rarely paid attention to television; seeing his brother sitting there, getting charged up by the news, unnerved him.

Lestor brushed his teeth and went back into the bedroom. He sat on the bed, next to Casey.

"He's going to kill someone," he said to her. "There's no doubt in my mind. Shazz is going to kill someone." He rested his forehead in his hands and shook his head. "I don't think this is over. Something very bad is going to happen."

"Lestor," Casey said, "he just set fire to a whole city block? Don't you think that's bad enough?"

Lestor said nothing at first; then spoke.

"When Shazz first came to our house, he was quiet for a long time. I mean, that's what my mother told me. I didn't notice. I loved him. He played with me. He took care of me, but mostly he stayed in the house, as if he didn't believe any of it was real; as if he was afraid that if he went outside, none of it would be there when he came back. He had a tough few years before that, what with his mother passing and his alcoholic father running the show.

"This was around the time of my parents' first big case: the Barker case. My parents were defending a black man who shot and wounded three white cops. It was all over the news.

"I was eight. Shazz was thirteen; he had only been with us for a few months."

Lestor sat up and leaned back against the headboard. He held a pillow over his chest as he spoke.

"You know that storefront church on the corner of my parents' block? That used to be a bar, and there were always a few guys hanging around outside smoking cigarettes. They weren't dangerous, just neighborhood guys, but we steered clear of them as kids.

"My father was becoming well known in New York. He was in the papers every day, standing next to Larry Barker, the 'cop shooter,' and he still took the subway to work. So one day, on the way home from court, he walks past the bar, and this guy, Frank, calls him a 'nigger lover.'

"My father was in shock: he was under the impression that he was some sort of hero in the neighborhood. So he ignored the guy and kept walking.

"When he gets home, he calls my mother into the kitchen and tells her what happened. He tells her not to walk by the bar anymore.

"I was outside, so I didn't hear any of this, but Shazz—he was in the living room; he heard the whole thing. And as soon as he hears it, he gets up and walks out the front door.

"Now this guy, Frank, was maybe twenty-five or thirty, I don't know exactly, but back then he looked like a full-grown man to me. He was a skinny guy with greasy black hair and a mustache; I think he was a tow truck driver or something. He was always outside the bar, standing in front of his truck.

"So I was sitting on the stoop, doing who knows what, when Shazz walks out of the house and heads down the block without saying a word to me, and I can tell something's up, cause he rarely left the house at that point. So, of course I follow, at a distance.

"Shazz was a pretty big kid, but Frank? Like I said, he was an adult; but this doesn't matter to Shazz. He walks right up to him, ignoring the two other guys who are there, and without a word, without even hesitating, he crushes Frank's jaw with a right hook: *BAM!* One shot. I heard it from fifty feet away. I saw Frank's hair snap straight up in the air, and his body dropped like a sack of potatoes... like someone flicked a switch in the back of his head to 'off' position.

"I couldn't believe it. I almost pissed in my pants. It was unreal. An ADULT, he hit an adult... he hit ANYONE! It was so out of character to what I knew about Shazz: he had been so quiet, so protective. So to see him in this capacity... like some sort of... demon—I just didn't know who that person was."

Casey was surprised by what she was hearing. She, too, had never seen that side of Shazz. Whenever she met him at their parents' house, he had always been such a responsible, doting son.

"So what happened?" she asked.

"Well, the other guys who had been standing there all jumped back as if their friend had just been shot. They didn't know what to do. Shazz was only thirteen. He had these two men backed against the wall, and was right in their faces, threatening them.

"'You fuckers ever say a word to my father again and you'll end up like that fucker' he said, pointing at Frank, who was out cold on the ground.

"I was four or five houses away, scared shit, and the next thing I know, my dad flies past me in his flip-flops to break it up.

"Of course, the guys get brave when people start coming out. The bartender came out; the guy who owned the deli next door; some of the other fathers from the block—and one of the bar guys says something to my dad like, 'You better control that kid before he gets hurt.'

"And Shazz pounces on him, and hits him like five or six times in two seconds, and the guy is balled up against a car and Shazz is yelling, 'What the fuck did I just tell you!'

"And then it turns into a melee.

"We found out later that Shazz's biological father had been sending him to boxing classes since he was, like, four: a real nut.

"Eventually, my mom gets down there and drags Shazz back home. And as they go by me, I can see that Shazz's face is all swollen, with these red knots all over it, not from getting hit, though I'm sure he took a few shots, but more as if something was rising up out of him, and trying to break free.

"And on top of all that, he had this big… serene smile on his face."

Lestor turned and looked at Casey.

"You have to understand; my house was like a hippie reservation: a world of peace and love. I had never known anything like this. It had my parents worried. They had a real long talk with Shazz after that."

Lestor took the pillow he was holding and slid it behind his neck.

"You know, as appalled as my father was about the whole thing, I think there was a part of him that was touched; you know, that Shazz was fighting for him."

Casey sat quietly. She was thinking about the fear she had felt when Shazz first walked into the apartment. She was thinking that maybe they should leave the city, and stay with her parents upstate.

"What do you think he's going to do?"

"I don't know," Lestor said, his mind still afloat in memories. "But I'll tell you one thing. After that, I never saw Frank at that bar again. Never. And my parents never had a problem with anyone in the neighborhood either."

CHAPTER 7

The next morning when Lestor walked into the living room, he found Roddy sitting on the made-up couch, holding a big mug of coffee in his hands. His eyes were sleep-swollen and watery, and he looked as if he had just woken up. He nodded to Lestor, then raised his mug in greeting.

A pony wall separated the kitchen from the living room, and Lestor could see Shazz standing in the kitchen with a screwdriver in his hand. He was fixing one of the kitchen drawers. Shazz made himself at home whenever he visited the apartment. He had lived there himself for a while. Usually he stayed for only a few weeks between tenants. He'd stay awhile and repaint, and fix anything that needed fixing. Once he stayed for half-a-year, but in the end, he always moved back to Brooklyn; parking was easier.

Shazz's black hair had grown a bit shaggier since the last time Lestor saw him, but it still didn't go past his ears. He wore a white, long-sleeved T-shirt with the sleeves pushed up past his elbows; Lestor could see that his arms were dark from working in the sun. Hard physical labor in the Florida heat had burned the fat from his body, and the muscles under the thin skin of his forearms moved like valves and pistons, as he maneuvered the drawer back into its place.

When Lestor walked into the kitchen, Shazz stopped what he was doing and gave him a piqued look of restraint. Lestor stopped when he saw this.

Uh oh, he thought.

"What happened?" he said.

He followed Shazz's glance toward the TV.

The sound was off, but all three of them watched.

On the screen was a picture of Lestor's friend, Colin.

BREAKING NEWS read the chyron across the bottom of the screen.

A body had been found in the fire; the cause of death was unknown.

The news was showing footage from the night of the riots, freezing the film when it got to Colin; standing off to the side.

Lestor turned back to Shazz.

"You killed someone?" he asked in absolute shock. Then he looked at Roddy.

"I didn't know nothing!" Roddy said. He looked at Shazz.

"That wasn't your fight, Roddy," Shazz said.

"Shazz," Lestor said, "Colin was my friend."

"Your *friend*?" Shazz shouted. "What the fuck? You saw him. You saw him just standing there. How many times did that piece of shit eat at our table? How many meals did Mom cook for him?"

Lestor was torn. He knew what he had tried to do himself, but he also knew the horror he felt at having come so close to making a bad mistake.

He turned back to the television. On the screen: images of his mother being dragged… Colin standing in the corner, facing the other way.

"It's not easy standing up to a crowd, Shazz," he offered weakly. "Not everyone is like you."

"Oh no! Don't even go there. Mrs. Greene was out there fighting! And the old man; he was out there too. They may not have had a chance, but they tried. You never know what might have happened. One more person standing up… a young man, like Colin, might have won the day."

Shazz tossed the screwdriver back into the drawer and shut it.

"I'm not sorry for what I did, Lestor. You saw what happened. The press wants to treat this like another fucking reality show, for people's entertainment, but it's not. Our parents are fucking dead. They were slaughtered like pigs in front of the whole world, and you can bet your fucking ass that there's going to be a price to pay. Blood for blood; there will be no forgiving and forgetting. "

Lestor froze. All the arguments in his mind—the lessons of right and wrong that had been drilled into him his whole life—seemed empty platitudes in the face of his current reality. He was just as angry as his brother. He wanted that block burnt to the ground. He wanted every one of those rioters killed… But still… Colin was dead. None of it seemed real.

He didn't feel these people were gone. It was too fast. It was all too fast. He still felt that at any moment, they would all come walking in.

"Look!" Shazz shouted, pointing to the television. "They're showing it again." He was seething. "You see. They don't give a fuck about us. Entertainment! That's all it is to them. No one is going to stick up for you but *you*. If we don't make them pay for this, Mom and Dad's lives are going to be a punch line on late-night talk shows in a month.

"Motherfuckers!" His voice had risen steadily and ended in a roar. He lifted the kitchen table an inch and slammed its metal legs straight down onto the floor. Then he stood straight up, his fists clenched by his side, trembling.

He realized he was out of control, and in an attempt to diffuse his anger, he unclenched his fists, spreading his fingers wide, then walked into the other bedroom.

On the television, the news was showing the riot again; the media's altruism had lasted only so long. The death of Colin had given them an excuse to start showing it again: "… to explore Colin's role in the event."

Lestor had turned just in time to see his mother being struck by the brick again. He turned away without a word and froze, his shoulders hunched as if against a cold rain.

Roddy quickly turned the television off.

"Enough of this already," he said.

A minute later Shazz came out of the bedroom and walked into the living room. He was calmer now.

"Roddy, let's go take a look at the block. I need to pick up some things anyway. We'll swing by your house too."

"Yeah, okay," Roddy said, and he put his empty coffee mug down on the end table.

Lestor watched as Roddy reached around the end of the couch to get his shoes and put them on.

"Do you want me to come along?" he asked Shazz.

"No, you need to be here with Casey."

CHAPTER 8

Shazz had been silent for most of the drive up from Florida. His hands gripped the wheel tightly as he steered his pickup north along the dark southern highways.

Roddy looked over and could see bits of black-crusted blood and glinty fish scales from their day of fishing, still stuck to the edges of Shazz's hands and wrists, but he wasn't about to bother Shazz with such nonsense. He had seen it too: the crime, and even *his* head had been fucked up. He could just imagine what was going on in Shazz's.

He looked down at his own hands and scratched a few spots of blood from the corners of his fingernails. Every so often, he stole another glance at Shazz: his expression hadn't changed since they left ten hours ago. It was a look of intense concentration, and his body seemed frozen, as if all its resources were being dedicated to the processes going on in his mind.

Sometimes Shazz's foot would grow heavy, and the car would creep up to dangerous speeds. Roddy would grip the door handle tighter as the pickup rocked a little too much as they rounded a corner or switched lanes.

In South Carolina, they were pulled over by highway patrol. When the lights started flashing, Roddy's heart iced over. He shot a look at Shazz, to make sure he wasn't going to do something suicidal. Shazz pulled over.

"Did you see what happened on TV the other day? In New York?" he said to the cop through the rolled-down window. "That was my mother and father. I'm going up there right now to settle things."

The officer checked out the name on Shazz's license; then went back to his patrol car and made a call on his radio. Two minutes later he was giving them a police escort to the state line. Roddy was so excited that he almost shouted with glee as they sped along the highway. But now was not the time.

That Shazz, he thought, *people were always helping him out.*

Shazz drove the whole way. Roddy nodded some, but mostly he stayed awake for his friend. When they finally popped out of the dingy, exhaust-tinted Holland Tunnel, into the crisp bright lights of the city, Roddy felt as if he could breathe again. Not because of the oppressiveness of the ride up, but because he was back in his home waters again. "You get tired of beach and heat and being cooked every day," he said. "It starts to drive you crazy."

Shazz didn't respond.

Roddy hadn't realized his issue with Florida living until that moment. He needed the change of seasons. He needed cool fall air moving down from the north, and trees with big, floppy leaves, and snow.

Give me a foot of snow, he thought, *a New York blizzard brings everyone together.*

He was glad their job down there was almost finished. It was fun for a while; a nice change of scenery: beaches and bikinis, fishing and four-wheel drive, but he wanted to get back home already.

They looped around lower Manhattan toward the Brooklyn Bridge; once on the bridge, Roddy turned to get a full view of the pristine downtown skyline.

It was evening. The buildings were illuminated, and the energy radiating from the island was visceral.

Roddy hadn't seen the sight in such a long time that it struck him deeply, and he understood for the first time, what a tourist must feel, when first gazing at the sight: it was like Oz.

They wended their way through Brooklyn, stepping down from parkway, to avenue, to quiet streets, until they were in their old neighborhood.

Shazz parked a few blocks from his parents' house.

"Why are we stopping—" Roddy started to say, until he saw Shazz reach under his seat and pull out a flat, zippered bag.

Roddy knew what was in the bag; down in Florida they all used to go to the firing range together. Getting a gun was easy down there. They all had one. The zippered bag, Roddy knew, was Shazz's gun case.

"I need you to stay here, Roddy," Shazz said. "I'm going to go check out the house."

"Shazz, it's okay," Roddy said, undaunted by the gun. "I'm here to help."

"Roddy," Shazz said, "no."

He reached into the back seat of the car and pulled out his work jacket then opened the car door and walked away.

Roddy was left sitting in the car. He watched Shazz in the rearview mirror until he disappeared around the corner.

"Shit," he said, then got out of the car to stretch his legs and smoke a cigarette.

The pickup was parked next to a small park they used to play ball in when they were kids. As he smoked, he leaned his forearms between the spikes of the wrought-iron fence that surrounded the park. He noticed that the parks department had sawed off the points of all the spikes on the fence. *They should have done that twenty years ago,* Roddy thought. He remembered having to balance with trepidation over the spikes as he jumped over to get a ball that had rolled out.

This used to be his neighborhood too. He grew up playing football and baseball in that park. That was how he knew Shazz. That was how everyone in the neighborhood knew each other.

It was Shazz who got him his job. In their senior year of high school, a construction site had sprung up across the street from the room where they had their last class of the day. And every day, they monitored the site's progress.

"Damn, that building's going up fast," Roddy would say, as they paid more attention to the building than the blackboard. They watched in admiration as iron workers climbed the bare skeleton of the building, guiding huge girders with a single hand as the beams floated downward on steel cables.

"I hear they get paid big bucks," Roddy said. "I wonder how you get a job like that. Probably gotta know someone."

They watched the building grow for months, and then one day after school, Shazz walked onto the job site and asked the foreman for a job. They must have liked him because they hired him right there. He worked part-time after school and sometimes on weekends.

Shazz's parents had always hoped that he would go to college, but Shazz convinced them that this was what he wanted to do. A few months later, after graduation, Shazz had a full-time job.

Over the next few years, Shazz put in a good word for Roddy and a couple of other friends; eventually he built up his own work crew. The bosses liked Shazz. He didn't clown around and he worked hard; not because of the principle of it, but more because he actually enjoyed work.

As Shazz walked along the desolate avenue toward his parents' house, he had one goal in mind. He unzipped the gun bag, took out his holstered pistol, and tossed the bag into a garbage can. He checked to make sure the safety was on and tucked the holster and gun into his waistband.

He turned onto the street adjacent to his parents' block. It was a small, poorly lit, one-way street. As he walked along the empty block, he peered through the driveways and alleys, into the backyards. In the dark, he could barely make out the backs of the houses on his parents block; their outlines floated in the darkness like the ghosts of old sailing ships. When he saw his parents' house, he closed his eyes, grit his teeth, and kept moving.

Near the end of the block, he saw the back of Colin's house. He turned down the driveway and started to put on his jacket. He put one sleeve over his left arm then slid the other sleeve over the same arm, making sure his fingers were well tucked in. Then he wrapped the bottom of the jacket around the arm also. When the jacket was secure around his arm he hopped the wall into Colin's backyard.

It all happened fast because he knew exactly what he was going to do. All the decisions had been made. All that was left to do, was execute.

Colin's dog was already barking as Shazz walked toward the back-door with his gun drawn. Without stopping, he put three shots into the lock then kicked the door in. When the dog jumped at him, he stuck out his wrapped arm and let the dog latch on.

He continued moving forward, dragging the dog along the way. Colin leapt from his couch and sprinted across the room toward the kitchen. He spun and dropped as Shazz hit him with two quick shots.

He put the gun down on a table, then grabbed the dog's collar and forced him down on his back.

"Bruno! Relax! It's okay. It's okay." He held the dog against the floor while forcing his forearm farther into his jaws. "Take it easy!"

The dog's aggression had been replaced by confusion. He knew Shazz, but not well. He squirmed a few moments—ears back, eyes wide—then gave up. Shazz pulled his arm from the dog's mouth, then stood up and led the dog by his collar into the yard. He opened the back gate and steered Bruno out with a shove of the side of his foot. He put his jacket on.

Back inside, Shazz looked at Colin. He lay where he fell: face up, his arms neatly at his sides. The upper half of his body was lying on the kitchen floor; his feet had never made it out of the living room. A dark liquid rapidly filled the void between his arm and his body.

Shazz remained resolute. He picked up his gun and walked farther into the basement.

Only half of the basement had been converted into an apartment. A door at the back of the kitchen led to the other half—a poorly lit storage area. There wasn't too much stuff; it wasn't cluttered like Shazz's parents' house. An exercise bike, an old television set, a cheap card table on its side… everything was orderly, pushed neatly against the walls. The center of the floor was open and bare: Shazz could smell the cool damp concrete of the unfinished basement floor. It was a smell he knew well from work.

He spotted what he was looking for against the right wall: the snow blower. He had seen Colin's father use it many times. And next to the snowblower, was what he really wanted: a one-gallon plastic container of gasoline.

He took the container back out through the kitchen then set it outside the backdoor.

He went back into the kitchen, where he had spied an unopened bottle of rum on the counter. He picked up the bottle and tossed it across the floor, into the living room. The bottle burst in the corner of the room; the sweet smell of rum filled the air.

He walked back into the living room, took a lighter off the coffee table, and lit a small pool of the clear liquid. The rum ignited with a soft puff: Shazz watched the barely visible blue flame race up the wall and couch.

He watched the flame on the couch, until it took hold and turned orange. Then he walked out.

By way of backyards, Shazz made his way down the block toward his parents' house, methodically dousing homes and setting them on fire.

CHAPTER 9

It was still morning when Shazz walked through the wooden police barricades onto his parent's block. The police recognized him with a nod, and let him and Roddy pass.

It was Shazz's first good look at the damage he'd done the night before. The west side of the block, across the street from his parents' house, was intact; its trees were green, and the small lots in front of the assorted houses were well kept.

His side of the block was a different story. About half of the twenty or so houses were damaged. Trees had been scorched, parked cars had been forcibly moved, and wet burnt debris spilled out from the lots onto the street. The worse houses were at the far end of the block; from his parents' house to the near end, the houses had little or no damage.

There was something refreshing about the block, but he couldn't quite put his finger on what it was. Then it came to him. The sunlight. His parents' block had always been a sunny block: a broad two-way street, tossed in among the narrower one-way streets of the neighborhood;

but now, with half the houses and trees cut down in size, more sunlight reached the street.

If it wasn't for the soggy ash, and burnt wood scattered along the street, he thought it would have looked pretty good.

"You know, they should take all those houses down and build a small park here," he said, "or something like that... a playground."

Roddy nodded. He had been a little unnerved after finding out about Colin, but he couldn't say it was a total surprise. In fact, he had a pretty good idea that something bad had happened the previous night; after all, by the time Shazz came back to the car, several fire engines were already streaking past them. So he had known that Shazz did *that*.

The most obvious sign that Shazz had probably shot someone, had been that he stopped his truck in Brooklyn Heights on the way to Lestor's place—then threw what Roddy assumed was his gun into the East River. Roddy had waited in the car again: staring out the window at the underside of the Brooklyn Bridge as Shazz walked off. To his left, was the same Manhattan skyline, that earlier, had infused him with so much excitement.

Roddy didn't condemn Shazz's actions. He wasn't sure he wouldn't have done the same thing. He'd think about it—that was for sure. But if he was absolutely honest with himself, he knew he couldn't have gone through with it. Now he was an accomplice. He knew that Shazz was purposely keeping him in the dark. He also knew that Shazz would die before implicating him in any crime.

The two men walked in the middle of the street, heading toward Shazz's parents' house. Their mood grew somber. They moved onto the sidewalk, conscious not to step on the street where the deaths had occurred. Shazz kept his gaze forward as he walked up the front steps; everything reminded him of "the scene."

Roddy had been there enough times to feel at home in the Milgram house. When they walked in, he went straight to the living room and sat down on the couch. He stretched his legs out and clasped his hands behind his head. He knew Shazz had things to do.

The sunroom stood at the front of the house. It was a small, mostly glass room, that overlooked the sidewalk and front stairs. Sunlight reached in through its windows to the living room, forming geometric patterns on the rug and over Roddy's outstretched legs. He closed his eyes and focused on the sun's warmth. He had not slept well at Lestor's. He was still tired.

One room over on his right was the dining room. There was no wall between the rooms, just an old rolltop desk. When Shazz had come in, he had sat down at the dining room table. The dining room had always served as his parents' workroom: the table was covered with paperwork as usual. Shazz smiled when he looked down at the organized mess.

After a short sit, he got up.

"I need to get some stuff from upstairs," he said. "Take whatever you want from the fridge. We're gonna have to throw most of it out anyway."

Roddy opened his eyes as Shazz spoke; he closed them as soon as he left.

Shazz went upstairs to his old room. He had moved his things out of his apartment and into his parents' house when he moved to Florida.

It was only a temporary job, supposed to last no more than eighteen months. His boss had asked him if he wanted to oversee a job down there. He said no at first. He was happy where he was. He had a nice apartment, a girlfriend, a nice car; he ate a good meal at his parents' house two or three times a week. What else could he want? It had been his parents who had encouraged him to go. They had always wanted more for him: more education, more travel, more experiences. They never realized that being home with his family was what he wanted most.

"Go!" his father said. "What an opportunity! You'll get paid to visit Florida. Your mother and I have always wanted to get a place down there, but we don't know the area. Scout it out for us. Let us know what you think. We'll come and visit!"

He had said it with so much enthusiasm that Shazz felt he had to go.

So he told his boss he'd take the job.

He ended up taking most of his work crew with him. They all volunteered to go.

All good workers, Shazz had thought. *We'll knock it out and get back home soon.*

Now the job was just about over.

Shazz went about his room taking out clothes and stuffing them into a gym bag. When he had enough clothes, he went to the bathroom for more supplies. Then he walked down the hall to Lestor's room.

In the middle of Lestor's twin bed was an obtrusive brown paper bag. Shazz lifted it and was immediately puzzled by its weight. When he uncrumpled the top and looked inside, he was so startled by what he saw that he gasped and dropped the bag back onto the bed. He laughed at his reaction.

He shook his head. *I'm going crazy,* he thought.

He reached down into the bag and pulled out a pistol.

Jeez, you can't get rid of these things. You throw one into the ocean and another one pops up.

He sniffed the gun's barrel and counted all the bullets and determined that the gun had not been fired. Then he took the gun and the box of ammo to his room and put them in his bag.

He wasn't sure how long he'd be staying with his brother, or even if he'd be going to jail. He also wasn't sure if he'd ever be able to spend another night in his parents' house again.

Not with these people, he thought.

He leaned on the windowsill and looked out the window. The back of his parents' house was offset from most of the others on the block. From his window, he was able to see six or seven backyards going towards Colin's house. A few houses down, he saw a middle-aged man shoveling burnt black sludge into a garbage can; the back quarter of his house was scorched. Shazz felt no remorse.

That's what you get.

Downstairs he heard Roddy rooting around in the kitchen. He heard a can of soda crack open with a fizz. He took his bag and went downstairs to join him.

He started going through the refrigerator and tossing all the perishables in the trash. He carried a half gallon of milk to the sink and poured it down the drain; he turned on the water to wash it down. Suddenly he didn't feel right about taking any of the food from the house. He went back to the fridge and started throwing everything out. Roddy watched from the kitchen table as Shazz loaded up the garbage can. Then he took the full bag out to the backyard.

He was about to leave when he saw the kitchen plants.

He stopped and leaned back against the counter. A line of plants hung from a ceiling rafter that separated a large alcove from the rest of the kitchen. Beyond the rafter, opposite Shazz, stood a bay window divided into twelve panes; each pane was framed by thick dark wood, and every ledge was lined with plants, so that a small overgrown jungle, burst around the edges of the window's light, cotton curtains, which shielded the lower half of the bay window.

"I have to water these plants…" Shazz said.

He took a small watering can with a long thin nozzle like the beak of an ibis, and watered each plant.

He had to refill the watering can many times.

Roddy went back into the living room to wait.

"Okay," Shazz said, when he was done. "This place is squared away for now. Let's go get some stuff for you."

"Okay," Roddy said. "Let's go."

Roddy had stored his things at his father's house in Staten Island.

Shazz threw his bag over his shoulder and they walked out of the front door; when Shazz turned to lock it, he noticed the glass on the storm door was broken. For a brief moment, he thought that maybe he should have burned down his parents' house too.

Roddy stood at the bottom of the stoop—a cigarette already dangling from his lip. He was peering toward the end of the block, where they had come through the police barricades. A small mob of reporters had gathered at the barricades and were waiting for them.

"They're back," he said.

"These guys…" Shazz said, as he descended the stairs and started walking toward the reporters. "They all think it's a game."

Questions started being lobbed at them as soon as they were within earshot; cameras jostled for better positions.

Already, they had marked Shazz as someone not media-savvy enough to hide his true feelings. He was someone they could easily goad into unfiltered, emotional sound bites: controversy. And more controversy equaled more ratings.

Shazz stopped in front of the barricades to address the press.

"Two good people died here, and the majority of these dirtbags just watched. I have no sympathy for the people of this block."

The two men walked away right after that. They went around the barricades and headed toward their truck; a police officer held the yellow tape high as they passed underneath it.

As they continued walking, they did their best to ignore the reporters, who bounced around them like electrons around a nucleus. They kept asking questions... once in a while someone would shout something obscene just to get them to look up into their camera. When someone put their hand on Shazz's arm, the only thing that stopped him from wrenching it off was the fact that the hand was so soft. He looked down at a small hand. It was a woman's hand. Shazz turned and looked into the warm, dark eyes of a woman he knew instantly. It was Manny. A lawyer who worked with his parents: a family friend.

"Shazz, may I speak with you?" she asked, as confidentially as the situation allowed.

Manny!" Shazz said, pleasantly surprised. It felt good to see someone who was so close to his mother and father.

"Well, we're not stopping here," he said. "Wanna go for a ride?"

Manny smiled. "Yes."

The three of them climbed into Shazz's pickup, which had been double parked behind a few police cars.

"And another thing," Shazz said out his open window to the reporters. "Stop showing that fucken footage already, you're starting to make people very angry."

He drove off.

CHAPTER 10

"Have you considered bringing in the National Guard?" a reporter shouts at Mayor Davis during his morning press conference.

National Guard! the Mayor thinks in alarm. *That's a first.*

They hadn't asked about the National Guard before.

God damn it! God damn it! he thinks. *"It was over. The riot was all over, and now this damn fire. People are starting to get worried!*

Riots are riots: people get angry, explode, and it ends, but this?... A response to a riot?

What's it called now... ethnic tension?

No! No way. Not in New York. Not on my watch. Things like this do not happen in New York City. This is not Rwanda. This is not Yugoslavia. We are past that.

Nervous tics are coming back.

The Mayor stretches his neck and juts out his chin, then looks down at his notes.

This ethnic tension angle must be downplayed at all costs.

He opens his eyes wide, then blinks a few times.

Nothing has been proven yet, he thinks. *The fire was an aberration, a one-off, a… Damn those kids. They won't even talk to us now.*

Lestor sneaks off. Shazz encourages violence. They're making things worse. What is wrong with them? How can these be Milgram children? They are nothing like their parents. They're fucking little… little fucking feral animals, running around with no concern for the general public.

He looks out into a pressroom full of ravenous reporters and forces a smile onto his face.

They're all ready to pounce, he warns himself, *searching for a scapegoat; waiting for one wrong word, and I'll be plastered all over the front page of the world, branded as 'not caring,' as 'out of touch.'*

They had already painted him as a rich guy with no connection to the working man.

It was like playing with fire.

If this situation were not handled perfectly, his political career would be over: another one-term mayor.

Yes, he thinks, *it's best to be right out in front of this thing from the start, to be proactive. It must appear like I'm doing everything that I possibly can, or this thing will blow up in my face. It must be taken seriously… Manny will reel them in….*

He looks down and shuffles some papers, and his burden feels a little lighter.

She can do it. She's a good person: a saint, just like the parents are, or were. They cannot refuse her.

The Mayor finally responds to the reporter's question.

"New York has the finest police force in the world. We have over thirty thousand police officers whose training is without peer. That is more than enough to handle these sporadic outbursts. We've beefed up patrols throughout the city and feel..."

CHAPTER 11

Virgil turned the volume down on his television and walked into the kitchen. He put his plate in the sink and took a long draft of orange juice from its container. He sat at the kitchen table and stared at his empty entrance hallway. He was going to go out tonight. He was going to attend the peace rally at Union Square.

He had never been to a peace rally before, nor anything like it; not the anti-war marches before the second Iraq War, not the spontaneous gatherings at Union Square after 9/11, not even the celebrations on 125th Street after the election of the first African American President. He felt uncomfortable at these things. He always had. He stood out in crowds because of his size. Even when he was thin, he was still taller than most people. He didn't like feeling so exposed.

He sat and thought about the election celebrations of 2008. He should have been there. It was late night when they called it. There was no traffic. It would have been easy for him to get uptown. He should have gone: for his grandmother. She had practically raised him. During the last few years of her life, it was just the two of them in that apartment. His mother had moved to Queens with his sister and her two kids.

Virgil's grandmother had been raised in the south, and he had grown up hearing so many stories of what she had lived through, that it had gotten to the point where he was afraid to leave the city.

How many times had she told Virgil about those children in Little Rock, and how grown men and women—whole families of regular-looking folk—were out there cursing and spitting on children (children!) just for trying to learn?

"It was the ugliest thing I had ever seen," she had told him. "The hate on their faces. It was like the devil trying to get out. They wanted to kill those children. They wanted to tear them apart. And they would have: if it wasn't for those soldiers…

"Just remember, Virgil," she had continued, "it's always there, right under the surface, and don't you ever forget it… and it wasn't that long ago either. Everyone acts as if it were a hundred years ago. Believe me, Virgil, it can all turn around in a second. So don't you forget."

She never forgot—and it hurt Virgil to see her that way. Someone whom he loved, living with part of their soul never truly free. And so on Election Day 2008, Virgil wished that she could have been there to see it; if even to release just a small bit of that pain; to give her a small, glowing… seed of faith in humanity, before passing on to the next world.

That night, Virgil sat alone in his apartment with tears in his eyes, as he watched celebrations taking place all over the world. He heard the celebrations outside his door, and he prayed to his grandmother, and his heart swelled with pride in his country: we were the first, he thought.

On the morning after the Brooklyn fire, Virgil had met Howard in the hallway. Howard had come up from his apartment on the first floor; he was greeted by a spontaneous outbreak of applause by the people of the third. The ovation was mostly tongue-in-cheek, but it was also heartfelt. Howard did his best to remain humble as he strode the hallway like a victorious Caesar at his triumph.

He had been in jail for only a few hours, but even so, days later he was still riled up.

When Virgil saw him, he had been cornered by the Boneheads. Drawn to his wounds like curious children, the Boneheads stood on either side of him, poking and prodding. They grabbed an elbow or lifted his shirt, and made a riotous fuss over any lumps or bruises they found.

"Oh! I *know* that one hurt!" they'd shout, or "Damn! They got you good here!"

But after each fuss, as if to allay any real concern, they'd show him a comparable injury of their own, giving graphic details of how it was sustained, as well as their prognoses.

Howard stood tall as he swapped stories with the Boneheads, and his own hurts faded as he listened to them laughing at their own pain.

He was now part of the club.

"So, Howard," Virgil said, joining the conversation, "are you going to Union Square tonight?"

"A peace rally?" Howard said. "Look at me."

He stuck out a swollen jaw and pointed a finger at it.

"After what they did to me, do you think I'm going to go to a peace rally? Shit. They'd probably beat my ass again, damn cops. No way. No. Way."

He stopped for a moment to think about it.

"Shit," he said. "You go to protest police brutality and what do they do? They respond with police brutality. They just don't get it."

Then, as if a great idea had just descended on him, his eyes lit up.

"You know what? I *am* going to go. I'm gonna show those TV cameras just what those damn cops do to people who protest peacefully. Fuck these cops. I'm gonna get that police commissioner fired. I'm going to get this face on TV."

Virgil regretted bringing up the topic. Angry talk made him anxious, but what did he expect? He looked at Howard standing there, bruised and battered, and felt pain too. He remembered a little six-year-old Howard, giving a piano recital in his mother's cramped living room…. Virgil had helped set up the chairs for a small group of family and friends. Everyone sat and waited respectfully as Howard got ready in the kitchen. A minute later, Howard walked out wearing his Sunday best, and a smile that warmed everyone's heart. Here was their hope.

He sat at the piano and played a few simple songs, and when he finished, everyone stood and clapped like mad.

Where did it all go? Virgil wondered.

It seemed like everyone was born perfect; born, and then covered, bit by bit, by defensive layers of armor, until eventually, even they forgot who they really were.

So much loss.

And that was when Virgil decided he had to go to the peace rally, regardless of his fear of crowds. It was a karmic debt he had to pay.

And so he promised himself that he would have the courage to face the chaos, and that he would walk into the unguarded crowd, and add his voice to the voices of those who wanted peace, and he thought in defiant prayer: *I don't know what you believe in, God, but if you want to take me while I'm standing for what I know is right, then so be it.*

Later that afternoon, after standing in his dark entrance hall for a long while, he found the resolve to open his door, and step out of his apartment. Without stopping, he marched down three flights of stairs, through the empty lobby, and out into the open summer air.

It had been a while since Virgil had walked in late afternoon sun. Breathing the warm air was unexpectedly invigorating. Where he lived, on the far, east side of the city, the streets were not crowded; but as he traveled further west, more people began to appear.

He skirted the edge of Tompkins Square Park and kept on toward the center of the island. When he reached Fourth Avenue, he turned north and stopped.

Already, as he looked toward 14th Street, he could see a crowd milling about the police barricades at the end of the avenue. He detoured into a deli.

Virgil took his time as he moved around the store's two aisles. He scanned the shelves as if perusing an antique store. Every so often, he'd pick up one of the dustier jars in the back and stare vacantly at its label.

Hmm. Pickled onions.

Eventually, after realizing that he might look suspicious, he grabbed a bottle of water from the fridge and made his way back to the front of the store. He picked up some junk food at the register, and asked for a couple of packets of aspirin from behind the counter.

He took the aspirins while still at the counter then stepped outside. A steady stream of people was making its way toward the park, as if drawn by gravity. Virgil watched them pass while he ate his snacks. When he was done, he tossed his wrappers into a garbage can, took a deep breath, and fell in line with the rest of the people.

Union Square occupied an area about the size of a full city block. The downtown end of the park rested on 14th Street and stretched north, against the grain of the rest of the streets, to 17th Street. While both ends of the park were capped by paved, open areas, its center, fully stocked with trees, was crammed with amenities intentioned for the public good: a restaurant, a dog run, a playground, a fountain, public restrooms, subway entrances, four or five statues, and a large flagpole resting on an eight-foot tall, concrete-and-bronze pedestal, plunked down in the park's heart. And all this had been laid out within a lattice of fenced-in pathways that rendered the grassy areas in the park, practically useless.

Virgil had never felt comfortable in that park.

When he stepped onto 14th Street, Virgil's eyes were struck for the second time in the past few days, by an open vista teeming with people. The streets around the park had been closed to traffic, and people roamed in and around the park like ungulates on the Serengeti.

The park rested comfortably within a cradle of buildings. And somehow, despite the park's broad pavements and areas of sequestered grass, it radiated an intense green in the summer gloaming, as if taking the rare opportunity of an afternoon without any traffic, to remind everyone of what they'd been missing.

Television crews peppered the area.

Virgil avoided the heavy crowd on the 14th Street end of the park, and began a slow patrol up the adjacent east-side street. As he moved north, he heard the garbled sounds of a speech shouted through a bullhorn, coming from within the park; every so often, the crowd's collective voice roused to an ovation. But as he moved closer to the top of the park, the speaker's voice melded with the rest, and all Virgil could make out was an occasional distant roar.

A heavy police presence blanketed the area, but none of the officers wore riot gear. The light blue shirts of the officers had relegated themselves to the outermost ring of the crowd; yet in spite of this loosely organized sprinkling of blue, the mood of everyone was harmonious. It eased Virgil's mind to see groups of police officers congregating in small, informal circles. They laughed and talked among themselves with little regard for the peaceful crowd around them.

The north end of the park had a different feel to it. Whereas the south end was bustling with proactive energy, the north end was a memorial. Disarmed by the curious scene, Virgil waded into the gathering, allowing himself to be carried along a flow that wended its way through the larger throng.

What an odd assortment of people, he thought. A true cross section of New York—a cross section of the world; and although Virgil had been born and raised in the city, he had been so long away from life, that it all seemed strange to him.

He drifted along, examining each display as if he were at an outdoor flea market. Many of the displays were moving: photographs of children, photographs of war, pictures of peace and love… and Virgil wondered: Were these people all really just naïve, as Howard had suggested?

No, he thought, *these were people doing their duty.*

Halfway to the other side of the park, a small field of candles had been set out. Virgil could tell that the field had started out as a simple peace sign of light, but had grown, as people had added their own candles to it. The peace sign had now become a focal point: people paused in front of the makeshift shrine for a few moments of introspection. On the ground, around the candles, lay flowers and pictures of famous peace activists: their eyes gazing out into different worlds, enticing hearts to rise just a bit higher, to see what they could see…

By now, the sun had sunk low in the sky, and the candles' lazy, orange flames were just beginning to glow beyond their vessels. A barefoot girl with thick blond dreadlocks sat on the ground beside the candles; she tended the flames and relit those that had gone out. Off to the side, a circle of guitar players was playing John Lennon songs; the mood was reverential. In the distance, sounds from the far end of the park could be heard occasionally, washing in like waves from a distant shore. Virgil's heart felt at peace.

When he finally emerged onto the west side of the park, he was in a daze. He would have liked to have stayed longer, but once again his size began to make him feel uncomfortable. He turned to go down the west side of the park, but after a few steps, he realized that he was heading into a wall of people. He veered off the street and moved directly into the park.

All along the park's pathways, people congregated in clusters. Virgil weaved his way through as best he could. Long benches lined the pathways, further constricting movement. He kept pushing on. He edged past a group of drummers who almost fully blocked the way. He moved on, finding himself more hemmed in at each step. He kept moving forward until, finally, he could move no farther. He had reached the end.

He stood on his toes and glanced from one side to the other. With his arms pinned to his sides by the crowd, he looked like a bear on its hind legs. He spotted a small opening at the very end of a nearby bench and waded his way there. He set himself carefully down on the end of the bench.

He sat facing downtown, his legs safely tucked in, out of everyone's way. He didn't stand out anymore. He was invisible. All around, the crowd continued to grow and boil, until soon he was barely able to turn enough to see who was behind him.

He sat quietly, his hands tucked neatly between his knees, closing his eyes on occasion, feeling the din of the crowd wash through his soul like an inexorable ocean current.

Okay, he thought, *here I am, right in the heart of it.*

CHAPTER 12

There is no fun, in shootin' people on the ground. Something just feels wrong about it.

Puffin' air on 'em… that's what it looked like. You pull the trigger and, if you can peek around the blast that temporarily tears open a gash in your consciousness… you see it: the slight flutter of clothing: the puff of air, so insignificant that it's repulsive. And then you feel a little sick—like, something inside of you has just turned to rot. It's the first time you really feel like you did something wrong. The first time you feel… *real* sin.

So you lay off firing at people on the ground. People lying in petrified lumps: in gutters, in between cars, behind trash bins; even though they all present themselves to you for slaughter; tempting you with huge targets: broad backs in bright solid colors, turned right toward you as you move past—so fucking obvious; impossible to miss with even the most indifferent shot.

Idiots!

Just lying there with their heads buried in the sand. As if by closing *their* eyes, *you* will cease to exist.

Run, stupids! Run! You never stop running when someone starts shooting! Never!

That big black lady in the purple top—she was not one of the protesters. Her groceries were all over the ground next to her. She had to have been dead already. She didn't move a bit when I leaned in between the cars and… Didn't move one fucken bit when her blouse… fluttered.

Bad.

It felt wrong no matter what color she was.

And I know now what we're all thinking as we move down the street: *Oh my God, I just made a horrible mistake…* But NO, we have to stop those thoughts right there. He told us to. He told us we'd feel them; Forrest did. He prepared us… told us it'd feel like the first time you went hunting and killed something; that sick feeling in the pit of your bowels when you're sitting next to a buck whose life is draining before your eyes.

And then he told us about that line, and how, for most of us it was far away; even beyond the horizon of our souls, or maybe, it was just *at* the edge of our souls: a flat Earth, ending in blackness… But it's there. We all have it; the line past which, if you make the decision to cross, there are no more rules, and the only key to survival once you *are* across—is to never go back.

He told us everything. He said: this would be our sacrifice; that *we* were the patriots now, fighting for our country. That the time had finally come, and that we were the brave ones; the first to step up; the founding fucking fathers.

And so now we banish all doubts from our heads at the instant of genesis. We kill them before they get a foothold in our minds.

But it's harder to banish feelings from your heart.

And so now we shoot, and we shoot, and we shoot, and I can't seem to miss… and the cops, they don't know what to do. They freeze. They run with the crowd. They hide behind cars. They fight the urge to flee; but I see the courage bleed from them. They try to do their duty, but we overwhelm them. No one knows how people are going to act when death's on the wing.

A brave officer at the end of the block takes a stand and gets dropped with a red spraying headshot: gone. Everyone near him turns and runs. It doesn't seem real to them. It doesn't seem real to us. "Shoot the officers, and the soldiers won't know what to do," Forrest said.

"Come on, motherfuckers! Come on! Bring it! Show me *something!*"

But there is no resistance. This is barely a fight.

No, they didn't expect this. They were supposed to be trained for the worst but they weren't trained for this. They didn't expect well-trained men; disciplined men. They expected maybe one nut, popping off a few shots with a cheap pistol and running, or falling to their knees and bowing obsequiously to their might. Not us. They didn't expect *us*. We already know our fate.

A fear-blind cop ducks behind the corner of a car; his arm wags like a lazy antenna over the trunk: waving his pistol at the sky.

What is the fucken point? I could throw a rock through that hollow trunk. We pour fire on him in thick streams and he dissolves.

From their rear firing positions, Floyd and Myrons do a man's job of taking out anyone who resists. Their shots crack like ball-peen hammers against steel tables: hard, violent, their .338s tear through the sky from out of the darkness half a block away. They're not tracers but I swear I can see them streaking through the air above me; angry molten hornets at three thousand feet per second. I see their vapor trails dancing and weaving above me as they furiously bear down on their prey: boring holes through skulls, punching through bulletproof vests, ripping holes through cars. Like Gods from above they hurl thunder at all who stand against us, and it suddenly hits me that tonight, we cannot lose.

Hardly a soul is in front of us now: and they start working on reporters and television cameras. I am so in sync with their thoughts that I feel like I am controlling their shots. My eyes rest upon a target—it falls.

If I look at you, you will die.

Forrest and I freeze in the middle of the block while reporters and photographers dive and roll around in a macabre circus act: their acrobatic moves amid the sparks are mesmerizing. In each face, an entire opera of drama unfolds as they realize they can't swim out of this storm. One by one they go down as the shots catch up to them. Floyd and Myrons are masterful, and they are unmerciful. I saw Floyd take down an eight-hundred-pound elk at a thousand yards with my own eyes. The elk was on the next mountain over. *This* is nothing for them. *Nothing!* This is what they dreamed of, they told me. This is what they dreamed.

We move again and I see flames to my right. The wooden front grip of Forrest's AK has caught fire. He's got a 75-round drum and he's been leaning too hard on the trigger. He jerks his rifle in tight quick movements, trying to get the fire out while continuing to fire down an empty street. *Bab-a-bap!... Bab-a-bap!*

In all our years of running around the woods playing war, I had never seen that. I turn back to our vacant street—and all at once our killing machine grinds to a halt. It's over.

I'm sweating profusely. I'm light-headed and feel sick, and all I can think is—how stress-induced vomit only happens in movies and not real life. It makes me so fucking angry to think that I might puke, or even faint. So I gnash my teeth and struggle to keep it together. I concentrate on taking deep breaths.

Like in a dream, this fucking polluted city suddenly seems clean and… strangely beautiful. Red and green traffic lights, fat and impassive, continue clicking away among a galaxy of smaller lights. It all somehow reminds me of Christmas, except that no one is here.

I suddenly notice screaming that has been going on since the start of our rampage, but I can't tell where it's coming from: *a woman—a young woman*—from inside the park. And at the hazy edges of my vision I hear people shouting, calling out names, shoes hitting pavement: *running*. But all these sounds and movements seem to disregard us, like actions taking place in a back room of a cavernous house.

Are we ghosts already?

"Forrest… Forrest…"

It's strange to hear my voice; a soft human sound coming from me. He's a few feet to my right.

"What now?" I whisper, which is funny… considering.

Even through his mask, I can tell by his eyes that he's trying hard to keep it together. He looks at me and answers as if he'd been reading my mind.

"I guess we don't die just yet, Carl."

He gestures for us to fall back. I guess there's no need for us to sit around and wait for the cavalry. Maybe we *can* make something more out of this kamikaze attack, although, at the moment, I've lost the taste for it.

We start jogging back down the street. The other guys join up with us at the end of the block. We keep our eyes forward, avoiding the nightmare we've left at the sides of the road. *We need to get out of this city*—and then you accidently look and...*Oh my God, I just threw my life away.*

Maybe Forrest was right. Maybe you *can* have guerrilla warfare in New York City. Why not? We've gone Third World in every *other* way.

We'll pull back for now; pull back and regroup.

Already I hear sirens, hundreds of them. Thousands. Like the light of the whole fucking universe being sucked into this one black hole... The whole fucking world is converging on this one spot.

"Keep a cool FUCKING head," Forrest spits out, more to himself.

Right. Get my head together.

Floyd and Myrons have already moved into new positions to cover our retreat, as Forrest instructed them to earlier. He's a planner: Forrest; he plans things out. He leads us to a safe house now. I barely have the strength to follow.

I never planned for it to last this long. Forrest did.

CHAPTER 13

When the shooting starts, the world slips into a dark dream for Virgil. He knows the sound right away: the flat unadorned *POW!* of a sniper rifle, and his ears jump to attention, and every nerve fiber in his body lights up.

Was that real?

He hears the sound and the blood flowing through his heart turns to ice—and he's up, frozen, staring in the direction of an approaching nightmare.

POWwwww!... POWwwww!

Single shots, tentative, gathering courage; each report followed by a slow burning echo...

He could move now, before anyone else grasps the significance of the sounds, but he knows he'd never clear the crowd in time.

Best thing now is to wait... any second now.

The people around him are preoccupied, babbling away, heads turning this way and that, like a crowded turkey farm before Thanksgiving: stupidly secure. The popping is barely registering at the back of their minds… and then it happens: a roar; a roar and then the whole upper portion of the park bursts forth like water breaching a dam.

At the speed of neural transmission, awareness diffuses through the crowd and suddenly everyone understands: *it's happening here.*

And then it's amazing to see how fast a park can clear. The whole top end of the park melts away like wax under a blow torch… the top quarter, the top half… the whole park… empty.

But Virgil doesn't run.

He stays where he is; where he *has* been for the past few hours, then takes a knee behind the bench. Warily, he peers over the back-rest, trying to get a bearing on where the shots are coming from. He's not being brave; it's just that, he has temporarily lost command of his body. It refuses to let him be trapped in a fleeing crowd when bullets are flying.

The gunfire is gaining steam, becoming angrier, and for an instant Virgil's mind fails him too. It tricks him into thinking he's in combat again, leaning on his weapon. But he's only gripping the cool ironwork of the bench.

A wave of adrenaline has crashed over him, and he's barely controlling his bodily functions. He ducks down behind the slatted back of the bench and tries to disappear. He sinks so low that his cheek almost touches the seat of the bench; for a moment, he's tempted to use the smooth green wood as a pillow, and close his eyes until it's over.

He stares at tiny scratches in the wood: pebbles between the slats, the shell of a sunflower seed; he hears his own breath and feels at the cusp of escaping into his own mini-verse where nothing can harm him. Far away, there's an unruly burst of gunfire… he clearly hears the patter of stray rounds striking leaves in the trees above him.

"Oh!" he shouts, and is snapped back into this world.

This is definitely not a safe place to be, he thinks while scanning the area behind him, searching for an escape route.

The shots are coming from the north side of the park—17th Street… the east side—and working their way west. There's more than one shooter, more than one type of weapon; but it all seems to be staying on the street bordering the park. Virgil can't get a clear view of what's happening: several trees and a large playground block his way. Suddenly he doesn't mind all the clutter of the park.

He hops up and crouches down and is about to bolt when he finally sees them: dark shadows, muzzle flashes. They are far: half a block away. They float past a small clearing in his tangled view… machines in factories come to mind: three in a line, arc-welding, fiber-optic pulses. Light and sound out of sync: sound, hitting his ears after bullets have already done their damage: have already killed. He's hearing the past.

They move methodically, like machines; as if all the "human," had been forced out of them; as if there were no such thing as *danger.* Again Virgil is dumbstruck by fear. He has just seen death walking the streets and has lost sight of it. Like a bad dream, Virgil is alone in a labyrinth. He is certain that death can smell the fear oozing from his pores and is already homing in on him.

"Move!" screams in his head.

He takes off down the path south toward 14th Street. He needs to put some distance between himself and annihilation. He needs to be near people. He makes it the fifty yards or so to the bottom of the park and skids down behind a heavy stone pedestal. Atop the pedestal is a statue of George Washington on a horse.

Nothing can make it through this, he thinks, while holding the corner of the stone.

He peeks around the base to check his situation. Nothing. No one is behind him. He's almost at 14th Street: too far to see anything at the top of the park now… but he hears it: more and more rounds sounding, overlapping bursts, firecrackers on an empty street…

With his shoulder leaning heavily against the statue's pedestal, Virgil notices his breath start to rattle. He didn't bring his inhaler. He takes a slow, deep breath to test his airways… then has to cover his mouth to silence a minor coughing fit. In the midst of this spasmodic episode he catches sight of a peace sign scrawled in chalk on the rump of George Washington's horse. It somehow focuses and calms him.

A group of police officers are running up the street on the west side of the park. Somehow Virgil knows they all are young. They don't see him hunkered down in the shadows as they rush headlong into the fire. He hears their shoes beating against the asphalt; the twenty pounds of gear strapped to each of them, bang and clatter like a chef's pots and pans.

What the fuck are they doing? he thinks.

"Wait!" he calls feebly; but they don't hear. He is too winded. He watches them run to their deaths.

It all seems too familiar.

After the first plane struck on 9/11, Virgil had watched an unending line of police cars and ambulances and fire trucks streaming down Varick Street, heading toward the World Trade Center. It was only much later that it struck him—like a punch in the gut—that they had all probably died.

Racing to their deaths.

Virgil had stood there on the sidewalk; a strong, able-bodied young man, wondering what to do. As if drawn in by a slow current, he meandered toward the disaster. Like everyone else on the crowded streets, his eyes were fixed upward, focusing on a plane-shaped gash in the North Tower. A flurry of confetti drifted dreamily about the sky, and Virgil wondered, *should I be helping?* But when he reached Chambers Street, the second plane hit, and a huge fireball warned him to go no farther. It was at that exact moment that everyone realized what was happening. Terrorism. This was the realization that struck Virgil now.

This is something big.

Pap! Pap! Pap-pap-pap-pap!

A loud furious exchange of gunfire lets Virgil know the two forces have met. The police are firing back with pistols; their sounds are anemic. No match for what rains down on them.

After twenty seconds, everything goes quiet.

Is it over...?

Virgil keeps still, one ear cocked. In the distance he hears sirens: growing, splitting, multiplying... He hears men talking over radios and feels some relief.

They're taking the city back, he tells himself.

He considers how to make himself known without surprising anyone. It could be dangerous to spring out of the shadows in front of a jittery cop. The radio chatter gets closer.

The police are regrouping and coming up through the park. Good.

Virgil shifts his weight to the other side of the statue and is about to step out when he sees him: a shooter, not thirty feet away. He faces Virgil. He stands on an unlit pathway that emerges from the center of the park. He is so still that for a moment, Virgil thinks his eyes are mistaken, and his fear ebbs. But then it flashes back; he *is* there.

He feels as if his heart has just been torn from his chest. He is dead. He is dead. He is so dead.

This shooter had gone south, while the others had gone west.

A thousand thoughts spring into his mind. He understands everything now.

How stupid I was.

The shooter is a giant; all in black, and bound in ropes and straps like a madman. His knee-high boots have laces running up long thick shanks, and his pants are tucked into them. He wears a tight flak jacket covered in straps: their ends dance and dangle at his sides. A balaclava has been drawn over the shooter's oddly small and rounded head, and it stretches down to fully cover a long and brutish neck, and together, this head and neck, seem to be straining to get as far away as possible from the body they are attached to—but they can go nowhere; the ogre-like body is firmly rooted to the earth.

Impassively, the creature faces Virgil—he has to see him there, crushed against the stone pedestal. Alarms are blaring in Virgil's head. He hears more radio chatter: garbled machine-speak; only now does he realize that the noises are coming from a hand mic on the flak jacket. He sees a weapon being held waist high and, as if they both realize its importance simultaneously, it springs to life—and slowly, as if nudged by a breeze, sways in Virgil's direction. But the arm that holds the weapon never tenses, and Virgil is now more mesmerized than frightened. Before his wits have a chance to come back to him, the dark apparition pivots, then jogs back up the path.

They are pulling back.

Virgil waits a few seconds, and then throws all caution to the wind. He takes off at full speed across 14th Street. He moves like a locomotive down Broadway. In his peripheral vision, he catches glimpses of crowds huddled behind cars and at street corners. He hears people rouse as he tears by; past arriving police cars, past ambulances… but he does not stop. It feels too good. He hasn't run for years. He didn't think he could. His knees don't hurt. His legs feel strong. His feet are barely touching the ground.

At each corner, a crowd stretches out into the street at the perfect angle of safety: away from Union Square. All necks crane over this invisible boundary, stretching toward the park; next to each face, a glowing camera phone.

Virgil keeps moving for another block before he realizes where he's headed. He turns left. He keeps moving and doesn't stop until he reaches Tompkins Square Park. He leaps the fence and lands heavily on the grass.

All around the park, bars and restaurants are crowded with patrons going in and out. As of now, no one in the neighborhood knows what's happened a few blocks away. But Virgil knows it happened... knows it *is* really happening, because he hears the sirens.

How can this end? he wonders.

He crawls backwards on his hands and heels until he's up against the smooth trunk of a sycamore tree. His body is on high alert; he won't underestimate his situation again. He expects one of the shooters to come walking around the corner any second.

A small group of teenagers are hanging out a few benches away. The rest of the park is empty. The teens congregate around a bench, smoking cigarettes and talking. *So free.* They know he's there, they saw him stumble in, but in this city full of madness, they soon forget him.

Just another spirit in the night.

Under him is a bed of woodchips; they stick to his meaty palms. He wipes them off. He taps the back of his head against the soft wood, and looks up into a night sky blanched sterile by lights. His wheezing is now drowning out the sounds of the sirens.

CHAPTER 14

Before the city had ground to a complete halt, a small construction crew was in the process of replacing the sidewalk next to Lestor's building. They had cordoned off the five or six squares of city sidewalk in front of the building, and jackhammered the concrete into a small field of jagged boulders. Understandably, Lestor had not been paying much attention to this construction project of late; but now, as he sat on his front stoop in the early morning light, he could see that the small boulders had been carted off, and the area had been swept clean. A smooth, lustrous layer of tar, now coated the sunken ground; concrete would come next.

Lestor stared at the tranquil pool of tar, which even now, after days of abandonment, glistened as if it had just been poured. Reflected images of the clouds above, drifted by Lestor's eyes as he gazed into the large shew stone, and just as his mind began making the connection that the surface of the tar reminded him of the still waters of a pond, he noticed (as if conjured by his own thoughts) three dragonflies resting on its surface.

The dragonflies were dead. They must have lit upon the tar when it was still warm, thinking, as Lestor had, that it looked like water. Now they were stuck forever. The small, stiff creatures hadn't contorted into agonizing poses to telegraph their situation; rather, they stayed perched, motionless, as if ready to rise with the next cool breeze.

Where had they come from? Lestor wondered. He couldn't recall ever having seen a dragonfly in the city. Perhaps, in the swirl of actions always taking place, the dragonflies were one of those things he had never noticed. The mind had more dangerous concerns at the forefront when navigating the crushing gears of the city.

Or maybe they were simply passing through, he thought.

It was sad. They must have thought they had found a place of respite in this alien, concrete world. *A pond!* It must have felt right. Now they would become fossils. Once the cement was poured, they would become part of this Godless stone world.

Lestor thought of drawings he'd seen in old textbooks: crude replications of three-foot-long dragonflies living three hundred million years ago—before dinosaurs.

Forever, he thought. *Now they will be frozen forever, just as they are today.*

The press had moved out from in front of Lestor's building the previous evening—during the shooting at Union Square. "Massacre at Union Square," they dubbed it, and they were right.

Thirteen people had been killed, including five police officers and a few reporters. Dozens more had been wounded. The Milgram sons were no longer top story. Replays and analysis of the Massacre at Union Square were the only thing on television now, and the shooters were still out there.

What *seemed* obvious, was that the shooting had something to do with the recent racial strife; but since the shooters had been cloaked from head to toe, and the victims were from a variety of races, even the obvious could not be established by any verifiable proof. Were they foreign terrorists? Homegrown terrorists? No one knew a thing about them. They had vanished.

Lestor was worried; not so much about a group of armed men still possibly wandering his neighborhood, but more that the whole world suddenly seemed so fragile. The civilization he had considered eternal, now seemed on the brink of complete implosion, and it had all been so simply done.

And buried not too deeply within his thoughts, was a tinge of guilt; not because he had skipped out on the Mayor's press conference, but more because... because he had given up. For the first time in his life, he had released the world from his control.

I don't care what happens anymore, he thought.

After watching his parents die, he had let go. And wasn't *that* the thing holding the world together—the unbreakable bonds of worry; the hallowed web, surging with the pleadings and exaltations of billions: *Pleeeeeaase,* and, *Hosanna.*

Our small planet, droning away into the void: our sacred Om.

Lestor had lain his burden down, and the freedom he felt from it was frightening. A new road lay in front of him. It was wide and clean and cut straight through the heart of the world, and on either side of it stood all the armies of man. He knew who was out there. He knew what those shooters were here for.

Lestor heard the door open behind him. It was Casey. Between the riots and the shootings and the press, most of the other tenants in the building had cleared out. The whole city in general had emptied.

Casey was still in her slippers as she carefully trod the coarse cement stoop. Lestor heard the soft fabric catching on the rough surface as she stepped. She sat beside him and rested her head on his shoulder.

Lestor closed his eyes. He tried to absorb as much of the feeling as he could, but he stopped himself. There was still too much to do. He couldn't relax just yet.

"Can you not do that?" Casey asked tenderly.

"Do what?" Lestor answered too quickly.

"You know, leave the apartment without telling me. I don't want to be left alone like that. Not now. Please."

Lestor could tell from her voice that she was a bit shaken; he knew right away what must have happened: she awoke, found herself alone in the apartment, and panicked.

"Sorry," Lestor said. He had not done it on purpose.

They had been up late the previous evening, watching the news, watching the madness once again. This time, only a few blocks from their apartment.

A little closer every time.

Watching it live was frightening. It didn't seem real. It seemed more like a B movie— shaky camera and all—until the view switched to aerial footage. Then Lestor turned it off. He kept expecting to see his parents come into view.

They sat quietly for a few moments before Casey raised her head to scan the empty street.

"Everyone's gone," she said, as if just remembering their situation. "Have you heard from Shazz?"

"No," Lestor answered. "I'm sure he's on his way. He's an early riser."

Shazz had called many times the night before to make sure they were okay. He had stayed at Roddy's father's house on Staten Island. He would have come back right then but the city was on lockdown because of the shooting. All the bridges and tunnels had been closed. Subway service had stopped. All vehicles leaving the city had to pass through checkpoints. Only official vehicles were allowed in. The Mayor was going all out; he had mobilized the entire police force. The press was all over him.

"So," Casey said, "what are we going to do?"

She motioned with her head, indicating the area where the press had been camped. "We can leave right now. No one's here."

"Shazz will be coming back soon," Lestor said.

"We can go up to my parents' house for a while," Casey continued. "Wait until everything settles down."

Lestor felt like he was stuck again. He wasn't sure what his next move should be; the only thing he was sure of, was that he needed to stay right there and wait for his brother.

"Shazz can come too," Casey said. "There's plenty of room. In fact, I want him to come with us. Lestor," she said, "I will never try to take you away from your brother. I understand that… with what happened… you guys need to be together."

"I know, Casey," he said. "I know. But I'm not ready to move just yet."

"That's okay too. Whatever we do, we'll do it together; as family. All I want to do is help you. I love you, Lestor," Casey said, tears starting to spill down her cheek, "and I loved your parents too."

Lestor hugged her desperately. "I love you too," he said.

They lingered in their embrace, rocking slowly, as a mother comforts a child.

"Come on, Case," Lestor finally said, "let's go back up."

As they stood to leave, they heard the low rumble of an engine. Lestor recognized the sound. It was Shazz's pickup. He had just pulled into view at the corner of the block.

"Here they are," Lestor said, with a little relief.

The truck turned onto their block: Lestor could see Shazz and Roddy in the front seat. He also noticed someone crammed into the small rear seat of the cab; but he couldn't make out a face as the back windows were tinted. All he could make out, was a person leaning forward, and a delicate set of hands placed in between the two front seats. The image of a ghost crab peaking from its seaside burrow came to mind.

Shazz stopped the truck in front of Lestor's building and left the engine running.

"Hey," Shazz said, while scanning the area. "Where'd everyone go?"

"They all left," Casey said.

Shazz threw the truck into park.

"That makes sense," he said.

Casey noticed Shazz's mood seemed to have changed, as if the bloodletting the previous evening had shifted the world around him. He still moved forward, but his mind seemed preoccupied, as if he were still trying to get his bearings.

"Manny…?" Lestor asked. He had been hunching over, trying to peek into the back seat.

Shazz smiled. He knew Manny was just what Lestor needed. She had stayed with them at Roddy's father's house.

"Manny!" Lestor blurted, and from the shadows of the back seat, a warm smile cradled by a shock of unruly dark hair, bloomed forth.

"Hi, Lestor!" Manny said.

Shazz got out of the truck and helped Manny out. She gave Lestor and Casey a hug.

"I got some stuff in the back," Shazz said. "Let's get it upstairs."

They followed Shazz to the back of the truck, where everyone picked up a bag or two of supplies. Shazz picked up two cases of bottled water and led the way.

Roddy was already waiting at the foot of the stoop. He had slung a small duffle bag over his shoulder, and he was holding a large paper bag filled with bagels.

"Aye," he called to Lestor while holding up the bag. "I got Lenny's." The locally famous bagel store from their old neighborhood. "I can't walk past that place without going in," Roddy said with a smile. "The smell gets me every time."

The rest of the day was spent in the apartment, picking at food and monitoring the world through television and social media. The same story was being rehashed all day: the same events covered from a myriad of angles. Every thread was pulled to its limit. In-depth exposés of all the players… an unending line of experts, acquaintances, and pundits, all taking their turns on the stage.

And then there were the rumors, attributed as aftershocks to the main event in New York. A "riot" in a high school in Kansas. A five-alarm fire in L.A. An unsubstantiated rumor of dissension among national guardsmen slated to come down to New York… should they be deemed necessary. All rumors—and reported as such by "concerned" news anchors; but by the time anyone began questioning these rumors, they had already been firmly planted in the public consciousness.

Lestor rested on the couch while these images flooded his mind. He began feeling as if he were trapped in a submarine, cruising through a world of fire and brimstone.

Stay inside where it's safe.

It affected them all, for during the long day, each person in their own turn, would saunter past the window and gaze out. It was quiet out there, which is what made it so unnerving. The streets were deserted. All was calm. All was very calm. But the television kept sounding the alarm.

Eventually, Casey did something they all wanted to do.

"Can we just turn it off for a while?" she said. She grabbed the remote and clicked the TV off with an angry punch of her thumb.

"Thank you," Shazz said, from the kitchen.

Lestor gave Roddy a look of surprise. "I thought you guys wanted to watch it?"

"Not me." Roddy said, as he continued staring at the blank television screen. "I thought you did."

Lestor watched Casey as she walked back into the kitchen. She sat at the table with Manny. As she sat there, Lestor recalled that the table in the kitchen used to belong to his parents. It was old and solid. They had bought it secondhand from a diner that was going out of business.

How many big decisions have been made at that table? he wondered, as he pictured his parents sitting there.

For a while the apartment seemed too quiet; but as the effects of the agitating news programs wore off, the mood in the apartment began to settle. Eventually, Roddy got up and went into the front bedroom for a nap. Lestor stayed by himself in the living room and listened to Manny and Casey talk. Their conversation calmed him.

He turned and lay on his side, resting his head on a throw pillow. Shazz leaned back against the kitchen counter, tinkering with an old flashlight; every once in a while, he added a word or two; but mostly, like Lestor, he just listened.

The conversation meandered along, always taking a pleasant path; and perhaps because they were skirting around such a huge canyon, that was exactly where Lestor's thoughts came to rest: the death of his parents. He started thinking about their funeral. Not in a morbid way, but spurred on by the warmth he felt in Manny's presence.

They had not made any arrangements yet, but Manny had mentioned that she had spoken with city officials about it already. And rather than finding himself dreading the event, Lestor had the urge to attend the service, and be among people who had loved his parents. Moreover, he wanted to be surrounded by people his parents loved, because he knew these would be good people: people like they were. It would give him one last chance to feel close to them, and make his proper farewell. But for now everything was on hold until the city was under control.

Manny had been a part of Lestor's life since he was a teenager. She had been part of his whole family's life. She had started out as just another of Stanley and Theresa's admirers; reading about their exploits in the papers, and seeing them on TV. And before she even truly understood what they were all about, she knew there was something special about them. They were just so… *ordinary*. What were such unglamorous creatures doing on the front page of the *New York Times*?

Yet, there they stood: unabashed in their imperfection, so ordinary that they were divine. Theresa, with her long gray locks pulled back and bunched into a barely controllable thicket, and Stanley, with the head of a twelfth-century monk: involuntary tonsure, scraggly beard, bobbing at the end of a stooped neck. And when they were not arguing someone's case to the world, they were always smiling; beaming, as if they didn't see the same world as the rest of us.

The Milgrams were not just role models for Manny, they had been a catalyst; a catalyst for a question that had always been there for her, hovering in the mists at the edges of her young mind; inducing it to finally descend, and coalesce into words.

What does one do with a life...?

And as soon as the question was put to words, all at once, the operands of this equation began falling into place, and tabulations began. Facts, memories, emotions—constants, coefficients, variables—all dropped into their allotted slots. She knew she had ability; she had known this from a young age: modesty had no place in this formula. She knew she could do anything, be anything, if she set her mind to it, and this troubled her... *Is it that simple?* she thought. The formula was missing something: *judgment* was called for.

Should she use her gifts to become rich?... Something seemed wrong about that. Is *that* what one does with a divine gift? And then, the answer became perfectly clear. It was the same catalyst that had started the whole process: the Milgrams, standing there, so plain, so ordinary... illuminated. *They* were making the best use of the lives given to them. *They* were using what they had been given, to help those in need. Wasn't that what heroes did?

It felt right. In her soul, she felt it *was* right... What better way to spend one's life?

In one inspired instant, Manny's course had been set.

Ten years later, she was interning for associate professor of law Theresa Milgram at Brooklyn Law, and attending their annual Thanksgiving dinners.

Lestor had not moved from the couch since late afternoon. He had napped for an hour or so, nodding off while everyone else was in the kitchen. Listening to their talking had given him a sense of security that lulled him to sleep. When everyone noticed him asleep, they were careful not to disturb him. They were happy to see him getting some rest.

When he awoke, Lestor sensed that everyone but Manny had gone. For a long while he lay motionless, listening to Manny in the kitchen, flipping through paperwork. Ever the workaholic, she had brought work with her from the office.

Lestor's grogginess was slow to wear off, and when it did, he automatically reached for the remote on the coffee table. He turned on the television and quickly clicked away from an angry, red-faced pundit, to the Yankees game. He kept the volume low. He figured sports would be a safe zone.

The team was playing in the cool northwest, and there were few reminders of their present situation on screen: no wide-angle views of towering grey buildings, no blimp shots of a shimmering Valhalla-like stadium amid the brick housing projects of the South Bronx; only the crisp greens and browns of an idyllic ball field. Only once did the play-by-play man's ruminating stray from the perfect diamond, to "what's going on back in New York"; but he quickly moved off the topic.

When Manny noticed that Lestor was awake, she put down her work and joined him in the living room.

"Lestor," she had said earlier that day, "just so you know—and I already discussed this with Shazz—the Mayor contacted me directly. He wanted me to talk to you guys about helping to calm the situation."

Had anyone else said this to him, he might have recoiled.

"But I was on my way here anyway," she said, and flashed a smile before dropping the subject.

That had been hours ago. It was night now, and Manny sat next to him on the couch as they watched the game.

"Did you know that Derek Jeter was from Kalamazoo?" Manny said.

They both laughed.

"Kalamazoo," Lestor said, "you can't write that stuff."

"I saw him once, walking along the street on the Upper East Side. People were trailing after him like the tail of a comet—businessmen, doormen, acting like kids and falling over themselves trying to get close to him."

Shazz walked in as they were talking. He stood next to the TV and looked at the game.

"His three thousandth hit was a home run, remember that," Lestor said. "*And* he went five for five that day. You can't write that stuff either, no one would believe it."

Then Shazz spoke up.

"Our parents, civil rights lawyers, killed by a black mob. Can't write that shit either."

Manny cringed; Lestor stayed quiet.

Shazz wasn't angry when he said this. He was more confounded; his mind still mulling over the images and emotions of the past week:

his parents dead on the street, Colin dead on his kitchen floor. As long as he lashed out, he didn't have to look in.

"You can't think of it like that, Shazz," Manny said reluctantly. She knew Shazz was not in the mood to hear anything reeking of platitudes, so she tried to move off of the subject. "You just need to keep your lines open, okay?" She was referring to his contact with the Mayor's office. "I know neither of you want to talk to anyone right now, and that's okay. I'm not here for that. You just need to keep your lines open. You never know when you might need them."

Shazz stood for a moment without saying a word. Manny was one of his people; he would never hurt her, in any way. He struggled to weigh his words before he spoke.

"Let me tell you something, Manny," he said, doing his best to tamp down his anger. "They knew," he said, pointing toward the window and everything outside it. "Those people knew exactly who my parents were. And they did it anyway."

Manny could see Shazz's hackles start to rise. She gave no response, only bit her bottom lip and looked straight ahead at the coffee table. Now was not the time.

"And that's why I don't give a shit about what happens out there!" Shazz said.

"Shazz," Lestor blurted. "Please!"

Shazz stopped, and nodded his head.

"Yeah, okay," he said.

Then he went into the kitchen.

A minute later, a sleepy Casey came walking in from the bedroom, holding a cell phone in her hand. She had just woken from a nap. She dragged herself over to the couch and plunked down on the other side of Lestor. With her eyes still half-closed, she raised her phone to start checking messages but quickly gave up and let her hand drop. Lestor smiled when she slumped against his side as if he were a big pillow. He was feeling much better after getting some sleep.

The game had ended, and Lestor began flipping through the channels again when Casey perked up.

"Wait! Hold on," she said. "Go back!"

On the television, a young black man was raging at the screen. It was Howard. The interview was from the previous evening at Union Square. It had been taped right before the shooting started.

"I know that guy," Casey said. "He goes to my school." She leaned in and stared intently at the screen. "I used to see him on campus all the time. He was some sort of activist. He lives over in the Riis Projects," she told them, pointing east.

On the screen, Howard raged on: "…I mean, they died, and that's too bad. They did some good things. But everybody seems to be forgetting about that baby sitting in the back of that bloody car. I mean, what's he gonna think when he grows up and sees that picture? He's gonna feel that for the rest of his life. Nobody's talking about the Martins, only about the two white saints!

"I mean, what's it gonna take?" Howard continued. "How long are we supposed to just sit around and take it? Doesn't my life have value too? How many decades are young black men supposed to just *accept* being murdered by the police? How many centuries? We protest and protest and nothing changes. Now look at this… two old white people get killed and things start happening! The Mayor's talking about it, the police commissioner's talking about it. Hell! The damn President of the United States is even talking about it! A little violence gets done and people start taking notice…"

Lestor changed the station.

Casey turned and gave Lestor a look of remorse.

"Don't worry, Case," he said. "We can't hide from it forever." And he reached out and gave her hand a squeeze.

Then he turned on another game.

As if on cue, Roddy walked in.

"Hey, the Dodgers game!" he cried, with an eager smile. He plopped down on the armchair next to the couch.

But Manny knew better. They had made a mistake in listening to Howard's interview.

She kept her eyes facing forward. She knew Shazz was standing in the middle of the kitchen, staring at her, indignant… but she refused to turn and look at him. She was not going to feed his flame. She knew exactly what his expression was trying to say:

"Do you see? Do you see what those fuckers are thinking! Do you see?"

And then the lights went out.

"What the fuuuuu—" someone let slip in the darkness.

And in the void, everyone's instincts leap to a higher state of alarm. A primal fear sets in.

Lestor had caught glimpses of this fear earlier in the week: gusts of it had flashed across the city like wind ripping across a field of tall grasses; but those had been false alarms. Now, in the darkness, for the first time, people of the city saw clearly, the fine line that separated civilization from savagery. It was a step, such a small step, and then everyone was naked and surrounded by death.

Everything is allowed with the lights out.

Thirty thousand police officers no longer seemed enough to handle a single borough, let alone five.

From outside they hear a few mock screams; a false show of bravado by a few of the neighborhood apartment dwellers; but they don't hear them again. A realization sets in fast, that for at least one night, there will be no law in New York City.

"Do you have any candles?" Manny asks, an instant before Shazz clicks on a flashlight, and she turns on her cell phone light.

"I have one right here," Casey says.

She reaches for a vanilla-scented candle that had been resting on the bookshelf for years.

Roddy takes out his lighter and helps Casey light the candle. She sets it on the coffee table and takes the flashlight from Shazz. She disappears into her room in search of more candles.

"I didn't realize it was *that* late," Lestor says, as he sees how dark it is outside.

Shazz has his head out the window now and is looking down at the city. The streets of the Lower East Side are old and narrow—and absolutely black. He watches a single car drive slowly down the street. Its headlights move, silent as a shark in the ocean depths. They reach the corner and blink out as they turn.

In a half-whisper, Lestor asks his brother, "What do you think's going on, Shazz?"

"I'm not sure," Shazz says. By now, half his body is out the window. He sits on the sill, one foot resting on the fire escape, and listens.

Manny and Casey are moving about the apartment, lighting dusty candles and setting them out on shelves and tables. Roddy is back on the couch again. By the soft candlelight, Lestor notices that he's starting to look old, but he wears a wistful smile, as if enjoying the quaint domesticity of the situation.

Everyone's movement slowly winds down until finally, they find themselves all stopped, and staring at Shazz in the window. No one says a word; they just listen, because that's what he's doing. They are waiting for something, but they're not sure what... And then it comes.

In the distance, shots...muffled: dry pet food, dropping into a plastic bowl, a popcorn machine down a long dark hallway. It's not so far away, but in these streets, these canyons, the sounds come like echoes from another world, and it's somehow quiet, and it's somehow immense.

A goliath awakens.

It's so quiet: the popping.

It fixes its gaze on them.

It's so quiet. It's so quiet. It's so quiet that it's the loudest thing any of them have ever heard: a whisper.

CHAPTER 15

Ed turned over and looked toward the door. Forrest was still standing there. He had been standing there for most of the night; hunched over and peering out through the door's tiny square window, the way a paranoid old witch from a fairy tale might. He didn't have much of a view, but still, he pressed his cheekbone hard against the cool thin glass, and strained to see as far down the skinny alley as he could. And when he wasn't at that porthole he was at the other, on the opposite side of the floor. That window at least was normal-sized, set horizontally, and ankle high to anyone standing on the outside; but since they were in a basement—a church basement—Forrest had to stretch high on his toes and prop his elbows up on the dank sill, to peer down the *other* skinny alley. And he spent the whole night scampering back and forth between the two.

Forrest seemed to be on the verge of losing it. Actually, he may have already lost it, but by that point, none of the guys really gave a shit whether he had or not. Half of them were angry: pissed that they had been stupid enough to follow that pedantic little know-it-all. The other half just sat around in stunned disbelief, waiting; as if resigned to a dawn's execution. The one thing that they *did* do, all together, was watch Forrest run back and forth in his cage, and secretly took joy in seeing him tortured.

He had done all right: Forrest. He had kept it together until they reached the church. Then he collapsed into a dark corner and began giggling hysterically for twenty minutes, before starting to shiver uncontrollably. Carl and Ed had taken pity on him. They dug around the basement and found some old church banners and a couple of New York state flags to toss over him. Then they left him and went to sit with the other guys.

Eventually, Forrest pulled it together enough to transform himself into the weasel-like creature that currently paced the floor; one that couldn't sit still for a moment; that had gone totally paranoid and didn't trust a single other soul to stand watch over *his* life. And they were fine with that. A better security guard could not be found.

After no one had come for them in the first few hours, the rest of the guys settled down. They stayed up late into the night, listening to police scanners and radios, and fidgeting with their weapons. Nobody talked much.

There were six of them: Ed and Carl, the two youngest; the two oldest, Floyd and Myrons; Joey Papas, and their leader, Forrest. Their sanctuary was the basement of a boarded-up church: a church whose upstairs had been damaged by fire and water, but whose downstairs was still sound. Its hardwood floors were solid, and even held a shine after a quick wipe-down.

The basement they huddled in was a large empty room. At one end was a stage built right into the structure of the building. At the other end, book-ended by a set of staircases, was a wall lined with thin, shallow storage closets. The longer of the two staircases rose from the west side of the building; it led up to the ruined church. Its stairwell had been filled almost to the ceiling with debris. Charred beams and piles of furniture had been tossed haphazardly into its space, leaving the route upstairs impassable. The smaller staircase—four stark concrete steps—led straight to the side entrance of the building—straight up to Forrest's tiny window and skinny alley.

The men had settled in at the foot of the waist-high stage. They lay scattered about the floor, mingled amid shadows and piles of gear. As the evening wore on, and as they finally felt it acceptable to do so, one by one they turned over to try and escape: through sleep… or just by hiding their faces in the dark.

All night they hovered just at the edge of wakefulness, fitful dreams and racing thoughts preventing any real respite. Instead, they slipped just beneath the surface and stalled, forever rising into disquieting moments of the night. They'd wake to hear Forrest in the darkness on the other side of the room… whispering… singing sotto voce:

World suits its own needs…

World suits its own needs….

Before quickly turning back over and trying to burrow down into sleep again… but there was no escape; nowhere to hide, and they were just realizing it.

By the time the windows warmed with the glow of the coming morning, most of them simply wished everything would be over already. At daybreak, they sat there, bleary eyed and exhausted, staring at Forrest tending his windows.

"This is the way things have to be," Forrest enunciated loudly, when the first rays of sunlight touched his face through the window. It was as if the sun on his skin had triggered the atavistic rooster brain within him. It scared the hell out of everyone. It was the first loud noise any of them had heard since the night before.

Forrest stood at the midpoint between the windows. He stood there with opened arms as if baring his soul. There was something almost holy in his gesture. His arms were not up and out, like the beckoning *Christ the Redeemer* statue, but low and wide, to the point where his outline resembled the innards of a peace sign.

"This is the way things have to be," he told his stunned audience.

Then he turned and slowly trudged back up the stairs to his window; his whole demeanor having changed from the previous evening. It was as if he had just ended the paranoid phase of his rebooting and entered the next phase, whatever that might be. It was the first glimmer the men had seen that maybe, Forrest was still in there.

One thing they *had* to admit, was that all the planning the "sane" Forrest had done, had worked out perfectly: they had all survived. But Forrest had always been good at things like that: planning and strategy. It was a point of pride for him, which he humbly never mentioned, but everybody knew. How could they not? One could not talk to Forrest for more than a few minutes without him mentioning weapons, or war. He had box sets of all the *Time Life* war documentaries, and entire shelves filled with books on military history. He collected war movies and gun magazines, and had scale-model replicas of most of the mechanized weaponry of World War II.

Of course it worked, Forrest thought during his long night's watch. *And why not? A plan is a plan. People don't think until they're told what to think… we surprised them.*

He had been down to the city many times before; long before the riot had taken place. He had walked its streets and studied its neighborhoods. He had surveyed his theater of operations through the eyes of a military tactician. He had walked around with a map of Manhattan, marking out all the important sites: police stations, abandoned buildings, subway stations; he had circled all the vantage points in the area he eventually selected as his home base. But these field trips had never been more than an obscene mental exercise; any plans he had were patchy at best. He never truly believed he'd see the day when his dystopian dreams would be at hand.

It was true the world had been at an increasing boil of late. He'd been monitoring outbreaks of social unrest all over the world. The fresh web of communication devices blanketing the planet, showed it to him all the time.

Yet even in the midst of all this turmoil, Forrest was still rattled when one of those outbreaks erupted on his doorstep. There had been protests before: all across the country, but any violence had dissipated quickly. Not this one. This one had a different feel to it. It was exactly what he had been hoping for.

The night the Milgrams had been beaten to death on live television, Forrest had flown into a rage. He leapt from his couch, shrieking and clawing the air in front of his TV. His mother, who lived quietly in the upper half of their house, knew to retire to her room.

He spent the rest of the night watching the scene unfold over and over again. He instinctively gathered his weapons around him, cleaning and cradling each one in turn.

He called the guys to make sure their TVs were on.

"Are you seeing this!" he shouted into the phone. "It's sickening!"

He called his doubters: the ones who had called him paranoid.

"I told you," he said. "I told you where this country was headed!"

They had nothing to say.

For the next few days, Forrest stayed in his house. He kept his television on at all times, and when he wasn't sleeping, or pacing, he sat at his computer, scouring the internet for news of any more injustices, and leaving a trail of incitive comments on message boards all over the Web. And when he came back around for another look, it nourished him to see that he was not alone in his hate.

There are so many like me out there, he thought.

But there were other things too: candlelight vigils popping up around the country, including the vigil being organized in New York.

"These *fucken* people," he said to himself. "They are *so* fucking stupid."

When images of the flames of Brooklyn reached Forrest's eyes, he felt many emotions at once.

Someone's striking back!

He had been angry—apoplectically so—but also indolent. For him to take up arms, to take that next step to action, would demand commitment. And big decisions like that involved hard work.

But that *is being alive,* he thought with a mixture of terror and anticipation.

At some point in life, everyone faces that decision: *what do you serve?* Otherwise you're left behind while everyone else who has already made that decision moves on.

The flames had inspired Forrest, and shamed him: someone out there was more of a man than he was. They had *acted.* They didn't just run around in the woods playing pretend war. He was at a decision point; so many of the small choices of his life had led him here. It took just one more step—*commitment*—to pass through to the other side. It was just a matter of that last step.

Everything is on the table now, he thought. *This is a new world.*

Things were moving too fast. He could hardly keep track anymore. Every day new ideas rose and rippled across the face of the Earth for everyone to try on, and every day the world adjusted one way or another. There didn't seem to be an agreed upon set of rules for right and wrong anymore. It seemed to him large groups of people no longer demanded things make sense. Maybe his ideas were not so far-fetched anymore. People's ideals changed when reality closed in around them. People were realizing they were not as open-minded as they once thought.

"People will accept me now," he said to himself.

The Milgram boys were the key. By now, everyone knew the story of the great American family: the "noble" parents, forever fighting for justice; their two sons: Lestor the teacher, Shazz, saved from a broken home. Forrest had heard the tale over and over for the past couple of days; but the fact that neither of these children had come out to call for reconciliation sunk a hook into him.

Could it be that they were nothing like their parents? Could the nightmarish spectacle of their deaths have pushed them over the edge? What a gift!

On the night of the fire, Forrest had been pacing around his couch, lost in thoughts, when he found himself stopped, leaning over the back of his couch and staring at the muted TV. The network had decided to go with a split screen to broadcast the conflagration: on the left, house-sized flames lapped the edges of a black sky; fiery bursts of ember and heavy smoke sprawled up, and into the darkness. There were no people on the screen, just a quiet ocean of rich colors: glowing streetlamps, and the spinning, flickering strobe lights from parked emergency vehicles, which all seemed to be patiently bearing witness to the great force before them….

On the right half of the split screen: a tall, sinewy man, striding up a Manhattan sidewalk. Surrounding him was a roiling pack of reporters, yipping and capering around him like a pack of smitten puppies.

It was Shazz.

He did it! was the first thought that sprung to Forrest's mind.

The sound was still off, and music streamed over his computer; so he didn't know what was being said. On the screen, Shazz stopped… and the small mob around him also stopped. And when he moved again, everyone moved.

Forrest knew the whole story simply by reading the chyron at the bottom of the screen:

Breaking News: Shazz Milgram arrives in New York

He wasn't what Forrest expected; he didn't seem a product of a "Milgram" household. He was too rough around the edges, and unlike the footage he'd seen of a timid Lestor, who always looked like a deer in the headlights, Shazz was absolutely unfazed by the hurricane he walked through. Forrest was mesmerized.

He started that fire. He was sure of it. *He dropped everything the moment he saw what happened and headed straight out to burn down that whole neighborhood… fucking crazy—no thinking, no planning, just action.*

And it worked; watching the fire felt good, like a *Dirty Harry* movie. And Forrest knew without even checking the comment boards on the internet, that if it felt good to him, it felt good to a whole lot of people.

Shazz was now a symbol. His fire was his message.

Now. All the country needed was a nudge.

That very night, Forrest rushed to the city for one last inspection, and when he came back the next day, he went a'preaching…

"Anything on the radio yet?" Forrest asked the men at the foot of the stage.

Joey's head popped up from a breakfast bar he was struggling with.

"No rebellion yet, boss," he quipped before returning to his bar, which stretched out like taffy.

Forrest was afraid. He had taken that next step. He had passed through the wall of fear. But he found out it wasn't just a wall. It was a boundary—a boundary to a new land—which was *all* fear.

CHAPTER 16

"What the fuck do we do now?" Carl whispered to no one in particular.

He sat cross-legged on the floor, his chin in his palm and his elbow on his knee. He sat in a small clutch, with Joey and Ed. Floyd and Myrons were off to the side.

"I don't know," Ed answered at the same volume. "Can't we just go home?"

In an odd way, with all of them just sitting there in relative peace, it seemed possible to simply get up and leave; but according to Joey's radio, there was a heavy police presence right outside their door.

"I think it's too late for *that*," Joey chimed in, before falling back onto his duffle bag. He put his small radio against his ear and began staring stubbornly up at the ceiling.

Ed froze for a moment, mouth ajar.

Shit, he thought. That was the problem. He *hadn't* thought this through. None of them had. None of them had thought more than one move ahead. More like, one move and a prayer… that things would work out after that.

He looked over at Forrest, who had finally settled down and was now sitting on the concrete stairs. *Forrest thought ahead,* he thought. But he was beginning to suspect that Forrest's whole thinking process might be a bit… *off.*

He looked at Floyd and Myrons, off near the side of the stage.

Those guys knew what was going to happen, he realized, and a bit of anger rose in him.

He knew their story but had never given it much weight, until now. Now he understood them.

Those guys knew where this was headed—and they were fine with it.

They had made their decision a long time ago, back when they were sitting in trailers outside of Las Vegas, piloting UAVs on the other side of the world.

Why didn't they stop us? he thought, and for an instant Ed's anger almost overwhelmed him, but it quickly deflated.

He had no right to be angry at anyone but himself. They had all stupidly volunteered to be here.

Floyd and Myrons were older than the rest of the guys; they didn't interact as much with the others, but they seemed to enjoy hanging around. Myrons took a liking to Ed, probably because Ed didn't talk much either. He told Ed about their stint in the Air Force: how they had loved it at first. They saved lives. Soldiers had thanked them personally for getting them out of jams. They were the all-seeing eye in the sky; pointing out threats, erasing danger from all around the good guys. But it wore on them: push a button *here,* and a moment later, deleting life over *there,* all while watching it unfold live on a small monitor.

"It didn't seem real," Myrons told him.

The actions happening—the push of a button, the delay, the explosion—seemed more of a coincidence, than cause and effect.

It was the delay that got to them: watching the small, dark figures casually moving about on the screen, not knowing that death was furiously racing toward them…

They had commanded death. There had to be a price for that.

Government absolution could protect you for only so long.

They could hold it at arm's length for a while, but it sat heavily, and it never left, and they would find themselves replaying footage in their minds, over and over, compulsively, wondering if someone had managed a quick escape from that truck, or that house, that they didn't see, in that last split second before the screen went white-hot blind from a strike.

They'd think about it behind the wheel on the way to work, or at the dinner table with their families; and like an addiction, it consumed more of them every day, bit by bit, until they both realized that they were entirely lost.

Floyd and Myrons, best friends from youth, had made up *their* minds the day they left everything behind in Nevada and moved back east. They knew where Forrest was headed from the start… and it was exactly where they wanted to go. They wanted to punish. They wanted to be punished; and so when Forrest pulled up to the front of their place with his van, they had no trouble stepping in.

It was the younger guys who hadn't known what was going to happen. They knew what the plan was supposed to be, but up until that very last moment, it didn't seem possible that it would actually happen. Deep down, they never totally bought into Forrest's preaching: that this was the right time, like Germany 1939, or that the country was so divided now that people would rise up and join them—but at the same time they kept going along. It felt good to believe him. Things had been rough for a long time. Only a few of them actually worked, and none of them had any real hope for the future. Forrest gave them an escape. And what an escape: an escape into glory.

He mesmerized them with tales of battle, told as only someone who was truly obsessed could tell, and his words carried *his* passion, to hearts that were passionless. Like a Bronze Age Mycenaean rhapsodist, he sung tales of epic battles of the past: the birth of urban warfare at the Battle of Monterrey: hold the enemy close, seize the stairwells, hack through walls. The brutish slaughter of a million soldiers at Stalingrad: as if Hell itself had burst through the Earth's crust and pure savagery raged over the open wound.... On and on he reeled them off: the Battle of Berlin, the Siege of Vicksburg: soldiers using shovels in hand-to-hand combat. Death had become so familiar to them that after a while it didn't seem so bad. They would stay up until dawn, drinking themselves sober with cheap beer; watching grainy, black-and-white footage of war documentaries in Forrest's basement, and he would weave them into his sagas and read quotations from his books...

Even Floyd and Myron's mood seemed to elevate during those long nights. They enjoyed listening to Forrest talk with such conviction of the long line of warriors that they now belonged to; and so, for a little while, they were able to ignore their pain.

Ed didn't care much about Forrest's talks, but he loved his weekends at Forrest's place. He hadn't really known where it was all leading but, when you were on a constant high from running through the woods, pumping round after round into all sorts of targets that Forrest had set up behind rocks and trees—blasting away until your ears were ringing and your hands were raw and covered in beautifully painful blisters and you couldn't wipe the huge smile off your face because you'd never had so much fun in your entire life... you lost all sense of anything beyond that first step.

At one point they even practiced in an old abandoned shell of a hospital: a wide, squat, four-story structure that hadn't been used for decades; now it stood alone in an overgrown industrial park, abused by man and nature.

As children, they had explored its edges with trepidation. Now they used it for war games. They'd mouse-hole through walls, moving room to room without regard for the destruction they were causing.

"They won't know what hit 'em," Forrest would say. "They won't know what hit 'em."

Afterward they would camp right out on the exposed concrete floors, the smell of decay all around them. They'd light a fire on the bare floor and sit around it, listening to a boom box that Forrest had picked up at a flea market—it had an old Bob Marley tape stuck in the tape deck, which miraculously still worked. Lost in a haze of alcohol and whatever other drugs they happened to have scrounged from someone's medicine cabinet, they'd imagine they were soldiers in some bombed-out city.

Floyd and Myrons would usually arrive after the most strenuous action. They enjoyed sitting by the fire and drinking the free beer.

Ed looked at the men sitting around the basement floor. They hadn't thought of the consequences during those fun times. They only thought of the glory.

But what glory was here? he thought. *What glory was there in mutilating another human being, no matter what... no matter what.*

No, Ed could not blame Forrest for being there, nor Myrons for not stopping him. One thing he finally understood, was that he could never blame anyone else for this; none of them could. This was all on him, and for some reason, he knew it was important for him to accept that right away.

CHAPTER 17

All morning, the men stared dumbly at a swarm of small patches of sunlight creeping across the floor. The soft touches of yellow moved at an almost imperceptible pace, feeling around the smooth wood as if searching. By afternoon, the soft touches had given up on one side of the floor and appeared on the other. There they pawed about for a few hours more, swirling slowly like stars in the night sky, all the while gently fading, until eventually, they were no more. It was only then that the men began to rouse from their stupor. It was only then that the steel grip of fear that had clamped down their thoughts, relaxed enough for them to think clearly again.

Ed leaned back against his worn canvas backpack and stretched his legs out in front of him. The bag cushioned his back from the hardwood paneling that lined the foot of the stage. He unscrewed the cap of his green plastic canteen and took a sip of water. It didn't taste right. He gave the bottle a swirl, then sniffed at the opening. He detected the odor of plastic. With a finger, he scratched at a molding seam running along the side of the bottle, and wondered for the first time if his canteen were actually a children's toy. He had had it since he was a kid, and never thought about it until that moment. Like most of the things he had gathered for this expedition, the canteen had been lying around his house forever. Actually, it was his grandfather's house, but he had grown up in it, and the house was now his.

Most of the things that he had gathered were old and somewhat desiccated. Some he found buried in the back of dusty closets, under piles of old shoes, and some he found in his barn, woven in among a tangle of miscellanea. His stuff was not top-of-the-line. Not like Forrest's. Not like the high-tech gear some of the other guys had sprung for. Ed couldn't afford it. He hadn't worked for a long time. He couldn't afford heavy duty ballistic body armor like Forrest had. He did have a Kevlar flak jacket that he had bought from an Army Navy store, but it didn't seem strong enough to do much good. Something seemed to be missing from in between its layers of fabric. Right now, it just seemed like two strong pieces of canvas sewn together. Ed stared at it, and in a moment of honesty, admitted to himself: *There's no way this thing would work on anything larger than a .38, and even then it would hurt like hell.*

Anything larger than that, and he'd be dead—or at least knocked on his ass.

Ed's grandfather had served in the Second World War. He hadn't gone to Stalingrad or Berlin, but he'd been in France; and although Ed was not the most charismatic guy in the group, that fact gave him a little cachet. It at least impressed Forrest.

Ed had lived with his grandfather for most of his life. His house was set on eighteen acres of land that abutted a national park; at one point or another almost every member of Ed's extended family had stayed at the house for a summer. That was how he had gotten all his equipment. He had uncles and cousins who had also served, and even today, every so often, he'd stumble across some olive-drab accessory in the barn or cellar, that could have been from any number of wars.

Ed had never joined. His grandfather had discouraged him, and he was glad of that. He doubted he could have handled it anyway: mentally. After seeing so many movies depicting basic training, he ascertained that due to his nature, he would not survive it. So he accepted at a young age that he would never be a man's man. But it didn't bother him too much.

He stared down into the mouth of his canteen with a sour look on his face. The water didn't taste fresh. It seemed stale. It wasn't fresh like he used to get from his garden hose when he was a kid. Come to think of it, he couldn't remember the last time he'd had a fresh-tasting drink of water. It was no longer safe to drink the well water on his property; some industrial chemical had leached its way into the water system.

He remembered the first time he saw water being sold in a store. His grandfather had laughed. Why would anyone buy water?

Now it was the only water Ed drank.

This water was from a rest-stop bathroom. He had forgotten to fill up at home, and so he filled up his canteen on the way to the city.

Water, he thought. *Water tastes different from other water... how is that so?*

He worked his tongue in his mouth; it felt irritated, numb.

Isn't water just water... an element or something?

Things were getting so confusing.

I'm not even old and I can't keep up.

He put the cap back on and put the bottle down.

He got up and walked toward the bathroom. He wanted to check the water there.

Forrest seems better now, he thought when he noticed Forrest standing up and stretching his legs.

Ed remembered the exact moment he had put boot to pavement the night before. Forrest had gone with Floyd and Myrons earlier, to show them the spot he had picked out for them; somewhere up high. When he came back, he and the rest of the guys piled into the van and drove the few blocks to their landing zone. Forrest parked in an open space in front of a fire hydrant; then they waited.

After a minute or two, Forrest received a text from Myrons. *G2G.* Good to go.

It was time. They swung open the doors and stepped out onto the street.

The moment was seared into Ed's mind. He remembered looking down through the opened door at his boot as it reached for the ground. *It looks ridiculous,* he thought. The boot was so tall, and had new brown laces running all the way up to his knee.

But even as those words scrolled across the outermost shell of his mind, the thing that most overwhelmed him was a blaring alarm going off in his head.

Get out of here! Get out of here!

The four boys staggered forward, huddled together like a small team of ducks. People smiled uneasily as they passed, sensing something was a bit off, but chalking it up to post-9/11 security.

They moved slowly along the street, toward the lights of Union Square. Their heads darting every which way, as the pressure on them built exponentially with each step. This was their last moments on the ledge.

It was Floyd and Myrons who had started things up. Forrest had picked out the perfect spot for them: a bare-bones building under construction. The building had a wide, unobstructed view, down the street the men were walking on. The two friends had picked out a sweet spot on the fourth floor. They laid themselves on the smooth concrete floor: there was just enough cover behind buckets and piles of equipment to not be seen.

They were the ones who forced everyone's hand. Up until the first shot, it was still possible for them all to back out. In fact, Ed expected that to happen. He could see Forrest wilting with every step. He could feel him about to abort, to tell them all to head back to the van. The whole thing could easily have been labeled a test run and they would have saved face. But then Floyd and Myrons began dropping people, and it became real.

Only a moment before, they had walked abeam a circle of reveling cops who were laughing and bullshitting with the crowd.

Now Forrest, Ed had thought. *Now is the time to break.*

They had one moment.

When the first, square-hatted, right-out-of-central-casting NYC cop dropped, everyone flinched, and Ed and his crew would have turned and run if others had not started dropping on either side of them. Like rats in a maze, big red meaty palms were dropping down on all sides but forward. When the cops regained their bearings, the first thing they noticed was the group of masked, armed men, standing right in front of them. Everyone was now committed. They all had one choice: move forward, or die with a bullet in the back.

Ed had never been so revulsed in his life.

Why are they shooting cops? The question screamed in Ed's mind.

Out of a dark side alley, another group of police officers came tumbling. They ran into the street like a troop of Keystone Cops; as if God himself had commanded them to proceed as quickly as possible to the middle of the street and set themselves up like clown targets in a carnival game. They were perfectly shaped, stationary targets, just like the ones the guys had been practicing on for years. The men perked up.

At one point, right at the start, they all saw Joey get hit in the stomach by what seemed like a blast of smoke. He staggered backwards a few steps, then plunked down on his ass the way a baby in a big diaper does; everyone stopped. In the corner of his eye, Ed saw a white puff of smoke coming from the first band of cops. *That's where the blast came from.* Then they noticed a swarm of small pellets dribbling on the street around Joey, and it dawned on everyone at the same time, cops included, that they were being shot at with rubber bullets and bean bags. Ed could swear he heard someone screaming with laughter, but with their masks on, he couldn't tell where the laughter came from.

The sting of the rubber bullets had made Joey livid, and he jumped up and started unloading directly at the human targets, which disintegrated just the way the paper ones had, and everything started getting louder, and angrier, like they were walking down the middle of a Chinatown street on Chinese New Year: explosions and smoke were all around them and popping in the air and they moved forward quickly, and Ed turned south right away and walked down the west side of the park alone; and as he walked, he made as much noise as he could, holding his AK at waist height and shooting it in the air and shouting at each side of the street like he was a mad dog snapping at a stream of water from a hose.

"Raar raar raar raar raar raar raar raar," he raved in tongues.

He sprayed the buildings on his left—stucco and brick-face crumbled, windows imploded. On his right he shredded trees, and leaves and branches poured down on the sidewalk and in the grass of the park, and right in stride he would pop out a clip and slap a new one in as clean as any soldier in any movie ever had, and everyone had disappeared from the streets, and he veered up a small stairway into the park and onto a small patch of darkness and he stopped, and with perfect firing-range form, he squared up to a thick Siberian elm and unloaded the rest of his clip dead-center mass.

Ed stood on the dark path hunched over, heaving, trying to catch his breath. He could taste blood from his raw lungs with each wheeze.

This is bad, he thought. *This is really bad.*

He had the urge to heave his weapon off into the darkness, but something wouldn't let him. He reloaded.

And then he saw the man. *There! Half in the dark.* The round, crouching, mountain of a man. The upper half of him, perfectly silhouetted against a massive grey pedestal; a man in the wrongest place of his life. He, on a stage: a soliloquy; the perfect parody of a man who had taken a wrong turn and found himself standing in front of a firing squad: a scene begging to be played out. He, slightly off-center a perfectly round yellow spotlight: well-protected from the static up above, at the top of the park, but for his current situation, dead; caught; naked as a child in war. A Japanese Noh actor, whose smooth moon-face, peered over a broad expanse of shoulder at Ed, fixated to the point of immobility. The amazed expression… expressionless, angled slightly skyward, as it seemed to hover above the huge body.

If he would have moved, Ed would have stopped him. He would have torn right through him the way he had torn through that tree. But he didn't move, and Ed felt something hold him back: a hand staying his heart, pulling him from the zone he was in. It was an uncomfortable feeling; something he had not felt before, and it gave him just enough pause for a thought to form in his mind. *I don't have to do this.*

And then it dawned on him that he hadn't killed anyone. He hadn't shot at a soul. And he felt relief. He still had a chance. And right then, that became his only goal: to not kill anyone. And that program locked in his brain.

How far he could make it in this game, he didn't know, but he knew what the stakes were: everything. He was ahead for now, but that was just dumb luck; and so he made up his mind right then, to get out of there as soon as possible. At the first glimpse of daylight, metaphorically, he would run. He didn't care what the guys would think of him. He would escape this Hell and go back to his land.

The weather would be changing soon, and he felt a powerful urge to breathe in the cool, rich air, of northeastern woods. He suddenly could not live without it.

He had no close family left... and he had made peace with that. The one thing that filled the void in his life was the land behind his grandfather's house: his backyard. After the death of his grandfather, Ed had felt nourished by that air; that moist, fragrant, over-oxygenated air. His backyard had become his cathedral.

He already had his perfect world, and he wanted to go back. He never really cared about what Forrest was saying. He just liked the camaraderie and hanging out in the woods.

He would go back; this time without his constricting flak jacket, or heavy boots, and clips weighing him down. He would walk lightly through those woods; climbing over downed trees and boulders, free to stop where and when he wanted, for as long as he wanted... and then he realized that there was no more gunfire, and panic overwhelmed him. He turned quickly and started jogging back up through the park to try to catch up with the guys: if they were still alive.

"Those ghosts... they catch up to you," Floyd spoke out of nowhere.

Ed started. He wasn't sure if Floyd was talking to him or not—he didn't seem to be focused on anyone in particular. He might have been talking to Myrons, who was sitting right next to him, but probably not. They seemed to be of one mind, and didn't need to speak to each other, especially not in the manner in which Floyd was speaking now: as if his long silence had merely been him pondering life's meaning.

"They catch up fast," he continued. "As fast as you can see; instantly: the speed of light. It comes in right through the lens but you don't realize it. Not until it's too late. Not until it's already in there. And it never leaves. Not during this life. You can't get rid of a ghost. You can't *kill* a ghost."

Everyone but Myrons turned to look at Floyd with wide-eyed concern. Myrons just sat there with a broad, closed-mouth grin. As if amused, that everyone there had just been let in on a big, shitty secret about their new world.

I've got to get out of here, Ed thought.

After the shooting, the boys had done as Forrest planned. By sheer luck, they had all converged back at the northeast corner of the park at the same time. They met at an anxious jog, and without stopping or even looking at each other, they took off toward the east side and its smaller side streets. They kept low behind the parked cars as they moved along the street. They hid their weapons as best they could; untucked their pants, ripped off hats and gloves, and weaved their way back into the night crowd, most of whom were still oblivious to what had just happened. Ten minutes later, they were all standing on the dark walkway at the side of the church. They had been in its basement ever since.

It was night again, and soft columns of ambient light streamed in through the windows. It was just enough for them to see, and just enough darkness for them to be alone again. Forrest had given up window duty long ago, but still sat at the front of the room. Carl and Ed were now the only ones who walked to the windows every so often to stare out longingly.

Joey was on the floor, lying on his side. He rested his head on a bag and kept his radio on the floor right in front of his face. Every so often, he would issue an update on the events outside.

"Swat teams are sweeping the streets around the park…"

"Mayor instructed everyone in the city to stay indoors…"

But he never mentioned any details about casualties, and no one asked.

Floyd and Myrons were still off to the side in the dark.

Forrest sat quietly with his back against the wall and his knees pulled up to his chest. Every so often he'd lift his hand to his nose and inhale deeply. He was trying to catch the scent of spent power. The smell had always given him a rush, but the scent was fading, and by evening, he couldn't tell if what he smelled was from his gun, or from the burnt timbers above his head.

Somehow, in an area swarming with cops, no one had managed to find them.

We must be just out of the search zone, he thought, *or maybe they figured we hightailed it out of the city.*

Forrest wasn't sure of what to do next, but he did know that they couldn't sit there for much longer. There had been little talk in the past twenty-four hours. Zero planning. Everyone just sat there, waiting for him to tell them what to do, and he could feel the pressure building.

Maybe we should *try to sneak out of here,* he thought.

But that wouldn't go over. With all the sermonizing he'd done in the past few years, he had painted himself into a corner. Now, he had to act, and he had to act bravely.

I could draw the cops in, he thought, as he ran through scenarios. He could turn it into a standoff, and get it all over the media. From there, he could stir the nation to rise. He could turn the burnt-down church into his John Brown's fort.

No, more likely they would make it his grave, and fast, and he wasn't ready to give up just yet.

For a moment, he got mad at the police.

How the hell could they have not found us, he thought—and he looked toward Joey and his radio. "Joey," he said. "What's going on, on the radio?"

Joey slowly maneuvered his body into a sitting position and faced Forrest.

"You know," he said, with some hesitancy, "they were just talking about the National Guard on the radio. There's been this debate going on. People are wondering why they haven't been called out yet… and then a few radio guys said there have been 'unsubstantiated rumors' of dissension within the ranks."

He raised an eyebrow in a look of mild surprise.

Forrest stared blankly at Joey for a few moments while the information leached down into his brain. Then he stood.

"You see!" he said, pointing at Joey. "I told you! I told you this would happen. People are going to join us! You'll see. Even the army is on our side. They see what's going on. This country is ripe for this."

And then all the lights from outside blinked out.

"They found us!" Joey jumps up and shouts. Everyone follows his lead and stands with rifles at the ready: pointing at windows, pointing at the door. They steel themselves, expecting to get hit at any moment. In the dark, they all concentrate on listening, but... nothing happens.

Carl tiptoes up the stairs to look out the window. He sees nothing: literally. It's pitch-black outside.

From out of the darkness, Ed speaks: "What's going on?"

"I'm going outside, everyone," Carl says from the doorway. "Don't shoot me."

They hear the door creak open.

Carl sticks his head out into the night air. He closes his eyes and takes a breath. He hasn't had the sky over his head in a full day. He can't remember the last time that happened. His body relaxes as he breathes in the fresh air. He steps into the alley. He hears some people howling on the street. He wants to go out and join them, but instead thinks.

They need to go back inside.

He leans back in the doorway. "It's a blackout," he says. "It's black out here. I can't see a damn thing."

From the front of the room, they hear Forrest.

"This is it. We need to go *now*. This is all set up for us. Remember, someone else started that fire. Someone out there is helping us. We are *not* alone. We need to go... *now!*"

No one says a word, and then from the back of the room, they hear the sound of someone chambering a round. It's Floyd's M-9.

Once again, a sickening fear sits in the pit of Ed's stomach. He had hoped *that* demon had moved on, but it's still there. Once again, they are back in Hell.

CHAPTER 18

Mayor Davis and five of his seven deputy mayors rushed around the rotunda and past the marble staircase where Abraham Lincoln had lain in state a hundred and fifty years earlier. Close behind this peloton was a larger group, comprising police brass, city councilmen, city agency heads, and their staff. Without pause the procession continued past the security desk and down the corridor to the Mayor's office. City Hall was running on generators.

Sensing the Mayor's heavy mood no one said a word. They had just broken from an intense late-night meeting with a room filled with more government officials than city officials. The meeting had focused on the state of the city. The President himself, or rather, his head on a large video screen, had made an appearance. He had chewed out the Mayor for letting it slip to a reporter that New York was "temporarily out of control."

There was just enough time for that statement to make headlines all over the world by the next morning: "NEW YORK CITY OUT OF CONTROL!"

"Come on, Mike," the President said calmly, yet sternly enough to let the Mayor know that he was, indeed, disappointed. "You know you can't go around saying stuff like that."

It took all the Mayor's strength to not scream, *Of course, I fucking know that!*

The Mayor was relatively new to big-time politics, but even he knew that it was probably best to just nod his head and eat his plateful of shit. The President was not only the leader of the country, he was also the head of his political party, and could be of immense help in the future... if the Mayor could somehow manage to extricate himself from this whole terrible ordeal without further destruction of his good name.

"I know, Mr. President," he said, glancing over at the Governor's unflinching gaze on another screen. "It was a mistake. It won't happen again."

The buck stops here, baby.

"Well, all right," the President said after a brief pause, as if weighing the sincerity of the Mayor's answer. "Now let's get working on getting this situation under control..."

Ten minutes later the President signed off, satisfied that the Mayor had understood the gravity of the situation.

The Mayor and his troop reached the end of the corridor and streamed into his office. There was a lot to calculate. Besides the obvious human element of the tragedy, politically the situation was dangerously close to turning into a full-out nightmare. As always, the electorate was delicately balanced: perfectly equal in size, perfectly polarized. Any scandal could sway the balance one way or the other. So race riots (if that's what these were) did not bode well for his political future.

The Mayor sat behind his desk while the rest of the group branched off into different parts of the room. They all lifted their phones and started making calls. The double doors of the office swung shut in their wake, as if pulled closed by the force of their draft.

When the riots had started, the Mayor had been getting hourly briefs from the heads of all the relevant city agencies. Now he no longer bothered with hourly meetings, his entire day had become one long, running meeting, with the agency heads never leaving his side. On every trip out of City Hall—to a burnt-down block, to a wounded officer's bedside—his new entourage stayed with him, feeding him constant updates.

Just a few hours earlier, the Mayor had been advised that the masked gunmen had returned.

"JESUS CHRIST!" he screamed.

The Mayor had been so upset by the news that he almost started to cry in frustration. He had just finished reviewing police deployment schedules for the blackout, when the reports came in. Between the previous night's shootings, the blackout, and now this, it was almost too much to bear.

In dealing with the new crisis of the blackout, he had almost forgotten about the shooters. He had been convinced by the people around him, that the shooters had most certainly left the city. Checkpoints at bridges and tunnels, a heavy police presence, and tons of PR seemed enough to contain the situation.

But the shooters were still here. And that spoke volumes. It reminded him of 9/11. He had been on the street watching the North Tower of the World Trade Center burning after the first plane hit, and all he could think of as he stared up at the plane-shaped hole, way up high on the building, was: *How on earth are they going to fix that?* But as soon as the second plane hit, he could think of only one word: terrorism.

I should have known. I should have known, the Mayor thought in disgust. He cursed himself for not trusting his instincts. He had based all his plans on the hope that this problem, the shooters, had simply gone away. But they hadn't. He should have taken more personal ownership of the situation. He had just sat there and agreed with everything the emergency responders recommended. It was all played by rote: pulled from the standard "emergency situation" playbook.

He needed to change his ways and face this monster head on.

"It's the same guys as last night, Mike," the police commissioner had told him. "I don't think they're planning on leaving."

A police cruiser had stumbled upon them, just standing there, in the middle of a narrow street. The blackout had rendered the streets of Manhattan surprisingly dark: dark to the point where those in the cruiser could see only what fell within their headlights. The cruiser had been tunneling its way through the murky darkness when it found itself face-to-face with a group of armed men. The two cops had just enough time to shout into the radio before their car was lit up.

In seconds, the vehicle was a shattered wreck; a small, intense fire smoldered beneath its hood. The gunmen pulled back, tossing road flares into piles of days-old garbage on the sidewalks; a small tree took flame.

Police immediately started flooding the area. A running battle ensued. The police pushed forward, the gunmen fell back. The East Village block became a war zone. The police gained ground fast as they moved along a runway illuminated on each side by piles of flaming garbage. They were overanxious. Cops had been killed the night before; this was personal.

The gunmen kept falling back; the police kept coming on strong. They tasted blood. They would have stories to tell. They would avenge their brothers. They would be heroes. They would kill these killers. But then shots began coming in from different directions.

Shit!… Is that us?

They tried moving forward but it became harder. Things weren't making sense.

Something's going on here!

Pops and sparks were snapping at their extremities. They couldn't move forward anymore.

And then it hit them: they were surrounded. They had run into a trap. Shots began raining in on them from all directions.

How many are there?

"There's too many!" someone shouted.

There was panic. Everyone fell back. The streets went silent.

Four more officers were dead; a half dozen others had been wounded.

"We got two of them," the Mayor was told. "We got two of them, and we're working on ID-ing them."

It doesn't matter, the Mayor thought, as his heart sunk deep in his chest. *It's over. They're going to roast me… Beame, Dinkins, and now Davis: one-term mayors ruined by riots.*

And now, he was hearing there was unrest in other cities too: Oakland, Seattle.

I am not responsible for those too, he thought defensively.

New York was the only city where people had died; the only place where violence had erupted—and now the violence seemed organized, which made it even more terrifying.

The mood in the country had been foul for some time, but was it possible for this to be the next step? Were the doomsday preppers and survivalists right all along?

No! the Mayor thought. *Impossible.*

Now he was expected to embrace the Governor's calling out of the National Guard, which was going to happen no matter how much he protested. The Mayor would have to stand there in front of the world and announce that he was a failure; that armed troops were necessary to control the city.

The doors to the Mayor's office flew open and people began streaming in and out again. The Mayor leaned over to look out through the opened doors. He saw that the corridor was filled with people. It was two in the morning, and City Hall was as crowded as he'd ever seen it. The Governor's team, federal officials, council members, lobbyists, security consultants, all stalked the halls, selling this and promising that. Somehow all these extra people had squeezed into the building, as if the pressure from outside had extruded them into the halls through gaps in the masonry. All these clawing people were adding to the Mayor's anxiety.

"Out!" he shouted. "Everybody out! I want only essential personnel in this building. Clear out!" He slammed his fist down on the desk. "There's an armed insurrection just a few blocks away and City Hall is wide open and lit up like a Christmas tree. Enough of this sinking ship!"

He froze for a moment.

"I don't get it," he said, more to himself than anyone else. "I thought we were through with this sort of stuff: riots in the streets? Aren't we supposed to be through with this sort of stuff?"

He kept falling for it. After each flare-up had burned itself out, he was certain that it was the last one. He was certain that this string of highly unlikely events had run its course... but another spark was always popping up: riot, fire, shooting, blackout... *second* shooting?

One after another, as if lined up and waiting their turn, the sparks kept leaping up and whirling across the city.

Enough already, he thought.

He closed his eyes and rested his forehead on his palms. People had begun draining from the hallway. His office was quieter.

It's the Milgram boys, he thought.

He still clung to the idea that they could make everything right, by getting in front of the cameras and calling for peace.

Rebuilding has to start from there.

"This is not what our parents would have wanted," was all they had to say. It would give people just enough pause—to take a breath and gather their thoughts.

As things were now, the longer they held out, the more the pressure seemed to build. No one said it; the news had even moved on, but the Mayor knew it. He could feel it. Their recalcitrance was jamming up the natural flow of the system; their unexcised wound festered just beneath the surface of everything, clouding every decision.

If the children of Stanley and Theresa Milgram cannot forgive, what hope is there for the rest of us? he thought. *They need to step up and make their statement.*

To say nothing when a group of armed men were running around the city, was tantamount to endorsing their actions. Especially since their first action was to set fire to the Milgrams' block.

The Mayor called one of his deputy mayors over.

"Miller, see if you can get Manny on the phone. Tell her she's got to get those kids in here now. *Especially* now! You tell her, at this point, it's criminally irresponsible for them to not make a statement… and she knows it!" He finished with a jab of his finger in the air.

He put his elbows on the desk and buried his face in his hands. He tried to rub away the sleepiness. He had hardly slept since the troubles began.

Unrest, he thought. *This is why it's called unrest.*

In his exhaustion, a thought floated into his mind.

Maybe I'm not the right man for the job.

At the thought, a wave of terror washed through him. He quickly collected himself.

"Toughen up," he mumbled through gritted teeth.

He started musing over lessons his mother had given him. She was tough. Her steel had been tempered in the first-grade classrooms of a strict Catholic school; she had been *his* first-grade teacher.

"Stability is just chaos at a slower pace," was her saying.

"Ugh," he grunted, then gave his head a quick shake.

Okay, he thought. *I can't sit here and cry that I have no experience in this sort of emergency. And I can't hide behind bad luck. People are dying.*

He had visited the families of slain officers that very morning, and was having a hard time maintaining his role as the city's "rational leader."

I must square up to this thing at every move, he thought. *No excuses. No excuses for me. No excuses for anyone. This situation must be ended now. Everyone is watching.*

He put his palms down on the desktop and closed his eyes. He took a few measured breaths to gather himself, and then began reciting, as if by rote, a civics lesson on representative democracy.

"What is my number one responsibility?"

Everyone in the room stopped and turned to him. It was a rhetorical question, of course.

"My number one responsibility is to the safety of this city. That is what a ruler does. That is why I exist."

He opened his eyes.

I get one shot at this, he thought, *and will forever be known by it.*

What he *had* been known by, was his less-than-effective leadership skills. He was a hard worker, no one denied him that; but after a few months in office, the public had already picked up on a vein of weakness in him. It drew out an instinctual aggression in them.

"He's not my *leader!"* people would think, with a tinge of indignation.

After two years in office, Mayor Mike Davis had already been pegged as a one-termer.

And now he was calling out the National Guard.

He was having trouble getting it all down. Not just what had happened, but what he was going to have to do to fix it all. He sat frozen in his chair, his eyes staring vacantly ahead, his palms still down on the desktop, as if bracing himself against the torrent of computations surging through his brain. He could almost feel his mind stretching and contorting like the jaws of a constrictor trying to swallow a meal too large. And while in this struggle, long-held, deeply felt ideals began to fall way. No longer could he afford to have faith in the better angels of people's nature. That was not his role.

He felt his heart quiver as more and more of the heavy chains that had once guided him began to lift away; and then, in a flash, the bonds were gone, and for an instant his soul floated in absolute freedom, and in that same instant, his diaphragm spasmed, as if his body innately knew to grab desperately for control again.

That was when the Mayor fully accepted his new role.

People needed to be controlled. Strict rules and boundaries were what lifted us from the animals.

"Okay," he said. "We can do this."

If they need a general, I will be a general, he thought.

"Billy," he called, before realizing that the police commissioner was still standing in front of him: hands clasped in front of his body, head slightly bowed, awaiting orders. "Billy, let's get things moving," the Mayor said.

Things were easier now. He could see each of his moves unfolding right down the line…

"Never waste a good crisis," he continued. "This situation gives us carte blanche and I'm using it. I'm throwing my full support behind the Guard. I will not have another police officer killed on my watch. This city must be secured.

"I want these lunatics locked up or dead before the end of the day," he declared. "I don't care what it takes!"

The Mayor's press secretary jumped up and ran out of the office. Deputy mayors and staff took that as a cue to start moving themselves; all sorts of electronic devices were pulled out to augment their phones. A slow swirl of people began filling the room again. The floodgates were now open.

The Mayor continued talking in the midst of the building gyre.

"If they want to sell us stuff, heck, I'm going to buy stuff. I'm going to buy every fucking thing they have to sell. And they're going to love me for it. Heck! Why was I even fighting this? This is the right thing to do. There are men with machine guns running around my city! I will buy every security measure these contractors have to offer. I don't care how much it costs. You can't go wrong in over-preparing."

In his excitement, the Mayor hopped up and began pointing at individuals who were racing in and out of the room, as if to say, "*Go get em!*"

"*I am going to save my career,*" he thought. "*I will be known as the Mayor who* saved *New York. This is a blessing in disguise. There is no future for an idealist in big-time politics. People respect strong leaders. I have an excuse now: a legitimate excuse to change my whole outlook on governing. I have an excuse and I have a stage.*"

He had it all worked out. He would rebrand himself. He would be known as the mayor who was tough on lawlessness. The mayor who carried a big stick! There was an entire nation out there who had yet to meet him. He would lock down the city, write a book, hit the lecture circuit, write another book, haul in the cash, and then—who knows?—maybe run for president. If he couldn't be a darling of one side, he'd be the darling of the other. He'd go where the love was. Everyone wants to go to where they are worshipped. It makes life so much easier.

"Back to the meeting," he snapped, with renewed vigor.

The Mayor and his troop reassembled and streamed back out of his office. Back down the corridor, round the rotunda, past the marble staircase, and back into the war room.

CHAPTER 19

"You know… you lose it," Virgil said. "You just lose it. You lose the time, and the only time you realize it is when you go outside, because that's where the change is. Things change so fast, you know… *you* change. You can tell by the way people look at you: their reaction to you. It's as good as an honest look in the mirror… once you start noticing. People look at older people differently."

Virgil was standing in the middle of the hallway, talking to Chris. He was near the end of an hour-long talking jag and was low on energy. He turned and leaned back against the wall, as if he were letting down the weight of the world. The painted cinderblocks didn't budge.

"Every time I go out," he said, "it's all new. When you work nights for as long as I have… every time I go back out into daylight, the whole city has changed: new buildings have gone up, new stores have moved in, a whole new batch of people are around. It's not just the styles or the music, these kids are so different. It's not like my younger days hanging out in the Village. Their programming is different. I don't know what makes them tick anymore.

"It's a whole new world out there," he continued, "and every step I take into it, is a step further away from what I know.

"When I'm out there I'm lost, and I just want to get back inside. Back to my apartment, where there is *no* time. Where things never change, except for the stories on the tube, and even they don't change much… Pretty soon I won't recognize anything out there, and what will become of me then? I will have become the past."

Chris looked up at Virgil and blinked his small eyes a few times. It was late. He understood very little of what Virgil was saying.

"You ain't that old," he said, after a short pause. "What are you, like forty?"

"I'm thirty-six!" Virgil answered brusquely.

After having survived his sprint from the Union Square battle zone, and his regrouping in Tompkins Square Park, Virgil had rushed back to the building. With the flood of adrenaline, his world had long since shifted into a dreamlike state; and so when he stumbled onto his landing, and into the Bonehead circus, he had taken it all in stride.

He had heard their hoots and hollers while still in the building's lobby, and when he stepped into his hall, he could almost see the noise issuing from their open door, like sparks from a turbine engine.

Instinctually, Virgil was drawn toward the commotion. He wandered into the Boneheads' apartment to take shelter beneath their shield of clamor. Chris and Ray and three of the video game kids were bunched on or around their heavy-duty, red corduroy couch. Virgil took a seat at the edge of the couch, where he sat quietly while they jumped and shouted at the TV. What had set them off this time: Howard was on the screen again.

Apparently, the story of the shooting at the park was only just breaking and no one knew how serious it was; so at that time, the clip of the day had been Howard, again, at Union Square, barking at the cameras. The interview had apparently taken place a few hours before the gunfire had erupted.

Howard was in rare form. He was going off on everything: police brutality, the bias of the media, the deification of the Milgrams. It was all very "angry black man."

As a means of establishing Howard's credentials as a legitimate voice, worthy of being heard (and replayed *ad nauseum*), the news station always made sure to accompany his current clip with his previous, slightly less dignified clip, of his "run in" with the police at the City Hall protest.

Virgil watched the television as the Boneheads filled him in on the details. He listened, but his mind was elsewhere. He kept expecting a gunman to walk into the apartment.

He didn't tell them what had just happened at the park. He didn't tell them that he almost died, and that he was frightened, and that he felt horrible despair.

The Boneheads stood in front of him, arms pumping in the air as they spouted off the highlights of Howard's second television appearance; but Virgil was concentrating on the reporter on the screen, broadcasting live from Union Square. The story of the shooting was just breaking.

He couldn't watch it. He knew the coverage would go on and on—until something bigger came along. He wanted it all to be over already, and everything back to normal, but he knew *that* wouldn't be for a long time.

He got up and left. He needed to take a shower. He wanted to wash the smell of gunfire out of his nose; the odor was faint in the park but he picked up on it right away, and it brought back memories. He wanted the smell off his skin and out of his clothes; so, when he got to his apartment, he took everything off and stuffed it in a pillowcase, then set the pillowcase next to his door so he'd remember to launder it right away. Then he sat under the cool spray of his shower and tried to control his racing thoughts, and heartbeat: *slower, slower.* After ten minutes of this meditation, to his surprise, the only thing that occupied his mind was not his encounter with death, but Howard. He was angry with him.

He got out of the shower, dressed, and went back out into the hallway.

Things had settled down; the noise had abated. Chris was standing in front of his apartment door, talking to one of the kids from the building. The kid had asked Chris about college, and Chris was joyously wending his way from experience to amazing experience; as excited now as he had been back then. Virgil wasn't paying attention to the stories, but he stayed there all the same. He wasn't interested in going back to his empty apartment. He did his best to act like he was listening, but his attention was more focused on the sounds coming out of the apartment. He could hear the news on the television clearly: the reporter's words echoing perfectly off of the bare walls of the Boneheads' apartment.

He heard that the reporter was still live from the scene in Union Square, but he also heard Ray and the other guys in the apartment, talking in a relatively normal tone now; they apparently weren't paying attention to the television. Virgil listened hard while nodding and looking at the people in front of him. He kept expecting Ray to come bursting out of the apartment and shout for them to get in there; to sound the alarm about a battle going on just blocks away. But he never came out, and every nerve in Virgil's body stood on edge.

"You know," Virgil dropped into the conversation blindly. "Chris tried out for the Jets."

He knew that would buy him more time to loiter outside the Boneheads' door without actually talking.

The high schooler's mouth dropped opened.

"No way!" he said, finally losing his cool. He had already been in awe of Chris and Ray, and he had tried his best to hide it, but this was too much.

As a safety, Chris had been much too small for the pro level, and he knew it; he was even too small for the college team he had played on, but his one true gift was speed. He was the fastest player on his team, and a phenomenal punt returner. And so, the summer after he graduated, almost as a lark, he had gone to an open tryout for the Jets.

"How'd it go?" the kid asked.

Chris stopped his normally frenetic movements for just a moment.

"Yo," he said reverently, while nodding his head slowly, "those are some big boys."

It was all he ever said on the subject.

Chris's attention shifted to something over Virgil's shoulder. He perked up again.

"There he is!" Chris shouted.

Virgil turned and saw Howard walking out of the stairwell. He was on his way to his aunt's apartment a few doors down from the Boneheads. He wore the same scowl he wore on TV, as if he were still too pissed to speak… as if he were the most wronged person in the world. He nodded at the three standing there. He didn't make eye contact with Virgil.

Virgil stared hard at him. He was livid. His hands were trembling. His rage against the stupidity of the entire human race was barely controllable; and right as Howard was about to slide past them without even stopping, Virgil lost control.

He grabbed Howard by the lapels of his polo shirt and slammed him against the wall.

"What the fuck is wrong with you?" he snarled. "Don't you know you have to set an example?"

Howard let slip a gasp. Virgil was twice his size, and when he looked up at Virgil's face, he didn't recognize him. But then, he had not really looked at Virgil for years. He saw that he had gotten older; that he had wrinkles at the corners of his eyes and grey hairs in his sideburns; and suddenly he remembered that the timid, easy-tempered Virgil was his elder.

He had never stopped thinking of Virgil as a teenager, sitting quietly on his couch while he played on the carpet in front of the television; Virgil, acting more as a sentry than a friend to play with. He remembered that Virgil had always been deferential to him, out of respect for his education, out of respect for what he expected him to become in the future.

For a split-second, Howard had been defiant, but at these remembrances, his shell of pride crumbled and he dropped his head.

"I was angry," he said. "I wasn't thinking."

"Look at those kids who killed the Milgrams, they weren't thinking either. And now look at what's going on. Go look at the TV!"

He let go of Howard's shirt with a flick of his fingers.

"Go back out there and…" Then he shook his head. "No. You can't go back out there. *You* can't call a press conference, because you ain't nobody, and they already got what they needed from you."

Virgil swept Howard past them with a firm but gentle hand. "Just think about your future. You've got to be better than this. You're right there. You are *right* there. Is this who you want to be known as? Is that who you want to be? People are getting killed out there. Get your act together."

And Howard was gone.

Virgil turned back to see the Bonehead troop, huddling together in their doorway like nervous children.

"I mean," Virgil said to them, "he's got to think. This thing is not a joke."

Virgil stayed up for the rest of that night, rambling on with the Boneheads until they went to sleep—and then he rambled on with whomever else happened to wander out into the hallway. He stayed up for most of the next day too; not getting to sleep until after a warm meal at Mrs. Gittens' place.

Mrs. Gittens had long occupied the role of hall grandmother. Something was always cooking in her kitchen, and her door was always open… during decent hours. She was also the unofficial babysitter of most of the kids in the building.

It was the next day around dinner time that Virgil found himself sitting at her table alongside the Boneheads. The Boneheads lived directly across the hall from her and had become permanently ensnared by the aromas emanating from her kitchen.

It was a scene that Virgil had never witnessed: the Boneheads slowing down enough to simply sit and eat. Virgil noted how they sat quietly as they enjoyed their meal, like polite children at the grown-up table. But Virgil was too exhausted to fully appreciate the scene, and his head was pounding.

After a second full plate of macaroni and cheese with a buttered bread crumb topping, his body told him that finally, he was done. He had stopped talking long ago. He had eaten without a word and was practically blind to all around him. He stood, put his dish in the sink, then dragged himself back to his apartment. He kicked off his shoes, changed into shorts and T-shirt, and crashed leadenly onto his mattress. There he slept soundly through the rest of the busy night.

Fifteen hours later, he awoke to a peaceful day. His mind had settled. His nerves were refreshed.

Oh, what a beautiful feeling it is to have nothing to do, he thought, as he lay in his bed; *to be able to burrow your head back into your pillow for another hour or so, if you feel like it.*

He wasn't expected back at work. His family was safely ensconced at the far end of Queens. There was no reason for him to move at all.

I never want to go back to work, he thought.

He had been working long hours lately; for weeks on end. He'd wake, go to work, come home, and go to sleep. He was exhausted. So he lay there, consciously restricting himself from searching for things to do, and let his body absorb as much rest as it could.

One thing the army had taught him was to get sleep whenever he could. He didn't forget what was going on outside. He remembered it all, but he let it go. He remembered his encounter with Howard, and did not regret it.

A cool draft came in through the window by his feet. He sensed an edge to the air: fall was on the way. He moved the drapes out of the way with his foot. Two, high wispy clouds, sped across an otherwise bright blue sky.

There'll be no fighting today, he thought. *Fighting cannot exist on a day like this… Then again, 9/11 was on a day like this.* He turned over to see the time, but inexplicably didn't see any digits on his cable box; he didn't think anything of it. He turned over and went back to sleep.

Eventually, he was lured out of bed by the luxurious aroma of coffee. His temples began to throb at the scent. He needed his daily fix soon or the throbbing would turn into a deep migraine.

He got up, threw on pants, and dragged himself back outside again.

Something seemed a little off when he opened the door to the hallway, but he was still half-asleep. He *did* think it a bit odd that most of the doors on the hallway were wide open. Light from everyone's windows reached through their apartments and into the hallway. It gave the impression of the nave of an old stone church. The serenity of the scene was disrupted by Chris hopping out into the hallway.

A burst of laughter almost slipped from Virgil's lips at the sight. There Chris stood, in his usual posture, elbows out, neck stretched forward and up, his body slightly crouched as if ready to spring forward, bristling with energy. He wore only a pair of gym shorts. He stood without pretension, like a prairie dog in front of his den: a big, pink prairie dog with tight white hair and a short brushy mustache, and Virgil thought him the most innocent human being he had ever laid eyes on. What faith that boy had, and he didn't even know it.

"Yo Virge!" Chris shouted. "Power's out." And then he quantum-shifted back into his apartment.

Virgil used to roll his eyes at Chris, him being one of those white guys who pretended to be black. One of those people so void of their own substance that they had to adopt a ready-made persona: the modern-day equivalent of blackface, turned loose on the street and dancing for acceptance; but he couldn't help liking Chris, and he found out that he *was* real, as if his personality had taken his cliché shell, and tweaked it in just enough places—the right places, the good places—to become an individual. But he had absolutely no knowledge of this process: he had no knowledge of anything whatsoever, except what appeared in front of his nose. He was a happy puppy, exuberant. Chris was exactly who he appeared to be… he needed psychiatric help.

What is *set in stone anymore?* Virgil thought.

Coffee.

Virgil quickly forgot about Chris and obeyed his withdrawal symptoms. He followed the smell of coffee once again into Mrs. Gittens' apartment. Mrs. Gittens turned off the small battery-powered radio that she had set on her kitchen table and got up to pour Virgil a mug of coffee.

"Oh!" Virgil said, when he saw the radio. "That's what Chris was saying. The power is out."

"I can still make coffee!" Mrs. Gittens said, and she handed him a large, filled mug. "If they took that away, then you'd see a real revolution."

Mrs. Gittens had a well-furnished apartment. Her husband had died a few years back and left her well off, in a middle-class kind of way. While Virgil sat at the kitchen table, Mrs. Gittens began to fill him in on all that had happened the night before: the blackout, the second firefight, the expedition that most of the floor had taken up to the roof. She hadn't joined them because of all the stairs, but Austin, a thirteen-year-old boy from down the hall, had given her all the details: about how they had all stood in a bunch and looked down onto the darkened city as it sparked and sputtered like a storm viewed from space.

"His words," she said with a smile. "He had just seen a show on TV about the last space shuttle mission. Now he wants to be an astronaut…."

Looked down upon from on high, Virgil's building had the outline of a small child with arms thrown wide. The long, horizontal arms made up the bulk of the building; two parallel "legs" extended from it. A smaller, squared head, jutted from the "top" side of the arms. Each appendage made up a different wing of the building.

When the expedition from the third floor exited the stairwell onto the roof, they found themselves perched atop a small black patch, floating in a black sky. They knew they were standing on top of the shortest wing of the building—the head—and so they all stayed huddled in a tight group, as close to what they hoped was the center, as they could.

A thin but sturdy arm reached out from the group and latched onto the back of Austin's T-shirt, to keep him from wandering; the arm belonged to his older sister.

The power had gone out; everyone had come to look down at the city…but Austin was looking up at the sky.

"Austin, Austin," his sister repeated. She tugged his shirt to shake him from his stuporous gaze into space.

Everyone else remained too frozen by instinct to wander. Some sat right where they were, to ensure that they themselves wouldn't accidently walk off the face of their cliff. But fear quickly morphed into awe, as their eyes adjusted, and they saw what was in front of them. Right there, on the other side of the river, three fires burned. The fires weren't close together: their flames blazed at three different points along the river, like torches lighting the way for passing barges. The two larger fires, the nearer ones, were about a mile apart in Brooklyn. The third, smaller fire, burned further upriver in Queens. They figured it was a trash can.

While the others were transfixed by the fires, Austin's gaze was fixed on the stars. "The Milky Way!" he gasped from the shadows, and if it wasn't for his sister's steel grip, he would have drifted away.

There, above their heads, a cloud of stars arched across all of creation: the serpent in the sky that had bewitched every consciousness that had ever laid eyes on it…. And stars twinkled, and Venus beamed a hard white, and Mars a pale red, and Austin had never seen anything so real in his life. The Milky Way. It had been a cartoon up until then, a picture in a book, but, to see it in a book and then, to see it alive, right above his head… There was something miraculous about it, and Austin didn't doubt it at all. But when he looked around for some sort of validation, he realized everyone else was staring down at their own stars, spread out below their feet: flickering, flashing lights—reds and whites and blues—moving this way and that, within the unlit grid of the city streets. Solid streams of reds and whites lined the FDR, while the foo fighters: the screaming emergency vehicles, raced with angular precision through unseen channels.

The group watched the colored lights moving along the darkened circuitry until a harsh noise drew their attention—a slow-burning explosion, like the volume suddenly jumping on white noise and then dropping back down.

Huh?

The sound came from behind them: from inside the city. Everyone turned from the river and shuffled a few steps toward the west side of the roof.

Because the Lower East Side was no stranger to fireworks, their first thought had been: *trash can filled with firecrackers, doused in gasoline and set ablaze.* But after the initial din—a period of silence;

then the noise started again, slowly: random pops at first, but quickly, the "thinking" behind the beats was discerned.

People.

The firing increased and echoed along the streets of Alphabet City. The group on the roof knew where the strife was coming from: they saw an orange glow on the rim of a flame-lit canyon. It was close; a few blocks away, but they couldn't see down onto the street. The noise had blossomed quickly into a hard fight, but then just as quickly, dropped off in a confused frustration.

Silence again.

Then, the only thing the group heard was sirens in the distance. But then came more firing. This time from right there in the projects, as if in answer to what they had just heard on the streets. The shots came from the next roof over. They could see flashes in the dark as a volley of shots went straight up into the air.

Austin's group quickly retreated from the roof. With flashlights and cell phone lights, they headed into the stairwell, trekking single file back down to the third floor, like a long procession of monks.

After hearing Mrs. Gittens recount the story of the events on the roof, Virgil's mood swung from happy and calm, to distressed once again. He left Mrs. Gittens in her kitchen and went into the hallway. With the power out, he had no idea of what was going on in the outside world. He had no internet, no cable; only Mrs. Gittens' tiny radio with bad reception. He needed, at the very least, to get a clear view of what was going on around the building; but according to Mrs. Gittens, the Mayor had told everyone in the city to stay inside.

Virgil looked in the Boneheads' apartment and saw Chris standing in his work clothes. Chris was a public school gym teacher; he pretty much wore the same outfit every day: a tight, light blue T-shirt bearing the name of his school, and tan shorts.

"You went up to the roof last night, right?" Virgil said. "Come on, let's go up there now."

Mrs. Gittens had told him about the National Guard being out there. He had to see this for himself.

"Hold up, hold up," Chris said. "Let me get my shoes on... there's rocks up there."

He ran into his room, then came back out a second later, wearing flip-flops and holding an oversized flashlight.

"Okay," he said. "Let's go."

Chris and Virgil entered the dark stairwell and began their long ascent to the roof. Chris led the way. He switched off the flashlight near the top because someone had left the door propped opened with an old metal milk crate. Sunlight illuminated the last few flights.

Chris shoved opened the heavy fire door with his shoulder. Its hinges gave way with a rusty pop. They were both temporarily dazzled by sunlight. Chris took a wire coat hanger that was attached to the outside wall and hooked it around the handle of the door to hold it open. Virgil sat on the milk crate to catch his breath.

"That's where the shooting came from," Chris said, as he walked toward the East River side of the building. "Right there," he said, pointing north to the next building over. "Some guys were on the roof popping off shots. We couldn't see 'em though... And then some shots started coming from the common area too. I guess everyone was trying out their new guns. We all started ducking and running for cover."

He laughed and threw his hands over his head to mime the fear they had experienced. "We had no idea where those bullets were going."

Virgil looked at the next building over. It was about a hundred feet away. He dabbed the sweat off his brow with a paper towel. Chris hadn't even mentioned the police shootout they heard.

"Hey," Chris said. "There're people walking across the bridge."

Virgil got up to look. He walked over to where Chris was standing—and sure enough, an unbroken stream of people stretched over the Williamsburg Bridge, heading toward Brooklyn.

"Oh shoot, look at that! The army's here too," Chris said. "Look, look… down on the fields."

"I guess that's the National Guard," Virgil said.

Mrs. Gittens had told him about them being there, but he hadn't thought they'd be camped right across the street. Of course, "across the street" meant across the FDR Drive, which was six lanes of highway, three north and three south… *plus* a small service road that ran next to his building… *and* a well fenced-in footpath or two on each side of the highway…and *then* the ball fields. But it was close enough so that they could see all the Humvees and a couple of transport trucks parked on the grass, half with jungle camo paint jobs and half in desert colors. He could see the soldiers setting up large tents, preparing a staging area.

I hope they know where the real trouble is, Virgil thought, as he imagined some petrified kid on his first day in green, walking around the big bad projects with a machine gun in his hands.

That could be dangerous.

There were also two large boats docked in the river alongside the walking path. One was a standard, military patrol boat; the other was something altogether different. The second boat was long and dark, and slung low to the water like something out of the Amazon. Its hull was over a hundred feet long, its fixtures made of wood and brass, with a lustrous, sturdy sheen.

The boat sat motionless, as if all closed up.

There were smaller boats too—lots of them—but they were local: orange pointed racers, with stand-up machine guns bolted to their back decks. These boats were part of New York's own anti-terrorist patrol unit; Virgil always saw them patrolling the waters around downtown and Battery Park. Now they hovered around the makeshift army base like mosquitoes around a campfire, all probably just coming to take a peek.

Virgil heard a commotion behind him. Ray popped out of the stairwell, followed closely by a couple of the video game kids.

"We couldn't see a thing in there!" they all came up shouting.

Chris turned and ran to join his friends; at the same moment they all heard a slow, guttural rumble coming from behind them. They turned to the west and saw it: a sharp gray machine, swimming through the sky toward them. A fighter jet, sweeping in low.

It was an awesome sight, hushing them all to silence. The jet flew much lower than ordinary planes, but it was still high enough to not be a threat. As they watched, the plane began to slalom like a lazy shark, making S-patterns, as if it had no particular goal in mind, and so wasn't sure how to act: a jet pilot's equivalent of twiddling their thumbs.

The jet thundered past them and then, even though it seemed to be going unnaturally slow, was over Brooklyn and out of sight in seconds.

"Holy crap," Ray shouted. "I've never seen anything like *that* before."

"Yeah… that *was* weird," Virgil said. But he had seen it before: on 9/11.

CHAPTER 20

Emmanuel died for a short time in her thirteenth year. According to the police, it had been for at least ten minutes—but according to her Aunt Ruthie, who was there, it was at least twice that. She said that, by the time Manny was fished from the lake and that, by the time the police had reached them and that, by the time Manny had been miraculously resurrected… that yes, it had been at least twice that. But then, that whole first winter in New York had been somewhat miraculous.

Manny had never even seen snow before, and on her very first night in the new world, not more than half a day after landing at a cold and dreary Kennedy Airport, the snow began to fall.

Her family had managed to squeeze in a viewing of Times Square and Rockefeller Center, before checking into their hotel for their first night's sleep. And they had considered that a full day; but around midnight, both she and her sisters were roused to witness the miracle.

The three girls sleepwalked to the window, dragging their feet along the way, and awoke gazing out into a beautiful new world.

While her younger sisters gave in to enchantment, fogging the windows with their breath and drawing hearts and smiley faces on the cloudy panes, Manny leaned her cheek against the cool glass and stared down onto a perfect snow-covered street. The scene reminded her of a postcard: a Currier and Ives Christmas scene. Central Park was directly across the street from the old hotel, and already the dignified old trees lining the park's stone walls were coated in white.

Oh what a beautiful world, she thought.

Without being prompted, her sisters raced across the room and started throwing on their new coats. Manny forgot her thoughts and raced after them, and together, with mother and father, they tumbled out into the hallway, and onto the elevator, and through the empty lobby, and burst out onto a deserted sidewalk.

Traffic had fled the oncoming snow, and the only movement not of nature, was the synchronized traffic lights stretching down Fifth Avenue. The five of them, like five children, clung together as they floated along the sidewalk, past elegant doorman buildings, beneath rich-green awnings with lustrous brass posts. Across the street, the Metropolitan Museum of Art sat gleaming like a national monument, its vast façade, well-lit, even behind its veil of snow.

The family crossed onto the park side of the street and stood in the lee of the museum's grand staircase. They craned their necks just to see its top. The small family, warmed by love, stared up into the dark sky, as heavy clumps of snowflakes drifted softly down into the yellow street light.

Mother and father held each other, and the children spun and spun and spun, their arms wide and their mouths opened to the sky to catch the falling snowflakes.

Day two and Manny grabs the red plastic handles of her round aluminum sled and races down a small hill in the heart of Central Park. Her glistening sled is her shield and she is Captain America, as she bounds with purpose and leaps and in one swift motion pulls her body up and under and lands solidly on her seat with two feet sticking forward. She has absolutely no control.

She speeds downhill awkwardly, bouncing and spinning her way toward the frozen lake at the bottom: a lake they had been playing on for the past twenty minutes. But this time, near the end of her run, as she's skidding backwards across the ice, her sled snags and is torn out from under her. She slams back and her feet fly up and the back of her head strikes the granite-hard ice.

At impact, her vision flashes white, and she detects the smell of death rising up from somewhere deep within her brain; somewhere so deep that even with its reaching, it barely brushes the back of her olfactory nerves. And though she's never smelled it before, she instinctually knows its seriousness.

She lies back, unable to move, unable to draw breath; all she can do is stare at the desolate, austere sky. Icy water trickles up the sides of her neck—and she can do nothing about it. She feels the ice shift under her and tilt... and she slides off into a muffled underworld.

From beneath the ice, she sees a glow; silver bubbles broil, they whirl and stretch like witches' fingers, feeling out the crevices of her luminescent cave ceiling. Bubbles, bubbles—and then... she has a vision.

From the top of the hill, Aunt Ruthie and her daughter had seen the whole thing. They had heard the crack of Manny's skull, and watched as she disappeared. It all happened so quickly—the slab of ice on which Manny lay, slowly, and mechanically, dipped below the surface for a moment, before popping back up into place: bare. The ice covering the lake was once again pristine. There was no sign of the tragedy that was occurring at that very moment.

Ruthie was confused. She didn't understand what was happening. Tragedies were supposed to be loud; accompanied by people running and screaming. Everybody knew when a tragedy occurred. The only thing that Aunt Ruthie heard was the soft rushes of wind that stung her ears. But then, thankfully, the tragedy was announced: someone began screaming hysterically.

Off to her left, at the bottom of the hill, a tall, skinny black man had jumped up from one of the stone benches that circled the base of a large fountain. Without hesitation, he started racing toward Manny, going right across the top of the frozen lake. He ran awkwardly, his arms and legs flailing about as he moved. Every third or fourth step, one of his oversized sneakers would break through the frozen surface; but he moved so fast that he didn't sink. His spindly legs pulled him quickly across the treacherous landscape like a marionette with strings attached at the knees, and he continued screaming the whole while in a blind panic.

"HELP ME! HELP ME! MY GOD, SOMEBODY PLEASE HELP ME! THE LITTLE GIRL! THE LITTLE GIRL!"

By the time he reached the spot where Manny had gone under, he was standing in waist-deep water. He plunged his bone-thin arms into the lake, making wild digging motions as if swiping the water away.

Over and over, he grabbed heavy chunks of ice with his bare hands and heaved them off across the top of the unbroken ice around him.

Aunt Ruthie's initial reaction had been one of terrible embarrassment. Who was this effeminate man: this ridiculous-looking thing with oversized sunglasses and a tiny cap of purple hair sitting atop his otherwise bald head?

Screaming like a woman, she had thought with revulsion.

And still, she stood there at the top of the hill, frozen in confusion, her daughter staring up at her. But Aunt Ruthie didn't snap out of it until she saw people all around her, running toward the lake. When she saw two police officers sprinting over from the Boathouse, she finally moved. She carefully hurried down to the water's edge to claim her niece. She reached the bottom of the hill just as two men and a woman pulled Manny's small body from the water. Her skin had turned blue. They carried Manny to shore and laid her down on someone's jacket; then people started to work on her.

In the twenty years or so since the accident, Manny had never told anyone about her vision. She had not told her family, nor her friends; she had never even mentioned it to Theresa Milgram, her mentor and life coach. (Who had a weakness for tasseography and those sorts of things.) She kept her secret hidden, not out of embarrassment, but because... well, the message had been for her.

It wasn't exactly a monkey who visited Manny, it was more of a... half monkey... and half human. And this creature, this Hanuman, sat beside her on the ground; not deferentially, but only because... that was the way, half monkey, half humans sat.

Manny stood tall—as if for a tailor: her head high and her shoulders back—while her visitor set to work. In the crook of his left arm he held a stack of masks, and one by one, Manny's mascareri lifted a mask to within an inch of her face, and one by one, he took them down.

It quickly occurred to Manny that she wasn't looking directly through the eyes of those hollowed-out masks, but was watching the entire scene take place in front of her, as if it were onstage. But at the same time, *she* was the one onstage.

The masks looked simple—plain and white—and seemed expressionless; but she knew they were not so simple, as each mask held a different emotion. And the face they were being held up to was not Manny's ordinary face, but a blank slate… her eternal face (her *Atman*?)… the face that always was.

As each mask went up, Manny felt herself putting on the emotion it possessed; and that would have been simple, if that were all there was. But Manny knew something else about the scene she was watching: it was a test, and how she controlled her heart, while trying on each mask, each emotion, *was* her test.

And so as this demigod held up each emotion, Manny, who stood back watching, had to work through her wheel of emotional control, to find the proper attitude with which to peer through the eyes of these masks of life; and she knew the answer was the same for each mask, but she didn't *know* the answer. Was it calm, was it impassive… was it some indefinably subtle mixture of feelings as of yet unnamed? No, those were just more emotions. Her wheel spun to emptiness… that wasn't it… Detachment? *Leave it all.* But no, that was too frightening…

And then she felt a smack on the center of her forehead, and just as her eyes snapped opened in shock, she could have sworn she caught the tail end of a bolt of light streaking up and off into the cold sky.

For an instant, her mind struggled between perceptions—her vision and… her sight—before finding herself distracted by the more immediate stinging sensation radiating from the blow to the forehead. She forgot all three when she realized she was lying in the snow at the bottom of the hill, surrounded by faces. She rolled onto her side and began to throw up.

When she finished, she wiped her mouth, caught her breath, and rolled back over.

"Did someone hit me?" she asked in perfect English.

She was answered with laughter and sighs of relief.

No one had hit her.

In the weeks that followed, Manny's family seemed to think that she had changed: she was no longer her carefree self. She didn't think it was so. She did spend a lot of time wondering about her vision. Did she pass her test? How could she have, if she didn't even remember her final answer?

She thought of these things, that was true, but not to the point where they affected her personality. No, she hadn't changed. This was just the first time they had ever really looked at her.

It had started on the flight over. Manny noticed her father was treating her differently. He was so worried about their move that he didn't have the energy to keep talking to her like a child; and sensing this, Manny, in turn, had to turn up different facets of her personality— facets that *she* was familiar with, but ones her parents hadn't seen.

Her father had been a pilot for many years. He had worked for the very airline they were flying; but on this flight, their exodus, he was just another melancholy passenger. Their flight attendant had taken a second look at him when she saw his AirEgypt carryon bag, and recognized him. He also knew the pilots of their plane. And so, later that night, when the lights of the main cabin had been turned off, and his wife and two younger daughters were asleep, he took Manny onto the flight deck for a tour.

They walked into the dimly lit cave, wallpapered with dials and switches and a million little lights, and shared the jump seat behind the two younger pilots. Manny's father talked when he was nervous— talking shop with the pilots helped him to even his keel.

The two pilots chatted with their eyes forward as they monitored the switches and dials. Manny was forgotten as the three men talked about planes and airports, or of their shared experience of serving in the military, and Manny's father had seemed his old self for a while. Manny rested against his shoulder and listened as they talked. The orange and red lights on the dash panel glowed warmly, and she felt like they were in front of a camp fire.

We should be over the Atlantic Ocean by now, she thought. *We've been in the air for hours.*

But every so often, she would see another white twinkling grid on the Earth below.

How can there be cities in the middle of the ocean? she wondered.

She noticed ice crystals forming around the edges of the windows. It scared her.

"That's Dublin," her father said, noticing her staring at the ice crystals. "After Ireland it goes all dark."

And a minute later, it did.

It was already late, and Manny was drifting in and out of sleep, dreaming of wooden sailing ships on ancient seas. She had tuned out the men and heard only hashed-out cross talk on the radio, which seemed to be leaking in from distant worlds.

So many people have crossed.

"There's barely any air out there," her father said to her. "Not this high up. I read about a man who broke the world record for highest sky dive. It was thirty years ago; a pilot, from the U.S. Air Force."

He relaxed and leaned back into his seat for the first time.

"Kittinger," he said. "That was his name. He jumped from a balloon... a capsule attached to a balloon. From nineteen miles above the Earth. That's three times higher than we are right now... he wore a space suit."

Manny roused from her stupor and looked up at her dad. She had never seen him speak so frankly. She noticed the other pilots were listening too. Their hands had stopped fidgeting, and their heads remained still.

"He peered out of this bubble—the Earth—into the blackness of space. He said it was beautiful... but he also said it was hostile.... Hostile.

"When he stepped off of a small platform on his capsule to return to Earth, he didn't even realize he was falling, because there was no air up there: nothing to rush against his body. No medium for sound to travel in. He thought he was floating until he looked up and saw his balloon speeding away from him, up into space... but it wasn't. It was *he* who was hurling down to Earth... Four-and-a-half minutes of free fall...

"*Excelsior* was the name of his capsule. 'Ever upward'."

The decision to move to a new world was not taken lightly by Manny's father. He knew he was gambling with the lives of his family.

It could all go wrong, he had thought.

A far-off voice sounded over the plane's radio. The pilots turned to attend to it.

Manny's father leaned in.

"This is where it all happens, Manny," he said. "Down here, huddled close to the Earth. Down here in the warmth."

He put his arm around his daughter and hugged her.

"We're in the middle of an unfinished time, Manny."

After her accident, Manny's family left their hotel and moved into Aunt Ruthie's house. This occurred ahead of schedule. They cut short their vacation week in the city and made their way to Astoria.

Their original plan had been well thought out. They would splurge during that first week. They would stay at a fancy hotel, see a Broadway show, visit the Statue of Liberty, go ice-skating in Central Park, walk across the Brooklyn Bridge, and do anything else they could squeeze in. Manny's parents wanted positive memories associated with this important time in their lives. And this one-week splurge would be worth it. After their quick whirl across the ballroom floor, they would settle back down to reality and move into Aunt Ruthie's basement apartment, until they were able to stand on their own.

"There's no hurry," Aunt Ruthie had told them. "There's plenty of room at the house."

It was only her, her husband Werner, and their daughter Zara.

For the first few weeks after the accident, Manny was given her space. Her parents didn't drag her out shopping every morning, or ship her off to another cousin's house with the rest of the kids. She was given time to mend. She was set up in her own room upstairs, next to Zara's, while her parents and sisters shared the basement apartment.

On weekday mornings, Manny and Aunt Ruthie had the house to themselves. Ruthie would spend most of the mornings in the kitchen, chatting on the phone and leafing through celebrity magazines; Manny spent her time on the living room couch, wrapped in a large comforter. She didn't feel bad at all. She could have gotten up and joined the rest of her family, but she made a conscious decision to be selfish; her family could manage on their own. She was going to take this time to figure out her new world. And so, every morning, she came downstairs after everyone had left, wrapped herself up on the couch and watched TV... and napped... and ate all the snacks Aunt Ruthie brought her.

In the afternoons, someone always stopped by the house—and Manny always happened to be napping when they arrived. She never heard anyone come in, and only realized company was there after being roused from her sleep by the sound of an unfamiliar voice. She'd open her eyes and look at the muted television, not letting them know she was awake, just so she could listen to the soothing tones of their conversation.

In the old country, her television was a small black-and-white, that was kept on top of the refrigerator and mostly ignored. But here at Aunt Ruthie's house, watching television was a luxurious experience. The set was as large as a picture window; its colors were sharp and bright, and she could burrow herself into the cushions of the sofa and change channels with a tap of her thumb. It was the first remote control she had ever used.

She parked in front of the television every day, until people started coming home around dinner time... and then, after dinner, they all watched more television together. She watched shows about science and history. She watched a special on the 1960s, and was convinced that the sixties was the most important decade in human history... But then she watched a bunch of *I Love Lucy*s, and thought that maybe the fifties were great too... and what about the forties? They battled for the world in the forties... And the thirties—were devastating... and the twenties—were wild... and the tens had revolutionary ideas... and the aughts had Model As and the Wright brothers; and back and back it went till probably the beginning of time.

She hadn't seen TV shows about the older times, but she was sure that every generation had *something* amazing that happened during its time, and she saw that the world was constantly *becoming*: billowing forth like clouds of smoke; inoculating itself against itself; struggling forward, expressing itself forward; and Manny was filled with excitement because she knew it would not stop.

On her first Saturday in New York, Manny spent the entire morning in her room. She had become spoiled: used to peace and quiet. But that morning, the kids had the run of the house. Uncle Werner had taken Manny's parents to Macy's right after breakfast, and the house was expecting company after lunch, so the children were not dropped off.

George showed up early that day. He was the man who had saved her life. He brought her golden marigolds for her night table and a small stuffed elephant. Aunt Ruthie had greeted him warmly when she opened the door; she had not been sure that he was going to show up. She hugged him, then took him right upstairs to meet Manny "officially" for the first time.

"How's my girl?" he said. "How's my little queen?"

He sat on a small wooden chair beside Manny's bed, and Manny sat up among the pillows and stuffed animals, and they talked as best they could and learned about each other, so that after a few minutes, Manny knew her family had a new friend.

"I just wanted to stop by to see how you were," George then said, almost apologetically. "I can't stay for long."

Aunt Ruthie protested.

"We have food! We have food!" Her usual argument.

"My friend is waiting for me outside," he finally confessed.

They looked out the window of Manny's room: a short light-skinned man was standing a few houses down. He wore no hat and had on a thin grey jacket. He fidgeted and stomped his feet while taking shelter behind a large Sycamore tree.

"*Aiee!*" Aunt Ruthie shrieked.

And before anyone could say a thing, she was hobbling down the stairs and out the front door, and Manny and George watched her through the window as she plodded across the frozen grass in her slippers to drag George's friend inside.

And Manny knew exactly what she was thinking to herself as she marched: *No way! There is no way I am going to fail God again so soon. Not here. Not now, with George right in front of me.*

Manny might have smiled about it, but Aunt Ruthie had taken the accident very badly; to the point of hysteria—once Manny was finally out of danger—and Manny had the feeling that Aunt Ruthie had made some sort of pact. She hadn't said anything to anyone, but Manny could sense it. George had not only saved her life, he had saved Ruthie's too. He had saved their entire family's future.

"Imagine if…" was all Ruthie could say before bursting into tears.

Never again would she question a man's worth, not when a man like this—someone she would not even have talked to the week before—raced, without hesitation, across the thin ice of a frozen lake, to save a total stranger. Forever, she would feel the shame of not being the one with such courage. George was now a part of her family.

Manny's parents came home to find Aunt Ruthie and her sisters plying George and his boyfriend with foreign delicacies at the kitchen table: the two were boxed in, and their wills were too weak to resist the onslaught.

Meanwhile, a cluster of children trampled down the stairs… and through the living room… and down to the basement… and out the side door… and around the side of the house… and back in through the front door… and back up the stairs. They had been loosed by the visiting relatives, who had arrived after lunch and who were now spread out all over the house.

As always, the first thing Manny's father did when he came home was make a beeline to where ever she was. He'd find out about her day and what new things she had learned and drop off a few *Archie* Comics, but that day, perhaps induced by George's appearance, he was a bit overwhelmed.

"Everything turned into a disaster," he said. "I wanted to make this special. I wanted to set you down in a wonderland; a safe and beautiful world. But now I'm sitting at the bedside of my daughter, who is so sad now."

Manny was shocked. She hadn't realized how much her father was suffering: he was kneeling at her bedside, like a man supplicating before an icon.

"What do you mean, Dad?" she said. "I am not sad. I am not sad at all. I love it here. Look!" she exclaimed. "Look at this house! We are surrounded by family here, we've made new friends, and I feel wonderful. I have never felt so wonderful in all my life. Did you hear about all those people who raced to save me?" She smiled a smile that couldn't be faked, and her father smiled too. He gave her a hug—and then they heard Aunt Ruthie calling from the bottom of the stairs, asking Manny's father to come and say hi to George.

Okay, she thought to herself. *No more lounging around.*

It was making people worry.

After her father had left, Manny leaned back among her pillows and looked around her. She loved her room. It was filled with pinks and purples and stuffed animals and white lace, and it was her exact image of the room of a princess. A burst of laughter came from the kitchen downstairs, and suddenly she felt herself at the center of some vast cosmic machine. She felt it. She felt the pulse of it: every player, every scene swirling, all of it flowing perfectly, the way it had to, and she shuttered at the glimpse of understanding, that every moment, was a perfect moment.

Downstairs in the kitchen, Manny's mother was holding up two three-pound bags of almonds; one in each hand. She had just come back from Costco.

"Can you believe it?" she said, with a huge grin on her face. "Look at the size of them!"

CHAPTER 21

Burns raised his small, balled-up fist, to knock on the door of Apartment 2C.

"It's Lestor's apartment now," he said to himself, before growing nervous and letting his fist drop.

It was still pretty early.

He cocked an ear to the door to see if he could pick out any of the voices coming from inside. He could not. But he did determine there were at least three distinct individuals inside: two males and a female… maybe. He could tell by the pitch of the murmurings. Even murmuring betrayed certain things; and after having spent his entire life moving through an overpopulated world of boxes atop thinly walled boxes, he had developed that one particular skill: reading the room behind the wall.

"It's Lestor's apartment *currently*," he corrected, and lifted his small fist again.

He stood in front of the door for another minute, fist paused; then, having calculated that the odds were good that he'd know somebody inside, he finally knocked.

Inside the door, Burns' tentative knock carried easily through the still air of the apartment.

Manny, who had been sitting on the couch texting for the past hour, stood, just as she was finishing off one last group message text to her family: *All is well,* she typed with two thumbs.

She hit the SEND button, then looked up at Shazz, who was standing in the doorway of the kitchen, waiting.

"It couldn't be Press now," she said. "Not this early in the morning. Not with all the shooting that's been going on out there."

She walked to the door and put an eye to the peephole.

"They still haven't caught these guys," she said.

She stared through the small lens for a moment, before lifting her head and snapping the lock open.

"It's Burns," she said, as she opened the door.

Outside in the hallway, stood a small man in an oversized Mets hat and a bright blue Mets jersey. His face bore a look of consternation, and his head fidgeted as if it couldn't bear the weight of a steady gaze.

"Burns," Shazz said, "come on in."

And with those words, Burns' true character was released. His look of worry lifted, and his face lit up with his well-known, tilted-head, open-mouthed smile—a smile that somehow managed to hide all his teeth.

"Oh-ho-ho, Shazz!" Burns sang out jovially with a high-pitched, airy voice. "Long time no see. Yah?"

He walked through the doorway, nodding his head and smiling at Manny as he passed her. Manny smiled back.

Everyone in the apartment knew Burns. He had lived in the building since the era of Stanley and Theresa, and he knew every person who had lived in the apartment since: Shazz, Lestor, Casey, and the few other tenants who had lived there in between. Even Roddy had met him once or twice at various Milgram parties: Burns, with the bent nose that looked as if it had been broken in a fight, yet was perfectly natural. Burns, in his ever-present sports gear. Burns, the man who never seemed to age because he had looked old since he was a kid.

Shazz gave Burns a pat on the shoulder, then turned to go back into the kitchen. As he sat, he could already hear Roddy start to get into it with Burns.

"You're still a Mets fan?" he said. "Didn't I tell you that team is cursed? Switch teams already, save yourself some pain."

"Oh no!" came the excited response from Burns, who loved nothing more than sports banter.

Manny followed Shazz into the kitchen, then sat down next to him. She turned off her phone because her battery was running low and the power was still out. She had spent most of the previous evening exchanging texts with the Mayor's office. Deputy Mayor Miller was her liaison. He provided her with updates regarding the movements of the gunmen as he learned them. She shared all the relevant information with the rest of the apartment.

The gunmen were only a few blocks away, the Deputy Mayor had warned—as if they hadn't heard the storm. *Two of the gunmen have been shot,* he had typed. The rest had somehow slipped away again. *Smoke, fire, and bullets can create a confusing situation,* he had added— and they had lost too many cops already. No more blindly rushing into things. They had to be *extra* careful. Better to lose them for a few hours than lose one more police officer.

The firefight had been captured by at least four different cell phones; it had been uploaded onto the internet minutes after it happened. The entire planet was in the process of having a collective conversation on the matter: everyone was throwing their two cents in.

As the deputy mayor fed the latest information to Manny, it was understood that what he was really doing, was begging her to bring in Lestor and Shazz for a sit-down. The Mayor's office desperately needed some good news: something to take everyone's eyes off of the clunky green trucks rolling down the FDR.

Manny also knew it was the right thing to do, not just for the city, but also for Lestor and Shazz. They needed to be rid of the attention so they could start moving forward.

So while Burns and Roddy talked sports in the living room, and Lestor and Casey were holed up in their room, Manny sat with Shazz at the kitchen table and wondered just how she was going to broach the subject.

She was surprised when Shazz spoke first.

"You know," he said, "I had just been thinking... before this... that things weren't so bad down there."

He sat back in his chair and held his head high, while still staring down at the table in front of him.

"No traffic, no crowds... blue water... the bar was right down the block from where we all lived. It was a real laid-back bar at a marina... one of the local guys in our crew kept his boat there."

How well did she know him? Manny wondered as she listened. She had known him for about ten years: Shazz, Lestor's older brother, always hanging around the edges of the scene when she worked with his parents at their house: on the front stoop, in the backyard, off in the kitchen, a friend or two always at his side.

She knew he was raised in that neighborhood, Alphabet City, and that both of his biological parents had died; his mother when he was very young, his father, a week before the Milgrams entered his life.

Burns' high-pitched voice came dribbling into the kitchen along a time-worn rill that had eroded down to the nerves in Shazz's brain. It grated on Shazz, Burn's voice. It was always at a shout—but because Burns was so frail, it never rose above normal conversation level, *and* it was half air.

"Yeah!" Burns "shouted' excitedly. "He's pitching tonight. He's a knuckleballer. You've got to *see* those games. You can't listen to that on the radio."

Shazz, who had never been a big sports fan, other than playing, had no idea who he was talking about.

"He says the pitch is like magic," Burns continued. "It's quantum physics stuff. The ball can *not* be hit… hard. The catcher can barely catch it. Even the umpire is confused as all get out… it's unfathomable!" he shouted in his weak airy voice, laughing at the word he had heard on the radio: "Unfathomable!"

Shazz looked up and saw that Manny was still focused on him. She looked different, he thought: her hair. She had always kept it pulled back tight and businesslike; now it was loose. It made her look younger.

Shazz had never let his gaze linger on her for more than a moment. Their relationship had always been courteous and at arm's length. They knew each other through his mother, and that was the extent of it.

He noticed that she had light-brown eyes that popped as she stared out at him from the center of a dark mass of hair. He could make out a band of freckles across the bridge of her nose that barely showed on her olive skin.

She had been downplaying her appearance, he realized; but then
again, he had never looked closely at her.

"The boat," she said.

Shazz smiled.

"Yes. It was a small boat," he said, "but big enough to take a few
of us out to the deeper water."

He remembered the exhilaration of being out of sight of land in
such a small boat, so easily skimming over the broad backs of cerulean
rollers... *Such hubris could not go unpunished*, he would think with
a dumb grin on his face, while holding onto the center console with
a fear-enhanced grip.

"The bar was right on the water too," he continued. "We were
friends with the girls who worked there. Some nights at closing, they
would just lock the doors, and we would hang out on the patio all
night... They had these schools of tarpon that would patrol the water
around the docks: huge, hundred-pound puppies with upturned snouts,
and people would feed them... and they would rise to the surface and
suck a shrimp out of your hand with a mouth like a steel trap. And
they had these huge metallic scales, two or three inches wide each...
prehistoric looking, and they glistened like silver armor when the
sunlight bounced off of them, and on late nights, they seemed to be
on autopilot, just cruising in circles beneath the boats, and they would
pass through the lights of the dock mechanically, as if dreaming... then
disappear back into the darkness, into some primeval world... I was
just thinking... *that* night... about how good it all felt: being there, in
the warmth, and the sea, and I could imagine going forth down there
and starting something—and that's when the television got me."

Shazz got up and walked to the doorway between the kitchen and
the living room. He leaned a shoulder against the wall and watched

Burns and Roddy continue their interaction. Roddy was trying his best to stifle a laugh. There had been a lot of tension in the apartment; Shazz could see that it was getting to Roddy.

"A what?" Roddy said to Burns.

"A presser. I'm a presser," Burns answered earnestly.

"A presser?"

"Yeah, a presser! Someone who presses things… suits and jackets and such. I work at the dry cleaner around the corner."

"Oooh!" Roddy said, through his snickering. He was laughing at himself for not understanding. "A pressure?"

"My mother was a dresser," Burns added. "She dressed actresses for Broadway shows."

Manny sat on the kitchen chair and watched Shazz as he impassively observed the two men. He had always been difficult to read, she thought, so she would often steal quick scrutinizing glimpses of him when no one was watching—looking for any tells.

The way he looked at people. It was as if, every second he looked at you, was the very first second he had ever seen you. He gave nothing away, and it unnerved her. But in spite of that she *did* know him, because she knew his past; because like any proud and worried parent, Theresa never stopped talking about her boys, and she told Manny Shazz's story.

His mother had died when he was young, and he had been raised by his father. He had a grandmother for a little while, but she passed soon after his mother, and his father was ill-prepared to raise a child. He was an alcoholic who was in and out of work.

Theresa had earned the trust of her new, reticent son, with patience, and persistence. And he had opened up and told her a lot; but he had never wanted to burden her with too much.

He told her his father had a temper, but never gave the details. He didn't say how his father spent most of his time sitting quietly on his chair in front of the turned-off television, or in an empty kitchen, and how every so often he would explode in fits of rage.

He could always feel them coming. The way an animal could feel a buildup of pressure before an earthquake. Days before, it would start to go silent in the dark apartment, and it was more than just a muffling of sound, it was as if a vacuum were slowly forming.

They'd start the way they always did, with a heavy thump: the violent stomp of an angry giant... a tripped switch. And then, faster than time itself, the shockwave would echo down through the steel and concrete of the building, off the granite sternum of the Earth below, and back up through the floor and into the bones of a young Shazz who, already, stood prepared for the next half of the tripped switch: the crash.

A demon had leapt from the depths and touched down onto the worn linoleum of his kitchen floor. With limbs of brute strength, it lashed out and did the only thing it knew how to do: destroy. It tore a cabinet from the kitchen wall; it ripped a door right from its hinges. Rage exploded like a thunderclap, and Shazz stood in his room, frozen like a rabbit in a storm.

But it was the words that were worst of all. Shazz could live through the soul-flinching crashes as the rampages wore on, but the words cut him deeply, and even as a child, Shazz could tell that they went too far over the line—the vulgarity, the spewing hatred of life, the sacrilegious desecrations of his late wife's memory. It was as shocking to Shazz as if he were witnessing his father's self-immolation.

And although, for reasons unknown, the rages were never aimed directly at him, he always put something in front of the door to his room when he went to sleep on those nights, just in case his father decided to deprive God of what was left of his family to torture. Something in front of the door would at least give him a bit of a warning.

But Shazz never really felt neglected. This was just the way things were. People threw fits. His father was strong. He was strong. The only thing that puzzled Shazz was…why was he still being provided for?

At the end of the rages, his father would collapse in exhaustion, and he seemed so small, so far away: alone, with no way for anyone to reach him—not that Shazz would ever try. He had learned at a young age to never trust his father.

One afternoon, Shazz came home to find the police at his door. They were looking for him. His father had gotten into a fight and fell, or was pushed, down the building's stairwell. Shazz's father, they told him, was dead.

"I could never truly explain the way I felt when I first met you, until you understood science," Theresa Milgram had told Shazz one evening many years ago.

The Milgram family were in their kitchen: Theresa, Shazz, Lestor, and Stanley. The boys sat at the table; Theresa stood, leaning back against the kitchen counter while gazing wistfully down at her sons. She had just finished washing a few dishes and was drying her hands off with a towel.

Lestor and Shazz sat facing each other. Stanley was comfortably ensconced on the inside seat between Shazz and the bay window that faced the driveway at the side of the house. He was peering through a large magnifying glass, reading a densely worded page from a legal encyclopedia. The heavy tome rested atop a pile of newspapers, magazines, and mail that covered most of the table.

Young Lestor wasn't paying much attention either. He half-heartedly leafed through a *Sunday Times* magazine, searching for something colorful to look at.

Shazz didn't look up at his mother, but he was listening intently.

It was night, and old, incandescent bulbs filled the room with an oversaturated, buttery glow. The rich yellow light spilled in thick angular columns from the two back windows onto the back porch; everything beyond the columns of light was black.

"You would have to understand what gravity was," Theresa said. "A force so… thorough… that not even light can escape it.

"The first time I saw you there, at the agency…" She paused then struck a new tack. "It's the only way I could have described it. The instant I saw you, I felt it. I *felt* it."

The day they met, she had not even come there to see him. She had come to see a friend of hers who worked at the agency. Theresa had heard a bit of Shazz's story earlier, but was too preoccupied with her own work to genuinely pay attention.

She met her friend in the reception area and had begun discussing work right away. When they went to sit down, her friend nonchalantly motioned for her to look into her office. The door was closed, but a large window occupied much of the wall that ran between the rooms. Theresa could clearly see the young boy, sitting there all alone: a little brave soul, sitting on an old orange couch, looking straight ahead at the empty desk in front of him—so courageous, so alone. And suddenly, everything she had heard about him but had not quite paid attention to, gelled in her mind, and she knew right then, without even consulting her husband, that she had another son. She was *drawn* to him. She walked right into the office, sat down next to him, and let him know he was not alone anymore.

Theresa finished wiping off the counter and tossed the towel into the empty dish rack. She turned around again and looked hard at Shazz.

"I thank God for you every day," she said, overcome with emotion. And she leaned down and grabbed him and pulled him in for an enthusiastic hug and a kiss.

"My baby Huey!" she said, as she crushed him.

Shazz bemusedly leaned over in his chair to accept her affection.

"You know what's *really* crazy?" Burns' raspy voice asked Roddy in the living room. "When someone hits a home run, and the crowd is going crazy, and the pitcher and catcher are trying to act like it's not happening; as if they don't notice fifty-thousand fans screaming in their faces. And they're wishing the next batter would hurry up and get to the plate, just so they can get the crowd to settle down…"

Burns' voice prodded Shazz into motion. He went back into the kitchen and took a seat.

"My mother was very sentimental," he said to Manny, as if knowing exactly what she was thinking about.

"I know," Manny replied. "Did you know she was still upset about the breakup of James Taylor and Carly Simon…decades after the fact?"

Shazz smiled wanly.

"She saw them live once," he said.

He reached over to the kitchen tool drawer and pulled out a metal utility knife. He pushed the blade opened and started lightly scratching at a splinter that was stuck in his palm. It had already been there for a few days.

Manny watched as Shazz deftly maneuvered the short razor around his upheld palm, as if painting an Easter egg. The hollow knife made a soft rattling sound, from the spare blades in its handle.

Theresa had always worried about Shazz, much more so than Lestor. She had been mortified the day he assaulted the men on their corner. She had dragged him home and plunked herself down at the kitchen table, at a loss for words. Shazz stood in the corner expecting a torrent of anger, but she said nothing. He saw that she seemed in shock, and then he saw that she had gotten some blood on her cheek, and he realized that she was wounded: not physically, but emotionally, and it startled him. He had hurt her, and this made him feel a pain he had never felt before. He felt ashamed.

"This trauma he's living with," Theresa said to Manny one day years later, "it could ruin his life. It can distort who he becomes—and I don't want my son to go through life stuck. I want him to be open to what the world is offering him. Life is hard enough as it is. I don't want him to have any excuses."

And so, she knew she had to expose him to something that was more powerful than any trauma he might have faced in his past. She had to expose him to things so… glorious…that they would blanch out that small patch of darkness at his start.

After his run-in on the corner, Theresa decided that the family needed to start traveling. Shazz had never left the tristate area. As it happened, Theresa had just finished reading *The Journals of Lewis and Clark*, and so was taken by the notion that, witnessing the grandeur of nature, like gazing upon the face of God, could purify any soul. All one needed, was to *really* see it: to catch a glimpse, just once…

At first the family traveled north. On long weekends and holidays, they would wake up early, load the car, and start driving.

For the first few trips, Shazz barely noticed a thing beyond the tangle of highways. He'd lean back into the pillows and blankets they kept in the back seat, and stare up at the trees streaming past his window. But after a while, on the long, boring drives, his eyes began to focus on other things.

In the crisp mountain air of Vermont, he noticed that the trees had changed. Here there were fewer soft, deciduous leaves. Here the highways were hemmed in by sharp-needled pines, and the cool air had them tuned up high, radiating an implacable green. But Shazz didn't really think much of it, because the trips were short, and soon they were home.

On their second summer together, the family loaded up and headed south… and then west, and Shazz noticed that the earth was different there also. Here lush green forests did not line the roads; and the farther west they drove, the more of the rich soil of the land seemed to have been dried out by the sun and swept away by time, until only the exposed skeleton of the Earth was left.

They made it as far as Arizona, before being drawn north, onto a forever dirt road, through the Painted Desert.

Desolate, desolate. The word touched softly in their minds like the white feathery seeds of a dandelion coming to a rest.

They followed the rolling and twisting but otherwise true north road through the badlands, and the silence of the land drew the silence from them. Every so often a small road would branch off from the main one and lead to a place of interest. The first site they stopped at had petroglyphs: whirling images scratched into the red earth a thousand years ago; at another, a forest of petrified trees had been laid low by a flood in the age of Pangaea and turned to stone... but one developed a tolerance even for these things after four or five stops, and the only thing that struck Shazz was a sign that warned of poisonous insects and reptiles.

Around the eighth or ninth stop, Shazz found himself alone atop a ridge. He stood on the hard rock ground, feeling somehow... bigger. Before him, below his feet, was the broadest vista he had ever seen. He'd seen it on TV of course: slow pans across desert scenery, the backdrop of cowboy movies, but to be in it: to be plunked down in the center of such an alien world, drew from him, senses as of yet undiscovered. He had to sit.

When they had pulled into the small dirt lot, it had hardly seemed worth the detour: to designate a scenic lookout just to see what was basically all around them anyway? Lestor and Stanley had gotten out first and followed a trail next to the car—it led downhill. Shazz waited for Theresa. When she told him to go ahead, he half-heartedly trudged up a second path, one that led up and along the spine of a short ridge.

Theresa sat with her door open and her feet dangling outside the car, enjoying the warm tranquility of her surroundings. There was no cell reception out there, and so she shuffled through a handful of maps that they had collected along the way, trying to figure out how far it was to their next hotel. When Shazz didn't come back right away, she looked up from her maps to see if she could spot him. When she saw him sitting alone at the top of the ridge, she got out of the car to join him.

Shazz had been a good sport about all the travel they had been doing lately. He seemed to enjoy it enough; but Theresa could tell he was mostly just doing his duty as a good son. Nothing they had seen had done what she had wanted: to plant the seed of *wonder* in him.

When she reached him at a small level area at the top of the ridge, she saw that his eyes were fixed outward, as if he were having a hard time understanding what he was seeing.

"It's so quiet here…" he said.

By this time in his travels, Shazz had seen mountains of all sorts, and trees, and old ships and beach towns, but he had never seen anything so vast, so infinite…. Its power had snuck up on him. His ridge was not a great height, but the land in front of it dropped off steeply, leaving him above an undulating sea of flat brown earth tones that stretched out to the horizon. The ancient earth had been baked by the sun to a hard, grainy rock, that seemed devoid of life, but above it was a riotous sky so fiercely blue and filled with wild slashes of white clouds, that it seemed alive and begging the Earth to rise up and join its dance. The celestial blue so dominated what he was looking at, that he felt as if he were looking down at it from low orbit; and while all these visual fireworks flared before his eyes, the only sound was a barely whispering wind.

"It's so quiet…" he repeated.

Miles away, he detected motion. A pronghorn antelope moved slowly up a berm. The air was so still that he could clearly see the animal's face. It was tired and seemed to be exerting itself as it climbed. Its thick neck, and small head, bobbed with each stride. It seemed from another age.

"I thought those things lived in Africa."

Shazz was sitting on a worn sandstone boulder. The gravity of the scene held his gaze. Theresa stood far enough back to not break its spell—and that's when she realized, she'd got him. She'd finally got him. Alone, in the silence, it had found him. Wonder, had risen up in him.

She sat down on the boulder next to him, and took in the view herself.

A short while later, Lestor came bounding up the path, followed by Stanley, and together, the family stayed there, until the first star of the night could be seen beaming a hard white in the sky.

Cars came and went. People got out and looked for a few minutes and left. And Shazz sat with his family, and for the first time in his life, he felt peace.

"You know what's a *real* mind-blower?"

Burns' voice came fluttering in from the living room like a big, sloppy parrot landing in a jungle canopy.

"When a pitcher faces another pitcher… I mean, it's supposed to be an easy out, but, I mean, it's *got* to be a mind blower!"

Shazz still had the utility knife in his hand. He gave up on the splinter, retracted the blade, and looked at Manny.

"I was really starting to like it down there," he said, and then his thoughts submerged.

A minute later, they resurfaced.

"Did she ever tell you about the time me and my dad got arrested?"

Manny shook her head. She knew they had gotten arrested together, but she hadn't heard the details.

"We were at a protest—that big one before Iraq—and I just knew he was going to get arrested," Shazz recounted. "He didn't say anything about it but I kind of had a feeling. So I went along with him, and at one bottleneck along the march, the old man starts rattling a barricade and getting people riled up, and the cops just lifted him up and over the barricade, and out of the crowd, and into a paddy wagon—all very neat and clean.

"I had to hop the barrier just to get taken in with him.

"Everything was alright at first, it was all just fun, until the cops realized who my dad was: the guy who got Larry Barker off. And they think it would be funny to toss old Stanley Milgram into a cell with some of the *real* criminals.

"Luckily, I managed to get one of the cops to send me with him.

"So they take us down the hall and shove us into a large holding cell, filled with a bunch of black guys, who all look pretty pissed off. And Dad is totally calm. He's still smiling."

Shazz shook his head in disbelief at the recollection.

"He's a baby," he continued. "A baby tossed into a dog pit. And I'm thinking, 'Okay, here we go. This is it. This is the Alamo' and my mind is gearing up for war, and then I hear some guy from the crowd say, 'Hey, that's the guy who got Barker off.'

"And just like that… it's a whole new world. Suddenly we're at a church picnic. People are shaking his hand and hugging him. People move out of the way to give the old man a seat. And he's talking to everyone, and giving everyone legal advice; there was a lot of love for him in that room.

"What a relief I felt. Such a burden lifted, because there was not a safer place in the entire world for him. And I felt like I didn't have to worry about them so much anymore… And then this."

He dropped the utility knife back in the drawer, sat down and began inspecting his hands again—alternately rubbing each palm—then clenched and unclenched his fingers slowly, articulately, as if they didn't quite feel right.

The deputy mayor, or DM, as Manny called him, had let Manny know that *they* knew Shazz had started the fire in Brooklyn, perhaps as a negotiating chip, or a wedge; but Manny had already known. What she was having a hard time facing, was that Shazz was responsible for someone's death.

Why wasn't she more repulsed? Was she numb, like everyone else there? What feelings she *did* have, were mostly selfish ones: she felt the loss of Theresa and Stanley; she even felt the loss of Shazz, who already seemed to be separating himself from the rest of them. His chair was pulled away from the table. He looked smaller... far away.

As if reading her thoughts, Shazz looked up from his hands.

"You're not born to live by rules written down in some book," he said. "You follow the ones you come with."

"I know," Manny said. Now was not a good time to push Shazz about seeing the Mayor.

The bedroom door opened, and out came Lestor, carrying a handful of dirty dishes. Casey trailed in his wake. They each wore a tired smile. They had been up for a while already, lounging in bed and trying to forget the rest of the world. Hunger and the need to use the restroom had finally stirred them from their cocoon.

On his way to the kitchen, Lestor nodded at Roddy and Burns. He put the plates in the sink, then came back out.

Casey stopped in the living room in front of Roddy. She made eye contact with him, then gave her head a derisive toss in Burns' direction.

"Mets, Mets, Mets," she said. "That's all he ever talks about."

Burns' face lit up with excitement.

"She's a Boston fan! She's a Boston fan!" he shouted hoarsely, as he rattled around in his big chair.

In the kitchen, Shazz got up and walked to the sink to do the dishes.

"I'll do those, Shazz," Lestor said.

"It's alright," Shazz said. "I gotta do something."

He turned on the water and started washing dishes. Manny got up to join the conversation in the living room.

The one good thing Shazz did get from his biological father was a work ethic. His father had also worked construction. And no matter how drunk he got the night before, he would always be up for work the next day—if he had work. Some mornings, Shazz would wake up early and lie in bed listening to his father making breakfast: the smell of bacon, the sounds of dishware as he shuffled about the kitchen in solitude… He would always leave a few strips of bacon for Shazz before leaving the apartment.

At night when Shazz came back home after staying away as long as he could, he would find his father passed out in the kitchen or on his chair in front of the television; more from exhaustion than alcohol. And that was what made Shazz most angry of all.

He thought of Theresa and cringed.

"I should have taught *her*," he thought.

He put both hands on the counter to balance himself, then he closed his eyes.

Behind him, in the living room, plans had just been made. Everyone had decided to go downstairs for some fresh air.

"Don't get off the stoop," Shazz called out over his shoulder.

Lestor and Casey went back into their room to change, and Manny went into the bathroom. Burns and Roddy waited for everyone to get back.

It should be okay, Shazz thought. Manny hadn't gotten any warning texts from whomever was on the other end of her phone, and Roddy would be with them.

Shazz had to take a shower. He hadn't showered in days, and even now he tasted burnt wood and salt air on his lips. He'd join them downstairs afterward.

He rinsed off the last dish and put it in the rack. He dried his hands with a dish towel and hung it on the cabinet door. Then he went back to the doorway to watch Roddy and Burns talk.

He looked at Burns sitting on the big chair. He looked like a child buried under oversized sports gear. His Mets hat was a least two sizes too big for his small, round head, and his oversized jersey made him look like a Mets beach towel slung over the chair.

Burns got on his nerves sometimes. Everything he did was to belong. It made Shazz angry that Burns was so weak.

Roddy and Burns had gone back to talking sports, and Shazz found himself beginning to get irked at the seriousness they were investing in such an unimportant topic.

"Who gives a shit," he spat with a little too much edge. "Live your own lives."

Burns froze, his eyes stretched wide in surprise.

"I can't even see you under all that stuff," he said to Burns.

Burns didn't understand what Shazz meant. He lifted his hat and rubbed his downy buzz cut head. He was older than Shazz, but had always looked up to him. For a moment he was off-balance as his mind searched for words to say. After no ideas came to mind, he surrendered; without thinking, words fell from his mouth.

"But it's just so good," he said.

Shazz couldn't help but laugh.

A few minutes later, all three of them were talking about a Super Bowl party that Shazz had thrown in that very apartment. The Giants had won that year. Even Shazz lightened up as they reminisced about the season and the party. Burns had roped him in.

Yes, they agreed after a few minutes of reminiscing, that season was a miracle. The whole damn season was a miracle.

"Forty-two," Burns said, with excitement. "Jacky Robinson! That was Super Bowl Forty-Two."

BOOK II

CHAPTER 22

It was still morning when everyone from Lestor's apartment spilled out onto the front stoop. Everyone but Shazz, who was still up in the apartment. The media had long since abandoned the Milgram watch and the streets were barren of movement. The power was still out, and it felt good to get out of the adumbral apartment and into fresh air and crisp light. The air was warm and the skies were clear, and even though they were not in a heat wave, they could tell that later in the day, the sun would be hard to bear. But at that moment, it all felt good.

Roddy stood at the top of the stoop, his back to the front doors. He took quick puffs of his cigarette while his eyes darted back and forth between the ends of the block. He had always smoked in that fashion: eyes scanning and quick puffs, holding the cigarette between his thumb and forefinger, the burning end hidden in his palm. He had developed this habit as a teenager while hanging out on his corner. He hung out with his friends in front of the pizzeria and kept a sharp eye out for his mom, who would drag him home in front of everyone if she ever caught him smoking. He had never relaxed his style.

They had all heard the shootings the night before, and Roddy's senses were on high alert. Lestor and Casey sat a few steps down from where Roddy stood. They leaned into each other, rubbing shoulders as they talked, oblivious to any danger. Manny and Burns stood together on the sidewalk at the bottom of the stairs.

"Hey! Hey!" Roddy said with urgency a few minutes after they had settled down.

The group looked up at Roddy, then followed his gaze to the end of the street. Alarm bells sounded in everyone's mind: a group of armed men were walking down the street, coming toward them. The men were spread out across the street: one man on each sidewalk, one man on each of the street sides of the parked cars. Something was "off" about their uniforms. They were not quite regulation. None of them matched.

"Is that the army?" Burns pondered loudly.

"Get inside. Get inside," Roddy said. "I have no idea who they are."

"It's not army," Shazz said, as he came walking out of the building.

He had spotted them from the window. His hair was still wet from the shower, and he was slightly irritated for letting them go out without him; but Manny had given him the all clear. She told him that the police had closed off the city below 14th Street, and were holding and waiting for the National Guard to transition in. He somehow failed to realize that this just meant they were now boxed in with the shooters, but so far they had only come out at night.

Being alone in the apartment had also given Shazz a chance to get the pistol he had taken from Lestor's room in his parents' house. Earlier, he had stashed it under the sink when no one was looking. Now he had it concealed in his waistband as he walked out of the building.

"Those are not soldiers," he said, as he walked by the group and stepped into the middle of the street to meet the advancing men. "Lestor, get to the basement door. If anything happens, run out the back."

Casey and Burns ducked down while moving quickly back into the building. They didn't stop until they were at the back of the lobby, holding open the door to the basement. From there they would be able to run down the single flight of stairs and make it out the back, if necessary. Lestor was only a few steps behind them; but once he was inside the building he stopped, and crept back to where he could peek over Roddy's shoulder and see the street.

"I think it's best if you move inside," Roddy said to Manny, who was still on the sidewalk, watching.

She cast a quick glance at Roddy, and then, reluctantly, began to move, holding her head high as she ascended the stairs, keeping her eyes locked on the men.

There are four of them, she thought. *Armed... irregular...* She checked off in her mind. *Not organized... They are not an organized force.*"

They moved wearily, like miners at the end of a long shift underground.

That's them, she knew. And they were there for what was left of the Milgram family.

The hair on the back of her neck started to rise.

She moved past Roddy and ducked into the building's vestibule. Her hand instinctively grabbed for her phone, believing she should let someone know, but she quickly changed her mind. Instead, she hunched down and turned an ear toward the door.

For a while she was effectively blind, because she was concentrating so hard on hearing what was going on outside; but after a length of silence, her ability to see what was immediately before her came back. She lifted her gaze and found herself staring at the building's brass mailboxes. Her eyes wandered over the surface of the tall thin boxes; they were scratched and battered but still solid; in between the scratches, the boxes still held a shine bright enough to offend.

A plastic label was affixed to the top of each box: last names in raised white lettering, all capitals, stood out like declarations on the black labels. The Milgrams' label was missing. From the looks of the gluey residue, it had recently been pulled off. Through the rosette cutout on the face of the box, Manny could make out the sharp vertical edges of several letters; there was also one envelope taped to the wall above the box. That envelope was addressed to, simply, THE MILGRAMS, which was scrawled in bright blue ink. In the corner of the envelope was the patriotic logo of one of the national cable news networks. On the wall around the letter were the remnants of other notes; ripped tape with bits of white paper attested to their having been there.

"Milgrams!" came a shout from the street.

Manny started.

"We're here for you!"

There was silence.

Roddy stood in front of the open doorway. He was tall and broad enough at the shoulders to block out most of the light: hiding in his shadow gave Manny a sense of security. When Roddy took a small step forward, more light spilled in.

"Lestor…!" Manny heard Casey call in a hard whisper. "Get back here."

She could hear Lestor's feet doing a soft-shoe on the tile floor behind her. She listened as his angst ran its course and his shuffling slowed to a stop.

"Wait," he whispered back. "I'm right here. I'm right here."

Lestor stood on his toes and stretched, leaning over to look past Roddy's shoulder.

Shazz was not far away. He stood in the middle of the street, just in front of their building, waiting. He stood for what seemed like a long time, not saying a word; just facing the approaching men. And then a shooter stepped onto the scene and came to a halt in front of Shazz.

The shooter was of average height and a bit thin: a high shouldered magpie, cloaked in all black, with a light dusting of white soot around the edges. He wore a flat black, ballistic helmet, which made him almost as tall as Shazz, and he cradled an assault rifle across the front of his chest, which he nervously clenched and unclenched, as if making sure it was always there.

A second gunman stepped into view. He stood on the sidewalk across the street. He was tall and thickset, but not muscular; his legs were like tree trunks and his torso was long. His arms were heavy, and his head seemed too small for his body, and he seemed a species of megafauna, a *Paraceratherium*, that had wandered onto the scene and proceeded to observe while chewing cud.

Lestor's body lurched to run, but he caught himself. A nightmare was at his front door. This was too dangerous. These were people to be avoided at all costs. Only bad would come to them. But he still felt shame over fleeing the Mayor's office, and seeing his brother standing alone on the street, he determined that he would not leave his brother's side, even if it killed him.

"Screw it to the sticking place," he whispered to himself, as he clenched his fists.

He craned his neck again. This time he could see the sweat on the man's brow as he stood facing Shazz, and his chin was ever so slightly raised, and all at once, Lestor knew they would be alright. They would be fine, because of Shazz—because of how he was, and because Lestor knew that people like that, ones who worshipped power, had always held a type of reverence for people like Shazz.

He who is strong can carry you.

Lestor had seen it his whole life: even when Shazz was a teenager, adults from around the neighborhood had treated him differently. Jim the deli guy respected him; he was working the day the local junky mouthed off to Shazz.

Everybody knew the guy, Keith… or Michael. Somebody's older brother from a previous generation: a belligerent character who was used to having crowds part for him when he stomped, half-crazed, around the neighborhood. Like a skunk, the boil-faced, malodorous waif of a man, had never come across anyone, other than the occasional pack of drunken teens, who was immune to his lecherous façade. But Shazz had never noticed him.

The deli was long and thin, and Lestor remembered being frightened when the man began to make a scene; all because Shazz was in between him and the exit. But before the man could get a full wind in his sail, Shazz grabbed him by the collar—and with one hand lifted and whirled him to his other side, dropping him in front of the exit.

It was over before anyone realized it happened. Shazz had gone back to counting out his change, while Keith… or Michael… was suddenly bathed in the daylight flooding through the plexiglass front door. He stood there for a moment, rubbing his chest and grimacing, waiting for his mind to catch back up to his body. And when it did, he pushed open the front door and walked out.

Lestor stretched, straining to listen as the armed man in front of his building spoke. He heard formal introductions: *"Forrest"*... *"Ed"*...*"Floyd"*...*"Carl"*... *"Shazz."* Then, bits of conversation: *"From up north..."* *"Two men lost..."* *"Here for retribution..."* *"Standing up for 'our' people..."* *"Save a dying nation..."* *"To be the spark..."* Lestor thought the armed man had a funny way of talking. As if a few *thees* or *thous* tossed into the man's sentences might not sound out of place.

He started to smile as he watched the gunman, Forrest, go on. He knew the look Forrest was getting from Shazz. It was the same he gave anyone who started talking to him. It was unreadable. There were no assenting nods or gestures. No body language or facial expressions to help the speaker gauge how his words were being received. You just knew he was thinking. You knew wheels were turning somewhere, but you had no clue as to *what* he was thinking. It had the effect of making one reexamine the words coming out of their mouth; the words hung there, exposed for a little too long. And if there were no faith behind those words, no power, they would simple fade away.

And so Lestor leaned his shoulder against the interior doorway, and watched the two men interact; and he could see Forrest start to crumble, and he remembered once again why, as a kid, he worshiped Shazz.

Forrest hadn't been ready when he had stepped up to Shazz. He'd been thrown by Manny—seeing her ascend the stairs as she had: a dark-haired fury with eyes boring into him from half a block away.... It had unnerved him.

Is she Spanish? was the only thought floating around his head when he came upon the sudden wall that was Shazz. He had to switch gears fast.

There was so much he wanted to tell Shazz: to make him understand and respect what they were doing… maybe even convince him to join them. What a perfect figurehead he would be! All Forrest had to do was get him back on the television screens and lean him one way or another.

Lestor wouldn't do. He was too soft. But Shazz, he was a working-class hero. And most important of all: he had already crossed the line. Forrest was sure of that.

In the shelter of the woods, Forrest's words had come easy. His patter lifted his men and stoked their anger; it made them feel good. But out there on the street in front of Shazz, his words wouldn't come, and when they did, they sounded thin and reedy.

Halfway through his patchy speech, Forrest's exhaustion finally struck him. His shoulders sank, and he realized his plan to recruit Shazz would go nowhere. In a desperate attempt to cling to something, he resolved that just meeting the Milgrams was message enough to the world. He had accomplished at least that: at least he had held the football for a while.

Finally, he just let out in a sigh, "We need a place to stay until tonight."

Shazz looked at him and calculated. Then he looked at the others and calculated. They were poison, he knew that; but apparently the Milgram name meant something to them, so at least everyone in the apartment would be safe from them.

By that time, Manny had crept down the stairs of the stoop and stood in front of Roddy. She stood like a statue, posed as if about to say something. When she saw Shazz uncertain of what to do, she waved him over with a quick fluttering hand.

Shazz walked over, shaking his head in uncertainty.

"Shazz," Manny said, keeping her voice low, "we can end this right now. No one else has to die. Things are going to be confused for a little while. I think we'll be safe till tonight. I can contact the DM and let them know to keep clear."

"No, no, don't say anything yet," Shazz replied.

"Think of the message it will send if you bring these guys in," Manny said. "What a way to honor your parents."

Shazz grimaced. This was way too dangerous, he knew; but Manny had pulled her trump card right away: his parents.

"You do know they're going to bring the whole army here," he said. "Right *here*." He pointed at their feet. "And when they get here, they're going to blow the shit out of *everything*."

"No, no, Shazz." Forrest spoke up from the other side of a parked car. He held up a police scanner. "Everything's closed off below 14th Street. Everyone's transitioning: between the cops and the Guard."

Shazz wrinkled his nose at the news then turned back to Manny.

"You know these guys are all dead," he said quietly.

"I do *not* know that Shazz."

Shazz eyed her.

"You know, you're not gonna change them."

He turned around and looked at Forrest, who, by now, had Ed and Carl standing next to him.

Who the fuck knows, he thought, for the first time seeing the three armed men as kids. *Maybe they do wanna surrender.*

He walked back to them.

"Okay, listen," he said. "You know the whole fucken army is going to be coming down on you soon. So you best have a plan to bolt. I want none of my people getting caught up in that shit. So stay until dark: sleep, shower, do whatever, but by tonight, if you're not planning on walking in peacefully, you *gotta* be very far away from here. Do we agree?"

The three men nodded.

Shazz looked over at Floyd, who was leaning against the rear of the parked car. He was paying no mind to Shazz. He was looking off at a pot of geraniums in a window box across the street.

"He's okay," Forrest said.

Shazz observed Floyd for a moment longer, then turned back to Forrest.

"There's an empty apartment on our floor. You're guests until then. Let's go."

The three gunmen nodded their heads and followed.

Ed Walks Into the Apartment with the Rest

Shazz led the new, larger group into the building and up the stairs. At the top of the landing, the soft glow of daylight poured into the hallway through Lestor's opened door. Everything on the stairs above their landing was dark as a cave. Shazz had not seen nor heard anyone else in the building since he got there. They had either holed up or abandoned ship long ago.

When he reached the first landing, Shazz moved to the side so that the others could pass. He motioned to a door a little ways down the hall on the right.

"That's the one," he said to Forrest, who had been right behind him.

It was on the opposite side of the hallway from their apartment.

Where the locks should have been on the door was a cluster of small, round holes, filled with daylight; the telltale sign of a vacant apartment.

Forrest had also stopped at the top of the landing. He stood across the stairs from Shazz as everyone filtered between them. He was thrown for a moment when Ed brushed past him with his head down and walked into the wrong apartment, but he had other things to worry about: he wanted another chance to talk to Shazz.

When everyone had gone by, Forrest sidled up to Shazz again. This time he spoke in a more confidential manner.

"Hey, I saw what you did in Brooklyn. You set that fire."

Shazz stopped and focused on Forrest.

"No, no," Forrest said quickly, to let Shazz know that he admired his actions. "I like your battle tactics. Like Andrew Jackson: arrive at a battlefield and shout 'charge'!"

Shazz continued to look hard at him while calculating the situation.

"Yeah, well," he said, not exactly following what Forrest was trying to say. "I just need to get clear of this situation. You go and get your rest," he said. "I'll talk to you later." And he walked into his apartment.

Forrest stared at Lestor's empty doorway for a while with his jaw slacking; then he turned to look toward his own vacant apartment.

Floyd hadn't gone in. He had taken a few steps past the open door then dropped down on the hallway floor. He leaned back against the wall, his legs sticking out—and that was all Forrest could see of him: his legs, softly lit in a shaft of light. The rest of Floyd's body was neatly cut off in shadows. Forrest couldn't tell whether he was asleep or not.

He walked into the apartment and saw Carl already asleep on the floor. His gear was scattered around him as if it were a shell that had popped off in pieces. He used his rucksack as a pillow.

There was a door to a skinny bathroom on the left when Forrest first walked in; a skinny kitchen was just beyond that. The rest of the studio apartment was a plain rectangle with two windows at its far end. The floor was bare; dust bunnies and bits of detritus had settled in every corner.

Forrest walked over to the windows and slid one of them open. He stuck his head out to check the fire escape. Its ladder rose right outside the window. They were only one flight up, and there was plenty of space out back.

Ed in Lestor's Apartment

Ed had trudged up the building's staircase with his eyes on the heels of the person in front of him. He hadn't seen Shazz point to the vacant apartment—and so, half-asleep, he followed Lestor and Casey into the wrong apartment.

They themselves had walked the length of the apartment and right into their room; closing the door behind them.

Ed barely managed to drag himself to the big chair across from the couch and plunk himself down; a puff of dust fluffed up around him when he sat.

He set the butt of his rifle on the floor and leaned its barrel up against the wall. Before his dust had settled, he slid off into a fitful sleep. His mind was racing but he hadn't the strength to lift his head… Myrons was dead, Joey Papas too. Images… fear… bubbled to the surface of his consciousness in a ceaseless patter. His only defense had become his mantra:

I have not killed anyone yet. I have not killed anyone yet.

It exhausted him…

Ed looks up. He is below street level, tucked into the outdoor stairwell of an old tenement building. Above him, a silhouette darts in and out of view, like the head of a giant raven, stabbing its beak out over the stairwell's concrete banister, spitting bursts of flame.

At his feet, the stairwell lay open like a black pit: a grave. But Ed knows there's a door at the bottom. It leads into a basement: a concrete-floored labyrinth, crammed with bicycles and pipes and a large water heater, parked like a submarine on a foundation that was nothing more than a huge blob of concrete… or at least that's as much as he could figure out from his quick pass-through earlier.

Above him the silhouette stabs out black against a crystal night sky, always with an almost imperceptible hitch in its movement: a hesitancy interrupting its flow. Sometimes it doesn't fire at all but freezes, as if thinking, and pulls back. And then sometimes it steps forth with a rage that lights up the world. It's Myrons.

Ed turns to look at what he's firing at, but he can't see much between the parked cars. He takes a step up and sees what he thinks is a piece of meat in the middle of the street, but he sees no indication of anyone hurt.

Violence is ugly, he thinks.

Police are suddenly swarming the street like crazed ants and the air around Myrons erupts and he seems to rear up like a serpent and he shouts loudly and clearly, "OW! OW! OW!" as if he were stepping on hot coals—and then he's horizontal in midair and kicks his feet straight out like a cartoon death, and his life is yanked out of him as if on a string.

Ed takes off down the stairwell in a blind panic. He crashes through the basement and out into the building's backyard. He hops a fence.

He smashes through another. He hears noise behind him and he's certain he's being pursued for the entire three-block run to the next meet-up point: a tall, prison-like public school building, with heavy gates over its windows.

Yikes, he thinks. *Imagine going there.*

His composure comes back to him, and he ducks around the corner and into a side door.

Manny Walks In

When Manny walked into Lestor's apartment, she couldn't help but notice the large man sleeping on the chair. He sat propped like an oversized marionette, his long limbs, loose and slightly disjointed. But his body had sunk far enough into the cushions to keep him from sliding down; and even though his legs were not stretched out, his bent knees still reached a fair distance into the center of the room. With his elbows resting on the short arms of the wing chair, and his light coating of soot, he resembled a statue, roughly hewn from marble.

Burns and Roddy had already taken a seat on the couch. They had followed Ed into the apartment, casting a perplexed eye at Shazz as they passed; but Shazz hadn't said a thing, and Ed had fallen asleep so fast and so soundly, that they quickly ignored him and picked up where they had left off on an earlier conversation.

"Ali, rope-a-dope! Ali, rope-a-dope," Burns chanted in a reedy voice. "Struck down Foreman like Saul on the road to Damascus! He rose up a changed man!"

"Ach," Roddy said. "Lewis defended his title twenty-five times, back in the *day.*"

Manny sat on the arm of the couch nearest the kitchen. She stared at Ed across the room from her, and then at the opened door. Shazz was still out there, talking to Forrest. She could see his back, slipping in and out of view; he wasn't concerned about Ed.

She got up and walked over to the window. She sat on the sill and leaned to look out. Down the block, she could see a smattering of people tiptoeing their way north up the avenue. They were civilians; probably headed to where the army had set up camp. Food and first aid were being distributed, and the camp offered safety.

She pulled her head back in and looked at Ed's face. His eyes were closed and his head leaned back, turned away from the window. His face was large and featureless, with hardly an angle on it, but he seemed honest: simple enough to be steered by a quick wit. He was younger than Shazz but older than Lestor. And his tall, worn boots made her think of Tolstoy and wheat fields. She recoiled slightly when her eyes caught sight of the lethal instrument leaning up against the wall.

Shazz walked back into the apartment and went into the kitchen. He sat at the table and didn't say a word.

He's mad, she thought, *but then again... maybe he's not.*

Whatever the case, everyone was there now and she had better make something good happen.

Shazz sat back in the kitchen chair. He stretched his legs out under the table and clasped his hands on top of his head. He leaned a little to the right and saw Manny in the living room. She sat, framed by the large window: backlit like an angel. She was staring at the floor with a look of anguish on her face. The strain was wearing on her.

Forrest and Burns Talking in the Hallway

Forrest sat cross-legged on the hallway floor. He kept his back to the wall and his rifle across his lap. He sat in between the two opened doors. He had a small radio turned on low, and every minute or so, he leaned forward, balancing on a hand and two knees, and looked down the staircase toward the lobby. He could see the lower half of the interior set of doors: the glass ones. Both sets of doors were now closed, but the exterior doors let in enough light to illuminate the checker-tiled floor of the vestibule.

He was picking at the barrel of his rifle when, to his alarm, he saw that it was clogged with a plug of dirt. *Must have happened last night when I fell in the backyards behind the buildings,* he thought. He quickly pulled a toothbrush from his chest pocket and went about using its sharpened plastic end to unclog the weapon.

A shadow dimmed the light in Lestor's doorway. He turned off his radio and slipped it into a thigh pocket. He turned and saw Burns' smiling face hanging out of the doorway. His smile was close-mouthed and wide, and he nodded his head every few seconds as if begging permission to be there. When he saw that Forrest had noticed him, he came out and crouched down on the floor next to him. Then he moved his head in close, and stared at Forrest's rifle the way a caveman might have stared at fire, and Forrest felt pride.

"It's beautiful, isn't it?" Forrest said, scratching at some char marks he had just noticed on the front hand grip.

"Yeah," Burns responded in his usual high-pitched, airy way.

"It's a famous weapon, you know," Forrest said. "The AK-47. It was designed by a Russian tank mechanic: a poet. It has only eight moving parts. This one is Bulgarian; pre-ban, milled receiver, fully automatic… Ed's got one too. But his is a copy.

He held the weapon up with two hands for Burns to get a better look. He tried to get it in the light.

"Carl's got an AR-15. Same as Joey had. The AR-15 was designed by some guy named Stoner." He chuckled. "Carl only likes it because that's what the military uses: it's the civilian version of the M4, but it's got no stopping power. Sure, it's more accurate, but we're in the city. We're not hunting coyotes. The AK hits hard. It's got a bigger round, a little more recoil… can't hit a thing at distance; three hundred yards, it drops about two feet…twenty-three hundred feet per second. The AR: thirty-two hundred f-p-s; drops maybe an inch the same distance…"

Burns was examining all the hardware Forrest was wearing. He had no idea what Forrest was saying, and Forrest knew it, but he didn't care. Rattling off specs grounded him.

"Floyd and Myrons are a different story altogether," he continued. "Floyd's got a .338: 200 grain ammo, pushing three thousand f-p-s; goes through vests like paper. That's what the police sharpshooters use. And Myrons…. he's just ridiculous: .375 magnum"—Forrest chuckled at an old inside joke—"in case he runs into a polar bear…"

Burns stared blankly at Forrest.

"Are you in the army?" he asked.

Forrest stops with a start.

"Army? Hell no!" He shook the idea out of his brain. "Pfft!… imagine that: putting your soul in the hands of a politician."

He looked back down and continued cleaning his rifle.

"Ha," he snorted, still shaking his head. "Imagine that."

Burns wore a heavy look of consternation. He wasn't sure what Forrest was saying, but it didn't sound right to him.

"You think an army man could do what I did?" Forrest continued. Another shadow upset the light from Lestor's door.

Forrest threw a quick look at Burns and whispered, "Give me a few more men and let me cross the Hudson and I'll take this whole goddamned country."

He looked over Burns' shoulder to find Manny standing in front of the door.

"I'm gonna go to my place for a while," Burns said, and he got up to go. He managed a smile for Manny as he walked past her; then he climbed the stairs to the third floor. The building's old stairs creaked and groaned, as if voicing the aches of Burns' old bones.

Manny and Forrest

"I understand you," Manny said.

Forrest stood up quickly. He made to lay down his weapon but changed his mind; instead, he leaned it as politely as he could against the wall by his side.

"I've seen it in my own family," Manny continued, "still trying to hold onto the old ways, from the old country. They're losing the world they grew up in: their culture, who they are, the place they feel safe… Our past means something. It's part of us… but then, I grew up with U2 posters on my wall." She shrugged. "Life's not the same for a moment. It almost can't be kept up with. You have to let go."

Forrest looked at her defensively. He was not sure where she was coming from.

"That's what you *want* us to do," he said.

Manny pursed her lips in disapproval. "So then, how is this going to end? You can survive. Your friends can survive. I can broker a deal," she said, and held up her phone.

"No!" Forrest said. "Don't call anyone."

"You can make it out of here and live out the rest of your days as a well-respected, infamous inmate… and you never know what the future brings; or, you and your friends can be torn apart by bullets, because that's what's on its way. And you know it.

"All you need to do is change the narrative in your head," Manny said, "and you can still play the game."

Manny could see the thoughts spinning in Forrest's head as his nose made small clockwise motions.

Apparently his faith was not pure, she thought.

"I mean," he said, "what's wrong with you people? Are you blind? Can't you see the world? Isn't it obvious? Look at every blighted spot on this planet. Do you want to bring that here?"

"All men are created equal," Manny pronounced, establishing the baseline for all further discussion. "So *now*, tell me why the world is, as it is."

"That's your answer?" Forrest said. "Ha! Well, good luck to you."

His pat answer irked Manny.

"If you thought people were going to join you," she said, "all those rumors were just that: rumors. This is just about wrapped up, so what it basically comes down to is, can you live with what you've done."

A sour snarl formed on Forrest's face. "Just because something hasn't happened yet, doesn't mean it can't," he mumbled.

Manny stared hard at him, taking him all in.

"Your view of the world is imprisoning you."

"Look at the world!" he snapped.

"*Fix* the world!" she snapped back.

"We're being overrun," Forrest said in frustration. "The ship is sinking. This brief period of political correctness has come to an end."

They both stood dumbstruck for a moment, like two fighters who had just met in the center of a ring and encountered a resolve equal to their own.

Then Manny enunciated slowly: "You're looking for your problems outside, when your problems are inside."

"I'm not a sheep," Forrest said. "I'm the only one who's standing up to fight."

Manny stopped. She had run across people like this before; usually they were forever bouncing around the criminal justice system, never at fault, flailing away at their own windmills. She could debunk every point in his argument, taking each one back to its very root; proving to him without a doubt that everything he was thinking was wrong. She'd even convince him: at that moment. But as soon as the lesson was over, like clockwork, he'd revert back to his original thoughts. He had a genuine personality disorder, she thought, and she could never change him.

She looked at him standing there, eagerly awaiting another treat to take a whack at; but she wouldn't play his game. There was only one offer on the table, nothing more. A sheepish grin began to form on his face, as if he realized that she had seen his secret. She would not engage him further. Finally he spoke up.

"What are you, Muslim or something?"

There was no maliciousness behind the question.

Manny was exasperated. She took a quick step into his personal space.

"No," she said. "I'm another human being. Can't you tell?"

And she locked his gaze with hers, just long enough for him to notice the color of her eyes, before pulling away and going back into the apartment. She was done with him.

Forrest stood there frozen. His heart quickened.

Shazz Observing Manny with Ed

Manny walked back into the living room and calmly sat on the couch. There was no time to be angry. She was starting to feel a sense of urgency: they were running out of time. They had to get out of there as soon as possible.

Roddy had gone back down for another smoke. Shazz was still in the kitchen.

She took out her cell phone and held it on her lap. She paused for a moment and took a deep breath; then she started tapping on the screen. She had to start managing information.

She had texts and emails to respond to, websites to monitor, public sentiment to weigh and sculpt, and she had never mastered the whole social media thing; she was about three years too old to have fully grown up in those waters. But she understood that she had to control the message coming out of the Milgram camp. She had to get to the virtual town square and start clanging a bell soon, before others did it for them; all that, and her battery was just about dead.

"Do you ever just shed identities?" came an unfamiliar voice.

Manny almost jumped out of her skin. She had forgotten that Ed was there.

His voice was soft, and had a muffled quality to it; and although she had been startled, she knew right away there was nothing to fear.

In the kitchen, Shazz raised his head.

Ed had awoken a few minutes earlier. He had opened his eyes and seen Manny, perched on the edge of the couch, peering down at her phone with furrowed brow. He watched her for a while, tapping out messages, reading replies, working so hard.

"Online, I mean," he said. "Do you ever just... delete all your old email addresses, chatroom IDs, gamer tags, comment board messages, and start anew?

"I've done it... several times," he continued. "I've stepped back, and flapped out my electronic history like an old blanket."

Manny kept her eyes glued on him. She shook her head slowly but didn't speak.

"Well," he said, thinking she was refusing to speak to him, and not blaming her. "You should try it; especially with all that government spying going on. Type one wrong word and you're downloaded for life."

He was about to close his eyes again but he felt a deep pain: the pain of her not speaking to him.

"How are you so sure what's right?" he asked.

Manny turned her hands over, palms up.

"Do no harm," she said.

"I've killed not one person."

"Hear ye! Hear ye!" Manny was just about say, while lifting a hand to mime a town crier clanging a bell, but the phone in her hand buzzed.

She looked down and saw it was a text from the DM.

We know they are with you.

The blood in her veins turned to ice as she stared at the small screen in alarm.

She stood and turned to Shazz in the kitchen. Then she held up her phone and mouthed: *"They know they're here."*

Shazz nodded.

She turned to go and confer with Lestor and Casey, then saw Ed looking up at her expectantly.

Another text came in. She looked down again.

Best to come in now.

She looked back at Ed, planted in the chair, not concerned at all with her texts.

"Sometimes," she said, "when you paint yourself into a corner, the only way out, is up."

She walked to the bedroom door, knocked lightly, and entered.

Shazz Talks to Forrest in the Hall

Shazz could hear it: all the way from the kitchen: the *clunk clunk clunking* of Forrest's boots on the soft hallway floor. It wasn't loud enough to justify being annoyed; but still, the nervousness of the beat became trying.

What the fuck? Shazz thought when the noise finally got to him, and he jumped up to put a stop to it.

His father, Stanley Milgram's voice, sounded in his head:

"A young man's got his pride."

He slowed down.

It was a line from a conversation he'd overheard one night at his parents' house. His mother and father were in the kitchen discussing a new client: a new friend of theirs. Shazz had been on his way out the door when he heard it.

Makes sense to me, he thought as he stepped outside.

Forrest had just sat back down on the hallway floor and was about to start cleaning his rifle again. He pulled a white cloth from a vest pocket. When he saw Shazz, he stood up and shoved the cloth into his hip pocket.

"Did you know the legal hunting age in New York is twelve?" he said. "That's what it is for most states."

Shazz didn't hear what he was saying; he was too busy focusing on Forrest's assault rifle, which was held level and pointing in front of him.

Forrest caught the distraction and put the rifle down, leaning it up against the wall next to him.

"I haven't been hunting," Shazz said.

For a moment, Shazz's murderee hangs in the air between them. Forrest decides to ignore it and gets back to his point.

"Every kid outside of a city's limits gets a hunting license as soon as they can. Same's as a car license. People like to hunt."

Shazz stared at him blankly.

"Who is it you're supposed to be shooting?" he said. "Black people? I only saw cops and old ladies go down."

Forrest pursed his lips against the shockwave.

"When I'm out there… I'll shoot down any man standing against me," he mumbled, "black or white; if they try to stop me."

He almost fell into a mood but remembered his point again, and spoke up with renewed vigor.

"You should join us, Shazz," he said. "What else are you going to do? They're going to throw you in jail too. Go out fighting!"

"Listen," Shazz said. "I've got a family to protect now… or what's left of a family. I've got to get my brother clear of this mess. That is the *only* important thing to me now."

"You don't have to come with us," Forrest jumped in. "Just get out there and start shootin' flares into the airwaves: like you've *been* doing. That'll get things moving. There are people all over the world ready for action."

When he saw Shazz pause, he continued: "Do it. That'll start the payback! And your hands'll be clean."

Had it been a few days earlier, Shazz might have jumped in, full force. He had come close to it, all on his own.

He wanted to destroy. He wanted to make the world pay for his loss.

He remembered what he had done and steeled himself again.

"Let me tell you what our plan is," he said. "Within the next few hours, we're gonna be moving out of here. We're gonna go see the politicians and make nice. Then we're gonna spend the rest of our days being venerated; maybe do a few charities here and there, and live upstate on some nice 'no animal' farm. At least my brother will."

"Well," Forrest said, "think about it."

He looked around quickly and then felt his pockets. He reached down and removed a dark holster from his thigh. He opened it and pulled out a long silver revolver with a walnut handle. It was so big and shiny that Shazz almost laughed.

"What?" Forrest said. "Look at it. It's beautiful."

"Who are you?" Shazz said, "General fucken Patton?"

Forrest looked at the jumbo-sized weapon and let out a small, self-conscious chuckle.

"It is big…" he said.

"Yeah," Shazz said, "but it's nice."

The small bit of approval lifted Forrest's spirits.

"It's a Blackhawk," Forrest said, and he held the gun in the palms of his hands and moved it this way and that, highlighting its artistry.

"Forty-four caliber, single action… hardwood handles… stainless."

He could have run off another ten minutes' worth of information about it but stopped.

"You take it," he said. He held the gun out to Shazz. "As a gift. As a thank you for letting us crash. And for all the hardships you've been through."

Shazz looked at him, and then at the gun. "You sure?" he asked.

Forrest smiled.

"Don't worry," he said, "I have another."

He slapped his right hip, where the other holster was strapped to his body. "Not as heavy, but more shots; and I don't want any cops getting that one… and don't worry, I haven't used it down here."

Shazz took the gun and its holster, telling himself that he was doing it to get another gun off the street.

"Okay," he said. "Now you better get some rest if you're gonna stick to your plan and get out of here by nightfall."

Shazz gave him a pat on the shoulder, then turned and walked back into the apartment.

Forrest nodded. He was happy to have finally gotten out what he had wanted to say, but then he became frightened at the thought of leaving.

He thought about Myrons and Joe Papas, and how close death was. He hadn't seen Myrons go down. He just remembered not hearing his rifle anymore. And Joey Papas: he remembered someone shouting, "He went down in the garden. He went down in the garden." As if it were something out of a fairy tale: all he could picture was a small child running, and hopping over a short garden fence, and crawling beneath a thicket to a safe hiding spot…

An image of him putting his gun to his temple flashed in his mind, but he banished it quickly. Being alone was terrifying.

Lestor and Casey's room

Time. Time. Time.

Casey sat cross-legged atop the queen-sized mattress that took up most of their room. She sat a little left of center (her side of the bed) and leaned over to peer into a small round mirror balancing atop a shaky pile of pillows.

Lestor lay at her side and gazed up at her. He was crushed by her beauty.

I should write a poem for her, he thought, as he breathed it all in: satin pillows, gossamer curtains, opaque cotton shades lowered just enough for privacy and swaying with an occasional soft breeze. The room was illuminated with perfect clarity.

She was Parvati herself: hands whirling about her crown: hair, comb, pins… lips. He was at the warm center of the universe, and she was in its womb with him.

For her part, Casey was unaware of his watching. She stopped her whirling for a moment to focus on an unruly eyelash. She peered into the mirror and plucked it right quickly; then went back to fixing her hair.

"To have faith is vanity," Lestor said, "and vanity is a sin."

"Not if you have faith in God," Casey answered, without taking her eyes off the mirror.

"To even think you can comprehend God is comical," Lestor returned.

"Not if you know you can't comprehend God."

Lestor mulled that for a moment.

"So then... you're worshipping nothing."

"Yes," she said curtly, "and if you were smart, you'd spend your life prostrate at the altar."

Lestor was quiet again.

"So where does the faith come in?"

"It's a rule," she said, "and, shut your mouth and keep moving, dummy."

Lestor's head fell back onto his pillows. He stared at the ceiling.

"Wanna have sex?"

Casey turned and looked at him seriously.

"No..."

And then they got into *that* conversation.

Eventually, there was a knock at the door and Manny's head popped in; when she saw that they were decent, the rest of her body followed.

"We need to go soon," she said. "They know they're here. It's not safe anymore."

"What did Shazz say?" Lestor asked.

"The only thing Shazz wants is for you to be safe," she said.

The answer didn't move Lestor.

"He's mulling it over," Manny added, "and when he realizes that this building has a big bull's-eye on it, he will come in here and agree."

"Well, I'm not going without Shazz," Lestor said.

"I know," Manny said, "but just remember, you have a pass for only so long."

"A pass?" Lestor asked.

"Yes. A pass before one side gives up on you, and the other side claims you."

Another text buzzed on Manny's cell phone. She looked down at its screen and then read the gist of the text aloud: "They want us to meet them around 14th Street and the East River. They're on a *boat*?"

"That's weird," Casey noted.

"Probably some police boat," Lestor speculated.

"Well," Manny said, "we should go soon."

She walked to the far corner of the room and grabbed a pile of clothes off a chair.

"You've got one of these too?" she blurted, when she saw the chair.

She dropped the clothes onto the adjacent dresser, not taking her eyes off the chair.

It was an old school chair, one with the desktop built right onto it, and a big square metal box underneath the seat for storage. It had to be over 50 years old.

She had been with Theresa when she had rescued them: a tall heap had lain in the middle of her building's loading dock. The Board of Ed was doing renovations on their floors; everything old had to go.

The chairs were perfectly fine. They were solid chairs, made of cast iron and wood, and built to last a hundred years. When Theresa had come upon the huge mound of sharp wooden elbows and metal legs sticking out like quills, it struck her to be as profane as a mass grave, and so she had saved as many as she could. She had even pawned one off on Manny, who kept it in her parents' garage.

Manny fell back into the chair as if it were an old leather baseball glove. She stretched her elbow out onto the warm wooden desktop, then pulled an ankle up onto the seat. Theresa had the same chair in her office too, only with different scars.

She used to love sitting in Theresa's office. She would sit in the old chair while Theresa sat at her desk rooting through stacks of paper. When she bent over to write, Manny would see only her hair moving behind the stacks. She was surrounded by piles of paper: on her desk, on the two additional fold-out tables on either side of her desk; even on the window sills.

How can someone so unorganized write such precise legalese? Manny would muse.

"I see you've dedicated your life to the fight," Theresa said to her one day.

It had taken Manny by surprise. She had been daydreaming when Theresa's voice snapped her back into the present. She looked up to see Theresa looking down at her from over her great bulwark of papers.

"It's an honorable thing to do, but please, you must put your own life first. You can't be selfless always. You need a copilot. You need a team. And if you don't have one, its absence will weigh on you."

Manny smiled shyly.

"It will come when I'm ready," she said.

Theresa had made a sour face.

Did Theresa realize how lucky she was? Manny wondered. She had met Stanley when they were still in school… and now Lestor and Casey were lucky too.

"The Mayor doesn't give a shit about us," Lestor spoke up. "He's just blowing smoke up our asses so he can save his legacy."

Manny looked at them and refocused.

"You're not doing it for him," she said. "You need to gather your strength, and keep it together long enough to read a prepared statement. Don't even *look* at the press. Don't take questions. The sooner we get this over with, the faster we lift off bottom."

"I'm not going to do it if—"

Just then the door opened.

Shazz stuck his head in.

"Okay," he said, "we need to get this thing over with and get out of this city. It's too dangerous."

They all looked at each other and agreed without a word.

"I'd say within the hour," Shazz said. "We don't want these guys thinking too long."

Manny and Shazz Come Out to Tell Forrest They Are Leaving

Forrest had taken a knee in the hallway. He still rested in the shadows between the two opened doors. Every so often, he felt a cool puff of air come from the open windows in Lestor's apartment.

It's not so bad out today.

He was thinking about Floyd and Myrons. They had been the engines of their fury: the unheralded superstars of their team. But now Myrons was gone, and Floyd was alone, and Floyd had barely said a word since.

Forrest looked back over his shoulder and saw that Floyd was no longer sitting against the wall as he slept. He had slumped down to the floor, and now slept on his right side. Mostly all you could see of him were his legs below the knees. He seemed dead; laid out in Paleolithic grace at the back end of a dark cave. All he needed now were wildflowers scattered about his body to complete the scene.

Manny and Shazz stepped out of the door to Lestor's apartment and stood in the center of the hallway. Shazz still had Lestor's 9 mm, in its holster, tucked deep in his waistband and under his shirt. Manny hadn't seen it.

Right behind them, as if attached by string, came Lestor and Casey. They turned right, onto the stairs, and walked out of the building without pause. Roddy and Burns had gone out earlier, and were waiting around the corner. Shazz had given Roddy Forrest's silver revolver, and told him to hold onto it just in case. All weapons were to be cleared from the apartment.

"We're leaving now," Shazz said.

Forrest stood and walked over to them. He moved slowly and deliberately, tottering like a toy soldier with stiff knees and raised shoulders; and when he stopped, he seemed on the verge of hyperventilating.

His smooth face had turned into a cartoon: a sad emoji with a perfect upside-down smile. His thin nostrils quivered as air rushed in and out of them.

Manny had seen it before, in courthouses, when someone was making life-changing decisions regarding whether to plea or not. They could be innocent of the crime they were accused of… but why roll the dice with your life?

Take the guaranteed two instead of risking twenty.

He would not be able to keep this up much longer, Manny thought.

"You have to calm down," she said, dropping her resolve to not care.

She reached out a compassionate hand to put on his shoulder, but he waggled his chest back and out of the way.

"Stop!" he yelped.

He stretched his neck and fidgeted with his shoulders and elbows, as if he suddenly didn't like the feel of his shirt.

Manny looked at Shazz in alarm, and he nodded for her to go.

"Okay," she said with a shrug; then she turned and walked down the stairs and out of the building.

When the door closed behind her, Shazz locked a hand on Forrest's arm.

"Never fight scared," he said.

Forrest froze like a cat held by the scruff of his neck.

"They know you're here," Shazz told him. "I wouldn't stick around too long."

Then he turned and left.

When They Leave to Go to Ida

The group stood on the sidewalk in front of Burns' Dry Cleaners. He didn't own it, he worked there: mostly as a delivery man. It was just around the corner from the apartment.

The gates were pulled down over the front of the store. There were two, heavy steel gates: a wide gate that shielded most of the storefront, and a narrow gate, that covered only the doorway. Burns unlocked a large padlock at the bottom of the narrow gate, and rolled it up with a clatter. They all walked in.

Lestor and Shazz had also worked at the store a few times during their high school years, each time covering for Burns; and so they knew the store.

Shazz had taken the gun back from Roddy, and he wrapped it together with Lester's gun, in an old T-shirt, then held them indiscreetly at his midriff as they walked into the cleaners. Once inside he steered Burns to the back room. Everyone else had stopped in the front of the store, around the counter, where they began poking around all the shelves.

"There's a radio on the middle shelf," Burns shouted over his shoulder.

The door to the basement was in the backroom. Shazz opened it and grabbed a flashlight from the inside of the door jam. He turned to Burns and opened the shirt just enough to show him what was inside his bundle. Then he disappeared into the darkness below. Burns held the door open and waited on the small landing at the top of the stairs.

Shazz was quick. He stashed the guns on one of the shelves in the basement and then came back up.

"Ditch them if me and Roddy don't come back," he said to Burns. "Just drop them in the river somewhere."

Burns had a blank look on his face but nodded his head quickly.

"They're both clean guns," he said. "*Don't* touch them otherwise."

They went back to the front of the store and clarified their plans. Burns and Casey would stay there. The rest of them would meet up with the Mayor to work out their role in the rebuilding process.

The group said their goodbyes, and all those who were leaving stepped outside. Burns pulled the gate down behind them.

The four of them—Manny, Lestor, Roddy, and Shazz—moved along the street at a hurried pace. They were to make their way to the East River, just north of the fields along the FDR Drive. It wasn't far, but they weren't going in a straight line. They were going to go around the Riis Projects, which stood between them and the river; they had heard gunfire coming from that direction the night before.

They headed south to Houston and then east to the FDR, walking in the streets the whole way. They took the long, car entrance ramp, down to the Drive and headed north, wading into a slow current of official vehicles and refugee-like stragglers. Everyone was moving toward the camp.

To the west, a line of identical buildings stretched out like the cliffs of Dover, barring their way back into the city: the projects. To the east, green playing fields lay veiled behind layers of fences; past that was the river.

All along the Drive, people were leaking out of the city. They crawled over fences and concrete barriers, separating the city from its parkway, and joined the migration north. Even the footbridges overhead were loaded with people—mostly young, and most in a festive mood.

Farther on, the soldiers came into view. They had taken over the ball fields and were still spreading. A small tent city had sprung up on the baseball fields, and food and water were being distributed.

The four decided to get off the road. They hopped the fence into the park area. They took a path that ran alongside the fenced in fields and followed it until it met up with the path that ran alongside the river. As they had been told, a long and low-slung vessel was moored alone, just north of the fields.

Ida: the name on the bow.

The boat was at least a hundred and fifty feet long and made of mostly dark wood and brass, and it looked as if it would have been more at home cruising the warm, muddy waters of the 1940s Amazon, than the cold steel East River of today.

Along the length of the boat's deck, they could see half a dozen men moving about like clockwork, appearing and disappearing out of doors and passages. A sturdy metal gangplank extended down from the vessel onto the grass alongside the walking path; a section of the promenade's railing had been disassembled and tossed off to the side to enable this.

"…This is odd," Roddy said.

"Well," Manny said, "let's go see what they have to say."

And she led the group toward the incongruous yacht.

Carl's Role the Night Before

Carl opened his eyes and the world was upon him. His shoulder ached. He had slept on a hard wood floor but he didn't mind. He had been so exhausted, he could have slept anywhere.

The apartment was gloomy, but it was peaceful. The room was filled with angular shadows, but it was still bright outside. He rolled onto his back and stared at the ceiling: blank, dry, eggshell… a black gossamer of dust hung in the corner above the window. He angled his head back and looked at the upside-down world out the back windows.

Above the buildings was a blue sky with a hard sun, but the apartment protected him.

Aside from his shoulder, he had slept well. The sleep had rejuvenated him. He felt energy welling up in him; then he remembered his situation, and his soul sank again.

Let this be my prison, he thought. *For the rest of my days, let me be here alone, forgotten in this far-off cliff-side cave. If it could end like that… I would take that deal.*

He heard a rustling from the other side of the room. Forrest was sitting in the corner.

"You know," Forrest said, "when the Vikings wanted to make their blades stronger; they would add burnt bones to their iron. Burnt bone is carbon, and adding carbon to iron, makes steel. They would add the bones of wolf or bear, to instill its power; or they would add the bones of an ancestor to give their blades mystical properties.

"That's what we're doing, Carl. We *are* the ancestors: the spirit of our people; and if we die, it will be fine, because our bones will make our people stronger."

"Please, Forrest," Carl said, "not now."

He turned over and faced the wall again. He needed time for his thoughts to settle. The images from the night before were fading too fast: like a dream upon waking. He had to go over them one more time…

He's perched inside an ornamental yew, in the tiny front yard of a four-story townhouse. Actually, it's more of a bush: no taller than the stoop it abuts, but it's old, and its branches are thick and ropey like the neck of an ostrich.

He rests comfortably on a solid branch, and watches the burning on the street.

The flare he had dropped in the garbage pile had gone up fast; the bags had been filled with mostly paper. On his left, another flame—a dark, orange-black flame—licks out from under a car hood, and in his mind a Van Halen song is rolling over and over.

Don't seem to can't *be aloooone.*

The song is *Ain't Talkin' 'bout Love*, but the words are his own.

Don't seem to can't *be aloooone.*

Followed by Eddie's hoary riff.

Baa, baa, ba-daaaaaa,

Don't seem to can't *be aloooone—Baa baa, ba-daaaa.*

A rope of flame leaps from the garbage pile and whirls into the center of the street before blinking out of existence. A bright orange ghost echoes on his optic nerve long after it's gone.

Forrest always did get off on theatrics, he muses. *Always blowing something up or lighting fires… are they coming for us now?*

Dark, clunky men, run past him and down the street. They don't turn his way.

He steps out of the bush, and steps out of the garden, then ducks down behind a parked car. He's about to sprint across the street to Ed's escape hatch, when he sees Joey running the wrong way across the street. He might be hit because he's moving awkwardly: his empty hands are bouncing at his sides like a small child, and his legs seem too short for his body and he leaps a small ironwork fence and falls face-first into a thick patch of ivy, and disappears down through it as if it were a cloud.

Fear overtakes Carl and he sprints across the street and jumps the gate into Ed's outdoor stairwell. Myrons is dead at the top of the stoop. Ed is gone. He takes the entire staircase in one leap then races through the building's basement and out the back and over fences and down the alley to the next street over—and somehow, Forrest and Floyd are there at the same time, and they run.

"He went down in the ivy," he says, as they race blindly down the dark street.

Everyone understands.

Behind them, a muffled clattering rages on, though they are long gone.

Chapter 23

Mrs. Gittens is laughing.

She's laughing so hard, it's making Virgil nervous, drawing his focus away from his magazine.

He's been on her couch for the past ten minutes, devouring a stack of celebrity magazines. Her coffee table always had a few.

He finally gives in and lifts his head from between the glossy pages and turns to see what she's doing.

Mrs. Gittens is doubled over, hands on knees, laughing at something going on in the hallway.

She's gonna hurt herself, he worries.

It's only then that he realizes loud music is coming from the hallway.

The Boneheads have a boom box, he thinks. *And batteries.*

He rocks forward, and with a grunt, lifts himself out of the couch. He's got to see what's going on.

With magazine still in hand, he walks over to Mrs. Gittens and peeks around the vestibule wall.

There he sees Chris, in the middle of the hallway, dancing. His stout, yet somehow thin body, is framed in the doorway. His dance moves are staccato, and strangely syncopated, as if his limbs are barely able to contain the energy issuing from him... but it looks kind of good.

The music makes a sharp cut to a Jamaican reggaeton, and Chris matches its changes as instantaneously as if they were entangled particles. Mrs. Gittens bursts into laughter again.

"It's Sandman," Virgil hears her say through the blare.

I need to go back to my apartment, he thinks.

He shakes his head and lumbers back to the couch—and sits.

This should be over soon, he thinks, as he stares at the blank television screen in front of him. *Army's on the street... back to work.*

He cringes at the idea of going back to work: the desolate lobby, the dirty, salmon-colored linoleum floors, the flat yellow paint on the walls, so dry that it leaves chalk marks on you if you brush against it... the never ending nights.

Just then, a blue pearl is proffered: Mrs. Gittens is holding out a coffee mug.

"It's beautiful, isn't it?" she says, her head still shaking free of the vision of Chris's cosmic dance.

"Miss Li from down the hall gave it to me... she got it on one of her weekend bus trips out of Chinatown. I've had it for months already but haven't used it. I'm afraid to chip it. But every time I opened the cabinet, I saw that beautiful blue peeking out at me. It finally just wore me down. Why keep such a beautiful thing hidden away?"

Virgil looks down at the blue mug in his hands. It's not that beautiful, he thinks. It was handcrafted, that was true, but it looked crude, as if someone with two graceless thumbs had smeared it into shape; even the Lapis blue seemed burnt and uneven... but it did *feel* good.

"Where have you been Virgil?" Mrs. Gittens asks.

"It's the night shift, Mrs. Gittens," he says. "I'm up late at night."

"I'm sure you've built up enough seniority by now, to switch over to days every now and then."

Virgil opens his mouth as if about to say something but doesn't have the strength.

"I'm just so sick of crowds," he finally says. "It's quiet at night."

Mrs. Gittens takes a closer look at him.

"Well," she says. "Sometimes you need to take a break, Virgil. You take your time. Do what you have to do, and then come back to us. We need you too."

She rubs his shoulder, then gives it a solid pat as if to prove his sturdiness.

"But don't take too long, Virgil; *tempus fugit*."

Virgil nods his head slowly.

"Yeah," he says, "I haven't felt too good lately."

He notices the warmth of the coffee mug in his hands. He takes a sip.

"And, Virgil," Mrs. Gittens says, "sometimes, times of hardship are rewarded."

She nods at the earthen vessel in his hands.

He looks at it again—and now it seems as if it were a thousand years old, fired in an open pit under a desert sky. Around the mug's circumference, blue, and every shade of blue, undulated over their own burnt edges.

"It *is* a beautiful mug."

Austin

Miss Li stood in the doorway of her apartment, looking up at Chris. She always got a kick out of him. Growing up, he was exactly what she had imagined an American boy to be like: a big-boned puppy, bounding enthusiastically in place. She had grown up in China during the Cultural Revolution; she had learned to keep her energy under control. But when she spoke with Chris, she felt her spirit lift.

Miss Li remained still as she watched Chris pump his arms and step his feet as he spoke, but she couldn't keep a bemused smile from her lips.

"Miss Li. Miss Li," Chris blurted. "What would Chairman Mao think of all these new billionaires?"

Without pause and still in good cheer, she answered: "He would kill them all."

She smiled.

Chris stopped.

"Really?" he said.

"Of course," Miss Li cried, and her body buckled and she fell back a step under the weight of her own self-conscious laughter.

Just then Austin popped out of the next apartment over. His nose was buried in the pages of a large picture book.

"Hey, Chris. Hey, Miss Li," he said, without lifting his gaze.

They "helloed" back and watched as he walked down the hall and went into Mrs. Gittens' apartment, still without lifting his head.

In the apartment, Austin walked past Mrs. Gittens in the kitchen, then plopped onto the chair at the head of the coffee table. Virgil looked up. Austin sat hunched over his book, flipping the pages mechanically. After a while he stopped and looked up at Virgil, as if he had just awoken.

"Did you know that we have a rover on Mars the size of a car?" he said. "It's not like one of those little ones they sell at an electronic store. It's a real car… a car!"

"Yeah?" Virgil said. "I heard about something like that; didn't know it was so big though."

Austin went back to his book.

They heard a commotion in the hallway.

Howard comes stomping in with Chris on his heels.

Howard was upset about something, and Chris was grinning and grabbing at his shoulders as if loosening him up for a fight.

"Virgil, Virgil," Chris said. "This guy is always mad."

"Of course I'm mad," Howard responds. "I just got a fifty-dollar ticket for riding my bicycle on the sidewalk."

Virgil's head pops up.

"Today?" he said. "You got a ticket today?"

"No," Howard said. "I just checked the mailbox. I didn't think that cop was serious when he wrote it. It was up near campus. I thought it was just a warning or something. Come on, man! A bicycle?"

"A letter?" Virgil said. "You got a letter?"

"They've taken all the fun out of bike riding," Howard ranted. "It's just another mode of transportation now."

"This city is too crowded," Virgil said.

"Shit," Chris chimed in. "You should see where I grew up. My nearest neighbor was one mile away."

"Did you have a car?" Virgil asked. "I'd like a car; I don't have a driver's license though. How am I supposed to find somewhere nice to live if I can't even drive around and look?"

"Shit, I'll teach you how to drive, Virge," Chris said.

"Don't they teach you that stuff in the army?" Howard asked.

Austin looked up from his book. "You were in the army, Virgil?"

"Virgil was in the war to get Saddam Hussein," Mrs. Gittens said from the kitchen.

"You fought in a war, Virge?" Chris said. "Wow!"

He took a step back and looked at Virgil in admiration.

"You a hero, man," he said.

"No," Virgil said quickly. "I'm not a hero. A hero does heroic things."

Just then they heard Ray call Chris from across the hall.

Chris turned and jogged out of the apartment.

Virgil and Howard looked at each other.

"Sorry about yesterday, Howard," Virgil said. "You know…"

"I know," Howard answered.

"Don't let that hate in you," Virgil said. "Cause it's hard to get it to leave again."

That was all they said about it until Mrs. Gittens came in from the kitchen, smiling and singing a Marvin Gaye song.

"Virgil, how is your mother?" she asked the next moment. "Didn't you say you were going to see her? I think you better wait until things have settled down. I don't think the trains are running yet anyway."

"I'll go see them once this is over," he said.

"Don't take a bicycle, man," Howard said. "They love going after people on bicycles."

Mrs. Gittens went back into the kitchen, still beaming.

Howard went around the couch and sat next to Virgil.

"Virgil," he said quietly. "Do you know the Boneheads have a gun?"

"I know," Virgil said, beginning to feel the gravity of that situation.

Just keep quiet, he thought. *Don't say a word. Get back to your apartment.*

But he didn't feel like leaving.

"Can you believe we landed a satellite on a comet?" Austin said. Then he looked up and abruptly closed his book. "Do you know that one day we're going to see dinosaurs, and cavemen, and everything. Because when the aliens arrive, they'll have it all on video."

"Yeah?" Virgil said. "When's that gonna happen?"

"We're not ready yet," Austin answered, and then with his best Captain Jean Luc Picard impersonation, he spoke: "I am asking you, for a leap of faith."

Then he opened his book again and went back to reading.

Sterm

Ray sat perched on the arm of his couch, peering out the window. Outside, between the buildings, a young man was peeking around the edge of a brick wall. He wasn't hidden: at least not from Ray's perspective. Ray had a perfect portrait view of the entire scene: the tall windowless expanse of brick wall (the stairwell of the next building over) on the left, and the overacting, Buster Keaton of a man, pantomiming nervousness, on the right.

What the heck? Ray thought, as he watched the man stoop and bob and peek around the corner of the building every few seconds, as if he were fearing snipers from out on the avenue.

But there was something familiar about him.

Chris came jogging in the apartment.

"What's up?" he asked.

"Look at this," Ray said.

Chris dashed over to the window and sat next to him. Side by side, they leaned over and stared out the window.

"Is that Sterm?" Ray asked.

They watched quietly for another minute, then burst out laughing. It *was* Sterm.

Third-Class-Sushi Sterm, they called him.

"What the heck?" Chris cried out.

Sterm was one of the delivery guys for a third-rate sushi place on Avenue D. He was meek as a lamb, and always stood slightly hunched, holding his hands at waist level, as if expecting to have to throw them up in defense at any moment. His head seemed a little large for his slight frame, and he chuckled nervously when he spoke; but Ray and Chris liked him because he knew a lot about video games.

"Call him. Call him," Ray said.

And they both shouted his name.

"Sterm!"

No reaction.

"I think he's trying to get to work," Chris said, noting that he was looking in the direction of the restaurant.

"Hey, get me the gun, get me the gun," Chris said. "Let's scare the shit out of him."

"Are you crazy?" Ray asked.

"No," Chris said. "I'll shoot way over his head, like 50 feet. It's no big deal. I grew up shooting guns."

"Okay, okay," Ray said.

He ran into the room and brought out the box with the gun in it. Chris took the box and set it on their end table—a plastic milk crate.

He opened the box, picked up the small pistol, and took aim at the wall high above Sterm's head. He squinted and puckered his whole face against the expected recoil.

"*STERM!*" they shouted one more time as Chris pulled the trigger.

A brick three feet over Sterm's head exploded and he flopped to the ground.

Chris and Ray both screamed. "*Holy shit!*"

Chris quickly dropped the gun back into its box.

"Oh shit," he said. "I didn't mean that! I didn't mean that!" His heart was racing. "I was aiming way up high!"

He slid the plastic end table as far away as he could, with his foot.

Their shock quickly broke into uncontrollable laughter when they looked outside again and saw Sterm sitting on the ground, looking up at them in bewilderment.

Just then Virgil came rushing into the room.

"What the fuck are you guys doing?" he shouted.

The Boneheads looked up dumbfounded.

Virgil stared at them—and at the gun—then looked out the window and summed up the situation.

"Gimme that thing," he said, and grabbed up the gun and its box. "I told you not to mess with this thing. Someone's gonna get killed!"

"Yeah, take it away. Take it away, Virgil," they both said, while making shooing movements with their hands. "Get rid of that thing."

Virgil walked out of the apartment, shaking his head.

I gotta get out of this place, he thinks.

Behind him the Boneheads are laughing again, howling over the fright they've just had.

Jays

Mrs. Gittens was back in her kitchen. Her apartment was empty for the moment. She walked around the table to the window, and raised the blinds a little higher. The summer was at its tail end, and the heat no longer had backbone; and so for the first time in months, the window was up and the screen was in. The air conditioner had been turned off.

"Oh," she said aloud and held up a finger. "This is it."

It had just occurred to her that this was the exact time of year—the creeping in of fall after a long, stifling summer—that was her very favorite season.

Outside in the courtyard the leaves of the sycamores were starting to dry; their rustling had a crisper edge to it.

The screech of a blue jay warned of a person walking by on the path below; the person passed, unaware of the bird.

Mrs. Gittens had been keeping an eye on that blue jay family since early spring. Sometimes she'd leave a few peanuts on the window ledge for them, and later, when she came back around to check, they'd be gone.

She leaned against the window frame and watched the noisy family hop up and down the fire escape on the next building over, thinking they were being discreet. Their needy chicks had matured.

I hope they come back next year, she thought.

Behind her, conversations from the hallway pattered on.

She looked down through the branches of the tree below her window. This was her favorite time of year, she thought again; but she always forgot, until it came around again, and then she could smell it: the breathing of the Earth, and she decided to rest for a while, and close her eyes, and soak in all she could. She pulled a chair out from the table and sat next to the window. There was nowhere for her to rush.

CHAPTER 24

The meeting with the Mayor was quick. Condolences and reminiscences warmed the air, and plans were set, and haloes were forged for those who were left to save the world. They were, after all, fighting the same battle. Even Shazz closed his eyes and allowed some self-righteous pride to swell in his chest, before quashing it.

No, he thought, *I will not talk.*

But he wanted his brother to: *he must talk,* he thought. He *has* to have been saved... by them. He has to have been saved because he was raised perfectly: always surrounded by love. He must stay pure for as long as he can, because that's what his parents were.

But standing in that room—a windowless meeting room at the front of the main deck of the boat—with those people... he wanted to smash something.

Oh, the bullshit, he thought. *The hypocrisy.*

He wanted to get away from them, so he stayed in the back with Roddy, handing the reigns to Manny and Lestor. He wanted Lestor to talk, and he did, though he often looked over at his older brother for affirmation; but Shazz only encouraged him to keep talking.

"You speak, Lestor," he told his brother. "You say something. And then we can all get out of here."

But Lestor honored his brother too much to think he could speak for both of them. *Why isn't he talking?* he wondered, and then he remembered… Shazz was a murderer.

And so Lestor and Manny made all of the arrangements for the next day's press conference. It would be held on the field next to the National Guard's press tent.

Manny was handed a list of points their official statement should touch on, and a few of the questions reporters were going to ask, and that was all that was needed. Once they had that, they could inoculate the public conscience at will. And all would be well; see you tomorrow.

The group made their way out of the floating conference room onto the main deck. The deck was higher than the shore now: it had been level when they boarded, but the tide had risen. Manny could see barnacles and seaweed clinging to some of the original bedrock of the island. The live stone crept up from the river bottom and disappeared under the island's concrete blanket.

At the top of the gangway, one of the deckhands stood handing out portable phone chargers to everyone in the group.

"The media guy wants to see you," he told Manny. "You too, Shazz."

Shazz stood behind Manny. He guessed what it was about and knew that he'd better go. It was best that Lestor be kept clear of that whole situation. He told Lestor and Roddy to wait on shore for them.

"Stay close," he told them.

Manny and Shazz followed the deckhand toward the stern, until they came to a passage that took them into the interior of the boat.

Shazz took it all in: gold carpeting, cherry wood wainscoting, with the walls above painted a saffron yellow.

Midway along the passage they stopped at an oversized set of sliding doors. The guard rapped twice then slid the doors apart. He nodded for Manny and Shazz to enter; then he let the doors roll shut on their own.

At first, all Shazz could see was a large golden ring: a bronze statue against the far wall—a life-sized Shiva, mid-cosmic dance, within a ring of flames. The ring of gold burned on his retina, and only after recovering from the stun of the museum-quality presentation, did the rest of the room begin to come into focus.

The room was mostly darkness. To his right, Shazz could sense a broad, open area, but he couldn't see a thing there. To the left, falling just within Shiva's glow, he could make out a set of wide, bare shelves on either side of a squat and shuttered liquor cabinet; on top of the cabinet stood a mounted white duck, posed the way any domesticated white duck might stand.

Wood beams on the ceiling, like the ribs of a leviathan, dipped just low enough to touch the light, and a thick Persian rug lay beneath their feet. And before them, and before the statue, stood a large, black, berm of a desk.

Manny and Shazz both jumped when someone stirred from behind the desk. Unseen at first, a thin, wick of a man hung over the back of a black leather chair. The man leaned in and gazed deeply into the center screen of a triptych of computers, as if it were a dark pool at the bottom of a soothsayer's bowl.

"Passwords!" he barked, without taking his eyes off the screen. "They make me change my passwords every few months… and it always has to be something new… and I can't just change one number, and I can't use a previous one, and it has to have a capital letter, and it has to have a symbol, and heaven forbid I ever type in the wrong password three times in a row; *then* I get locked out and have to call some operator down in Tampa to get it reset… and I've got twenty different passwords to deal with!"

He smiled pridefully at the implication that so many passwords made him important. Then he popped a final key with a long boney finger before lifting his head as if catching a scent; the statue's light, tangled in his peach fuzz hair, gave his round head a shallow nimbus.

He was taller than they thought, and thinner, but seemed sturdy. He wore a tight, peach-colored T-shirt, which struck dark against his opaque skin, and his long vascular arms hung at awkward angles from his body.

Is he old? Shazz wondered. He couldn't tell. If you gave him an oversized jacket and a backward baseball cap, he could have easily passed for a teenager.

The man quickly made himself proper: donning a worn tan derby and rose-tinted glasses. He picked up a navy, velour, tracksuit jacket, from off the back of the chair, and swung it on as he made his way around the end of the desk to greet them. He disappeared in the dark for an instant as he rounded the far end of the desk; when he reappeared, he seemed a new, more affable man.

"I've been wanting to meet you"—he held out a wide, ungainly hand to Manny and nodded politely to Shazz, who stood off a ways behind her left shoulder—"to extend my deepest condolences to you and your family, and to let you know that we will be behind you all the way; assisting you with all our resources, to get your positive message out there, and to calm these stormy waters."

Against her instincts, Manny took his clammy hand in her own and shook.

"I've been following your texts," he said to her in a confidential manner.

"And who are *you*?" she asked right off, seeing his game.

"I'm Ida," he said, a little surprised. "Didn't you see the name on the boat?"

His words dropped in clips, which made him seem foreign, but he had no discernable accent, and he smiled a lot, as if he were constantly pleased with himself.

"Who am I?" he repeated. "I am an advisor, a partner... a comrade in arms with Hizzoner... in the good fight... and a major resource gatherer."

"And what do you want with us?" Manny asked.

"I'm here to help," he said. "I'm here to calm the world down. So I needed to meet you; to get a feel for you; to see how we're going to run with this."

From the back, Shazz stared at Ida in bewilderment. *What is this guy?* he thought. He didn't seem white... or black, and not really anything else. He had a long, featureless face, even below his hat and gold-rimmed glasses, and Shazz thought that if he were to grab him by the face, he'd probably, accidently, sink a thumb right through his mottled skin.

"You guys must become the conscience of this play," Ida said, "the superego that defeats the id: if you know what I mean. I mean, the waters must be stilled."

"So," Manny asked, slightly perturbed by Ida's cavalier attitude, "what do you want us to do?"

"Oh, nothing," Ida answered. "Hardly a thing… just stand in front of the cameras. We'll take it from there."

He gravitated back toward the bulk of his desk, then stood directly in front of it. Manny had not moved closer, leaving an uncomfortably wide gap between them.

"You know," Ida said. "… I have access to this place in Morocco. It's a palace, really; a *palace.* And it's like… in the desert, and like, a thousand years old and surrounded by five hundred acres, and a ten-foot wall, and its gardens are so beautiful that it's almost biblical.

"After you're finished here, you and your people should stay there for a few months. It'll be a great place to heal."

Who is *this guy,* Shazz thought. *This skinny little…?*

No one spoke, and so Ida offered up more.

"Before we go any further," he said, looking at Shazz, "I want you to know that we had nothing to do with your parents' death. I assure you that."

"Why would you even say that?" Manny said.

"Well, you know what I mean," he said, "people love blaming the media. I mean… sometimes a plotline *does* run a bit long… and then something pops…"

"Like Forrest," Shazz said.

"Ah," Ida said, smiling and nodding. "You know him."

They stopped talking.

"You know," Manny said, "I'm not comfortable working with you. I think we're going to ask the Mayor to work with someone else."

"The Mayor?" Ida guffawed. "God bless him. He's a good man. He really is; a good Catholic school boy, still trying to impress the nuns. Doesn't quite connect though; that's cause the real him was covered up long ago, when he was first trained to be a man. But God bless him, he tries so hard… and, you *don't* have to work with me."

"You're the media guy, right?" Manny asked.

"I'm the director," Ida said. "The movie is always on—I just choose which scenes to cut to."

He turned again to Shazz. "Shazz, I know you like the ocean, right?" he said. "I once had *this* boat, atop a boil of sardines that was eight miles long and a hundred feet deep. It was like a crusading army rolling up the coast of East Africa, with half of the ocean's biosphere following along after it: a village of smiths and sewers, and wainwrights and brothel owners; all living off of the troops."

Manny looked at Ida, her mouth hanging open.

Did he think he was going to steal Shazz?

She was so absolutely certain that Ida was barking up the wrong tree that she let out a snort of disbelief. He was selling Shazz the wrong dream. She knew Shazz well enough to know that all he ever wanted was peace: to have a normal, suburban, lawn-mowing life.

How wonderful it would be.

Though, she thought, he had been careful for so long: walking along that long fragile pathway toward his dream, which now lay in a shattered heap… Maybe she did have to worry. He might not have shown it, but she knew he was devastated.

"You know, Shazz, you're a rich man now," Ida said, ignoring Manny's guffaw. "Well, at least reasonably well off. Your parents did well: with the books and all. You're not a *slave* anymore."

Shazz had not even thought of it till then, and he distinctly felt a small mount of guilt rise within him.

"Now you'll feel the pain of the taxman," Ida said, with a knowing smile. "And they're trying to take more every day… though, after this episode, I doubt people will be talking about tax hikes for a while."

"Taxes?" Manny said.

Ida looked at her as if he had forgotten she was there.

She glared at him.

"And so, who's your director?" she asked.

"Ah," he said, with sudden enthusiasm. "Jabba." He clicked his heels and did a quick nod. "The man's a financial genius. A wizard, who can take time and space and sound, and whorl it around like pizza dough, and slap it back down on the table and, ta-da! There's a pile of cash there so large that it would make you shit your pants. And it's all legal."

At first, Manny was taken aback by Ida's unabashed display of— squalor of soul. Her face recoiled in disgust at the reek, before remembering that, *that,* was her enemy, and then she got angry.

"And so you guys are racists?" Shazz spoke up from behind.

"Racists?" Ida asked, not knowing what Shazz was talking about at first. "Oh… no; racism is stupid."

"They're stealing as much as they can!" Manny shouted.

"Hey, we're operating within the parameters of the system!" Ida shouted back, followed by a somewhat apologetic, "What can you do: capitalism… it's a living thing."

"People will evolve," Manny said. "And your beast will die. Greed will start to feel ugly. We *will* evolve."

"I don't think so," Ida said. "It's hard-wired into the machine."

"It will collapse from exhaustion," she said.

Ida smiled at her perceived naivety.

"The Greeks considered hope to be an evil," he said, with a smile. Then, after a beat: "Shit, you should be happy these guys are only in it for the money. There are all sorts of nut jobs running around out there, pointing their ray guns hither and dither."

"So what do you want?" Shazz asked.

"They're afraid," Manny said, with gathering strength. "They think we're all like them. And so they're guarding themselves against themselves."

"What do we want?" Ida said, irritated by Manny. "We want to stride through the firmament like Gods. We want King Djoser. We want Ramesses the Great. We want Teotihuacan."

Manny looked at him in confusion.

"You know what I think?" she said. "I think your kind don't stand much of a chance anymore. I think you are all about to be devoured. Real soon!"

"Listen," Ida said. "You know that Solomon story about the baby? These guys would be the bad mother. And that's why they'll never lose."

"Yeah, well," Manny said, "everybody sees you now."

"That's the whole yin and yang of it," Ida said. "You're more locked down than ever; a flash here, and you run there; like a herd. No, not even a herd; like a school of fish, a murmuration of starlings."

"You are the leftover crap of the past," Manny said, "congealed into a scab, and the scab is the hardest stuff yet, but it's the last stuff. A new age has come!"

"Aye, but an old human still lives."

Shazz stood back and watched as they went at each other. He felt slightly embarrassed at what seemed to him like childish behavior;

but he was not of their world, so he couldn't judge for sure what was going on.

Manny seemed on the verge of physically attacking Ida. He had never seen her like that. He had heard his parents talk about it with wry smiles. How infused with the spirit she became when defending her beliefs.

Her nostrils flared. Her hair seemed to rise like the hood of a cobra. She held nothing back, but she didn't lose control.

"Don't you fear your future?" she finally asked.

"No, no, no," Ida said right away, and he stepped forward again. "Ida won't flinch under the gaze of the great terror. When I stand before the scales of Anubis, I have absolute confidence my heart will rise: 'I did what I had to,' and I will slide right by."

"Into oblivion," Manny said.

Ida smiled wanly.

"All paths lead to God."

"*Aiye!*" Manny spat and threw up a hand with a flourish. "Why even talk to you?"

And now Ida's ire rose.

"You ain't holy just yet, Manny," he said, and he tapped his thumb on his chest and sneered. "I'm the most enlightened person they is!"

And he would've started cursing and spitting and leaping in place, if Shazz hadn't been there. But Ida's dark cloud quickly whisked past and he returned to tranquil.

"You know," he said, "I'm kinda surprised at *you*, Manny. After all that your family's been through. You know what's out there. Your dad stole away in the dead of night to give you girls a chance. And now you made it. After this… you're going to *bank*."

Pushing the metaphor as verb, Manny thought, as she scrutinized each word he said.

"I mean," he continued. "You can quit working so hard and raise a family. You can join TV shows, and get big books advances. You're a brand now.

"Do you know how much money you can make, by just letting yourself be happy? You can be the next Martha Stewart—"

Normally Manny would have laughed at such obviousness, but right then, hearing it from him, made her angry: he had mentioned family. That was Theresa's job.

"—changing the world between pumpkin pie recipes," Ida continued.

He moved toward the dimly lit liquor cabinet. His stuffed white trophy stared at him. He stopped.

"I can have you applauded at awards shows," he said.

"You're so selfish!" Manny admonished.

"Come let us not talk falsely now," he sang.

Manny was finally thrown by Ida's peculiar behavior.

"Yeah, well," she let out. "I'm just trying to be the best person I can while I'm here."

"Yeah, I see," Ida said, as if he were waiting for this exact moment, "by setting murderers free. Thank you. You are the best tool I've ever had. I just hold up your great works and the whole nation shifts right."

"Just make sure you tell the whole story!" Manny shouted.

Ida was happy now; satisfied that he had made her lose her cool.

"When you two realize how dilute of character your world is," he said, "you'll go for the money."

He looked at Shazz.

"You saw it, Shazz," he said. "This trash ain't worth fighting for. Grab what the fuck you can and get out. Cause it ain't worth saving."

Shazz didn't speak, and his face did not betray.

"Well, just so you know," Manny said, in control again, "we've already decided to step up and try to end this thing, because it's the right thing to do, *not* because it's costing *you* business."

She turned and walked to the doors.

"I label thee hippie," Ida said, and made the sign of the cross in the air.

Manny gave the sliding doors a heavy push open and marched out.

"Simmer, simmer," Ida said, as the door slid shut behind her.

Shazz had made to follow, but she had moved quickly, and he knew he still had business with Ida; and so he stood there, waiting his turn.

"I tell ya, Shazz," Ida said, as he strolled back toward the shadows beside his desk, "don't let 'em drag you into their warped thinking. If I did what you did, I wouldn't lose a drop of sleep over it… dragging those saints into the ugly pages of history. It's unforgivable."

Shazz felt his temper rise. He didn't like Ida mentioning his parents.

"I like you, Shazz," Ida said. "You give no quarter. It's so hard to find a clean-thinking man like you, nowadays. Not in this country."

He reached into the darkness against the wall and lifted out a tall bass guitar. Shazz hadn't noticed it before.

Ida carefully lifted the wide strap over the top of his hat and tucked his shoulder through.

When he stood, the bass seemed wider than he was tall.

"I've got band practice now," he said, smiling again. "Online stuff."

Shazz got his best look at him yet. He *was* old. And he would have looked funny with his oversized glasses and undersized hat, if it wasn't for an unnerving stare, which never let up, no matter what the rest of his face was doing.

"Nobody really knows what happened, Shazz," he said, distracting Shazz from his scrutiny. "And from where I'm standing, it doesn't look like anyone's asking."

The mention of his crime set off alarms in Shazz's mind.

"You can't believe the things that are out there, Shazz," he continued, while adjusting the strap around his neck. "You're a guppy in a mud puddle. There are crystal-clear oceans out there Shazz… oceans, with turtles and seals, and overgrown bamboo forests with shoots as thick as cedars, and deserts unchanged since the first man, with the first man still in it. And you're kicking around this piss-soaked piece of concrete. You're wasting your life.

"You know, a man of your caliber is owed a higher station."

He looked at his fingers, high up on the neck of the bass, and started working his way through a riff. The bass wasn't plugged in, so the notes sounded soft and far away. He had the awkward fingers of a dilettante, but he was tenacious; after a few attempts at a 12-note run, he managed to get it right once.

Then he looked up at Shazz. "You *must* see the old world!"

He looked back up at his fingers and ran through his riff again.

"Don't worry, Shazz. Everyone is going to be alright once the money starts rolling in. Money is the great protector. Once the money starts rolling in, everything will be wonderful. You'll see. Money is the great path clearer, like Ganesh. And then you can save everyone you care about."

He turned around and started walking toward the open doorway to the left of the statue, then he stopped and looked back.

"I gotta go," he said. "I can't be late for practice. Our band leader is strict, like Miles."

He smiled again, pleased at his dropping of the name.

He plucked out a few more deep, hollow sounding twangs, then turned to leave again.

Shazz watched him walk: bow-legged; the long neck and oversized headstock of the bass throwing off his gait.

He seemed smaller now.

Had he been standing on a box? Shazz wondered.

He looked down into the darkness around the side of the desk but couldn't see the floor.

"Shit," Ida said. "You haven't lived until you've heard *Bitches Brew* off the coast of West Africa under a full moon."

He started a new riff, one that he knew how to play.

He started singing, "I'm Gonna Booglarize You Baby," by Captain Beefheart as he side-stepped around the back of Shiva's wall, twanging his bass along the way.

Shazz stood alone, looking at the empty doorway; then he looked at the empty desk with the huge bronze statue hovering above it…and then he realized that the pattern on the rug was exactly the same as the pattern on the rug in his mother's living room: reds, browns, and greens. *It's a garden,* he finally realized after years of having seen the rug. And he suddenly felt an urgency to get out of there.

Path of least resistance! Path of least resistance!

He turned around and walked to the doors. He reached out for the handles, but they weren't there. He felt around in the shadows and was on the verge of panicking when his fingers slipped into the recessed handles and he threw the doors wide.

The bright light in the hallway stunned Shazz, and he stepped forward dumbly into a blurry yellow tunnel. He turned and moved along the passage toward the exit, and as he moved, the colors made him feel as if he were wading through the tall amber grasses of a primeval savannah. He hurried his step and blinked to clear his vision, and at the end of the hall, he turned toward the open hatch and daylight. The late summer sun, rich and fiery, hung low in the sky between the buildings framed by the exit; and now he felt as if he were being drawn from the depths of a Neolithic temple toward the dawning of a spring equinox, until he stepped across the boundary between inside and out, and was knocked to a stop by the visceral scents of salt water estuary and diesel fumes.

He put his hands on the railings and looked down to see Manny, standing on land, looking up at him, and he took his first breath in what seemed like minutes.

The group gathered around a bench on the pathway, then headed north to stay clear of the commotion downtown of them. They'd go up and around on the way back.

Traffic on the highway was sparse; every so often, a line of Humvees would buzz past heading for the encampment. Manny and Shazz walked together at the rear. Roddy and Lestor walked up ahead.

"Whether you like it or not," Manny said, "everyone's watching." And she left it at that.

After a few blocks on the empty highway, they veered onto the long descending off-ramp to 23rd Street. Already near the bottom of the ramp, Lestor and Roddy had slipped between two concrete barriers into a parking lot that was under the highway. It was a shortcut to get back onto the streets below.

Shazz had already decided to stay away from Ida. All his instincts warned him to keep clear.

Bad things are gonna happen around that guy, he thought.

And then he heard shouting coming from beneath the highway.

Shazz took off down the ramp, sprinting toward the shouting. His triangular window onto the stage grew larger as the ramp sloped down and the highway stretched above. He saw an empty parking lot: a square, boxed in by long concrete barriers on either side.

In the ring, two strangers—two young black men—had already squared off against Roddy and Lestor. They were average-sized guys, Shazz noted.

We walked right into it, he thought with anger. *The city is still not safe.*

Roddy and one guy were already tangling, but Lestor was falling back fast. As soon as he ran out of space, he'd be dead. And there was one more element to the equation: out in the sunlight on the other side of the lot, another man was on his way.

This could be trouble, Shazz thought.

The new man was huge, rippling with muscles, and just about as wide as he was tall. He strode confidently toward the arena with a smile on his lips.

Three: three.

Shazz hopped the barrier and made it into the lot first. He took one step and froze, as if stuck in information overload; and then, through sheer force of will, he had a breakthrough. In a flash, he saw the solution.

Chunks of concrete lay scattered about the parking lot; they had fallen from the underside of the highway. He leapt to the closest, softball-sized clod, snatched it up and took off at full sprint toward Roddy.

Roddy's opponent had his back to Shazz.

When Mr. Big saw Shazz move, he realized the game was afoot; his body shuttered as his muscles jolted to life. But his path was not clear: there was lots of side-stepping for him to do: between parked cars, between concrete barriers—he was not designed for that. This gave Shazz the extra instant he needed.

Manny had let out a scream when she reached the lot's entrance at the bottom of the off-ramp. She grabbed hold of a barrier and braced herself as she watched the violence unfold.

Halfway to his target Shazz took to the air like Superman. He landed with an explosion as he brought the brittle chunk of cement down onto the back of his enemy's head. The concrete burst into a white cloud on contact and the man dropped.

Roddy was free.

Three: two.

The giant's hands were already grasping the far side barrier. His arms looked powerful enough to cast the stone blocks asunder. Roddy turned to sacrifice himself.

"No!" Shazz shouted. "Lestor!"

And they took off.

Lestor had now fallen back into the farthest corner of the lot. He stood with both hands up, parrying, trying to push away the grasping hands of his attacker.

Roddy and Shazz bore down on them.

In the split second before Shazz made contact, Lestor's tormentor lifted his chin as if sensing something, and then Shazz hit. He drove his shoulder into the soft ribs beneath the man's shoulder blades and collapsed him into the rusty chain-link and plywood fence on the north side of the lot. When he rebounded off the fence, the man dropped to the floor. Roddy arrived a step later, but Shazz was already done and had turned to face the next opponent.

Lestor and Roddy had managed to figure out what was going on by then; they turned, just in time to give the muscled giant a moment to think. He stopped ten feet from them and threw his hands up wide as if inviting them in.

Three: one.

The three fell back slowly, their hulkish stalker following them pace for pace. Shazz could see struggle in the man's face, as he was unable to bring himself to rush their three-man wall; and as the stress overtook him, he began working himself into a frenzy and flexing his 'most muscular' pose while repeating, "Skinnnnnn tight. Skinnnnn tight."

He was expending tremendous amounts of energy and working himself further into a frenzy until finally, he tore his shirt off over his head and continued flexing and following them closely.

It made Shazz furious: to have to back away from such a clown, and right as they swung back around toward the entrance where Manny was still standing, frozen to the concrete barrier, Shazz halted a step, feigning attack. With that, their attacker's face fell blank, and his body reflexively leapt back, and he froze with his balled-up fists directly in front of his eyes and his elbows sticking out and his feet level… before regaining his composure and putting his hands down again and puffing out his chest.

Shazz smiled.

He doesn't know what he's doing.

He felt Manny's small hand grab the back of his shirt and pull him back; then the four of them resumed moving backwards across the lot to the other side. They slipped out between the barriers and a couple of parked cars. When they popped out onto the street, they took off at a jog.

Manny couldn't wipe the look of astonishment off her face. She hadn't even had a chance to be scared. She kept looking over at Shazz as they bound down the middle of the street, Lestor and Roddy leading the way again.

Shazz finally looked back at her.

"Big dude, huh?" he said, and popped his eyes wide for effect.

She was giddy. It all seemed so gleeful to her. As if the violence had never happened. The four of them raced down the street like children running from a cranky old man. Manny's hair, bounced and floated around her face as they ran.

CHAPTER 25

Ed raises his eyes to the night sky and breathes in deeply. Fall is in the air. He can sense it. Even way down there at the bottom of the stone city, the first cool breaths of the coming season are bleeding their way down from the north: a stream within a current… a rivulet, branching… molecules: parts per parts per million, finding their way into the depths of his olfactory system; even through the overpowering stench of dried piss that coated the anemic hedge he hid behind.

He lies on his right flank; his long body, flush against a patch of earth that had been tramped to a smooth, marble-like polish, from decades of foot traffic. He propped himself up with an elbow. His head rested in his palm.

The hedge he lay behind was long and patchy, and ran the length of the projects on the avenue side; the other side of the projects was bordered by the FDR. The grass he lay upon was part of a patchwork of lawns around the buildings, separated by a crisscross of walkways.

Calling them 'lawns' was a stretch: most of the green had concentrated into tall thick tussocks, scattered amid patches of bare earth, as if the grasses had contracted for safety's sake. And he couldn't smell the grass, nor the hedges, nor the soil; everything alive had sealed itself off from the abuse.

But the air, he thinks... The breath of a mountain range could not be denied... but not just yet; now, only a trickle.

Behind him, across the avenue, stands a decrepit old walk-up, whose narrow face is almost fully obscured by the heavy iron latticework of a fire escape.

He knows Floyd is atop that building; hanging over its edge with his rifle; swaying to and fro like the beam of a lighthouse; thinking... searching. The last time he saw Floyd, was on his climb up, through the iron cage: up and off into the darkness.

Carl had stopped at the first floor. Ed couldn't see him either. And Forrest, he rooted around the murky shadows along the base of the building.

It's not a very strategic setup, Ed thinks.

He can't see any of them, and none of them can see him, but every so often, he thinks he catches the glint of Floyd's scope up on the roof... searching.

"You have to smell the earth," he hears his grandfather say.

He feels a sharp pain in his calf. He'd been digging a finger into the top of his boot for a while now without even realizing it, thinking a buckle must be out of place and stabbing him.

He pulls his finger out and lifts it to his nose: sharp, metallic.

A wave of fear rises up when he realizes his finger has been playing in slick viscous blood.

I've been shot! he thinks... but it couldn't be.

He reaches a finger down again and taps gingerly around the area. His alarm dampens when he realizes that there is no deep wound.

With the back of his finger—his nail—he feels a round object, stuck in the thick leather of his boot.

It's a bullet; a smooth unblemished slug.

From the inside of the boot, he plays with the weight like it was a loose tooth, until eventually, it pops out and drops onto the stone dirt.

"Let him stay," he hears his grandfather's voice again.

They are out in the back of his house: his grandfather's house—and his mother is there too, and she is alone.

He is sitting on the tall step at the back of the house, looking up at his grandfather.

His grandfather is a tall, handsome man with a square jaw, and he's framed by a pale winter sky. Smoke from his cigarette streams back past his ear, and the short, greying hair above his collar, flutters in the wind like the feathers of a bird.

"He'd be bored to death," he hears his mother say. *But he needs space,* she knows.

The decision had already been made. She'd be close by.

"I doubt it," Grandpa says, and he turns and walks back to his old work shed.

That was all the convincing he was going to do.

Ed warms at the remembrance: set a boy out there like Huck Finn and… how does one get bored of infinity?

"Thank you, Papa," he whispers.

Ed rolls onto his back and looks up at the sky again.

Auroras comes to mind.

He reaches over to the bush and strips a twig of its leaves. They are small and round and practically succulents, and he begins to snap them in half, one by one, catching the broken pieces in his palm.

He lifts them to his nose and inhales. This time he smells the green, and with it, he feels he can recall every instant of every day he had ever spent exploring the woods around his grandfather's property: the house he grew up in.

He sits up and pulls the cap off his head.

The smell of wet fall leaves, he thinks.

He looks down at his body.

He is all bound up in straps and laces. And everywhere his clothes are bunched has been rubbed raw. He can't stand it any longer. He reaches down and pops the buckles on his thigh holster. The heavy pack drops off.

It's so uncomfortable.

He reaches out and rips open the Velcro straps of his kneepads. He feels instant relief as each one falls to the ground; they had been chaffing him the most. He knocks the backs of his heels against the dirt a few times to unbunch his pants around his knees.

He sweeps his cast-off gear aside, then wriggles off his Kevlar vest and long-sleeved shirt in one piece, like the shell of a turtle. He plops it on the ground next to him, where it holds its form for a few moments, before gravity wins out and it begins to deflate.

He sits there in a new white T-shirt that practically glows. Now he's really starting to feel the air.

He looks down at his feet. Those boots. He feels numb from the knees down; and so he starts dragging the gnarled and crusty laces from their eyelets.

He flicks each lace off into the darkness, then whacks his heels on the ground a few more times to break the seal the boots had made with his feet. Once cracked, the boots slip off easily... then the socks... And then he is sitting there wiggling his toes in the air.

T-shirt... bare feet... unbound. A breeze washes over him and cools his mind.

I haven't killed anyone, he thinks.

He stands up and faces the eastern sky.

God, this weather is beautiful.

When he feels his feet firmly beneath him, he turns and steps through the hedges, emerging onto the sidewalk.

The pebbles in the concrete pavement shock his senses awake.

He steps off the sidewalk onto the smooth blacktop between the parked cars.

He stands and looks up at the roof where Floyd is supposed to be. He doesn't see a thing.

He sets off down the street, his bare feet slapping against the cool asphalt.

Carl sits wedged into one end of a narrow fire escape. He leans his head back against the iron bars and draws his knees in close. He can see only one way down the avenue. He has no idea what's happening behind him.

He had followed Floyd up the fire escape ladder but stopped at the first landing; he sensed that if he climbed any higher, the whole cage of corroded ironwork might tear free from the brittle bricks and crash down onto the street.

Floyd had kept climbing, and Carl felt his heavy footsteps resounding through the whole iron web, long after he had already settled in. When Floyd finally stepped off the fire escape and climbed onto the roof, Carl felt the whole structure slacken. From that point on, Carl imagined Floyd hanging over the edge of the building like a stone gargoyle.

Carl hears a clicking sound coming from behind him: the steady beat of claws against asphalt. He turns his head to track the sound as it moves through the void and out onto a section of moonlit avenue.

A huge loping beast steams out of the darkness.

It's a lion, he thinks, *a female.*

... but the gait's off.

It's a Great Dane... with a long curved tail, and floppy ears, and the short tight pelage of a savannah cat.

It disappears off into the darkness. The clicking sound echoes on.

Lights burst on, klieg bright, coupled with a blaring clamor. A roof party has just sprung into existence on the building across the avenue.

The roof is too high to have any real view of the party, but Carl catches a glimpse of an elbow and shoulder in glittering white.

There must be a hundred people up there, he thinks.

He looks down at the base of the building where Ed should be, but it's still dark down there; all he can make out is an even darker line. The hedges.

He must be scared, Carl thinks... *Don't do anything stupid, Ed.*

Forrest is somewhere down below too, but Carl knows he doesn't have a clear shot, and so would not give up their advantage... he wasn't *there* yet.

And Floyd: *He's probably beading on them right now.*

And that makes Carl nervous.

If any of them popped off a shot now, it would be all over fast.

No one lets off a shot.

They all watch. They have to, because there's nothing else to see.

From below, he hears a voice:

"They dance like fucking monkeys."

It's Forrest.

"Yeah, well," Carl says, "maybe we should dance like monkeys too."

The power cuts off and the party disappears, and for the rest of the night, all they hear is a murmuring crowd: an intermission audience, blending so well with the night air that after a while, they're not sure if they are really hearing anything at all.

Forrest made his way along the dark and narrow sidewalk. He could barely see a thing. He moved forward as if moving through tall grass: holding his hand out in front of him, deflecting the things that leaped out of the darkness: an enormous sycamore on his right, a bunch of metal trash cans on his left; even the sidewalk juts up suddenly in spots where tree roots had muscled up the concrete squares.

How fucking long is this block? he thought as he stumbled forward.

He changed his stride to an awkward march: kicking his foot out in front of him with each step to ensure the path was clear.

Ed, Carl and Floyd dragged along behind him in single file. No flashlights were used.

The Guard had been out earlier that evening. A curfew had been set for ten, but people were still milling about for an hour or two more. On the corners, people bantered with self-conscious guardsmen, or danced around the bright lights of the news cameras. Eventually, the groups dwindled, until at last, a lone man on a bicycle did a final few loops then rode off for home. By midnight, even the Guard seemed to have disappeared.

"One-two-three-fff…" Forrest took a quick count.

He stood in the hallway next to the stairs counting his men. He'd been peeking out the front window all night, until finally: he saw the chance to move.

"One-two-three-fff wait." His mind jumped into a state of panic.

"We had four when we got here! What happened?" he said.

His mind raced and raced as his men stood staring back at him with blank expressions.

"Oh," he realized, "I'm the fourth."

Forrest knew there was a clearing at the far end of the block; a wide avenue, across from which stood the projects. That was where they would go.

At first, all he could do was feel it: the open air, the wide-open spaces between the buildings; but as he stood on the corner staring out into the great void, different shades of darkness began to appear. He saw a thin line of bushes running the length of the sidewalk in front of the buildings. Ed would go there. Carl and Floyd… up the fire escape. He'd root around curbside and pick himself out a place in the dark.

He gave the word. Everyone set out for their positions.

CHAPTER 26

Theresa and thirteen-year-old Shazz waded forth into the onslaught of humanity that flushed back against them; they were part of their own flush too: at their heels, an entire subway train's worth of commuters had just burst forth with impressive energy at the Times Square station. The opposing forces clashed mid platform and souls swirled off here and there, like particles in a supercollider.

Shazz was out of his element.

He looked up at the large hand Theresa had clamped onto his forearm and thought: *There's no way I can break that grip.*

She dragged him along, keeping him in her lee.

When the current became too strong even for her, she turned sail and slipped into a calm eddy in a nearby corner.

She looked back at Shazz with a mad grin on her face, as if checking to see if he was having as much fun as she was.

"Look," she said, as they waited. "Look at that wall."

Wall?

He stared across the terminal at the dirty white tiles: same as the ones in his old public school's bathroom... and then he saw orange.

Through the haze of people who rushed past like snowflakes in a storm, he could see a whole wall of colors.

...*Oh*, he thought. *It's a thing.*

There were swirls within the wide washes of colors... patterns... and textures, as none of the tiles were flush or uniform of shape; even the colors themselves were never exactly the same, and the waves metamorphosed into new and beautiful shimmery colors... And for a while, Shazz couldn't see a person at all...

Shazz opened his eyes at the sounding of the cleaner's front gate lifting. He tilted his head to the right to get a straight-on view of the front door. Roddy was doing his best to lift the gate as quietly as he could, but the heavy steel still rattled in its tracks like an empty subway car.

Burns hung over the store's recessed door frame, watching Roddy as he lifted. When the gate was halfway up, the sidewalk in front of the store radiated a golden sunlight into the dark store, making it seem as if Roddy had just lifted the lid of a treasure chest.

Roddy did a quick peek under the gate to make sure it was safe; then lifted the gate neck high. He swung his head beneath it, and stood scanning the streets while the gate rested on his shoulder. Already, a cigarette dangled from his lips.

Shazz watched from atop a mattress of freshly bundled laundry bags that he had spent the night on; a foot above his head, a hedge of dry-cleaning bags hung from the clothes on the rack above him. The gossamer-thin bags undulated in the warm currents of air.

Burns was quick to detect movement behind him and turned with a hop to face Shazz.

"Those guys!" he shouted, and took a breath, "they still haven't caught those guys!"

Shazz squinted against the glare from the street.

Roddy leaned in. "You think they left the apartment?"

"They left," Shazz said. "They said they would leave. How's it look out there?"

"Seems pretty calm. Still no traffic. I saw some people on the avenues."

"Anything on the radio?"

"Just what he said." Roddy nodded toward Burns. "No new attacks last night... at least."

Shazz turned to the wall opposite him, inside the store. Manny had bed down on her own makeshift mattress behind the counter. She was sitting up, waiting for him.

Home

Theresa shrugged her shoulder heavily to keep her pocketbook from slipping off and spilling out onto the front stoop. She also danced with three overladen shopping bags, as she tried to unlock the front door.

Shazz stood behind her, waiting patiently, keeping a wary eye on this whirlwind before him: her bags, her long winter coat, her spiraling grey locks bursting out from beneath a wide-brimmed Gorton's fisherman hat. For all he knew, she could have been a wicked witch leading him into a gingerbread house.

He looked up at the pointy roof of the house. It did look a bit like a gingerbread house: yellow stucco outlined in dark wood trim. Tudor style. And yet it shared a common wall with the neighbor's house to its left—a house covered in mint-green aluminum siding. On the right side of the house ran an empty driveway, wide enough for a car to park in.

Finally, he heard the door unlock and watched as Theresa kicked it open and marched in. Shazz followed.

They stepped into the small entrance hall. It was unlit but still bright enough to see by. A staircase at the end of the hall led to the second floor; to the right, at the base of the staircase, stood the real entrance to the home.

Theresa walked through that doorway onto the main floor of the house without hesitating. She kept on toward the back of the house while Shazz slowed at the door's threshold.

The main floor seemed like one large room, but it was actually four. The entrance opened right into a large dining room, most of its space taken up by a heavy wood table covered in papers. To its right was the living room, which was practically empty but for a long couch against the far wall, and then a sun room lay just past that: it overlooked the front entrance and the sidewalk.

Shazz hadn't even noticed the overlooking windows while waiting for Theresa to unlock the door. It wasn't until he stepped into the dining room, that he realized a small child had been watching him from the window.

The small boy still watched him.

More interesting still, was a bearded old man sitting at a rolltop desk. The desk served as a boundary marker between the dining room and the living room. The man sat at the top-heavy desk as if he were a honky-tonk piano player: his knees were high and spread wide because the wooden office chair he sat in was too short, and he kept having to balance the old chair because of a broken recline mechanism.

As Shazz took in the scene, the old hillbilly fell deliberately back in his chair and threw his arms wide to the sky. "Oh, Calliope!" he wailed. "Help me to find a higher key!" before diving back into his desk.

Shazz could see an open, airy kitchen at the back of the house. Beyond that, he saw a porch out the back window, and a small yard beyond that.

The bearded man slapped his hands on the desk in surrender.

Shazz flinched, and froze.

"Eh," the man said, as he rested his hands on his knees. "It ain't Chekhov."

There were other people in the kitchen, but no one seemed to pay any mind to the old man. The wheels of the house kept whirling along.

Theresa had moved through the dining room into the kitchen. Shazz had been pulled along in her wake, though, the old man had slowed his drift.

Manny and Shazz

Shazz slapped opened the steel bar that held the cleaner's backdoor shut. He put a hand against the cool metal of the door, then popped it open with his shoulder. The door flew open with a sharp screech. He hadn't been back here in years.

The cleaner's back yard was small, but there were no fences on the adjacent lots. Most of those properties were owned by the surrounding businesses—who kept their doors permanently barricaded against thieves. Wilderness had reclaimed that end of the block: a tangle of bushes and vines wove a thick mesh over most of the area.

The cleaners' back patio was more of a glade in a small woods. It was mostly paved, and lipped with dark, trodden earth. A pebbled birdbath stood near the far end of the yard; currently it was used as a flower stand. The birdbath was crowned with an overflowing flowerpot of colorful petunias; next to it stood a cast-iron chair and a cheap outdoor end table. An old park bench had been pushed against the cleaner's back wall.

Manny had followed Shazz out the door and sat down on the bench.

Shazz walked slowly around the edge of the clearing to see what had changed. Burns apparently still used the place: a gallon-sized plastic soda cup stood on the ground next to the chair. Burns drank two or three a day.

The big tree had been cut down… but two smaller ones had grown in its space.

No more woodpeckers, Shazz thought. *But the jays will still be here, and the cardinals.*

"Who would have thought a place like this existed back here?" Manny asked.

"This is where we used to hang out between deliveries," Shazz said. "I worked here a couple of times back in high school."

He looked at where Manny was sitting.

"That bench has been here since before the cleaners."

Manny straightened up to look down at her wooden seat. It was an old park bench with ornate ironwork and wooden slats painted green; an unruly bush with long grasping tendrils reached around each end.

"Oh," Shazz said, his gaze coming to a shoulder-high sapling. "It's an oak."

Manny gave him a puzzled look.

"Oak leaves," he said, reaching out and turning a sharp-lobed leaf toward her.

Strange how that small patch of earth grew, he thought. That's what he had missed about the northeast: its dark rich earth, almost an oil.

Shazz was still a little freaked out about the fight the day before. What was that all about? What if he hadn't been there? His mind was starting to roll when Manny interrupted him.

"So what are you going to do?" she asked.

"I'm going to get my stuff and get out of here," he said. "You guys go to the press conference and take care of that stuff. I can't be there."

Manny didn't respond, and her silence finally set Shazz off.

"I can't be a part of something I don't believe in," he spat. "How do you know what justice is? Who makes up all these rules?

"What's right is right," he concluded. "If I had my way, I'd kill all those guys."

He felt bad as soon as he said it. Not because he didn't mean it, but because he saw how it hurt Manny. Her entire frame deflated, as if she, too, had been on the fence about how she wanted justice to be served to the monsters who had danced with glee around the bodies of the people she loved… such good people.

She wanted them dead too. She wanted them crushed, just like Shazz did. But she knew it was wrong. She knew *that* demon should never be let out: violence was always wrong.

In a defeated voice, she spoke: "You *are* the Milgrams now, Shazz."

Shazz dutifully trailed his mother through a maze of circular clothing racks. A gangly teen, he was already a foot taller than her.

He scanned the vista before him; a lazy stream of evening shoppers flowed along the walkways bordering their field of apparel, but the field they crossed had only a few grazers.

He had a hard time keeping up with his mother as she went her way along their serpentine route. The path was narrow, and the dry wool jackets of the clothing racks, roughed the outsides of his arms, forcing him to twist sideways as he moved.

By the will of God, they came face-to-face with a former neighbor of theirs, right at the center of the maze. They knew Milisandra from before the exodus. Theresa had never been close with her, for no reason in particular, and when Milisandra had moved out of their neighborhood, they had not kept in touch. She had been part of the tribe that had up and moved across the longest bridge around, when "the others" had moved in.

Upon seeing Theresa after such a long time, Milisandra physically latched onto Theresa: holding onto her arm and not letting go. With desperation in her voice, she began pouring out her tales of woe: she was on nine different medications, her job was trying to screw her, her son's girlfriend was rude to her (so she'd teach them a lesson by turning off her son's phone!), she had lupus, she had RA, she had PTSD, she had diabetes, and on, and on, and on…

Theresa assuaged as many wounds as she could before remembering: some people's troubles never end. After ten minutes, she managed to pry Milisandra off of her, and leave just at the limit of politeness.

After they broke free, Theresa headed in the straightest possible line toward the exit. She was visibly flustered.

Shazz followed.

Theresa looked over her shoulder at him.

"Don't be a Milisandra, Shazz."

Theresa's Party

The house was open: its doors thrown wide; even the windows on the side of the house were raised up high. The Milgram team had just won a big case—one of their biggest—something to do with justice. And everybody involved was invited to the party.

The decision had been rendered earlier that morning, and the day was still bright. Everyone had been caught off guard by the sudden settlement, and the Milgrams had nothing planned.

Theresa had sent Stanley and the boys off, to pick up some food from all their favorite places. They would feast. They would celebrate.

Not everyone had arrived yet, but the ones who had, mostly crammed into the kitchen; a few had spread into the backyard. A couple sat together on the living room couch.

The dining room—where most of the team's time had been spent during the past few years—was empty. But the table was covered in a paperwork mess.

Manny lingered alone, by the back edge of the table, near the windows. She was still in a daze. The case she had been working on for so long had suddenly vanished. The lack of pressure was disconcerting.

She moved a document here or there with a finger, but didn't lift a one.

She had performed well; not because she was brighter, but because she had worked harder. It was finally over, and she had become the Milgrams' unblemished Lancelot.

The Milgrams had made her their media spokesperson. She had no media training; no scripts, and she had a penchant for straying from strictly businesslike tones and letting her emotions get the better of her. The Milgrams loved it. The media loved it too. She was now as beloved as the Milgrams.

Manny circled the table slowly. Papers that had been in neat piles earlier, now lay scattered. She had just gotten off the phone with her father, who kept insisting that she make a conscious effort to take it all in. They had, after all, beaten City Hall. But she was too numb to feel anything.

In the kitchen behind her, the din of the party was starting to rise; everyone was giddy. Theresa stood at the head of the table, recounting, to hilarious effect, how she had geeked out on a famous actor at a recent fundraiser.

There was a commotion as Stanley and the boys burst in through the backdoor, laden with food. Stanley hopped into the kitchen holding a large platter of calzones in each hand. He mimed a crab as he walked sideways through the door and chased his wife.

Startled by their sudden appearance, Theresa leapt out of the kitchen and into the dining room. By the time she landed, she had already realized the humor in her overreaction and was laughing uncontrollably. She landed right in front of Manny, who was still hovering around the table, dreaming.

Without a word, she hugged Manny, then dragged her back into the kitchen to feed her.

Shazz and Lestor stood beside the kitchen table, smiling at their parents' silliness.

Casey and Lestor

"Lestor!" Casey shouted, upon opening her eyes and seeing Lestor opening the cleaner's backdoor.

Lestor jumped.

"What!" he said a little too loud. "I'm just going out back!"

They looked at each other dumbly for a moment, before bursting into giggles.

"Come check it out," he said.

"Later," Casey replied. She turned over and buried her head back into a comforter.

"Okay," Lestor said. He opened the metal door as quietly as he could.

He had been a bit unnerved when he awoke a few minutes earlier. He had dreamt that he died… or rather, he woke at the instant he was about to die, and his heart was racing. He had looked down at Casey and felt safe again.

They had slept at the back of the cleaners, behind an old Singer sewing machine. They had the whole area to themselves. They laid out a pile of down comforters and sat in the middle of them like birds in a nest. Between them lay a small radio, which played quietly all night.

Rumors, and rumors, and more rumors from talk radio, floated in the darkness around them; but Lestor had learned that rumors always blossom at times of crisis. He remembered sitting in school on 9/11 and listening to them float in.

Teachers and parents had run in and out of the classroom all morning: it was two planes, it was ten planes; at one point eighteen hijacked planes were in the air, hovering over the city like the sword of Damocles.

It wasn't until the cleaners' back window warmed with the glow of dawn, that Casey and Lestor had both finally drifted off to sleep.

Shazz and Lestor

"How much can that crane lift?" Lestor asked his big brother.

"That thing?" Shazz answered. "That's nothing. Watch."

Shazz walked over and grabbed the crane's hook, which hung six feet from the ground.

The steel hook was part of the overhaul ball assembly: a "headache ball"—a two-hundred-pound iron ball that kept the crane's cable straight; the hook hung at its bottom. Most people struggled to budge it, but Shazz grabbed it and swayed it toward him as if he were drawing a giant arrow to be shot at the sun.

The crane operator was still sitting in his cab, catching his breath after a hard day's work. He had been watching. Everyone at the site knew Lestor—Shazz's little brother—he often stopped by on his way home from high school.

The crane operator saw Shazz making as if he were in a battle of strength with the crane—holding the hook down—so he began revving the engine to sound as if the great yellow machine were straining… but alas, to no avail. The operator threw up his hands in defeat when Lestor looked over at him.

Lestor thought it was funny every time. Not so much the idea of Shazz being that strong—he didn't think it beyond the realm of possibility. It wasn't even because Shazz used to do the same thing with Lestor's toy trucks when they were younger, and now they played the same game with an even larger toy set. It made Lestor joyful because it made Shazz happy, and Shazz smiling and taking time for something childish was such a rare thing.

Lestor and Shazz stood at the foot of the tangled copse behind the cleaners. They had stood there before, once or twice, long ago, when Shazz had filled in for Burns.

Lestor stooped and peered into the wall of hedges before them. Archaic brick structures arose here and there like Roman ruins; a slunken chain-link fence, rusted to the color of the underbrush, was woven through with vines. He remembered. He had almost begun to think of this place as something he'd dreamed.

There was not much of a path into the bush, only an area where the flora was somewhat sparser; and so Shazz and Lestor had each taken a step into the wilds on parallel tracks. But one could only go so far into that wilderness. If they ever wished to venture farther, they'd need equipment—and then, after hacking their way through about eight lots worth of dense jungle, they'd emerge onto a wide plain of empty, fenced-in cement yards. They'd never gone that far before; never even tried. After so many years, they could still get only a few steps in.

Manny was in the yard too. She sat perched on the lip of the park bench, keeping a wary eye on the grasping tendrils of an unwieldy forsythia that came at her from all sides.

She'd given the brothers space to talk.

Shazz had told Lestor about the gun he found in his room, and the revolver that Forrest had given him; and Lestor had told Shazz the whole story about the strange man who had shoved the bag into his hand… but he still left out his run on Colin's apartment.

"That was Ida," Shazz told him, still a little disturbed by their meeting. "That's the media guy we saw. Do *not* trust that guy. There's something wrong about him. Keep clear of him. Don't trust *anyone* out there. Don't trust anyone Mom and Dad didn't trust. Manny knows. Manny can guide you.

"Make your speech," he advised, "and then get away from here. Go north. Stay at Casey's parents' for a while; maybe the whole winter.

"I'll head south," he informed Lestor, "and come back when things calm down—and then we can figure out what we're going to do. The guns are stashed. I'll get rid of them when no one's around."

"Wait, you're going?"

Lestor was flummoxed. He didn't want to be the voice of the Milgrams. He had walked a few steps along the family path: he'd done marches and picket lines, and slept a few nights with the Occupy Wall Street movement. It had all been fun. But he wanted his own life. He wanted to start a family, and he wanted his parents to instill their values in his children, and he wanted Shazz to be an uncle. But now all that was gone. He had no family to grow into.

Lestor's eyes began to well up.

"We need to be strong now, Lestor," Shazz said. "We can mourn later. Right now we have to work."

The backdoor opened with a short screech, and Roddy poked his head out.

"What's up?" he asked.

"Take a walk with me to check out the apartment," Shazz said.

He turned back to Lestor.

"We'll be right back. I just want to make sure the apartment is clear. We'll figure this all out later."

He and Roddy left.

A minute later the door opened again, and Casey came out, followed by Burns.

"Those guys!" Burns shouted with a hoarse voice. "They went out."

He was carrying a fresh, 64-ounce cup of diet soda, a long red straw sticking out of its top. He walked over to his iron chair and sat down.

Casey walked over to Lestor and embraced him for a long, quiet moment. Then they sat on the bench next to Manny.

I just want to get out of here, Lestor thought.

But every time he thought of them all hopping in a car and driving north, the same roadblock kept springing up: Shazz had murdered someone—and that would never go away.

"How could he have done that?" Lestor said aloud.

Manny and Casey perked up.

Burns sat like a statue, his hand attached to his big cup of soda.

Lestor was surprised himself that the words had slipped from his mouth.

He looked at Manny and Casey on either side of him and spoke: "He doesn't believe it. He doesn't believe all these things I'm going to say. Why should I?"

"Lestor, you need to do this," Manny said.

She was afraid she was losing two battles now.

And where Lestor would have normally smiled in the past—acquiescing at the slightest pressure to avoid conflict—this time he didn't.

He got up and walked back into the cleaners.

Shazz's father stood at the center of a crater in the middle of his kitchen: *he* had been the bomb, and all streams of debris pointed back to him. His head was bowed, his arms hung at his sides, his palms facing forward, beseechingly.

Shazz had just missed it. He had come from his friend's apartment down the hall; from a place of happiness and light, to this: a black hole of despair.

Shazz didn't know why his father had exploded. He didn't care. He was used to it by now—the blight—and he could leave anytime he wanted. His friend's family knew about his father: they wore a look of concern and shook their heads when they talked about him. His rages could be heard throughout the building.

They had given Shazz a standing invite to stay over any time he wished.

In fact (Shazz thought, upon seeing his father standing there) he would pack up some things from his room and head right back out. Why stay?

His father stood like a statue, stunned, overwhelmed by the rage that had just coursed through his body. He quaked like a hyperventilating child at the end of a hard cry.

Shazz walked into his room and closed the door.

Lestor steadied himself with a hand against the wall at the top of the stairs. He was inside the cleaner's stairwell to the basement. He couldn't see a thing. While the interior of the cleaners was comfortably illuminated by the daylight that seeped in, once the door to the basement closed behind him, Lestor's world went black. He kept a hand on the wall because he knew that a few inches in front of his feet, a narrow staircase dropped down steeply.

Even when the electricity was on, the two bulbs hanging from the basement rafters were not enough to see much. That was why the owner of the cleaners always kept a flashlight on the inside of the doorjamb.

Lestor stood in the dark for a while before turning on the flashlight. Beneath his hand he could feel the timeworn cinderblocks, crumbling at the slightest pressure: he heard the light patter of sand raining onto the wood beneath his feet.

He turned on the flashlight and saw the stairs. The passage down seemed hewn from solid stone. He had never been down there, but Shazz had: his brother used to scare him with tales of giant insects. But Lestor wasn't afraid of any insects now—he was too angry—and his vision was blurred by teary eyes as he made his way down the rickety stairs.

He had seen Shazz and Burns go down earlier… and it wasn't hard to figure out why. He saw the look on Burns' face when he came back out.

Lestor found the guns right away. They had been wrapped in a white T-shirt and slid under a pile of shovels.

He reached in and picked out a large chrome revolver. He had not seen it before. He walked back up the stairs and returned the flashlight.

When he opened the door back into the cleaners, he saw Burns walking in from the backyard.

"Lestor!" Burns shouted on seeing the gun.

Lestor ran out the front door.

Theresa and Shazz sat atop a whale-sized outcropping of grey Manhattan schist. They were in a small Brooklyn park, right across the street from Shazz's high school.

Lately, he'd been finding it difficult to sit in class all day. Not while the wind roared through the park right outside his windows. Theresa (who knew everyone at the school) had just found out.

The park they sat in was mostly open space, a few blocks square. It was the top of an old, undevelopable hill: the unusable remains of an otherwise built-up neighborhood; a WPA-era stone wall, barely cinched in the dark earth of the park, lifting it five feet up from the sidewalk all around.

Old trees lined the park's borders and roughed its crest; a hidden playground in the far corner, a city tennis court around the bend.

The stone they sat upon was wrought: striated with deep scars from ice ages past… North south, north south: a thousand-foot wall of ice—a continent-sized glacier—had rent the earth to its bones. North south, north south… they could still feel its power beneath them.

A little farther along the hill, a gnarled Himalayan pine, stooped like a Nihonga cliché. It leaned over a perfectly auburn pool of its own needles.

The colors were pleasing… its scent. The tree was in its perfect place: protected in the shadow of a small hill, shielded from the steel gaze of the Manhattan skyline.

They had come to an agreement. Shazz would finish high school. He had a plan. Other plans would be formed. The world would go on.

It was almost three. They would both go to pick up Lestor from his school. He'd be excited to see Shazz: to show him off to his friends.

Theresa stood up and slapped pebbles from her jeans.

"You know what?" she said. "Let's go to Riis Park. We'll pick up your brother, and drive to the beach."

"But it's winter," Shazz said.

"Have you ever *seen* a beach in winter?"

Forrest

Forrest stared down at the street from his second-story vantage point. It was daylight, and they were in another walkup; this one at the very end of Lestor's block. Behind him, Carl and Floyd were sleeping.

Carl had set his body upright against the far wall, his backpack still on. His legs stretched out toward the windows, his head lolled back. He drifted in and out of consciousness, every so often opening his eyes to find Forrest silhouetted against the tall, bright windows, like a child pining to go out and play.

Floyd lay on his side beneath a cheap folding table in the corner, his back toward the room.

They were in the same building they had been crawling over the night before.

After a night of no action, at dawn, Floyd had entered the building through the rooftop door. He made his way down to the second floor and broke into the apartment, whose fire escape Carl sat on. The apartment had been empty, as the whole building seemed to be.

When Floyd opened the window to let Carl in, Forrest popped up from behind a green dumpster. Right away, he ran around to the front door of the building and forced himself in. Once again, he kept guard at the windows.

Forrest wasn't certain of what he was seeing when Lestor ran by down below. He was exhausted; the best his mind could do was translate the entire scene into a single image—a comic book panel: a Jack Kirby action shot: Lestor, midstride, holding a large silver revolver, chest high, barrel to the sky; as if holding it upright were keeping its contents from spilling out.

But once Forrest *had* confirmed in his mind that yes, indeed, he had seen Lestor run by with *his* gun in his hand, he leapt to his feet.

"Get up," he shouted, and ran to the door. "This is it! Lestor's on the move!"

Carl opened his eyes and stared vacantly.

Forrest didn't hesitate. He reached down and grabbed Ed's AK, which he had salvaged the night before, along with his last two clips; then he ran out the door.

Floyd hadn't budged. Carl closed his eyes again.

By the time Forrest made it down to the sidewalk, Lestor was gone. But he could have gone only one place: the projects right across the avenue.

That's all there is! he thought. *That armada of identically insipid brick buildings, anchored in a sterile green bay.*

He ran across the street, weapon at the ready. This was how he was going to go out. *Pow!*

He ran between the parked cars and into the midst of the buildings. The path curved to the right and so he curved to the right then stopped, in front of the first building.

The entrance was all brushed aluminum and heavy duty plexiglass. Soft daylight fell halfway into the lobby; beyond that were shadows.

Forrest burst his way through the front doors.

CHAPTER 27

"...I awoke one day with the urge to own copper," Jabba said. "Not burnished ingots or foul, stinking pennies, but nuggets, plucked up fresh from the earth."

Jabba was on a talking jag.

"Those were the days before I had ascended," he continued.

"I had to go to a mineral show, to find the nuggets: all gnarled and shiny weight; with rocky inclusions like generations old chewing gum, wedged into the corner of some public building's lobby... but they were too bitey: like the rasping teeth of a baby nurse shark.

"I worried the element in my hands for days, before I realized that it was too strong: its fields were too harsh.

"But I needed it to be close by.

"So I buried the element in the soil in the back of my residence."

Eh?

Jabba's focus was broken by the pale visage of Ida, floating quietly in the darkness at the other side of the room.

Jabba had forgotten that Ida was there. He had forgotten that he was even talking, aloud. Thought it was all going on in his head... *Ah well, no mind.* He zoned in on Ida sitting there and continued.

"And that's when I knew what we are."

His face twitched, subducting his eye like a frog.

"Element, delivery," he said. "We are at the planet's beck and call. Entropy."

Ida never felt quite at ease in Jabba's office. It was buried in the bow of the boat, and was small and airless, and set up all backwards. They were at the *back* of the room, speaking across the length of a wooden desk, and everything in front of the desk lay in darkness. The only light in the office came from the bathroom, and a small group of computer screens on the desk.

Jabba stood in the doorway of the bathroom as if he were on a tall narrow stage. He presented himself in profile, as he usually did; this time in pear shaped silhouette, against the well-lit bathroom.

Ida sat awkwardly on a smooth wooden bench. He rested on his hip, like a merman who had just scrambled onto a seaside rock: his legs pointing toward the darkness in front of the desk, and his head, toward the exit door in the corner next to him. The upper half of his body twisted at a grotesquely acute angle to upright, so he could watch Jabba. The tips of his toes hung just a drip from the floor.

...barely knows I'm here, he thought.

Ida had learned that it was best to just let Jabba rave on under the influence of whatever molecules he happened to be currently working with, to peg his senses to a high static. Round and round he'd go; over and over his senses would roll, independent of consciousness; under and around, he'd reach out through his screens and feel the world the way a blind man reads until, with one quick scoop, he'd capture it: a sure thing. And then both of them, Ida and Jabba, would shower 'neath falls of riches.

"You look like you have gas!" Jabba shouted at him from across the room.

"I'm getting claustrophobic in here," Ida barked in surprise when he saw that Jabba was now focused directly on him.

He slid his body to full upright position, still holding his feet a tad off the floor.

"We gotta go," Jabba said. "The Jodies are heading back out east."

"Ach," Ida said, "*those* people."

He had never met them.

Jabba had gone back to staring distractedly into the bathroom mirror: left eye, right eye, left eye, right eye; chin held high, looking down his nose at his reflection. He wore only an oversized pair of boxer shorts that were pulled up high on his belly. Tufts of hair, leeched of all color, sprouted above each ear like flames from a gas burner.

"So where're *they* going?" Ida asked.

"I don't know," Jabba said. "Some mountain fortress? The Jodies get tired. They need to regenerate."

"Regenerate?" Ida said. "How do they do that? By sticking a zip drive up their ass?"

"The Jodies know everything and they are always right," Jabba said, before falling back to mirror-gazing.

Ida focused on the paneling on the wall behind Jabba to get his balance. It was the only well-lit area of either room, but it was off; its dark, cherry wood, ran horizontally instead of vertically. The paneling of both rooms ran the wrong way; even the ceiling seemed off, with long uniform planks running its length. The ceiling itself seemed to arch down sharply right in front of the desk, but everything in front of the desk was lost in the darkness.

Ida felt as if he were on the inside of a rolltop desk.

"Daotoo!" Jabba yapped.

Ida flinched when this name from his past was said aloud.

"Jeez," he let slip, but stopped.

He didn't want to start Jabba off on a huge explosion of Daotoo's flying this way and that.

"Daotoo, Daotoo, Daotoo!" Jabba cried. "This well has run dry. We must move on."

"No worries," Ida said. "You know the market."

"No no no," Jabba said, while dancing in place on his toes and balling up his fists. "Don't ever, ever, *ever,* think that you know the market. That will make it mad."

"We're getting them at noon," Ida said.

Jabba stopped and turned back to the mirror. He realized the glare from the string of bulbs over the mirror was giving him a headache.

"What's all this talk about tax hikes?" he said.

He stepped closer to the mirror and began to unscrew one of the bulbs until it went out.

"Why does everyone keep talking about tax hikes? Isn't there anything else going on out there besides tax hikes?"

He began going down the line of bulbs, twisting each of them until they went out. When there was one bulb left, he turned and drew the shower curtain open, then began running the bath.

"Three-point-nine percent," he said. "What's wrong with people?"

He reached out and swung the door shut. It closed with a clean brass *click.*

A moment later, the light from under the bathroom door went out.

Ida and Mayor

"By Oak, Ash and Thorn!" Ida cried, as he popped his head up from behind his desk.

He'd been leaning over his chair and fighting with his computer again.

"It's the Mayor and his spark plug of a police commissioner," he said. "… One second."

He leaned back over his chair and started jabbing the computer screen with a long gnarled finger.

"Alright! Alright!" he shouted. "Cancel already! Cancel already! It didn't take this long to scan for viruses last time. Why is it taking so long this time?

"Do you know what it's doing?" he asked the room. "It's reading everything on my computer. Damn these computer guys!"

After finally, getting his computer to obey, he came around the desk and greeted his guests.

The cabin was brightly lit this time, and the unlit Hindu god behind his desk barely registered within the topography of the rest of the room. The larger right side of the cabin seemed a forest scene on an empty stage: its ceiling was a foot lower than the rest of the cabin, and thin wood columns sprouted up along the floor at regular intervals. The columns were painted a flat red and had black capitals in a simple, Egyptian lotus design. A single, out-of-place aluminum light fixture with long florescent bulbs, was mounted on the ceiling between the rows of columns.

Ida wore a saffron-colored Nehru-type jacket that hung well past his waist; an oversized red baseball cap with a wide brim shaded his eyes. The entire silhouette of his body angled down to the point of his soft black slippers.

Ida guided the Mayor to the high-backed lounge chair waiting in front of his desk. It was the only place to sit in the room, aside from Ida's own chair, which always remained tucked into his desk.

The Mayor sank deep into the cushioned chair when he sat. The police commissioner stood deferentially at his side.

"You know the kid's a murderer," the Mayor said. "He's a psychopath, and he shot that guy."

"Wait a minute, wait a minute," Ida said, blocking the Mayor's conclusions with a waving hand. He hopped onto his desktop to sit. He crossed one knee over the other, rested his chin in his hand, then looked down at the Mayor.

A thin slice of mottled, marble skin, showed above the top of Ida's sheer black sock. It was disconcertingly close to the Mayor's face.

When the Mayor looked up at Ida, he felt like a bug under a giant mustard-colored fly swatter.

Ida's leg began to pump.

The Mayor leaned back and tried to slide the chair away, but its pointy legs were caught in the thick carpet.

"A tiger jumps out of its cage and kills someone, you have to put it down," Ida said. "But, a nutjob jumps into a tiger's cage and gets mauled, well, the guy's a nut. He deserved it."

"That's a faulty comparison," the Mayor said.

"I don't think so," Ida replied.

Ida dropped off his desk and walked to a point equidistant between the Mayor and the police commissioner.

He liked the commissioner. He was a cliché; a short, square-jawed man with a permanent five o'clock shadow; a man who had risen through the ranks and worked hard at hard things, like night school, while working full time and raising a family; a man of unquestionable integrity; a man who always stood shoulders back, like all ex-military, and when anyone looked at him, something primal within them said: *law and order.* Ida loved clichés; how quickly they disseminated information. It made Ida happy to see the commissioner had risen in the ranks.

"I'm the Mayor," the Mayor said. "I need to make declarative statements."

Ida began gesturing like a politician and reciting like JFK: "Only through advancements in education can we save our nation."

The Mayor was a little put off by Ida's mocking tone.

"Listen," Ida finally said. "He's not going anywhere. At the right time, just make sure his bed's made up nice."

"And the shooters?" the Mayor asked.

"That guy's crazy for sure," Ida said. "But he knows his stuff. You know he wants to take his band of merry men across the Hudson."

He smiled even wider.

"But don't worry," he said. "It's over this afternoon. Then you can have your announcements and declarative statements."

"It isn't going to be easy dealing with the press?" the Mayor said.

"No, no, no," Ida said. "This is the *best* time to work with the press. We've achieved neutral buoyancy."

The Mayor shrugged his shoulders. *Eh.* He wasn't sure what Ida was talking about, but he had learned to trust him. Everything worked out right, when he was around.

"Well," the Mayor said. "Everything is set up on our end. Let's just hope that kid shows up. He's a runner, you know."

"They'll show," Ida said. "Manny will make sure of that. She knows how close they are to being declared legally insane in the public theatre. And if that happens, well... hey, if a kid's nuts..."

"That girl makes me nervous," the Mayor said. "That's all we need: one brave, photogenic girl to start making a scene."

"I don't think she's so brave," Ida spat. "She's just got some sort of, psychological issues, she's working out in public."

The Mayor furrowed his brow as he pondered his future.

"This is a blessing for you," Ida said. "The whole world knows who you are now. You have brand recognition."

The Jodies

"*Who are the twins? This is who we are,*" their voices sang through the noisy connection.

That was how the Jodies summoned him.

It was some sort of password thing, although they had never officially worked it out. Jabba just always knew what it meant: time to meet.

The Jodies were a tow-headed, brother-sister duo, who always looked as if they had just jumped from the pages of a Dick and Jane children's book, and were racing off on some adventure. Jabba suspected them of being immortal, as they once sang to him: of waking at the foot of a great stone Lamassu, in a stone room, overlooking a wide valley with mountain ridges in the distance.

For each meeting, Jabba was summoned to some bright, chaotic, embarkation point. This time, it was the downtown heliport: a concrete pier jutting into the East River.

Jabba awaited their appearance outside the heliport's terminal.

Opposite him, at the far end of the pier, rumbled an immense palanquin covered in gold and ivory. It seemed to have more than two rotors, but it was hard for Jabba to see because of the tumult it was creating and the harshness of the naked sun overhead.

"You want we should leave now!" Jabba shouted into the blinding gale.

The Jodies sprang from a side building he had not seen before: a geodesic crystalline structure.

"It's asking the wrong question," comes back, high and reedy, in the roaring stream of air.

"Eh?"

Jabba barely held to the ground with the tips of his tennis shoes. He held his arms tight against his sides while the wind bent him up and backwards like a reed.

Tip-tap. The Jodies flitted across the concrete pier like butterflies in a gust of wind. They alit atop the stairs in the dark maw of their flying fortress.

They defy gravity, Jabba thought.

"Air, rock, water; it's all pressure," he hears the sing-song voices high up in the wash.

Jabba's face had been angled toward the sky, and the harsh rays and gale force winds locked him in place like the talons of a giant falcon.

And the singing was repeating now.

"… and there is time, and there is warmth, and there is here, and there are connections, and there is the line… and there is time, and there is warmth…"

And from behind Jabba's head, the warm glow of sunlight bloomed in its intensity until he wondered, *Is this it? Has enlightenment finally arrived? I've heard about the glow... though, false alarms are aplenty for the presumptuous. Though, if it is to happen, it is to happen; no matter the 'I'.*

The fortress lifted and pulled away with a blast and Jabba was back in his dark cave.

Where else should one go to recover from an overexposure of solar rays?

That is how they always are, Jabba thought.

They never told him what they wanted.

CHAPTER 28

Virgil's body knows the sound, even before his mind does: it knows the sound of automatic weapons fire inside a building; it knows the percussive feel, no matter how far away it was, and the dams of adrenaline burst. If he had been alone in his apartment, his mind might have slipped. He might have found himself hiding in a dark corner of his room… under a mattress… behind a dresser, lingering in a nightmare-like trance until the next day. But he's not in his apartment. He's in Mrs. Gittens' hallway, and Austin is staring up at him with a primal look of existential concern, and a different emotion takes over Virgil: protection.

"It's okay," he tells Austin. "It's probably just those kids playing again. Go inside and keep away from the door. You never know… and try to stay low."

Austin walks slowly back into the living room, then drops down onto the couch. He picks up his book and begins leafing through it.

Virgil looks into the kitchen. He sees Mrs. Gittens smiling away and cleaning up after their breakfast. She's wearing big yellow dishwashing gloves, and is oblivious to the situation.

He had come to Mrs. Gittens' apartment earlier that morning, before any of the other doors on the floor had opened. The power was still out, and sunlight smoldered beneath a few of the doors along the dusky hallway.

Virgil turns back and leans an ear toward the buildings hallway... Nothing. He waits a few beats and then cautiously peeks out. The hallway is still deserted.

He steps out and quietly pulls the door closed behind him.

The shots had come from the front of the building. He steps tepidly in that direction.

The stairwell door is half a hallway away. The door hovers like a black monolith at the end of the hall.

There is still no sound, but the silence intensifies, like a forming vacuum that has to pop at any moment. He sidles up to the black portal and listens... Nothing.

He turns to look into the darkness of the stairwell, and as his head breaks its plane, the stairwell lights up with fire. He screams and falls back against the wall. He rights himself quickly then races down the hallway, sprinting toward the back stairwell, certain that he is about to be torn apart. Behind him, fire and steel grind away the world like the angel of death.

Forrest Stairwell

Forrest steals across the empty lobby, then disappears into the stairwell. It's a doorframe with no door: a black rectangle at the back corner of the lobby.

Once inside, he stops.

Where the fuck is he? he wonders about Lestor while panting. *Did he go into a different building?*

He catches his breath and focuses—listening for gunfire—but he hears nothing. His hackles are slowly starting to rise.

Still time to escape.

He detects a soft glow from above; from up and around the first landing. He figures the light is coming from the second-floor hallway.

Someone's up.

His nerves are shocked to high alert when he hears two male voices coming from somewhere up high in the stairwell.

He hears the building's front door open behind him.

He leaps out of the stairwell, slings his AK around the edge of the tiled lobby wall and sprays the building's front entrance.

He scurries back into the stairwell and hides in the dark.

The voices from up in the dark are now focused in his direction.

Now!

"Blitz!" he shouts and pulls the trigger.

He starts up the stairs, lighting his way with bursts of fire. He climbs and shoots, and climbs and shoots, feeling concrete shrapnel raining down on his face as he moves. He leaps out onto the second floor and falls to kneeling position. He looses several shots straight down the hallway—changes clip—and holds.

Where is everyone? he thinks, over his heaving chest.

The hallway is silent. All the doors are closed, and the only light comes from under the doors. He hears nothing from above, nor below. He is alone, and the silence is driving him into a panic. The only safe place is beneath the noise.

Quickly!

He jumps again, back into the stairwell, lighting and shredding; up and around the second landing to the third floor. This time there's no stopping. This time he's making it louder and louder as he marches down the hallway, shooting left and right at the ceiling, kicking doors like a drunken college student tearing through a dorm. He marches right past a confused old woman in big yellow gloves standing in a doorway. He runs the remainder of the hall and disappears into the stairwell at the far end.

He stops firing and blindly leaps down flights of stairs, using only the railing to guide him; down and around, down and around, next level down, next level down, until he is as deep as he can go.

He drops down onto a concrete floor smooth as stone. He's at the bottom of the stairwell. He knows there has to be a fire exit near, but he can't see a thing.

He wraps his arms around his knees and bows his head. His rifle hangs in one hand, its barrel rests on the floor.

"Oh Jesus," he says. "When is this going to end?"

There is silence, but for the high-pitch ringing in his ear, and he's not sure if it's from the gunfire or if the whole stairwell had been rung.

He lifts his head and leans it back against the wall behind him, and stares into the void.

He can feel the gravity of the building—the density of the stone around him—as if the whole building had been poured out in one giant block of concrete.

The King's chamber, he thinks, *Khufu's Pyramid. This must be what the King's chamber feels like; safely buried under a million tons of stone.*

And for a moment, he feels peace.

"And the sound of struggle roared and rocked the earth," he whispers. "Screams of men and cries of triumph breaking in one breath."

That was how Homer described battle. That was how he had always imagined his great battle would be.

And then he realizes again where he is, and he listens. There is no sound. There is no reaction to his action, but he knows his peace will be short-lived, and he closes his eyes in the dark for one more moment, takes a deep breath, and stands.

His rifle is out of ammo, but he still has a pistol. He is safe as long as he has one bullet.

He knows an exit is near. He sticks a hand out in front of him and shuffles forward.

"*Hello… hello,*" he says, as he sweeps the air before him.

"*Hello… hello,*" he whispers, as a form of echolocation.

"*Hello… hello…*" he says a little louder.

"Hello," comes back at him from the void.

Forrest lets out a yelp of terror right as he's hit by an invisible force that lifts and crashes him out through the fire door, planting him on his back in the blinding sunlight. It's Virgil.

The wind is knocked out of Forrest. His eyes are slow to adjust. All he can make out is the silhouette of a great Minotaur, risen from the Earth and standing above him. He struggles to breathe and blindly paws the ground for his rifle.

Virgil sees what he's up to. The rifle is on the ground at his feet. He grabs it by the barrel and flings it off. It cracks high up against a brick wall and falls to the grass in pieces.

The noise frightens Forrest and he fumbles for his pistol now; all the while, his wild eyes stay peeled on Virgil.

Virgil is ahead of him again. He yanks the pistol out of its holster and points it at Forrest's chest.

Forrest freezes. He is completely helpless—and they both know it.

Virgil has every intention of pulling the trigger as he steps back and aims true. He knows who this guy is. There's a good chance he killed someone in his own building.

I am justified, he thinks.

But as he is about to pull the trigger something rises up in him, and he stops.

No.

Forrest flips over and scrambles away on all fours.

Virgil watches him scurry along the curved path toward the avenue, second-guessing himself the whole time; but he is also thrown. He's thrown by the feeling of that *thing* that had risen up to stop him.

And he realizes he's having trouble breathing. His asthma is kicking in.

He needs his inhaler, but all of the inhalers in his apartment are empty. He needs to go to the drugstore.

He starts wheezing. He needs to get an inhaler *now.*

Right across the street from the projects is his drugstore.

No way they're open now, he thinks; but in desperation he goes, following the same path as the shooter.

Shazz Back at Cleaners

Shazz had one picture of his biological father, aside from the small one that was on his driver's license. It was taken long ago, pre-digital age, in front of their building. It looked like some variation of a Polaroid, but was backed by thick white paper. It was age-faded and had long horizontal cracks running across its top quarter. A neighbor lady from his old building had given it to him after his father's passing.

Shazz came across it in Lestor's apartment, when he'd gone back to check it. He hadn't seen the photograph there before. Lestor or Casey had put it up on one of the corner shelves, thinking they were doing a nutritive thing for Shazz, but the photo just made him uneasy.

He knew his father hated pictures; and looking at this one, he could tell by the un-posed posture, that the photo had been taken without permission.

His father stooped toward the photographer with his elbows slightly flared and his chin tilted up, as if he were saying something. Behind him, a frozen snowdrift lay against a brick wall, and the fenced-in grass stuck up in frosted tufts like the wind-blasted prairies of the Great Plains.

With his straight, black hair and high cheekbones, his father's picture reminded him of century-old daguerreotypes of Native Americans, looking uncertain—as if their whole world had been spun out from beneath them.

The picture had probably been taken in fun, but anyone who saw it knew right away, there was no fun there. Shazz was certain his neighbor had given it to him because it somehow seemed a violation.

Shazz took the photo with him. He didn't want it in his brother's life. He alone would bear its burden.

When he and Roddy got back to the cleaners, he was met by everyone in front of the store. They were in a panic. Lestor had just taken off.

Shazz was still trying to understand the situation when Manny snapped at him for not going with his brother to the press conference.

"He's free to do whatever he wants," Shazz said.

"No," Manny implored. "He is not free. He's tied to you! And he won't leave without you because he knows *you'd* never leave without him."

Shazz was flustered.

Casey grabbed his arm.

"He's got a gun, Shazz," she said.

"What?" he said, and looked at her for confirmation. She nodded her head, and Shazz put all the pieces together.

"Everyone stay here," he shouted, and he started running down the block.

He was so angry, he could barely contain himself.

"Everybody! Everybody!" he said through gritted teeth as he ran. "I'm so fucking tired of picking up after everybody!"

He was going to find his brother and drag him back to the cleaners by the hair, if necessary. And then he was going to leave the city forever.

This crowded shithole of a city.

When he heard shooting coming from the projects, he shifted into another gear....

"No no no," he thinks. "Please, don't be him!"

He sprints across the avenue into the projects and sees someone running away from the first building. That's where he heads.

He rips open the outside door and throws a shoulder into the interior door. Its lock bursts open.

He runs across the lobby, sprinting into the stairwell—and stops. Everything has gone silent.

Slowly, he makes his way up the stairs, listening intently. It smells like his firing range. He gets out on the second floor where the scent is strongest and walks into a desolate hallway.

The first door he comes upon is the only door open on the hall. Dust and smoke drift slowly before its sunlit opening—but there is silence. The scene is dreamlike to Shazz as he approaches the open door.

He sticks his head into the bright entrance, and his eyes adjust just in time to catch a woman, taller than himself, leaping at him like a raptor: all claws and crest.

But Shazz is in a foul mood—when the woman lands on him, she lands on a rock. She flails and flails and Shazz feels the sharp sting of nails on his exposed neck and he shoves her back violently against the hallway wall and that stuns her for an instant, before she attacks again, slashing at his face.

The stinging continues and Shazz's anger rises, and he turns full force on his attacker.

He shoves her back and they both fall into her apartment and he's shouting in tongues— vengeance and injustice—and there is no reason in him, just mindless rage, and his hands are wrapped around her neck and her eyes are bulging and he's about to pop her head clear off and he's killing again when in a brief moment of clarity he sees two small hands lying on his wrists.

He lets out a cry of shock and leaps backwards, away from the hands, and against the far wall, then slides down to the floor.

He sits on one side of the kitchen, the woman lies on the other, beneath the kitchen table, coughing and struggling for air; her crying child is on top of her, trying to gather her up protectively.

Such courage, is all Shazz can think.

"It's okay. It's okay, baby," he says, to try to soothe the hysterical little girl. "Everything is okay."

He gets up and leaves.

Howard

Howard stood frozen behind his lobby door. Something had just happened, and he wasn't exactly sure what: a flash and a loud noise, then holes in the plexiglass wall panels to the left and right of him.

Huh?

The noise erupted again. Gunfire from inside the stairwell.

He turned and ran.

He ran out of the building and down the front pathway. He jumped the short chains and cut across the grass of the inner court. He hid behind a corner of the opposite building.

He was torn over what to do. Should he run back into the building? His people were there.

He had no phone. There were no police around.

He is about to step out from behind the wall when he sees a man running in from the avenue. The man ran right into his building and broke through the inside doors.

Is he armed?

He didn't know, but he was sure that he didn't belong there.

He has to be another shooter.

A minute later, a different man comes running out from around the far end of the building. He was hunched over, almost running on all fours, as he scurried out of the projects and into the street.

Should I tackle him? he wondered.

Howard was frustrated.

This is bullshit, he thought. *I'm an Ivy League graduate. I'm out of here.*

He took off, jogging toward the National Guard encampment.

Virgil at the Drugstore

The pharmacy's storefront looks as if it had been blown out by a rocket. Its metal gate blooms outward like a jagged lily. Virgil doesn't hesitate at the entrance. He has no choice but to enter. He cannot breathe.

He steps in through the gaping maw. His shoes crunch onto a field of sparkling broken glass. He stumbles down the center aisle toward the prescription counter in the back. His feet slog through a tide of small boxes: everything has been swept from the shelves onto the floor.

This is his drugstore. He knows where everything is. He knows the asthma pumps are in the back.

A long rattling wheeze rips through his throat with every gasp for air.

Hhhhhhhhhhhh.

His exhale sounds like the screams of a thousand tiny witches.

No! No! No! his mind screams. Real fear begins to overwhelm him. *This can't be it! I can't die now!*

The pharmacy section of the store has its own separate metal barricade: one that pulled down from the ceiling to a chest-high counter.

This is where the treasure was kept. That gate, too, has been breached: peeled up and bent over like the page of a metal book. Virgil sees pill bottles all over the floor in front of the counter.

He's sure asthma pumps must be there somewhere; looters would have been concentrating on pain pills. To his relief, he sees the familiar shape of the box of an asthma pump, on the floor at the base of the counter.

He lunges for the box and tears it open... and just as he's freeing the pump from its inside packaging, he catches the glint of a bright silver revolver in the corner of his eye. He reacts.

Virgil goes at Lestor like an offensive lineman: shoving and shoving and launching him backwards over an overturned garbage can of construction debris. The gun flies and disappears beneath the clutter on the floor.

Lestor recovers his senses just in time to see Virgil drawing a discarded steel pipe from the overturned can. He barely has time to reach out and grab something for protection.

Fortuitously, his hand finds another pipe and manages to raise it up and over his head just as Virgil's pipe smashes down. A shower of paint chips and dirt fall all over him and rain down into his eyes.

A horrifying wheeze rips through Virgil's throat as he tries to draw in more air.

HHhhhhhhhhhhh

Lestor is almost blind as he tries to rise while holding up the pipe protectively.

Virgil strikes again, and Lestor drops back down.

HHhhhhhhhhhhh.

Over and over, Virgil lifts and smashes, and lifts and smashes; and each time he knocks the pipe from Lestor's grip, and each time Lestor barely manages to lift it back in time.

The struggle seems eternal: as if it's the only thing either of them have ever done; as if it's the only thing they will ever do....

Lift... *"HHhhhhhhhhhhhh"*... Smash.

Lift... *"HHhhhhhhhhhhhh"*... Smash.

Virgil wheezes so loudly now that it wakes him from his own nightmare, and he sees Lestor as if for the first time.

He is almost buried. Only his arms and head rise above the debris on the floor. He's coated in a fine white powder and looks like a statue, straining to break free from the earth, while holding his steel pipe up, against the rain of blows from above.

Shazz hits Virgil like a cannonball and bounces off of him. He lands on the floor next to Lestor. Virgil's momentum is slower to get moving. His body pauses for an instant, before being forced to take its first, stagger-step, backwards, through the river of boxes: one heavy step... two... two, tip and crash against a set of metal shelves, taking them down to the ground with him.

Shazz is up before Virgil even lands. With one hand, he lifts Lestor to his feet by the scruff of the neck; then he steps forward to finish the job.

With fists of stone, he advances toward the large man on the floor: now hopelessly tangled amidst the debris.

One shot to that bulbous temple—one steel-tipped boot to the liver—and this debilitated man, struggling for air, will die.

But Virgil doesn't see them anymore. His eyes are vacant, as he tries to right himself. He reaches out, feeling around for something that is not there.

The brothers stop and watch. The sound of Virgil's breathing is painful to hear, and for a moment, they actually fear for his health.

There is no danger here, Shazz understands, only someone who needs help.

He sees the blue inhaler on the ground, the same type Lestor used to use when he was a kid. With a foot, he slides it over to Virgil. Virgil grabs it desperately then raises it to his mouth and starts pumping. His mind slowly comes back to him.

The three men look at each other and realize: none of them has any desire to be in this situation.

Lestor puts his hand on his brother's shoulder. They back away and leave the store.

Outside, the traffic lights are blinking; the power is back on.

The brothers walk down the avenue and turn the corner onto their street, heading back to the cleaners.

As they pass their apartment, Shazz stops.

"Please," he implores his brother. "Go back to the cleaners. Then go right to the fields and read your statement. I will meet you there."

Lestor does not question this time. He nods and walks off in a daze.

Shazz had seen Forrest's elbow in their apartment window as they walked by.

Of course, it's not over, he thinks.

Stairs

"I never told you guys," Forrest said, "but I wiped out of basic… I never really got along.

"I *wanted* to fight.

"What better place to die, than on the battlefields where Alexander himself had shed blood?"

Since making it back from the projects, Forrest had managed to convince his remaining cohorts to go back to Lestor's apartment. It felt safer there, in the middle of the block, and the Milgram apartment had a comforting air to it.

"Alexander left home at twenty-one and never returned. He spent the next twelve years of his life, tearing across the known world... supposedly in revenge for the burning of Athens a hundred years earlier by the Persians... that's Iran.

You see. Greece... Iran... there have always been lines in the sand.

"Alexander avenged the Greeks. He beat the Persians... but he never stopped. He kept on to India."

Forrest thought about it for a while.

"Funny how his biggest problem was probably racism. His troops didn't like him dressing in native garb or marrying native women, or bringing Persian military officers into his ranks... that's probably why they killed him."

They heard the building's door open downstairs: someone started walking up. None of them moved.

Halfway up the stairs, the person stopped.

"Guys," Shazz called. "It's me."

There was no response.

Shazz climbed the rest of the stairs, then poked his head into the open door of his parents' old apartment; the three men looked up at him.

Forrest sat in the chair next to the window; Carl and Floyd sat on the floor against the walls.

"You need to get out now," Shazz said, slowly and adamantly. "Your time is up. Just leave the weapons here, and I will bring you in safely. 'Cause you are all about to die if you don't. This is it. No more fucking around. It's over."

None of them made any effort to rise.

"So," Forrest said. "It comes down to the Triarii."

Floyd stood abruptly and started to walk out.

Forrest jumped up quickly and followed.

"Floyd, Floyd," he said. "Wait up. You're racist, right?"

Floyd stopped and looked down at him flatly.

"Sheeeet," he said, in the deepest, darkest minstrel show voice he could muster. "Black or white don't matter. Black man in the army fighting for *my* life. That's good enough for me."

Forrest stood frozen in his tracks. His eyes stared vacantly, as if his CPU had overloaded. He had absolutely no comprehension of the sounds that had just come out of Floyd's mouth.

Thoughts battered around in his head as he struggled to remember: had he ever even heard Floyd's voice before? Those guys never talked: Floyd or Myrons. Mostly only Myrons talked... a little. *"You guys going shootin'?"* was about all he'd ever say.

And then Floyd spoke again; this time in his natural voice.

"Shoot me like a soldier; don't hang me like a dog."

He dropped the magazine out of his rifle and cleared the chamber.

Then he turned and walked out, still holding his weapon.

Shazz moved aside to let him pass.

Forrest was still staring at Floyd as he walked out. Then, as if awakening with a start, he rushed out after him... but not before picking up the magazine and single brass bullet.

He ran off, holding up one in each hand, like a waiter holding two champagne flutes.

Shazz followed them into the hallway: he stopped at the top of the stairs and watched as Forrest hurried down after Floyd.

Carl lagged. He moved past Shazz and onto the staircase. When he was two steps down, a huge blast sounded from the building's front entrance. Shazz dropped to the hallway floor and buried his head in his arms.

The blast fades and he lifts his face to peek over the top step. Forrest and Floyd are gone.

Downstairs the inside of the front entrance now looks like the outside, as dust and smoke swirl around bright new shafts of sunlight. The walls and front door have been shredded by gunfire.

Shazz stares disbelievingly, until he becomes aware that Carl is face-to-face with him. He still stands on the stairs, but he had been turned around by the blast.

He looks down at Shazz, lying on the hallway floor.

"Kid," Shazz says, "you don't have to go."

But he can see the resolve on Carl's face.

Carl rights himself. "Sometimes you deserve to pay," he says, then turns and resumes his walk down the stairs.

Shazz's whole body clenches, knowing exactly what's about to happen.

"NO!" he screams an instant before the next blast hits.

He covers up again.

When he looks up, he sees Carl, still standing…but he's off, as if confused. He faces askew of the front entrance, but still tries to walk out. He staggers, like a drunk trying to get a key in a lock, until finally, he takes a small, deliberate step, over the building's threshold, into open air, and a third blast hits.

When Shazz looks up again, Carl is gone.

Shazz springs up and runs into the vacant apartment behind him. He crouches in the middle of the floor with his thoughts racing. He has seconds. Already he sees smoke and dust drifting up into the hallway from the staircase. His eyes race about, looking for an escape.

The two tall windows at the end of the apartment are bare: no curtains, no shades—just wide-open daylight and a fire escape.

A bright-green tree branch, reaches just high enough to be seen in the window: an *Ailanthus*. Its rows of leaves are crisply delineated in the rays of light: layer upon layer, interleaved, multidimensional. The branch sways as serenely as a palm in a tropical breeze. He wants to make a break for it.

He knows he can make it up the fire escape and onto the roof easily. He could go a few buildings over to a friend's apartment and lay low for a few days; then he could disappear back down south again. Ida would probably leave it at that.

But he has to move *now*.

Already a racket in the front entrance can be heard. The first boots are on the front stoop.

Shazz bolts across the hallway into his parents' apartment. He stands in the middle of the living room and turns slowly, looking each direction.

This is where you should be.

He drops down onto his knees in the middle of the thick carpet. He lies flat on his back, his feet toward the window, his arms are thrown wide.

He waits.

Ray and Chris

The Boneheads' door opens a crack, and Chris sticks his nose out like a nervous prairie dog emerging from its den. His eyes are bulging.

"Whoa," he says. "What was that?"

Ray's head pops out above Chris's. He looks left, then right, down the empty hall.

"Is everybody alright?" he calls out.

Slowly, doors begin to open.

Light trickles back into the hallway.

BOOK III

CHAPTER 29

Petrichor

Shazz raced alongside his new family, back towards the car. They had held out for as long as possible at their lakeside picnic, but now, a mountain-sized cloud mass was rolling in on them.

The sight inspired a primal terror, but there was also elation, as they were in the middle of a heat wave, and every living thing in the baked green Hudson Highlands had been crying out for relief.

The family laughed and tumbled across the fields, their arms filled with chairs and blankets and baskets and bags; and just as their feet crunched down onto the dry gravel of the parking lot, Theresa yelled, 'Stop!' and held a finger up.

A smattering of heavy raindrops had already started to kick up the dust around them. Pollen was being knocked into the air; the low scent of ozone was growing.

The clouds had snuck up on them. They had spilled over the ridge at the far end of the lake, and were now gliding across its rippling water, so laden that they could barely stay aloft. A deep guttural growl preceded them. Lightning was about to crack. But Theresa still held her family back with a finger.

They huddle together as other families race past, squealing with glee. Shazz is excited too. He can't wipe a smile from his face. He can't stand still either. Eagerly he looks up at Theresa for a cue, but she's not looking at anything in particular, and so he's not sure what's going on. His smile begins to relax. His thoughts spin and spin and search for meaning until...

Oh...this.

"Okay," Theresa shouts. "Go!"

Fleurette Africaine

Virgil stepped through the dugout entrance onto the East Side playing fields. The section of playing fields he was on, were four baseball diamonds, daisy-chained and swaddled round by a twenty-foot-tall chain-link fence. The media and various relief agencies had set up shop over most of the outfields, and the area resembled more of an outdoor festival than anything official.

Virgil had entered through the first base side of the north field. A loose crowd milled about its infield, awaiting the start of the press conference. A wide stage had been set up at home plate.

City officials were taking turns at the podium, speaking to a mostly uninterested crowd. Everyone was biding their time, waiting for the main event: Lestor Milgram.

In his hands, Virgil held a shoebox. Inside it were the pieces of three handguns: the pistol he'd taken from Chris and Ray, the pistol he'd taken from the gunman, and the revolver that had been dropped at the drug store. He had disassembled the weapons and tossed all the small pieces into sewers on his way there. He was there to turn what remained over to the authorities.

He scanned the crowd in front of the stage and didn't recognize anyone. He scanned the back of the crowd and saw Howard standing across the field, near third base.

Howard's body faced first, but he didn't see Virgil. He wore an indignant scowl on his face and didn't look in any one direction for long. He looked off toward the buildings looming large over the outfield fence, then he looked back toward the crowd in front of the stage; and as his view swept between the two, his body rocked in place like an elephant driven to madness by being chained to one spot.

The crowd roused, and Virgil turned to see what the commotion was. He looked back toward right field and saw a small group of men making their way toward the stage. He recognized the person at the center of the group. It was the kid from the drug store. It was Lestor Milgram—he realized just then.

The group made their way down the first baseline toward the stage. Lestor stood a head taller than the men around him. When they reached first base, the two tall men—Lestor and Virgil—faced each other alone, above the group.

Lestor recognized Virgil right away, and initially both of their guards were raised; but on seeing each other clearly, under the light of an open sky, they each quickly seemed to understand the seas that they had all been swimming in.

Lestor stopped, throwing his handlers into a tizzy. He ignored them and reached his hand out through their protective wall. The two men shook hands then parted without a word.

Virgil watched as Lestor continued to the stage then stood beside the Mayor. Then Virgil walked across the field to where Howard was standing. He took Howard's hand and put it atop the shoebox.

"Come on, Howard," he said. "Let's get rid of these things."

Ed

Ed lay back on the unmown grass with his arms thrown wide and his palms facing the night sky. He rested his head against a jutting stone from the base of a well.

His grandfather had built the well: a crude stone structure of scintillating white marble. He had scavenged the stones from a local quarry. He had heaped the irregularly shaped blocks into a coarse ring, with thick, slovenly bands of concrete in between each heavy stone, and *on* each stone and… sixty years later, it still looked as if he had suddenly realized, that building something as simple as a round wall was a lot harder than it looked. But Ed loved it.

He used to fear those stones. Their crevasses and overhangs held spiders and snakes; but on this night, he would have simply brushed them away.

It had taken him almost a full day to get home. He had walked the length of Manhattan, and crossed the GW Bridge, just as the morning sun rose at his back.

He spent the next six or seven hours walking barefoot through the vegetation alongside the Palisades: north, always north. All the while, the naked sun glared down at him mercilessly.

By the time he was offered a ride by an elderly couple, he felt as if he had just crossed the Judaean: his lips were cracked, his face was burnt, his feet bruised and bloodied.

A couple had seen him sitting on the curb at a rest stop parking lot; they had figured him to be a lost addict in need of help.

They didn't have shoes to give him, only a pair of oversized, ankle-high rubber galoshes, which flopped around Ed's bare feet as he walked.

He didn't say much during his long car ride north, and the couple didn't ask many questions. They had done a good deed. That was enough for them.

The sun was well down by the time they dropped him off; close enough to walk the final few miles home.

The field that Ed lay on sloped gently down from his grandfather's house: down to a gravel road that ran for miles before hitting asphalt. A tangle of tall loose bushes and a few stout willows, shielded the field from the road. Behind him, a short line of dark green firs shielded the house from the field. The only other things on the small field, aside from the marble well that was tucked into a corner, were a few anemic apple trees.

Ed's grandfather had conjured it all. He had built the house, planted the trees, dug the well, fenced a garden, and constructed a long pergola for grapes.

Ed's own Proustian trigger involved the Concord grapes that hung from the pergola. Just catching a hint of their ambrosial aroma transported him back to his youth, when he used to sit in the shaded tunnel, as if in the mouth of a giant cornucopia, and pick the ripest grapes of the darkest hues from all around him. He'd pop them out of their skins and into his mouth, and osmose only the very richest of their essence, before spitting them out and picking another.

How had he forgotten that?

Ed's father and uncles had helped with many of these projects; but none of them were around anymore, and so now the house, and the property, and all the dreams born on it, belonged to Ed.

He caught the scent of burning wood. Someone down the road had a fireplace going, but for an instant he thought the smell was coming off of his clothes, and it reminded him:

Oh God, what did I do?

A near full moon illuminated the world around him, and Ed gazed out into the dark crystal sky: an airplane... a satellite... stars. Constellations began to reveal themselves the longer he looked: Cassiopeia... Perseus... And as always, when staring into the firmament, he mused on the past: the ancient Greeks, and Persians, and, even earlier, forgotten civilizations, and he imagined families sitting around fires and staring out at the same obtrusive patterns he looked out on, and making stories about each of them to entertain their young.

A gust of wind washed through the cottonwoods bordering his field. Its slow, patient sound, like a straw broom being drawn across a floor, temporarily hushed a soundscape filled with layer upon layer of frog callings and insect stridulation; and then, for the first time in his life, he saw it: the Northern lights: a great green silence rushing through the sky like blood through capillaries.

Oh, if only they could have seen...

The air was crisp and sweet, and Ed could feel it already healing his wracked body. He closed his eyes and inhaled the breath of the Earth. And he felt grace.

"I will never leave this place again," he promised.

The trees rattled, the insects chirruped; the night choir's song bloomed out into a sky burning with life.

Ida

Ida sat high up in the cab of his big yellow wheel loader. The two-hundred-ton beast was the largest one they made. Ida had just spent the last few hours on a football field–sized patch of earth, ripping the ground and tearing into huge spoil banks.

Oh, how full of the universe that smell is.

The ship was down in the half moon bay being resupplied, while Ida played on a manmade plateau at the top of a looming mountain: a copper mine Jabba was part owner of.

This was where Jabba had first found Ida decades ago; back when he was Daotoo: a shoeless, shantytown orphan, sweeping up for handouts. Now Ida came back once a year or so, to live out his childhood fantasy of driving one of the big rigs.

He stayed off in a secluded area, away from the pit, and no one but the person who ran the mine, knew exactly what his connection to the operation was. The few others who were there on the night tour, figured he was a mechanic, testing out the machine.

Garbed in safari wear, complete with pith helmet, Ida trundled through the darkness with floodlights smoldering for so long, he began having delusions of sailing across the abyssal plains in an underwater ship; and, like in nightmares, only the areas within his sphere of light were safe and known, while just beyond, horrible monsters circled in the darkness.

He shut down his machine and took his helmet off. He wiped his brow with a small towel.

He was feeling melancholy after having failed to win over Shazz.

He would have been a strong piece, he thought.

"Ach," he said, shaking his head. "I did it all wrong. I shouldn't have brought him in that way."

Shazz had been strapped down to a gurney and carried from the Milgrams' apartment into a waiting ambulance. From there he had been driven directly to the National Guard's camp.

A dozen men, all in white, tightly encircled Shazz's gurney as it was wheeled through the crowd. All the men were dressed as doctors: all in white, with masks and caps; all facing forward, none of them saying a word.

At one point, one of the men, in a clean white mitre, began casting glances down at Shazz. Shazz looked back quizzically, until the man finally pulled his mask down and smiled broadly.

Initially, Shazz was too taken aback by the odd-looking face to recognize it: the pinhole eyes, the amphibious jaw. Then the man winked and pulled his mask back up, and he managed to disappear in plain sight by falling back in sync with the other clones. By the time it hit Shazz who it was, he had been dropped off in the center of a large black tent befitting a Bedouin sheikh.

A few minutes later, Ida came rushing in like an excited middle schooler who had just gotten away with a prank. He had changed; now he wore a banana-yellow, velour tracksuit with a white racing stripe and a white terry cloth bucket hat. His glasses were back on: oversized and amber tinted.

"Have you heard about the Catatumbo lightning storms?" he began, while going to work, undoing Shazz's ankle straps. "It's a lightning storm that's been going on for centuries. It's at the mouth of this river in Venezuela.

"It's so consistent," he explained, "that ships use it as a natural lighthouse."

He paused before resuming. "And we're gonna park right next to it!"

He stopped working on the straps and looked down at Shazz to see if he was paying attention. Then he started again.

"The Ganges," he said. "Palenque… the trickling wall at the head of the Amazon… castles. There is so much going on out there. Have you ever been in a castle? They don't have real ones here, but they are everywhere in the old world. What a feeling one gets inside a castle, safely buried beneath so much stone. You can feel its gravity."

He moved up to the chest straps and stopped again to think.

"… or maybe the pure harshness of the Siberian wilderness. You'd love that. To feel the cold breath of a Russian winter in the taiga." He looked down and nodded again in affirmation of his own statement. "Dangerous even with a lifeline."

He started to undo the chest straps.

"… Or perhaps, an uninhabited atoll in the middle of the Pacific; you walk just a bit into an island forest and look up, and you're surrounded by angel terns of the purest white, and they hover all around you… like real angels."

Shazz didn't speak. He kept a wary eye on Ida as he undid each strap.

"… A pilgrimage to Mount Fuji… the silent sand deserts of Africa… the Mongolian grasslands… Northumbrian megaliths… the Levant…"

Ida finished undoing the last strap and tossed it over Shazz's body to the other side of the gurney. Then he took a step back.

Shazz sat up and scanned the tent. There was no one else there.

He hopped off the gurney and walked out.

Ida sat back in the cab of his loader and shook his head again.

I did it all wrong, he thought.

But he cheered up quickly.

Ah, but life is long.

In a few hours he'd be setting off in the dark, on a terrifying journey across open water.

Jabba

Jabba walked into his bathroom: nude, with a blinking, vibrating, purple butt plug, firmly ensconced in place, and three brilliant ideas, freshly hatched in his mind. He repeated his ideas in his head so as not to forget them; then he quickly jotted them down on a notepad that sat on the bathroom counter.

A word for each would suffice: to help him recollect later... Also, he needed to make a list of which drugs to get rid of quickly, while he still had the strength. They had completed their task of lofting him up and into a high plane—just long enough for him to receive his ideas.

He scribbled down one final reminder—*CALL IDA*—before stepping into the tub.

He had gone stale for a while and needed a boost, but it was best not to linger too long in the death zone. Be thankful, be humble; get out fast.

"Elements," he mumbled, and stepped into the bathtub.

He swung the bathroom door closed and turned off the lights.

Certain elements needed to be removed from his environment or they would dominate it.

On his desk lay a ten-ounce bar of silver, which he worried to help maintain equilibrium. He also had a short, but weighty chain of pure gold that he would wear atop his head… for equilibrium; jasper, lapis, hematite; onyx, alabaster, turquoise, carnelian. The Jodies' had never told him about these things, because they didn't care if he burned out. They had a whole roster of guys like him.

Elements were what helped him maintain the fields around him.

He drew the shower curtain closed and lay down in the bath tub.

"The elements must be gotten rid of. The elements shall be gotten rid of."

Shazz

Shazz stood at the foot of the aluminum staircase at the side of the stage. It was a short set of steps: only three, up to the stage and podium from which Lestor had just spoken. Shazz had stayed there while Lestor read his statement and answered questions.

Lestor had addressed the media, flanked on either side by Casey and Manny. Behind him stood the Mayor and a gaggle of public officials and religious leaders; in front of him stood a small legion of press, aiming their weapons at him.

The rest of the gathering was filled with well-wishers and first responders. Shazz recognized many of the people in the crowd: friends of the family, others from the "movement." A few even recognized him and came over to express their condolences and support. With the feeling he was getting from the crowd, he half-expected to see his parents come walking up to him at any moment.

Lestor had been relieved to see Shazz already at the fields when he arrived. He stood with Casey and Manny beside the stage. Roddy and Burns had stayed back at the cleaners, waiting for Shazz. None of them had heard about what had happened at the apartment, until Shazz told them. They were shocked, but they carried on.

When they had come off the stage, Lestor and Casey both hugged Shazz and then ran off to see a group of Lestor's students, who had shown up to support him.

Shazz could already see that their demeanors had lightened. When they joined with the high school students, an emotional dam seemed to have burst, and the couple began to beam as they always had before.

Manny had stayed back with Shazz and watched the jubilant reunion.

Shazz knew those fields well. He had played on them when he was a kid: before he met the Milgrams. He took a deep breath and caught scent of the old sycamores lining the pathways of the park. His nostrils flared when he also caught the acrid smell of the powerful antiseptic, used to clean the nearby public restrooms, but it passed quickly.

God I had fun here, he thought.

He remembered a diving catch he had made at third base, and how it had happened so naturally. How he didn't even think about it; it just happened. He didn't even play third base. But there he was, making a perfect Craig Nettles dive. He didn't throw the guy out at first; but still, decades later, he wondered about that catch.

How the heck did I do that?

Shazz was surprised when he looked over at Lestor again, and saw that the family of the couple who had been killed by the police was there also: the Martin family. Everyone in the family was tall and thin and well dressed, and one of the men was carrying an equally well-dressed eight-month-old. He was the boy who had been on the front pages of all the papers.

Shazz was alarmed at first, but then, he realized there was no reason to be. He watched the interaction with fascination: the instant bonding, the hugs, the smiles. The boy was passed to Casey, who held him for a while before handing him off to Lestor.

The press seemed to have forgotten about the group; no one was paying much attention to them anymore. The students around them were laughing and carrying on… one or two were taking video of the meeting with their phones. But Shazz watched as his brother held the child, and the two youngest sons smiled at each other as if old friends.

Shazz had been impressed by how well his brother had done. Speaking to the press seemed to come naturally to him. Perhaps it was a result of having grown up around these sorts of events, or perhaps he only had good things to say.

Lestor looked up with a smile still on his face, and noticed his brother watching him.

They locked eyes, and Shazz smiled with pride for his younger brother.

Lestor would be fine, he thought. He hadn't noticed until then how much his brother had grown while he was away. And now here, among his people, he could see that Lestor was at home.

The smile remained on Lestor's face, but his eyes softened as he realized that Shazz was up to something.

Shazz stood facing him with one hand on the railing. When he put a foot up on the first step, Lestor understood. And Shazz could swear he saw his little brother grow taller when he realized what he was going to do—and then all was right in his world again.

He was about to ascend the stairs when he remembered Manny. He had to tell her *something*.

He turned to see where she was and flinched, because she was right next to him—a beatific visage of compassion.

She had seen what he was going to do and moved to go right with him.

"No," he said.

He thumped his chest with his thumb a few times: "I'm on me."

Whatever fortune left is mine, and I alone must atone for my crime.

Manny said nothing.

Shazz turned back toward the stairs. The stage was now a chaotic patch of real estate. People in suits stood around shaking hands and negotiating who was going to speak next. Stagehands and sound technicians were scampering about making adjustments.

Shazz took a deep breath and stared up into the cloudless sky.

I have my strength, he thought. *I have my strength.*

A gentle breeze rolled in from the north, and beneath all the noise on the fields, he heard the rustling leaves of the sycamores.

He put his hand back on the cool aluminum railing and ascended.

Manny walked up the stairs besides him.

Lestor and Casey

Lestor and Casey sat shoulder to shoulder on the top step of his parents' front stoop in Brooklyn. All evidence of the nightmare that had taken place there had been cleansed: washed away by a river of flowers and prayers. A shrine had sprung up at the Milgram house: flowers and candles, signs and photos.

The two seemed to be sitting atop a falls of offerings—a falls that flowed from their front door, down the brick steps, and pooled on the sidewalk in front of their home.

It had brought them to tears when they first saw it that morning.

They went in through the backdoor and spent most of the day cleaning.

When they came out for air, Lestor had to move aside a poster and some large candles so they could sit. LOVE CONQUERS HATE, it read.

"Is that a Bible quote?" Lestor asked.

Casey spent a few seconds looking it up on her phone.

"It's derivative of Marvin Gaye."

They both laughed.

There was construction going on down the block. A few of the houses that had fire damage were being repaired. They could hear hammering and electric saws. A couple of workers were shouting to each other. The sounds started and stopped with a calming regularity.

It was almost dinnertime, and one of their neighbors was cooking something spicy: Jamaican food?

They heard more sounds of life: children playing, the gentle clacking of dishes being set, and in their minds, whole household scenes were being imagined.

Lestor held the wind chime from the back porch in his hands. He had finally taken them down from the awning. "Should I get rid of these?" he asked Casey.

Casey looked them over, while Lestor tapped two of the bamboo tubes together, to remind her of the sound they made.

"No," she said. "Let's just move them over a bit."

They smelled Spanish food now, from another neighbor.

Casey inhaled deeply, then made googly eyes at Lestor. They hadn't eaten since breakfast.

"Should we order?" Lestor asked.

He began running through a list of nearby restaurants they could order from: Chinese, Indian, Mexican, Italian, Thai...

"Let's cook at home," Casey said.

She turned and faced him, then took his hands in hers and smiled.

"Are you ready?" she asked twice. Once with words, and again with her expression.

Lestor pulled his head out of the clouds and really looked at her.

There she sat. The woman he loved.

Their bodies mirrored each other.

Their eyes linked. Together, they rose to a higher level.

"Go," she said.

CHAPTER 30

Laughter echoed throughout the hallway: the city was alive again. Inside the Boneheads' apartment, there was a gathering: Chris, Ray, the video game kids, Virgil, Howard, and even Mrs. Gittens, had been drawn in by the commotion; and a new person found himself at the center of the mass: Sterm, the star of the show.

Everyone in the apartment was packed on—or around—the heavy red couch, as if it were a lifeboat at the center of a tan linoleum sea. In front of the couch stood an old rear-projection television set, the size of a large china cabinet. Austin and the younger kids sat on the floor, forming left and right stage wings. And front and center, three fools leapt in equal ecstasy.

Sterm was besting Ray in video football!

The revelation of it had been so startling that it was subliming.

Shy, timid… Third-Class-Sushi Sterm, was beating all-American Ray. Ray, who was all-American at everything.

Epiphanies bubbled to a froth, and Ray and Chris roared glory! Everyone did.

There at the center of the universe, the three men wove all of reality into being. Their hearts flared and their souls beamed, and all of creation swirled right along with them.

The game continued. Beads of sweat formed on their brows, smiles were plastered on faces. The crowd hollered, and the two competitors gave it their all.

Kids in the Basement

"All clear!" shouts the lantern-jawed cop as he lets the basement door slam shut.

He turns to his partner, who's standing outside and holding the building's front door open.

They look at each other expectantly.

The two officers are dressed in identical riot gear: all blue and black, with helmets and vests. They look like twin action figures, but for the different shades of their skin.

SWAT teams had been sent to thoroughly search the Riis Projects from top to bottom. They needed to make sure no more active shooters were present anywhere in the area.

Weapons and casings had been collected. EMS had responded. No injuries were reported.

Cop number one had just finished clearing the basement of Virgil's building.

Cop number two was anxious to move along.

"Is it clear?" he shouts back to cop number one, having not heard him the first time.

"All clear," came back. "Nothing down there but a bunch of kids."

He jogs out of the lobby to join his partner.

"They ain't doin' nothin'," he says, as they meet up.

They jog off to the next building.

The lobby sits empty for a while, like a stage awaiting its players... and then there is movement. At the back of the room, in the small window of the basement door, a face appears. The face looks left then right: straining to see as much of the lobby as possible, before pulling away.

It's Raj.

Inside, at the top of the long stairwell, Raj stood in the dusk. All of his friends were in the basement, huddled quietly in the shadows. They were all waiting on him.

But Raj didn't rush. He selfishly took a moment of peace, and closed his eyes and breathed in deeply... Dank concrete, roach spray...

He opened his eyes and started down the stairs.

He made it down to where he could see the single bulb, hanging in the center of the large room.

"All clear," he called.

And people started moving again.

He clomped down the remaining steps and found a quiet spot at the edge of the room. He sat up on an old dresser and watched the empty circle of light beneath the bulb. It was hard to make out anything else. All the clutter of the basement had been shoved against the walls; only the center of the room was clear.

Raj could see the glistening corner of his radio on the other side of the circle. It sat on some cardboard boxes against the far wall. It was an old radio; one that still played cassette tapes, and he had a whole shoebox full of them. His father had recorded most of them right over the airwaves, back in the day. Raj and his friends were still in the process of discovering them all.

The volume on the radio was still turned down; Raj could see the lights on the equalizer bouncing along to music they could barely hear.

Elbows, shoulders, legs and feet; the billowous dark curls of a serene goddess: all flashed by the edges of the circle, as people milled about in the dark.

And it suddenly occurred to Raj that he was experiencing something beautiful.

A hand reached out from the darkness and gingerly twisted the volume knob higher.

The song was one they hadn't heard before. A familiar beat, but woven through with strains from the other side of the world.

At first, the song was left on as a lark but soon… they were all hooked.

Raj closed his eyes again and let the vibrations wash through him: the twangs of a sitar, the rhythm of drums, the heartbeat of a bass; everyone in the basement fell into sync.

The light bulb was tapped and began to sway in an easy circle.

They were celebrating. They didn't know why: the change of seasons, the end of strife, or maybe it was just the spontaneous blooming forth of life.

They were celebrating as people had always done.

Raj leaned back and squinted, till all he could see through blurry vision were flickering lights and silhouettes: dancing celestials, whirling round the leaping flames of an open hearth. And he felt a powerful stillness…

The music stirred. The lights swirled… and swirled.

The circle began to fill.

EPILOGUE

Theresa and Stanley sat facing each other across a small table. The table was knee-high and had a round top, roughly decorated with colorful mosaic tiles.

Stanley was serving his wife tea.

The tea set had been a wedding gift from his aunt. The table, had been inherited from Theresa's side: a grandfather's trip to Morocco decades ago. It had been a fixture in her room while growing up. It had sat in the corner, buried beneath clothing and toys through her whole childhood. She had been saving it her entire life for this very moment.

They sat in the sunroom of their empty house. They had just moved in.

Tink, tink, tink, were the only sounds in the cavernous space.

The young couple glowed.

Stanley poured out a clear riffling stream of tea into Theresa's porcelain cup; then he filled his own.

The sun streamed into the room from every angle, as if they were at the center of a blazing sun.

Bliss.

Then they picked up their cups and held them with both hands, feeling their warmth. They bowed their heads and looked down into the golden tea… and they were thankful.

Their hearts were sated. Grateful, humbled, blessed.

"Divide and conquer"

—*Hüsker dü*